PRESENTS

THE Dark Side OF THE SMOKY MOUNTAINS

McGhee Tyson Airport
33
Lakemont
Rockford
Springs
S.H.S.
Seymour
Shennendoah
35
411
Newell Station
411 441
Knob Creek
Dupont
Walden Creek
ville
129 115
Little
Wildwood
334
Alcoa
Sam Houston Schoolhouse S.H.S.
tion
Eagleton Village
Maryville
Alynwick
MOUNTAIN
Reed
335
Maryville College
Crooked
CHILHOWEE
Walland
Hesse
Montvale
Townsend
336
73
Little River
Ranger Station
G.S.M. at Tre
FOOTHILLS PKWY.
Tuckaleechee Caverns
Look Rock
Ranger Station
Abrams Falls
Cades Cove
Laurel Cr. Rd.
Abrams
Abrams Creek Ranger Station
Cades Cove Visitor Ctr.
Ranger Station
Cades Cove
W. Prong
Rabbit
Mill
Pammel
NORTH CAROLINA
Thunderhead Mtn. 5527 ft.
Little
One Way (Closed in Winter)
Gregory Bald 4949 ft.
Bunker Hill 2767 ft.
Tennessee
EE AL
Shuckstack 4020 ft.
Eagle
WE
Calderwood Dam
Deals Gap 1955 ft.
Ranger Station
BENTON
Hazel
Fonta
e
Fontana Dam
Tapoco
Cheoah Dam
Fontana Lake
MOUNTAINS
Fontana Village
APPALACHIA
129
28
Tuskee
Yellow Creek
Yellow
CH
Cheo

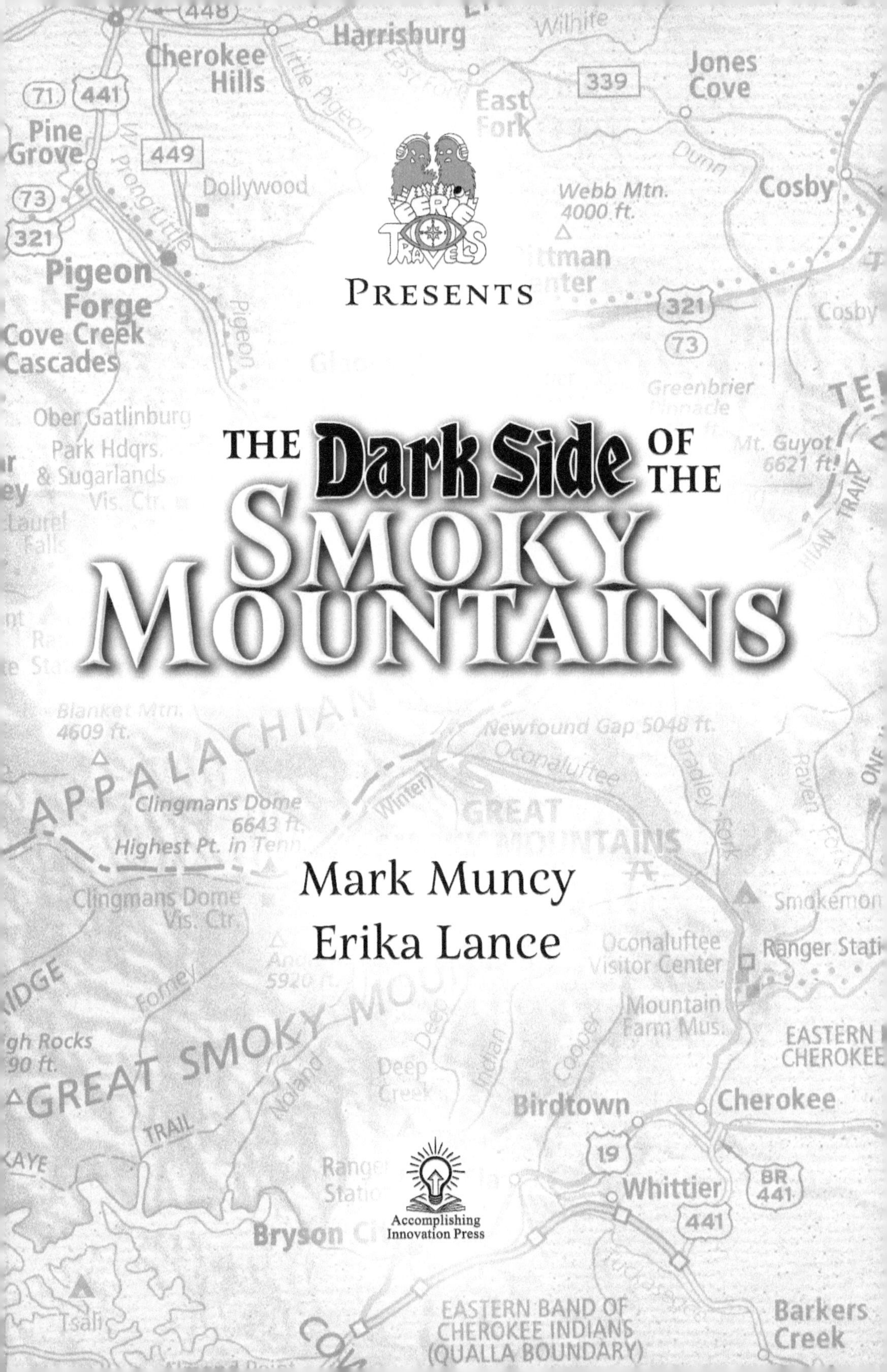
EERIE TRAVELS
PRESENTS

THE Dark Side OF THE SMOKY MOUNTAINS

Mark Muncy
Erika Lance

Accomplishing
Innovation Press

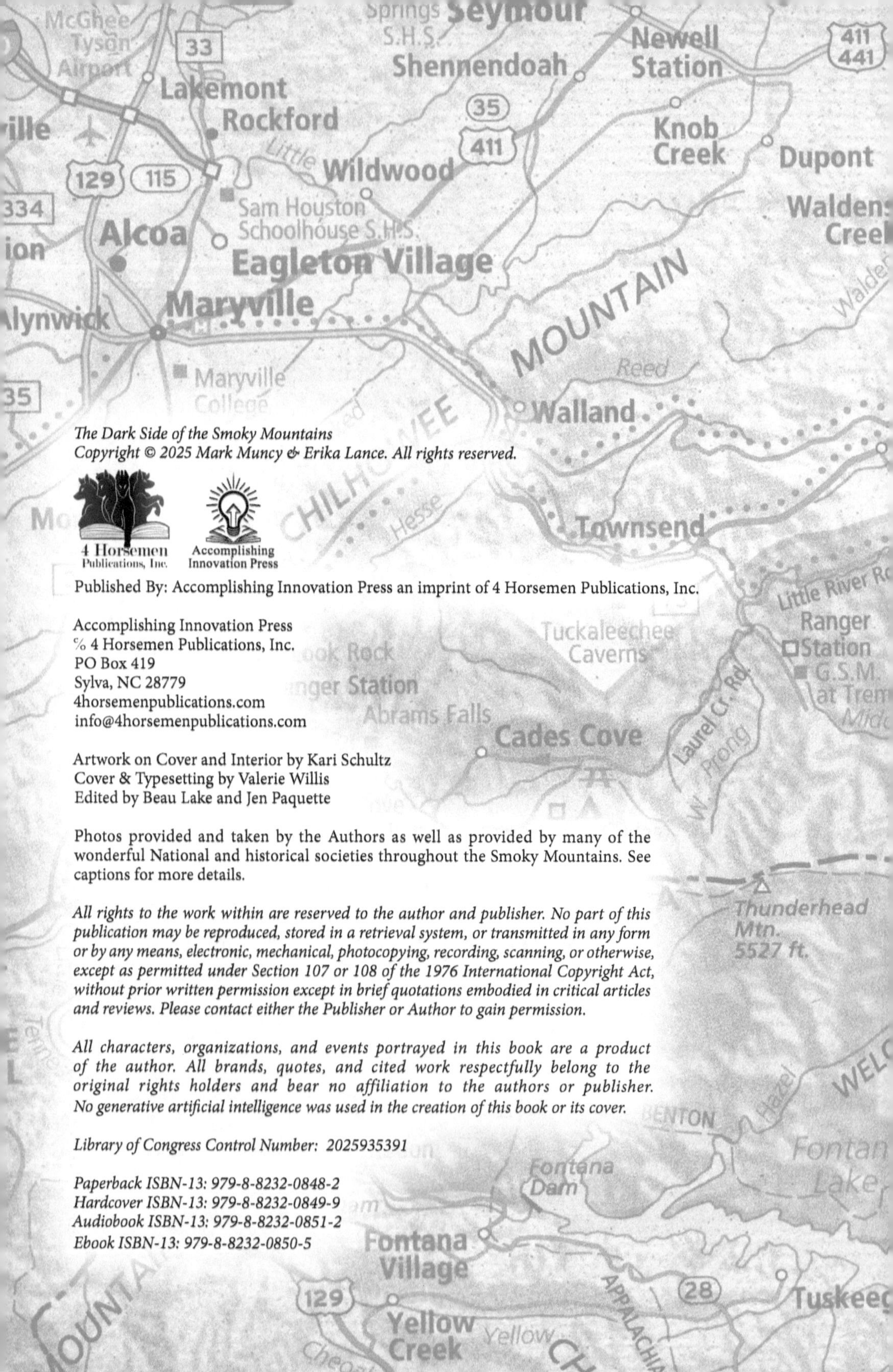

The Dark Side of the Smoky Mountains
Copyright © 2025 Mark Muncy & Erika Lance. All rights reserved.

Published By: Accomplishing Innovation Press an imprint of 4 Horsemen Publications, Inc.

Accomplishing Innovation Press
℅ 4 Horsemen Publications, Inc.
PO Box 419
Sylva, NC 28779
4horsemenpublications.com
info@4horsemenpublications.com

Artwork on Cover and Interior by Kari Schultz
Cover & Typesetting by Valerie Willis
Edited by Beau Lake and Jen Paquette

Photos provided and taken by the Authors as well as provided by many of the wonderful National and historical societies throughout the Smoky Mountains. See captions for more details.

Library of Congress Control Number: 2025935391

Paperback ISBN-13: 979-8-8232-0848-2
Hardcover ISBN-13: 979-8-8232-0849-9
Audiobook ISBN-13: 979-8-8232-0851-2
Ebook ISBN-13: 979-8-8232-0850-5

Dedication

To all our Travelers, thank you for this journey with us.

Special Dedication

To Beau, Kari, & Jonathan who keep us a little less crazy.

Additional Dedication

To all those who were affected by Hurricane Helene and those who stepped in to help these communities through one of the worst disasters in Smoky Mountain history. You are truly amazing, and we are proud to be part of your community.

The Smoky Mountains living up to their name. Photo by author.

Table of Contents

THE **Dark Side** OF THE **Smoky Mountains**

the **Dark Side** of the Smoky Mountains

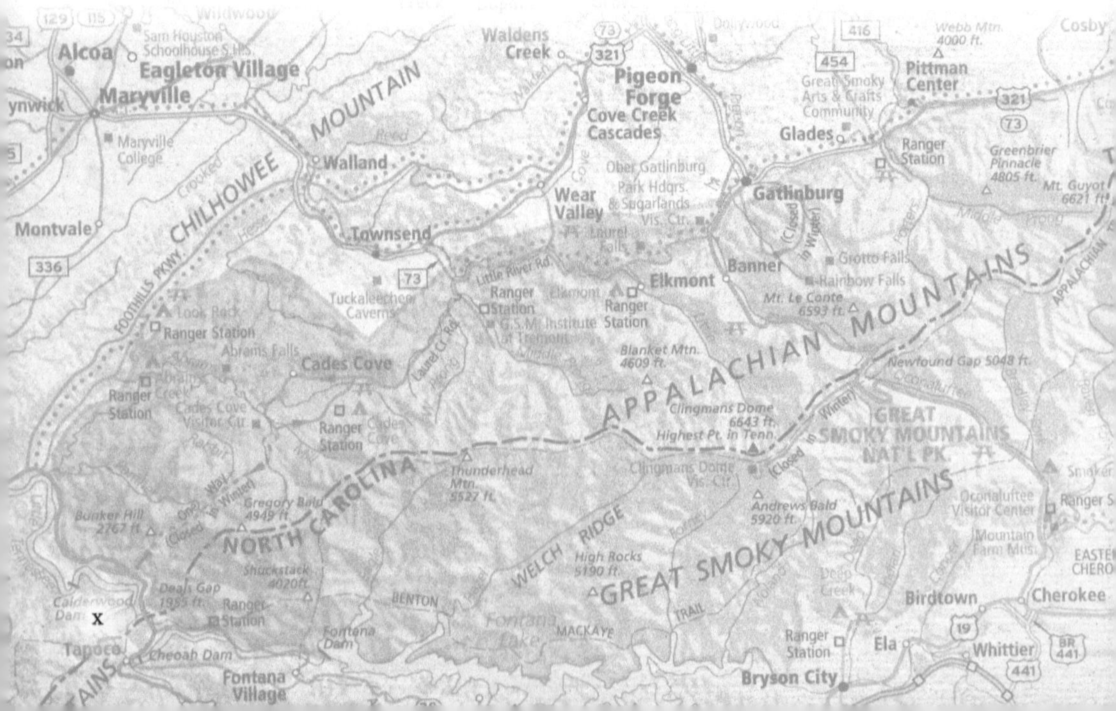

INTRODUCTION TO THE DARK SIDE OF THE SMOKY MOUNTAINS

ERIKA: So, Mark, we are headed to the "Dark Side" of the Smoky Mountains. Where are the Smoky Mountains exactly?

MARK: Well, Erika, I'm glad you asked. Plus, this is a fun way to show how we'll put in these asides to our Travelers.

THE GREAT SMOKY MOUNTAINS STRETCH FROM TENNESSEE into North Carolina. They are a subrange of the Appalachian Mountains in a part of the Blue Ridge Province.

The Blue Ridge Province covers from Pennsylvania, through Maryland, West Virginia, Virginia, North Carolina, South Carolina, Tennessee, and ends in northern Georgia.

The Smoky Mountains contain large sections of the Appalachian Trail and the Blue Ridge Parkway. They are called the Smoky Mountains due to the natural fog that often comes off the mountains and creates large fields of smoke when viewed from afar.

The Smokies, as they are also referred to, have several amazing ecosystems throughout their mountains and valleys with over 180,000 acres of old-growth forest.

This is the largest primary forest remaining east of the Mississippi River. These diverse ecosystems include black bears, elks, salamanders, skunks, chipmunks, bats, squirrels, otters, foxes, armadillos, deer, and snakes.

THE **Dark Side** OF THE **Smoky Mountains**

More than 1,500 species of flowering plants, 240 types of birds, and more than fifty types of fish call this area home. It is with little wonder that it was designated a UNESCO World Heritage Site and is the most visited National Park in the United States.

ERIKA: I feel like you have become a Park Ranger.

MARK: There was a time I wanted to be a Park Ranger, so for our Travelers, I will assume the role and tell you about the park itself.

The Great Smoky Mountain National Park was commissioned in 1934 and certified by President Franklin Roosevelt in 1940.

By the time it was established, it had been decimated by logging and farming for over a hundred years. The mountains had to regrow over one hundred native tree species and even more native shrub species to return them to their natural state.

The area was originally referred to as the *shaconage* by the Cherokee natives. Its name means "the place of blue smoke."

We believe the natives of the area started with the prehistoric Paleo Indians. They hunted and built settlements in these hills for thousands of years.

Archaeologists have found traces of early life here as far back as nine thousand years. While much of this is lost to antiquity, it cannot be understated that these mountains have a history going back much further than we will ever truly know.

ERIKA: We always talk about the fact that we need to work on not losing the history of a place because so much can be learned from it. But my guess is that you have even more?

MARK: Of course! We're just getting started.

In 1540, the Spanish Conquistador Hernando De Soto led his men into the mountains up from the panhandle of Florida. He had early encounters with the native Cherokee of the area who had inhabited the region for several centuries before his arrival and documentation. Not finding the gold he sought, he continued his expeditions elsewhere.

Introduction to the Dark Side of The Smoky Mountains

MARK: Now before you all feel we are skipping some important cultural eras, we will get into the history of the Cherokee and pre-Revolutionary War periods of the area later in this book as they tie to specific tales and locations. Needless to say, the area is steeped in blood and dark history.

ERIKA: The title of the book begins to unfold… The DARK SIDE…

MARK: As I said, there's plenty here. Even more later. Hold your horses.

In 1775, botanist William Bartram made his way through the southern Appalachians and explored much of the Smoky Mountain area.

The first non-natives began to clear homesteads in the area in the 1790s. The Cherokee natives were forced to relinquish their lands in 1819, leading to the Trail of Tears in 1838.

The Civil War came a short while later, and it had the mountain people divided on both sides. Raids were common in the mountains with livestock and supplies seized by both Union and Confederates frequently throughout the conflict. While no major battles took place in the mountains themselves, the effects on the area were still very deep-seated.

ERIKA: I guess we are not seeing many Civil War ghosts then.

MARK: There will be plenty more than I think you will expect.

After the war, we saw the lumber camps begin in the early 1900s. They brought booming business and so the population exploded.

They also carried with them the tall tales and legends that lumberjacks loved to spread to keep entertained. While entrenched only for a few decades, they too would leave a profound impact on the area.

Thankfully, the mountainous terrain kept much of the old growth forest safe from the logging industry.

the **Dark Side** of the **Smoky Mountains**

ERIKA: This is something to be thankful for since you and
I get to look at it every day from our porches!

After the declaration of the area's intent to become a National Park, almost 80 percent of the forest had been destroyed. The bulk of the remaining land belonged to over a thousand families and companies.

It took Tennessee and North Carolina years to buy out all the loggers and landowners to begin the restoration. Numerous families were forced out by eminent domain actions and remain bitter to this day.

With all this stated, it is easy to see how so many shadowy bits of history combine to make the Smoky Mountains so fertile with legends, folklore, and encounters with the unknown.

Countless historians have spent lifetimes here trying to uncover all the hidden history lying in the mists. So, Travelers, this is how we begin your journey into the Dark Side of The Smoky Mountains.

ERIKA: I hope you brought snacks!

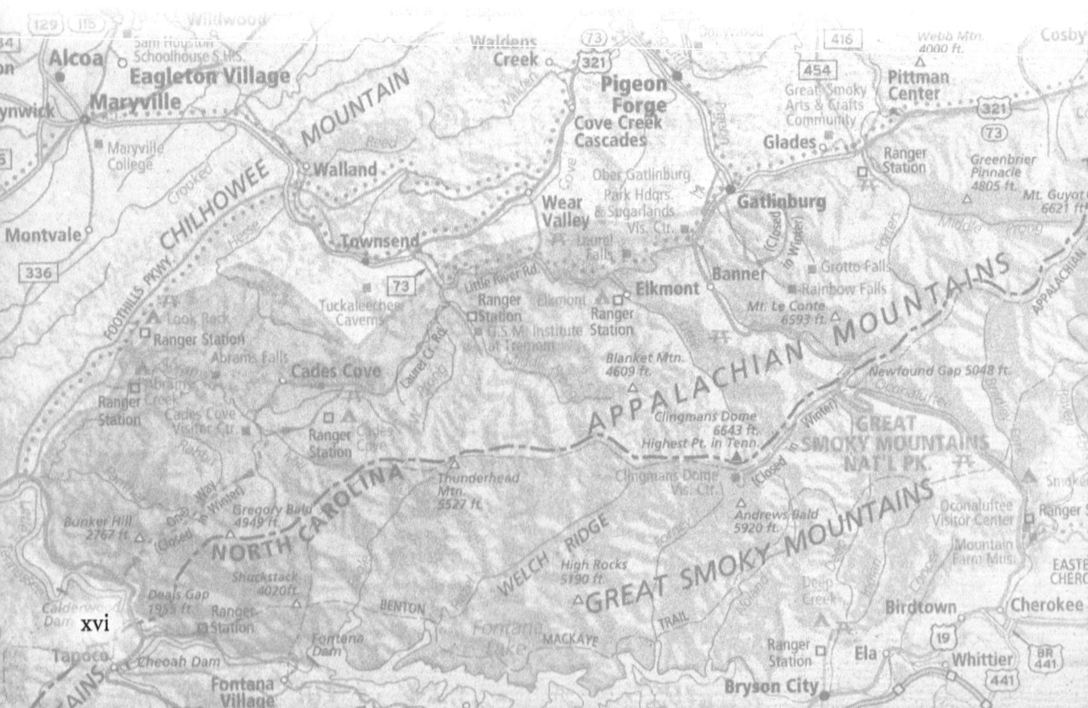

Chattanooga, Tennessee

LOOKOUT MOUNTAIN, CHICKAMAUGA BATTLEFIELD, AND OLD GREEN EYES

WE'RE STARTING OFF IN EASTERN TENNESSEE, JUST WEST of the Smoky Mountains proper. This is the gateway to our eerie road trip ahead.

Tennessee River bisecting the city acts as the transition between the Appalachian Valley and the Cumberland Plateau which leads into the Smokies. According to *Ripley's Believe It or Not*, the city has the fastest internet service in the Western Hemisphere.

ERIKA: So, it is time to load up our playlists (or Eerie Travels podcast) and maps?

MARK: I would recommend it since cell phone service can be unpredictable as we head out into more rural areas.

ERIKA: Playlist and maps are downloaded. Let's do this!

The early history of the area dates back to the Upper Paleolithic period around 10,000 BCE and has a history of continuous population ever since. The city is believed to have gotten its name from the early Creek word Chat-toto-noog-gee, which roughly translates to "rock rising to a point." This likely refers to nearby Lookout Mountain which is a great place to begin our trip.

MARK: Let's hop into the Wayback Machine.

ERIKA: The Wayback Machine is loaded with snacks and

> with Kari (your amazing wife) at the helm, we are
> ready to go. Where are we headed?

We'll go back to 1818 with Elias Cornelius, a traveling cleric, visiting the nearby Brainerd Mission, a local Cherokee school, who mentioned the first written account of going on a tour to the peak of Lookout Mountain.

Then in 1838, James Whiteside was given a huge tract of land containing the peak after the forced removal of the Cherokee, who had inhabited the area since at least the early 1700s.

> **ERIKA:** I don't think I will like the next part of this story.

> **MARK:** No one should like this next part.

It was in that year that the U.S. government forced the Cherokee and many other tribes to Oklahoma in what became known as The Trail of Tears due to the fatalities and extreme tragedy of their exile.

> **ERIKA:** This journey is definitely dark from the start.

The city of Ross's Landing was where the largest of the internment camps or "emigration depots" were located. The horrors of the Indian Removal Act should never be forgotten.

> **ERIKA:** Agreed! It is vitally important that we don't forget
> and don't make the same mistakes ever again.

Less than a year later, Ross's Landing would be incorporated as the city of Chattanooga. It became a boom town for river commerce and exploded in population with the arrival of the railroad in 1850.

An ancient Indian path led from the town and up to the peak of Lookout Mountain. This is where Whiteside built the Lookout Mountain Turnpike and began to develop the northern summit.

He would go on to build a resort hotel and nearby attractions like Rock City, Lula Falls, and Point Lookout. He was optimistic that they would soon begin operations.

> **ERIKA:** Seems like he had some big plans for this land.

> **MARK:** That Whiteside did. Just pay attention and see
> what he did.

The **Dark Side** of the **Smoky Mountains**

However, early construction on the hotel was plagued with a string of unusual construction issues. This led to many of the workers claiming the area was "haunted" by evil spirits.

A number of the slaves at that time believed the area had bad magic. They felt that the loa, or Vodou spirits, had claimed the mountain top as a view for Bondye, the supreme Creator.

ERIKA: That sounds terrifying. I would say that with everything that happened around this land, it would not be surprising to find that negative energy was left behind.

Even with these rumors and stories, the issues were worked around and the hotel opened to visitors. It was an immediate hit, spurring tourism from all over the fledgling United States.

It was a short-lived boom as the Civil War began.

ERIKA: War does tend to put a damper on vacations.

In early September of 1863, General William Rosecrans of the Union pushed the Confederate troops out of Chattanooga. Braxton Bragg called out for reinforcements from the Confederacy for his Army of

"BATTLE OF CHICKAMAUGA" IS NOT HISTORICALLY ACCURATE. HOWEVER, IT IS HIGHLY REGARDED BY CIVIL WAR ART ENTHUSIASTS. PAINTING FROM KURZ AND ALLISON 1890.

Lookout Mountain, Chickamauga Battlefield, and Old Green Eyes

Tennessee. The men arrived later that month, and they began their siege of Chattanooga.

Between September 19th and 20th, Bragg launched his counterattack on the banks of nearby Chickamauga Creek.

With both sides suffering heavy losses, Bragg forced Rosencrans to flee but failed to press his advantage after his victory.

> **ERIKA:** What does that mean?

This meant that the Federal troops were able to secure themselves within Chattanooga until Ulysses S. Grant arrived shortly after to reinforce the Union troops. This allowed them to resecure the entire town.

Over the two days of the battle, Bragg had gathered over 60,000 men thanks to reinforcements led by General James Longstreet.

They repeatedly attacked the remaining Union, which was anchored by a corps led by Union General George Thomas. Thomas held his position with heavy losses. Longstreet's reinforcements arrived, and he advanced just as General Rosecrans was shifting his troops. As his men pushed through, the Federal lines collapsed, and they then retreated into the town.

Bragg refused Longstreet's request for even more reinforcements to take the town. He was dealing with over 20,000 casualties and the loss of ten Confederate generals, including Texas's own John Hood who had to have his leg amputated. Longstreet and General Nathan Bedford Forrest wanted to pursue the enemy again the following day, but Bragg was still reeling.

The Union suffered over 16,000 casualties themselves. This made the Battle of Chickamauga one of the largest costs of human life in the entire western theater of the Civil War. The bodies were everywhere. It was here that tales of something unusual began to circulate among the soldiers.

> **ERIKA:** I didn't think there were civil war ghosts in this story. Are there?

> **MARK:** Not exactly a ghost, per se.

What was reported were sightings of a strange half-man and half-beast wandering amongst the sea of dead and wounded on the battlefield.

> **ERIKA:** Umm... what?

5

It walked on two legs and had long stringy hair down to its waist. The creature had two large, glowing green eyes and huge jaws with two sharp incisor fangs sticking out. It was draining blood from the bodies strewn across the battlefield.

> **ERIKA:** There was a blood-sucking creature roaming the battlefield? Can you imagine what that must have been like for those that saw this monster in the middle of all that horror?

> **MARK:** Well, Old Green Eyes is still seen walking the battlefield even today.

> **ERIKA:** NOPE!

Witnesses describe the creature as floating along the old battle lines; some hear the echoes of ghostly gunfire and battle sounds when it is encountered.

Edward Tinney, a former Chief Ranger at Chickamauga-Chattanooga National Military Park, who tended the grounds from 1969-1986, said ghost sightings at all Civil War battlefields are not uncommon, but old Green Eyes is unique.

> **ERIKA:** That is an understatement.

"Green Eyes is rumored to be a man who lost his head to a cannon-ball, frantically searching the battlefield at night for his dislocated body," Tinney told us. "Those who lived are the ones who saw it and started the stories."

> **ERIKA:** Of course! How can he fight a battle if he doesn't have a head?

> **MARK:** That story doesn't exactly mesh with the vampiric nature of some of the other reports of the creature.

There are dozens of other ghosts seen all over the battlefield with hundreds of documented sightings of soldiers and even phantom brigades. Old Green Eyes, however, may predate the battle.

Lookout Mountain, Chickamauga Battlefield, and Old Green Eyes

There was a training encampment for soldiers getting ready for the Spanish-American War adjacent to where the battlefield now lies. Hundreds of soldiers died of typhoid fever during their time at the encampment. There are stories that Old Green Eyes preyed on the victims of that disease long before the battle occurred.

There are even older stories that say the spirit may have stalked the early Native Americans that lived where the battlefield now stands.

> **ERIKA:** So, we have ghosts, a monster, and an ancient spirit?

Tinney told us that one night he saw something he himself could not explain. He said, in 1976, he was checking on a group of re enactors who were camping at the park.

He saw a man walking on Glen Kelly Road who was over 6 feet tall and wearing a long black duster. He had long, stringy hair and bright green eyes. The figure rushed at him, and Tinney ran to the other side of the road for fear of being attacked.

The man smiled a devilish grin at him from across the road.

> **ERIKA:** NOPE!

THESE CANNONS MARK THE LOCATION OF BRIDGES BATTERY AT THE CHICKAMAUGA BATTLEFIELD, A LOCATION FREQUENTED BY THE SPIRIT OF OL' GREEN EYES. PHOTO BY AUTHOR.

Just then, a car came down the road. When its headlights hit the man in the duster, he vanished. While not saying that it was Old Green Eyes that he encountered, Tinney did say that it still haunts his dreams at night.

He also said that, during his tenure as chief ranger, people frequently claimed to experience all sorts of supernatural activity all over the park.

> **ERIKA:** Sounds like that place is very spiritually-charged, but that is not surprising with everything that happened there.

There are quite a few more ghost stories on the battlefield. One of which is the "Lady in White" who searches the field near Snodgrass Hill, which saw some of the fiercest fighting in the battle. The Snodgrass family cabin served as a field hospital in the battle for both sides. The Lady in White is thought to be a specter of a nurse or perhaps someone looking for their lost loved one on the battlefield.

> **ERIKA:** You know my thoughts on the "Lady in White." She is observed in so many places, but I often wonder if it is because of all the loss in a certain area.

> **MARK:** That is possible. It is all preternatural, A.K.A. stuff we do not understand yet.

There are other sightings, including a skeleton in a Confederate uniform who constantly calls for someone named "Amy." Ghostly horses with phantom riders are observed occasionally charging through the hills, and dark, shadowy soldiers are often accompanied by the echoes of marching or fierce skirmishes.

> **ERIKA:** I am thinking I may want to get back in the Wayback Machine at this point.

The National Park Service very specifically says there are lots of stories about the battlefield, but they don't have any "official files" on the hauntings. The current ranger would only say that they don't deal with ghosts, and "We certainly have no files on Old Green Eyes."

> **ERIKA:** Of course they don't.

Lookout Mountain, Chickamauga Battlefield, and Old Green Eyes

Okay. Now we are getting back into the Wayback Machine because in the two months after the Battle of Chickamauga, the Confederates had placed the city of Chattanooga under siege once again. The Union still held the city. General Ulysses S. Grant arrived and took over command. He was able to assist the newly promoted Brigadier General Thomas, now known as the "Rock of Chickamauga," in a decisive victory over the Confederates in the Battle of Chattanooga and the poetically named "Battle Above the Clouds." This freed the city and Lookout Mountain for the Union for the rest of the war.

One last point of interest here is Sunset Rock.

In that fateful October of 1863, General Braxton Bragg and James Longstreet stood on Sunset Rock on the western side of Lookout Mountain to view the army below and plan their attack.

Today, it is a popular destination for hikers and rock climbers wanting to watch the sunset. It is on West Brow Road, but there is very little parking for it, so plan to go on a slower weekday if you can.

Feel free to watch the sunset and keep your eyes open over the battlefield below for old Green Eyes or the Lady in White.

ERIKA: Way to make this pretty and yet terrifying.

If you come at the right time of the year, usually in early October, the Green Eyes Festival is held at the Chickamauga Visitor Center.

This cryptid and ghostly themed event is filled with vendors and food trucks for a fun time. Old Green Eyes is even their mascot, and you can pick up a cuddly plushie of him to remember this amazing place.

ERIKA: I want an Old Green Eyes plushie!

MARK: We'll have to get you one.

Now, let's head a short distance to one of the most famous locations in the area—with our twist, of course.

ROCK CITY

Mark: Faeries, ghosts, and legends await at our next location.

Erika: I have mixed feelings for this then already.

Since we've talked a lot about Lookout Mountain, we should head up to it, but our GPS seems to be a bit confused as we are heading up the hill.

Erika: If you say we have gone into another dimension this early in the trip, I will be mad. Especially since you didn't even warn me.

We're not dimension-slipping, but we are skating through various states. As you might have noticed, we crossed the line from Chattanooga, Tennessee into Georgia, then back into Tennessee, and finally back into Georgia, all within a few minutes of reaching the top of the mountain. This is because while the summit is right on the state line, Rock City itself is properly in the town of Lookout Mountain, Georgia.

Erika: Weird...

Mark: Before we go in, we've got to fire up the Wayback Machine again.

Erika: I would say I'm surprised, but we just went through a bunch of states and are on top of a mountain. Where are we headed?

Mark: We're going to the early 1800's.

Rock City

ERIKA: No air-conditioning. Well, this should be fun.

While there is certainly historical evidence that Native Americans inhabited Lookout Mountain, it is difficult to study exactly how long any tribe stayed on the mountain. However, in 1823, two missionaries named Daniel Butrick and William Chamberlain climbed Lookout Mountain to minister to the tribe currently residing at the peak.

Butrick noted in his journal on August 28, 1823 that the natives lived in "a citadel of rocks" atop the mountain. He noted the immense size of the boulders he found, and he also mentioned that the stones were arranged in a way that denoted streets and alleys.

MARK: Architecture. I am sure that was amazing, although not surprising.

During the Civil War, both the Union and Confederates held the mountain at different points in time. Both sides claimed that you could see seven states from the summit. These are independent accounts recorded in different journals.

ERIKA: I wonder if you can see seven states.

THE VIEW FROM LOOKOUT MOUNTAIN IN ROCK CITY. YOU CAN SEE A "SEE ROCK CITY" BARN FAR BELOW ON THE LEFT.. PHOTO PROVIDED BY ROCK CITY.

THE Dark Side OF THE Smoky Mountains

MARK: You aren't the only one to wonder about that.

It wouldn't be until 2007 when a scientist from the University of Tennessee would be asked to verify this claim. He noted that you likely could see the high peaks of distant states from the peak of Lookout Mountain back in the time recorded in those journals, but now, pollution has made it difficult without the benefit of telescopes or binoculars.

ERIKA: It is understandable why you would want to hold a summit like this during a war.

Even back then, "Rock City" became a well-known location for hikers.

ERIKA: I get the name now.

MARK: Exactly. See, I get us there in the end.

It didn't become the destination it is today until the 1930s. Garnet and Frieda Carter began to develop a neighborhood themed after European folklore on the mountain and called it Fairyland.

ERIKA: Be careful what you wish for...

Garnet intended to build a golf course but decided to miniaturize it due to the complex nature of the mountain's geology. Tom Thumb Golf is now recognized as the United States' first mini-golf course and the second in the world, created here by the Carter family.

ERIKA: I love mini-golf!

Besides the mini-golf course, Frieda set out to develop the property into a giant rock garden which would enclose over seven hundred acres. The Lookout Mountain Fairyland Club was built by architect William Hattfield Sears and would encompass ten cottages and a main clubhouse. These would be the prime places to stay. In 1935, Frieda and Garnet hired painter Clark Byers to paint barn advertisements throughout the Midwest and Southeast of the United States. By 1969, Byers would paint over nine hundred barns with the "See Rock City" ads in over nineteen states.

Rock City

ERIKA: Early billboarding. You must admire the idea. Also, I love the idea you hired a painter and said, "Go paint barns and say this!"

MARK: It was a great idea and drew people from all over.

Rock City is one of those places where a mere description on paper is never truly sufficient. It really is a place you must see for yourself. The Enchanted Trail laid out by the Carters hasn't changed much. It is full of quirky attractions, geological wonders, majestic waterfalls, botanical gardens, caves, forests, and art exhibits. All the while, you'll stumble on mythological creature sculptures displayed by the founders for nearly 100 years—including little gnome statues that would become a national craze.

ERIKA: This is true. It is absolutely indescribable.

Some places of interest here include the Needle's Eye. It is a narrow crevice you have to squeeze through between two large boulders.

ERIKA: Nope.

MARK: Thankfully, there's a side path to avoid it.

There's the Swing-a-Long Bridge that spans a 200-foot-long ravine. It offers an amazing view of the Chattanooga Valley.

ERIKA: Again... nope. What else?

MARK: Again, there's a stone bridge that avoids the bridge with a slightly less breathtaking view.

A short turn from there leads to the 90-foot-tall High Falls Waterfall, which is stunning to behold and feeds into a beautiful pool. It is a true highlight of the garden trail.

ERIKA: That is amazing!

The trail then leads to Lover's Leap just atop High Falls. It is on a rock that juts out of the mountain and is probably the most famous landmark at Rock City. Cherokee legends speak of it being named after two lovers from warring tribes that had a forbidden love affair. A young

A VIEW TOWARDS THE LOVER'S LEAP OF ROCK CITY WHERE THE 7 STATES VIEW IS LOCATED. PHOTO BY AUTHOR.

brave named Sautee was captured while attempting to woo the beautiful Nacoochee of the rival tribe. He was thrown off the cliff into the valley below. Nacoochee jumped to her own death after him. Their spirits are said to be wandering the mountain.

ERIKA: I would not consider that to be a happy ending.

MARK: Not exactly. Except to say that they are together for eternity.

ERIKA: I hope the next part is not as sad as that.

On our way back to the entrance, you'll see the more mystical side of the gardens as this was where Frieda really went all out decorating the place. You'll pass through Rainbow Cavern, which is a small tunnel with windows that cast rainbow colors on the opposite wall.

ERIKA: Is that a unicorn charging down the hall?

MARK: No. Because charging unicorns are dangerous in tight spaces. That would have been bad.

Rock City

This leads us to Fairyland Caverns. It's not often you see a cave entrance on the top of a mountain, but that's just part of the charm of this place. Inside, there are hundreds and hundreds of fairies and shiny things. It's incredibly unique, and most of the fairies have a properly scary appearance.

ERIKA: Yep. Previous warning about the Fae stands.

It's so gloriously unique. Words do not do the place justice. The Hall of the Mountain King and Mother Goose Village are also part of the caverns and filled with even more unique sights and sculptures. It's no wonder that everyone who visited decided they wanted their own yard gnomes.

ERIKA: Are we done with the creepy fairies yet?

There are a few other locations to visit before we head out; Balanced Rock is a 1000-ton rock balanced on a much smaller stone. It is a great photo op where visitors can pretend to be Atlas holding up the world since we're already among so much mythology here.

Fat Man's Squeeze is on the way down the trail and even the smallest person will likely have to turn sideways to fit through. Thankfully, there is a bypass for those of us who like to eat solid foods.

ERIKA: Though, I don't think it is the solid part of the food but more the type and quantity of said food.

MARK: I'm never going to be a skinny man. There are things like Little Debbie Swiss Rolls—and fried chicken.

There are many events here depending on the time of year you visit. Irish heritage is celebrated in March when it turns into ShamRock City. Fairytale Nights are in early spring. Rocktoberfest features German food, music, beers, and storytelling with the Troll King. The Christmas season brings the Garden of Lights complete with Santa and Ms. Claus and plenty of hot cocoa.

ERIKA: I love me some hot cocoa with extra marshmallows!

THE **Dark Side** OF THE **Smoky Mountains**

MARK: Make sure you do that after Fat Man's Squeeze.

On your way out, don't forget to grab a "See Rock City" birdhouse from the gift shop. Yes, you too can celebrate the ingenious marketing scheme created by the Carter family that continues to draw people to the amazing Rock City.

Overall, plan for about two to three hours to see everything that makes this place one of a kind. Be sure to keep an eye out for the spirits of Garnet and Frieda Carter as they have been spotted wandering the paths of their amazing creation.

ERIKA: Now you bring up the ghosts? What the heck?!
Let's go grab a snack.

A FAMOUS "SEE ROCK CITY" PAINTED BARN. TOUTING THE ATTRACTION AS THE "8TH WONDER OF THE WORLD." – PHOTO PROVIDED BY CHATTANOOGA HISTORICAL SOCIETY.

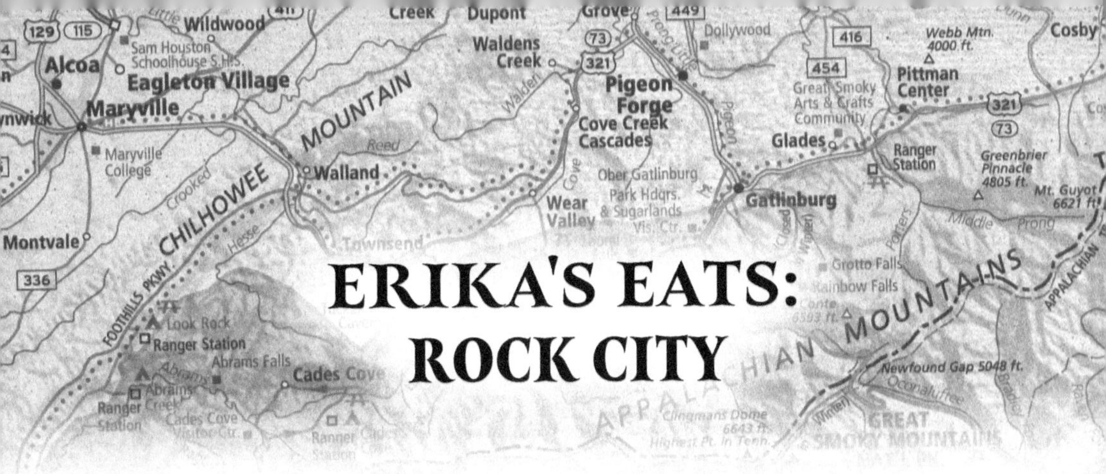

ERIKA'S EATS: ROCK CITY

BECAUSE YOU ARE ON A MOUNTAIN, THERE ARE ONLY A couple of options nearby, but if you are hungry (or want some hot chocolate like Mark promised), you can go here:

Cliff Terrace

This place has amazingly fun and delicious food right near Lover's Leap, including pizza and other classic snacks for the trail.

Cafe 7

This is also just at the Lover's Leap and a great place to look at the Seven States view. I, of course, love peach cobbler with vanilla ice cream while Mark will grab an air fried apple pie any chance he gets.

Big Rock City Grill

Just inside the main entrance, you can head to their short-order style restaurant, have a made-to-order hamburger or sandwich, and enjoy the mountain views.

Before we head back down the mountain, Travelers, if you have an extra day, you might also want to visit Ruby Falls just under Rock City. Well, not exactly *just* under—it is one thousand feet under Rock City. It's an impressive location with incredible tours of the caves below Lookout Mountain.

MARK: What are you wearing, Erika?

ERIKA: It's my mask. I thought we were going to hang out with some racoons. I wanted to look the part.

THE **Dark Side** OF THE **Smoky Mountains**

MARK: Not exactly. Though, we are headed to the
Raccoon Mountain Caverns!

ERIKA: Oh. That makes a little more sense, but I am
keeping the mask on.

THE RAINBOW TUNNEL IN ROCK CITY HAS BEAUTIFUL COLORED GLASS THAT PROJECTS COLORED RAYS OF SUNLIGHT ONTO THE FAR WALL. – PHOTO BY AUTHOR.

RACCOON MOUNTAIN CAVERNS

ERIKA: We just saw a bunch of caves. Why are we headed here?

MARK: We're going to be spending the evening at Raccoon Mountain Caverns and staying at one of their cabins.

ERIKA: Umm... what?

MARK: The property has a campground with full-service RV sites and primitive tent sites as well. After traveling through Lookout Valley, it is convenient to head right up Raccoon Mountain to the campground.

ERIKA: At least you did not say we are staying in a tent.

MARK: Nope. But before we head into the cabin, we need to take a quick jaunt in the Wayback Machine to 1929.

ERIKA: Good thing I have my hot chocolate. Why are we headed back?

MARK: Because history is important for context. Why else would we do this?

THE **Dark Side** OF THE **Smoky Mountains**

THOUGH THE CAVE SYSTEM HERE WAS FIRST DOCUMENTED way back in 1853, it's assumed that the Native Americans were familiar with these caves far before then. By the 1920s, the land was owned by The Grand Hotel and used as a farm for its restaurant.

There were stories of the farmers visiting cavern fissures to cool off on particularly hot days. This led Leo Lambert, a local spelunker, to the area. He had recently discovered and helped open Ruby Falls to the public.

Lambert quickly surmised that the cool air blowing out of the fissures meant there must be a large cavern somewhere beyond the crack in the mountain. He began to carve out a larger entrance and quickly discovered hundreds of feet of cave passages that were well-adorned with beautiful geological displays. He built trails and installed a series of electric lights. By June of 1931, Lambert opened Tennessee Caverns to the public.

> **ERIKA:** I love an adventuring spirit that would say, "Yes, go deeper into the cave!" We both know that would not be me.

Lambert's tour of the caverns circled an area called The Crystal Palace Room due to its large cave structures resembling a medieval castle. His route would be the staple tour for decades.

In the 1950s, the Smith brothers had taken over managing the cave and discovered a small hole just off the main room of The Crystal Palace. They squeezed through an opening of less than eight inches in diameter and crawled for about twenty feet. There, they found even larger rooms which led to even more discoveries.

> **ERIKA:** What is it with everyone trying to squeeze into tight spaces in mountains?

> **MARK:** I'm no spelunker, but I kind of get it. The thrill of exploration.

Needless to say, by the 1960s, a full half-mile loop including these new areas was opened to the public for tours. It is known now as The Crystal Palace Tour.

It is the home to many wonderful species of salamander and a unique spider species known as The Crystal Caverns cave spider, or nesticus furtivus for its scientific name. Though discovered in 1938, it wasn't officially

RACCOON MOUNTAIN CAVERNS' CRYSTAL PALACE TOUR PROVIDES EXCELLENT VIEWS OF THIS UNIQUE CAVE SYSTEM. KEEP AN EYE OUT FOR THEIR ENDANGERED SPIDERS. PHOTO PROVIDED BY RACCOON MOUNTAIN CAVERNS.

described until 1984. It is currently only known to exist within the Raccoon Mountain Caverns. Due to this unique spider, no pets or even service animals are allowed in the caverns for fear of endangering the spider's environment and unique ecosystem. Pets and service animals are, of course, welcome at the campground itself.

ERIKA: I do love pretty spiders, as does Kari, your amazing wife.

MARK: Kari has several spiders as pets. Not the Crystal Caverns cave spider of course, which you <u>legally cannot make into a pet.</u>

For those with a bit more vigor, there is a full spelunking tour available known as Wild Cave Expeditions. These tours were added in the 1970s and allow travelers to explore the undeveloped areas of the cave outside of the commercial tour areas. They have discovered over five miles of passages that have been mapped. New cave discoveries are being made there to this day.

21

THE **Dark Side** OF THE **Smoky Mountains**

While the caves and the unique spider are the main attractions, there is a little history here; that is why we had to place this on our "Must Visit" list. One of the spelunkers who passed away here has never left.

His spirit haunts the caverns, and he particularly likes to interact with female visitors. He will blow in their ears or run fingers through their hair as they walk through the tunnels.

While visiting, make certain to ask your tour guide or the employees at the gift shop about the ghost of Raccoon Mountain Caverns.

Lastly, you will want to head over to the remains of the old cable car that used to travel to the top of the mountain. While no longer in service, this cable car is a fun reminder of the area's touristy history. It's right around the corner from the cavern entrance and makes for a great photo op.

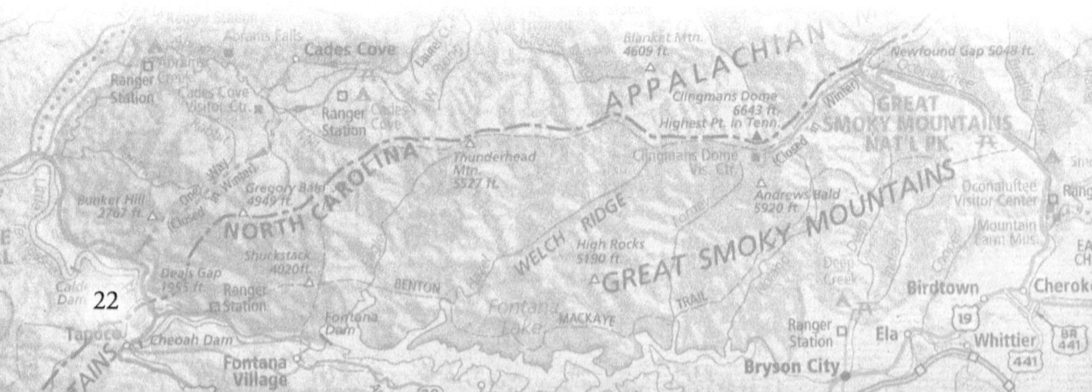

"

THE GHOSTS OF CHATTANOOGA'S CEMETERIES

AFTER SPENDING THE DAY AT CIVIL WAR BATTLEFIELDS, Rock City, and the Racoon Mountain Caverns, I think it's time we spend our last bit in Chattanooga before we head out on the rest of our trip visiting the final resting places of some of the city's residents. We might even get to see some local restless spirits as we walk amongst the tombstones.

> **ERIKA:** Somehow, I just knew we would end up in a cemetery.

> **MARK:** Hard to do an eerie trip without a few at least.

> **ERIKA:** Of course, you'll take us to even more before this over.

We'll start at Forest Hills Cemetery just down the mountain. More than 44,000 bodies are at rest here. It is a beautifully landscaped Victorian-era cemetery. It makes you realize why Victorians visited cemeteries as often as they did public parks. Many famous and notable people call this cemetery their final resting place.

> **ERIKA:** Pretty flowers do not make me want to hang out with ghosts.

It is not just pretty flowers that make this place unique; it's history. General John Wilder, who famously led one Union Brigade at the Battle of Chickamauga and who would later be mayor of Chattanooga, lies interred here. Also, Senator Newell Sanders lies here with his wife Corrine. The senator led the charge for women's suffrage which, in turn, led to Corrine being the first woman to cast a vote in the state of Tennessee.

ARTICLE PROMOTING JACKIE MITCHELL'S HISTORIC PITCHING AGAINST THE NEW YORK YANKEES IN CHATTANOOGA. CHATTANOOGA TIMES FREE PRESS, APRIL 2, 1931.

The Ghosts of Chattanooga's Cemeteries

Erika: That is awesome. The voting, not the dead bodies.

Mark: Grace Moore's grave is also here.

Erika: I feel like I should know this, but who is
Grace Moore?

She was a movie star and opera singer of great renown. She was called the "Tennessee Nightingale." Her films helped to popularize opera for the masses.

Grace was nominated for an Academy Award as Best Actress in the movie *One Night of Love*. In 1947, she tragically died in a plane crash while in Sweden.

Erika: That is sad, but she sounds amazing.

Although not the first female professional baseball player, Jackie Mitchell is interred here, and she has an amazing story. She played professionally for the Chattanooga Lookouts.

On April 2, 1931, 18-year-old Jackie took to the pitcher's mound in an exhibition game with the New York Yankees. First up to the plate to face her was the legendary Babe Ruth. Her first pitch was outside and called a ball. Ruth swung and missed the next two pitches. With her next pitch, she struck out Babe Ruth.

Erika: She sounds like a bada**.

Mark: How do you pronounce "**?"

Of course, Babe Ruth handled it like a gentleman. Just kidding! He reportedly threw down his bat and argued extensively with the umpire before being sent to the dugout.

Next at the bat was Lou Gehrig. Just like with the Babe, Jackie struck him out. This time in three straight pitches. She received a standing ovation from the crowd.

Erika: I would have given her one as well. That was no
small feat.

She unfortunately walked the next batter and was immediately pulled from the game. However, the story of the teenager striking out the two heaviest hitters of the Yankees blew up in newspapers and newsreels all over the country.

Sadly, her fame was short-lived. Baseball Commissioner Kenesaw Mountain Landis voided all women's baseball contracts. He stated that baseball was "too strenuous" for women.

> **ERIKA:** Sounds like he needed to be hit in the head by
> a fly ball.

Jackie ended up playing in exhibition games until she was 23. She may have only played two-thirds of an inning against the Murderer's Row of the Yankees, but she earned her spot in legendary baseball history. She died in 1987 at the age of 74. Her grave is here in Forest Hills.

> **ERIKA:** Sounds like the perfect place to put a baseball on
> a grave to recognition of how awesome she was.

> **MARK:** Remember to take only pictures and pay your
> respects. The groundskeepers here have enough
> to worry about without extra baseballs.

This cemetery boasts monuments of Gothic, Victorian, and even modern art styles. There are sculptures of biblical figures, Greek gods, and even effigies of the deceased themselves. You can also find stained glass windows adorning grand mausoleums.

The land here is full of trees and flowers propagated from cuttings from all over the world. Drive or walk through this magnificent cemetery at the base of Lookout Mountain and admire graves of Civil War soldiers, officers, entertainers, police officers and fire fighters, and many that made Chattanooga their home.

> **ERIKA:** Okay, I see how people might find this place
> beautiful. However, with so many people
> buried here, I am sure there are some ghosties
> hanging around.

> **MARK:** Well, of course there are.

The Ghosts of Chattanooga's Cemeteries

ERIKA: I can tell I spoke too soon.

There is one more area we must mention in Forest Hills: the unmarked graves of the children of the Vine Street Orphanage.

Section D of the cemetery has several markers from the orphanage. Many have only first names. The bulk of the burials are from the early 1900s. The orphanage only took in white children and those considered adoptable. However, there is a hidden bit of history here.

ERIKA: Of course there is.

The Seele Home for Needy Children nearby took in diseased, crippled, "feeble-minded" children over the age of 10, and black children.

Almira Steele helped found this institution while the town of Chattanooga was recovering from an epidemic of yellow fever which left many of the town's children homeless and orphaned.

ERIKA: That is horrible. I think that we forget that although we do not have the greatest systems in place now, at that time, there was nothing in place when you lost your parents.

This home is regarded as the South's first orphanage for African Americans. After only 19 months of operation, arsonists burned down the facilities on Thanksgiving of 1885. Thankfully, everyone escaped the fire unharmed. Donations flooded in, and the old wooden buildings were rebuilt into a substantial brick building with over 44 rooms. It reopened in May of 1886.

ERIKA: It is great that no one was hurt, but you have to hate that people would try to destroy something that was actually trying to help.

Sadly, many of the children were unable to be adopted and many died. They are buried in Forest Hills as well—many without grave markers.

ERIKA: That got really sad. Although not marked, at least they gave them a burial. Is there anything even darker you want to share?

THE **Dark Side** OF THE **Smoky Mountains**

MARK: Not really. Sorry to end on a bummer. Just think
about bada** Jackie Mitchell.

After our detour at Forest Hills, we'll do a quick tour of some notable cemeteries that should be included on our trip.

ERIKA: Great. More ghosts.

The first stop is Aetna Mountain Cemetery, near the Whiteside area of Chattanooga. It was once called Running Water by the Cherokee Nation before they were forcefully removed in 1835.

ERIKA: I like their name better.

The graveyard here dates back to the early 1800s, and there are graves here that may go back even further. It takes some off-roading to get here, which lends itself to the ominous sense of desolation you will feel here.

ERIKA: Wonderful. Ghosts, sadness, and abandonment. I
see we are making this fun for our Travelers.

MARK: Not everything, as you know, is fun and rainbows.
I am hoping the site can be restored, and more
historical work can be done to see just how far
back this cemetery truly goes.

ERIKA: That would be good. This place could use some
care. Where to next?

Next up, Kings Point Cemetery was rediscovered by Keith Harper, also known as "The Cemetery Detective."

ERIKA: Is that a job? Could I be a Cemetery Detective?

MARK: You would have to be willing to go out to find
places where bodies are buried. So, no, I don't
think you would want that job.

Kings Point was another mid-1800s cemetery that fell into disuse in the early 1900s. There is a strange legend here of a man buried in the lone

The Ghosts of Chattanooga's Cemeteries

mausoleum. He was apparently unkind to his wife and felt remorseful about this. He supposedly changed her dress weekly until her body had decayed. The legend says that his spirit is seen walking into the mausoleum to change her clothes even today.

> **ERIKA:** He was crappy with her in life and decided a wardrobe change would make up for it? Well, at least that would be a mostly harmless poltergeist.

Our third stop is the Long Cemetery Number 2 in Mullins Cove. Well, the part that's not underwater.

> **ERIKA:** I am assuming this is where the "2" comes into play?

MARK: I think you're getting the hang of this.

When the Hales Bar Dam was built in 1913, the water in Mullins Cove rose and surrounded the cemetery which was located on a small hill. After Hales Bar was replaced by the Nickajack Dam, the water rose even higher and forced the cemetery underwater.

There are only three gravestones still visible which is, in itself, a little spooky. Even more scary is the legend that a ghostly funeral procession is said to walk to the gravesites on moonless nights.

> **ERIKA:** Nope! I'm out. I am having visions of floating bodies.

MARK: Okay. Maybe something a little more your jam.

Head over to Greenwood Cemetery. It is home to the "Green Lady," one of Chattanooga's most infamous spirits.

> **ERIKA:** The Green Lady? Okay, I have to know this story.

The story goes that a rather wealthy businessman lived just across the lake from Greenwood Cemetery. His wife fell ill with yellow fever and was forced to become a wheelchair user. The man, ever the dutiful husband, found himself a mistress within a week.

THE **Dark Side** OF THE **Smoky Mountains**

ERIKA: What an a**.

His wife recovered from her illness, but it was discovered that she would never be well enough to leave the wheelchair. Her *wonderful* husband decided to push her into the lake and drown her.

ERIKA: I am sensing one of my favorite kind of ghosts: a vengeful ghost!

MARK: I knew you'd like her.

The story goes that her spirit rose up from the lake as a choking green mist that slew both the husband and his new mistress. Her spirit is often seen as the green mist rises from the lake again and again.

ERIKA: I did not love the middle of that story, but the end made me happy. I, of course, do not want to see the mist, so where to next?

Well, there are a couple more cemeteries with haunted hot spots we should mention before calling it a night. Chattanooga Memorial Park, once known as White Oak Cemetery, has reported sightings of a shadow person waiting under a stone archway on its hill.

ERIKA: I do not love shadow people.

Then there's the Chattanooga National Cemetery which was founded in 1863 to mark the battle of Chickamauga. By 1870, over 12,800 soldiers were interred there. While 8,865 of the soldiers were identified, 4,189 are unknown.

Many people have been reinterred in this cemetery. A "reinternment" is when they dig up a grave and move the body to a new location for reburial.

ERIKA: So, they are adding more bodies?

It is also the home of dozens of German POWs from World War I. In 1935, a monument was erected there by the German government to mark the POWs interred at the cemetery.

ERIKA: I do not know about you, Mark (and Travelers), but before we head to the ghost tour tonight, I am hungry. I definitely want something yummy to eat before heading back out to the realm of the dead.

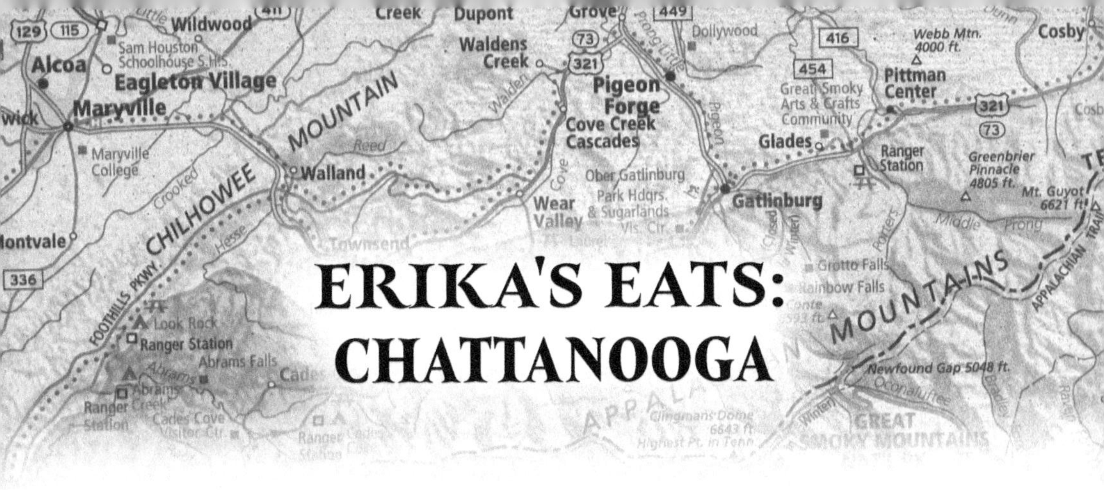

ERIKA'S EATS: CHATTANOOGA

HERE ARE SOME OF MY TOP PICKS FOR FUN PLACES TO GRAB a bite, a drink, dessert, or a coffee while in and around Chattanooga, TN:

Frothy Monkey

I personally cannot live without caffeine. Even if you are not a caffeine addict like me, you should check out Frothy Monkey. They also have a fun menu of yummy food and a bakery full of mouthwatering breads. Grab their signature Monkey Mocha, my favorite, before you leave. It is a great mix of their house made chocolate with banana syrup. Mark loves their shrimp and grits.

State of Confusion

This is a fun restaurant that is open late and has breakfast, lunch, and dinner service. Their menu features a lot of yummy options, including one of Mark's favorites: a fried baloney sandwich. They also have mini-pies and one of the yummiest drinks: a hibiscus mule.

Julie Darling Doughnuts

Did someone say doughnuts? You know Mark goes crazy for a good doughnut. He said it himself—he would plow through an army of ghosts for one. If you plow through any ghosts or monsters to get here, you will not be disappointed. You will, however, have to choose between a banana split filled doughnut or one filled with Granny's Apple Pie. Or if you arc like us, you will get one of each!

Aretha Frankensteins

Whether it's for breakfast or lunch, this place cannot be beaten for the spooky at heart. The menu features anything you could want to eat with some delicious twists. If you go during busy times, you might have a little bit of a wait. It is worth it. If you are up for the challenge, you should have the Super Dave Scramble with four eggs or the Elephants Gerald waffle with ice cream on top.

The Urban Stack

Sometimes you want a burger—a good, juicy, meaty burger. This is the place. Locally sourced, it is considered one of the best burger places in town. Of course, the fact that it boasts fried baloney sliders doesn't hurt in convincing Mark to join me. With a ton of burgers— including my favorite Good Day, Sunshine—you are bound to find something that fills you up before heading back out to face those things that go bump in the night.

ARETHA FRANKENSTEIN'S IS A MUST STOP ON A VISIT TO CHATTANOOGA. PHOTO PROVIDED BY ARETHA FRANKENSTEIN'S.

CHATTANOOGA, TN GHOST TOURS

ERIKA: Okay, now that I have eaten (a lot), where are we headed?

I THOUGHT THAT BEFORE RETIRING FOR THE NIGHT, WE can recommend a few tours that have a spooky edge.

There's the Murder & Mayhem Haunted History Walking Tour by Chattanooga Ghost Tours. It will take you on a tour of Chattanooga's darker side of history with an emphasis on the supernatural.

By Your Time tours offers the ChattaBOOga Ghost Walk as well. This is a fun walking tour that visits the Hamilton County Courthouse and discusses all the fires, floods, disease, and war that make this city such a haven for visitors from the other side.

Another fun experience is the Ghost & Booze Tour of Chattanooga—for those over 21, of course. You'll walk through the Historic District and get to hear some scary tales while enjoying drinks at some of the best local taverns. There are other options for tours in town so check ahead, but you will get your money's worth from any of these.

THIS POSTCARD FROM 1962 SHOWS THE HISTORIC ENTRANCE TO CHATTANOOGA'S NATIONAL MILITARY CEMETERY. PROVIDED BY CHATTANOOGA AREA HISTORICAL ASSOCIATION.

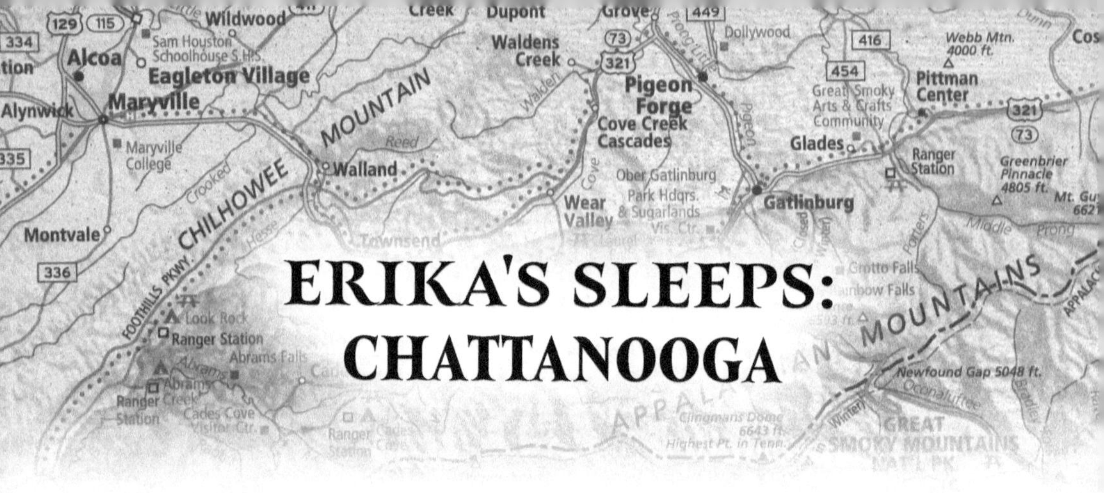

ERIKA'S SLEEPS: CHATTANOOGA

ERIKA: Aka where to rest your head… well, maybe?

The Read House

Want to stay in a haunted room? I don't, but if you are like Mark and Beau, you may want to have a spirit to be your roommate for the night. Book room 311 at the Read House, but if you can't sleep, don't blame me.

The Mayor's Mansion Inn

There are not a lot of stories about hauntings, but this establishment is beautiful and built from the bricks of Fort Wood. Oh, the stories they could tell…

The Hotel Chalet

You can stay in a train car! Yes, it is as amazing as it sounds. It is a unique experience even I couldn't turn down.

Chattanooga has been fun and well worth our extra day here. Let's hit the road bright and early as we've got a few miles to go before our next stop as we enter the Smoky Mountains proper.

HOTEL CHALET OFFERS THIS WONDERFUL ROOM INSIDE A REMODELED TRAIN CAR. PHOTO PROVIDED BY HOTEL CHALET.

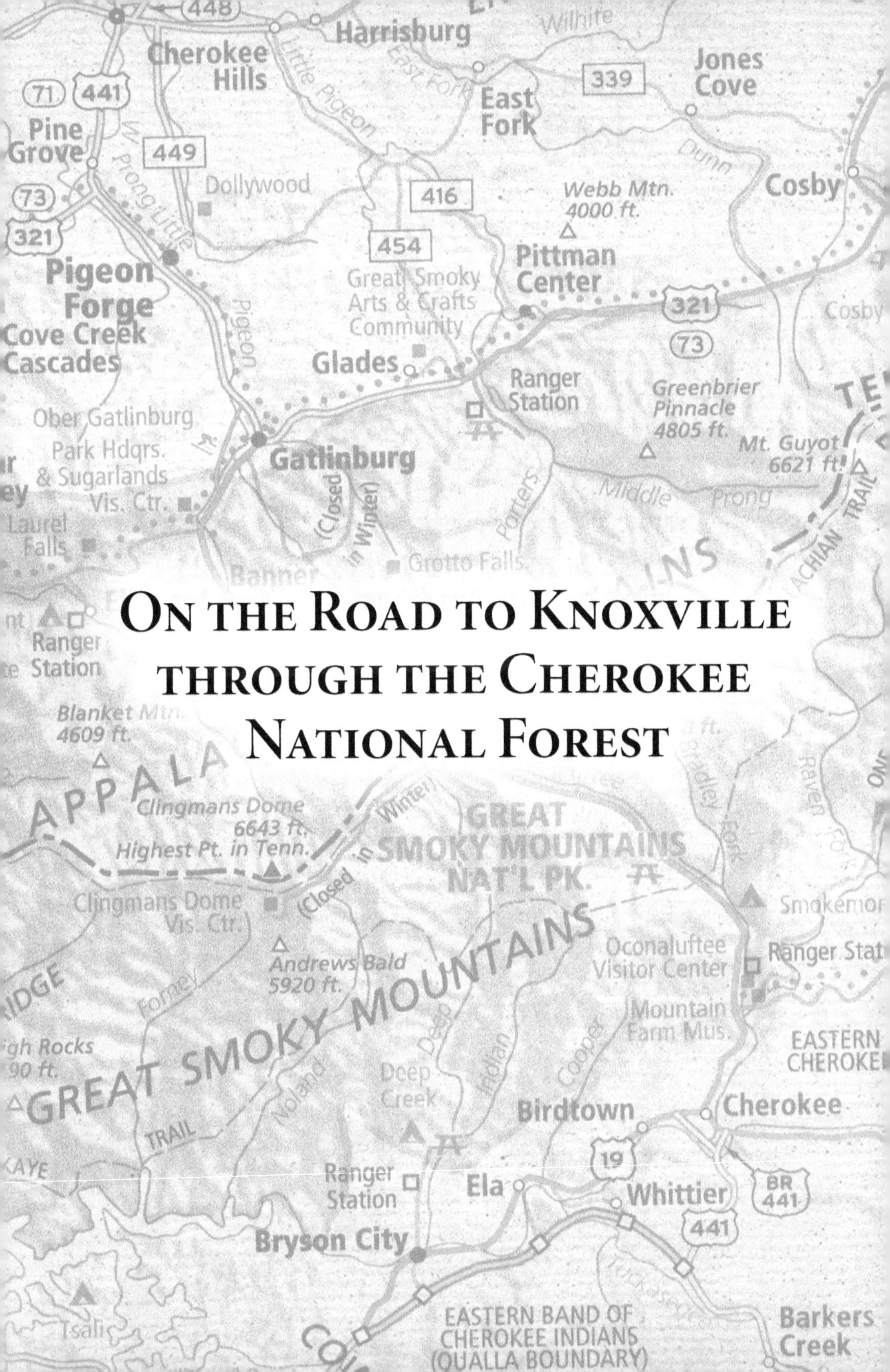

On the Road to Knoxville through the Cherokee National Forest

THE CHEROKEE NATIONAL FOREST

From Chattanooga, we'll take I-75 toward the border of the Smoky Mountains. We'll be hitting much of the Blue Ridge Mountains. What's fascinating, geologically speaking, is that they are all subranges of the Appalachian Mountains, though the Blue Ridge and the Smokies are actually the same subrange.

Mark: I'm probably the only one who really thinks that's cool. Well, besides some of our geology nerd Travelers.

Erika: Mark, there are definitely other nerds like you who will think that's cool.

As we continue along the eastern Tennessee border, we're passing the large northern portion of the Cherokee National Forest. We'll be passing through the southern section on the way back at the end of our journey. There's a lot of history in these woods—legends too.

Erika: Travelers, make sure you have your snacks for the road.

Mark: Time to rip off the Band-Aid and dive right in.

Early road sign in 1941 for the main road into the Cherokee National Forest. Photo provided by The Tennessee State Library and Archives.

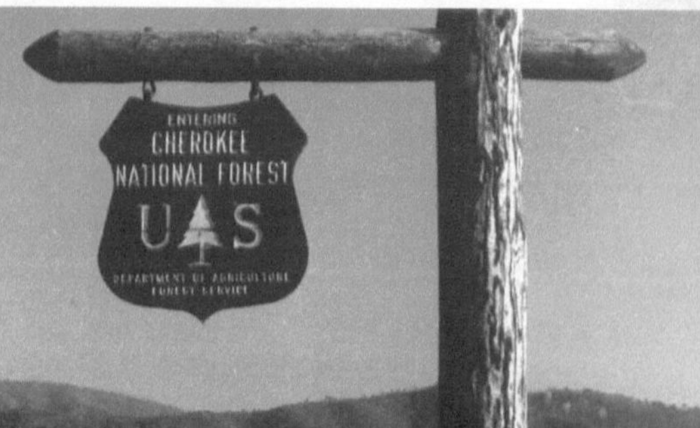

THE STORY OF SPEARFINGER

THERE'S A BIT OF A DRIVE TO PETOS, TENNESSEE, SO I thought I'd break up our trip with a story that haunts the hills here. Since we are heading deeper into the darker side of the Smoky Mountains and the southern edge of the Appalachian range, I figured it was time I told you about the Stone Witch of the Cherokee who is said to wander the mountains along the Tennessee and North Carolina borders: *Spearfinger*.

ERIKA: One of my favorite creatures. I love this story!

It appears that the legend started as a cautionary tale to protect the younger members of the Cherokee people, particularly in the area of the Great Smoky Mountains. This ancient story tells of a powerful shape-shifting witch armed with a finger-like spear and an appetite for human livers.

ERIKA: A female Hannibal Lecter, if you will.

The Cherokee people feared her. She was no ordinary witch. Spearfinger was made entirely out of stone. The index finger on her right hand was long and tapered to a point like a spear tip. Her strength was well known, as she could effortlessly lift and throw huge boulders. The warriors of the tribe were often told to be very wary of U'tlun'ta or Spearfinger in English.

I first heard this legend from Kathi Littlejohn, a very talented story-teller of the Cherokee. Her family has centuries of history in the Cherokee Nation told through the generations. Oral storytelling is central to the Cherokee culture, so storytellers like Littlejohn are venerated amongst the tribe and essential in keeping their history alive.

She told me, "Cherokee believe in three worlds. Of course, we believe in the upper world which is where the creator lives. Then, the middle world where humans live, animals, birds, insects, and reptiles. But then there's another world, and that's what we call the underworld. Humans are not meant to go there."

THE **Dark Side** OF THE **Smoky Mountains**

ERIKA: I don't want to go there.

She went on to explain that there are portals between our world and the underworld, and that's where the story of Spearfinger comes from. She came from a portal somewhere in the Nantahala of Western North Carolina, or possibly near Chilhowee Mountain where she would prowl near the Little River in what is now Blount County. Many say she roamed much farther—all the way to Frozen Head in the Crab Orchard Mountains of Tennessee.

According to Littlejohn, Spearfinger is of a group of immortal beings called the Nûññë›hï or anglicized to Nunnehi. They only appear to humans when they allow themselves to be seen. Many of them were kind and helpful to the Cherokee. Often, they would appear to lost travelers and guide them back onto proper trails. They would appear as normal Cherokee to those who witnessed them, only giving away their true nature when they would suddenly vanish.

ERIKA: I am glad they were helpful, but the popping out of existence thing would scare the crap out of me.

Famously, during the Civil War, in the town of Nikwasi, which is now known as Franklin, North Carolina, a group of Union soldiers approached the town to burn it to the ground. A group of Union scouts reported back to their officers that that town was heavily guarded and held many warriors. Due to this news, the Union soldiers changed course for Atlanta and burned everything in their path. In truth, the town was defenseless. The Cherokee say it was the Nûññë'hï that saved them from destruction. Sadly, the trick didn't work a second time, but we'll talk about that when we get to Franklin near the end of our trip.

ERIKA: I appreciate a good ruse to keep war at bay.

Similar to angels in some religions, the Nûññë'hï were mostly helpful, but there are those who have fallen to evil urges. Spearfinger is one of these. She could change her shape into that of a beautiful Cherokee maiden with long black hair and dark eyes to lure young men into her embrace. She could also change her form into that of a frail and elderly crone to seek sympathy and compassion from children or travelers. These disguises often allowed her to infiltrate villages to hunt for her prey.

The Story of Spearfinger

No one was truly safe from Spearfinger's malevolence. She had a profound hunger for the human liver. She would use one of her disguises to get close to her intended victim. Once they let their guard down, she would reveal her long, obsidian index finger, which she would use to steal the liver of her victim.

U'tluna'ta' is her Cherokee name which translates into "the one with the pointed spear." The wound she would leave would sometimes be nearly undetectable. On occasion, her victims would last for days without knowing what had happened. She was a clever hunter and would take the form of a slain victim in order to ingratiate herself with the tribe and family to gain even more victims.

In autumn, the Cherokee traditionally started small brush fires so they could hunt the fallen and freshly roasted chestnuts. Spearfinger would be drawn to these fires like a moth to a flame to reach out for wandering children. She would call out saying, "Come, my grandchildren, come to your granny and let her dress your hair." She would let them lay on her lap while she played with their hair until they went to sleep. Then she would stab them through the neck or back with her finger. Sometimes, the victim would have no memory of the attack but would grow ill and die several days later.

She would wander the mountains singing a strange song called "Liver, I Eat It" to her friends, a group of ravens. It went something like this: "Uwe la na tsiku. Su sa sai. Liver, I eat it. Su sai. Uwe la na tsiku. Su sa sai."

THE Dark Side OF THE Smoky Mountains

ERIKA: I would assume that it sounds *much* better
in Cherokee.

Her only enemy was known as The Stone Man, Stone Head, or the Great Stone Face. Like Spearfinger, he had the power to move boulders and rocks. He also ate livers, so they were competing for the same food source. At one point, they made a stone bridge together to move from mountain to mountain; this angered the beings of the upper world. Spearfinger and The Stone Man had encroached on their territory, so they destroyed the bridge with lighting.

ERIKA: Note to self: do not get on the beings of the
upper world's bad side.

MARK: Now you see why I rarely fly.

The remains of the bridge are right on the Georgia, North Carolina border in Jackson County. Whiteside, also known as Thunder Mountain, offers some of the highest cliffs in the Appalachians. It is a site to behold. We'll be visiting it on our way back.

ERIKA: What did the Cherokee do about two liver-eating
baddies preying on their people?

The Cherokee called a great council of the nearby towns. Tomotley, Chota, Setico, and Tenae all came to discuss ways to destroy the liver-eater plaguing their tribes. The medicine man, Adawehis, knew many of Spearfinger's hunting tactics but had no idea how to kill her. They did decide to set a trap for her and hoped they could find a way to slay her.

ERIKA: I like this plan.

They dug a great pit outside the village near Chilhowee Mountain which they covered with brush. Then they made a great fire with green saplings in order to create a huge amount of smoke that would be sure to convince Spearfinger they were preparing to harvest chestnuts. Spearfinger did not take long to be drawn to the smoke.

She appeared as an old woman and claimed she had come from a neighboring village. She said she was lost and needed assistance into the town. Knowing it was a trick, the medicine man threw his spear at her.

The Story of Spearfinger

It harmlessly bounced off her as she was made of stone. All the warriors attacked, but their arrows and spears could not penetrate the stone.

> **ERIKA:** I feel like this is not going to end well.

> **MARK:** You know, you really are like that kid in *The Princess Bride*. We're getting right to the good part and you have to chime in. Shall I continue?

> **ERIKA:** All right. I'll listen. What happened next?

Spearfinger was greatly angered by the attack and showed her true form. She charged at the town with her long obsidian finger poised. She fell into the pit but was unharmed by the stakes there. The warriors continued firing countless arrows at her, and she swatted them away. Taunting the warriors, she sang her song about eating their livers.

The "Celestial Beings" of the Cherokee decided to send a messenger from the upper world to assist. A Utsu'gi—or, as we call it, a titmouse—flew down and landed on Spearfinger's shoulder. It sang out "un, un, un," which to the warriors sounded like "u-nahu," the Cherokee word for heart. The warriors concentrated their attack on her chest. Yet again, the arrows and spears bounced off her stone skin. The warriors were so angry with the titmouse that they captured it and cut off its tongue. The Cherokee now call all titmouse birds liars.

> **ERIKA:** I love the idea that a little bird appears, swelling the hope of the tribe, only to give them the wrong answer.

It wasn't that the bird lied; it just wasn't specific. The celestial beings sent another messenger. A Tsi'killi'—a Carolina chickadee—came down and landed on her right hand, just above her flashing obsidian finger. The warriors didn't take long to start aiming for her hand. Though she kept her hand in a double fist, they could see her heart beating in her palm. While the arrows could not break through her stone hand, they were finally able to sever her wrist. With a great scream, she sank to the ground and died. It appeared to be the end to the curse of Spearfinger.

> **ERIKA:** I am happy they defeated her and yet sad because she had some pretty cool powers.

THE **Dark Side** OF THE **Smoky Mountains**

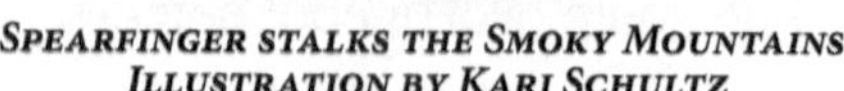

SPEARFINGER STALKS THE SMOKY MOUNTAINS.
ILLUSTRATION BY KARI SCHULTZ

The Story of Spearfinger

The Stone Man heard the cheers of the victorious hunters. He came to the village and saw Spearfinger's hand embedded on a post outside the village. According to the legend, he considered himself warned and stayed away from the towns, but he still continues to sing his songs of war, hunting and eating livers as he wanders the Smoky Mountains by rolling around and causing tremors and earthquakes.

> **ERIKA:** Of course he does.

Now, the chickadee was venerated and is now known to be "the truth-teller." Should one perch near your house, it is meant to be a sign that you will return home safely from any hunt or trip. The poor titmouse is now the "liar bird" and was cursed with a small tongue.

> **MARK:** So, you'd think with her slain, that would be the
> end of Spearfinger.

> **ERIKA:** Umm... I am guessing, no?

Sadly, the Cherokee are convinced her spirit is still walking the hills. It is said that her song can still be heard in the forests. Temperature drops and shadow forms with a long spear-like finger are seen throughout the Smokies.

Park Rangers in the area often get reports of visitors in states of unease and strange songs echoing near their campsites. Despite efforts to debunk the legend, she still holds a spell of fascination in the area.

> **ERIKA:** It seems to me that these types of creatures
> are never truly dead. I mean, where would
> horror movie franchises be if you could *actually*
> kill them?

Kathi Littlejohn says, "When you think that these stories have been handed down, some of them since we believe from the beginning of time, because we have quite a few stories about how the world was created and how people came to be in the world. How animals came to be and look like they do. A lot of the stories have really deep meanings and lessons. So, if we pass those on and teach the other generations that are coming up, then it benefits everybody."

She continued, "If you look at our past and all of the efforts that were done to eradicate us, move us, destroy us, and the fact that we're still here, and that we can still tell our own stories, instead of only reading about them in a book somewhere, I think that is the underlying point of anything that we do.

Our dress, our arts, our festivals, our dances. Everything that we do not showcase, but that's our life. That's our culture. We are the only people in the world who do something in a certain way. The efforts we are doing now to save our language and the stories we tell are a big part of that. They draw us together and are another tradition to keep and pass down."

ERIKA: I love that she said that!

MARK: I couldn't agree more. She's amazing. If you see her at any of the Cherokee Storyteller festivals, tell her the *Eerie Travels* team says, "Howdy."

Let's get to our next location before dark. We'll stay clear of any mysterious figures along the way. Pay close attention to the right hand of anybody we talk to. Also, keep an ear out for any singsongs drifting through the mountains while we're here.

ERIKA: Don't worry, Mark. I am confident I can outrun you.

THE CAROLINA CHICKADEE IS THOUGHT TO PROVIDE GOOD LUCK TO TRAVELERS AFTER ASSISTING THE CHEROKEE IN THEIR DEFEAT OF SPEARFINGER. PHOTO PROVIDED BY THE NATIONAL AUDUBON SOCIETY.

BRUSHY MOUNTAIN STATE PENITENTIARY

AS WE TRAVEL THROUGH THESE WINDING ROADS OFF THE interstate on our way toward Frozen Head State Park, we've got to take a quick journey in the Wayback Machine before we get there.

ERIKA: Okay. Where are we heading?

We have to head back to the end of the Civil War. The end of the war led to a huge boost in railroad construction and the need for lots and lots of coal to fuel these railroads. There was a huge expansion of the coal mining industry throughout the Appalachians and particularly in this area of eastern Tennessee. Because many of the regions where coal veins were located were so remote, most of the mining companies provided housing and collected rent from the wages of the miners that lived there.

ERIKA: That doesn't seem completely fair. "Hey, come work for us in the middle of nowhere, but you have to pay your rent"?

The companies also opened on-site shops to sell food, clothes, and necessities at hugely inflated prices. The debts of the miners quickly added up. Combining this with the dangerous working conditions, the plight of the miners was great indeed. The Coal Creek miners in this area were being pushed to the breaking point. They decided to strike for better pay in the winter, when they knew demand for coal would be at its highest point.

ERIKA: Good for them!

This tactic worked for a brief time until Tennessee came up with the convict lease program.

THE **Dark Side** OF THE **Smoky Mountains**

ERIKA: The what?

The prison lease system allowed the local jails and prisons to lease out their inmates as labor. This gave the mining companies a cheaper workforce that couldn't strike. Soon, other states in the South began to adopt this program. The Southern states' economies had not recovered after the Civil War, and this was a cheap way to feed, shelter, and get clothes for their overcrowded prisons. They couldn't afford to build new prisons anyway.

ERIKA: This seems like a terrible plan. How did they get away with that?

It also worked to help bypass the new Thirteenth Amendment of the Constitution. Slavery had been abolished, but "involuntary servitude" was allowed as a form of criminal punishment. As the federal troops began to leave the southern states in the late 1870s after Reconstruction, state officials who were hostile to former slaves used this loophole. They would hand down extreme prison sentences, including life without parole, for even petty crimes. This made the blacks the majority of the prisoners in the South.

ERIKA: I hate history sometimes.

MARK: It's rarely pretty. However, we must remember it, or we may be doomed to repeat past mistakes.

By 1891, the Tennessee Coal Mine in Anderson County had been mostly staffed through the prisoner lease program. The regular miners in the area were about to lose their jobs despite the meager wages. They came up with a plan and attacked and burned the nearby state prison. They burned its stockades, buildings, and its mine. They then loaded all the prisoners and guards onto a train and forced them out of town.

ERIKA: Wow! That is one way to approach the problem.

The mining company called for federal troops to be sent in to quell the strike. There were months of skirmishes leading to many deaths of both troops and miners. It came to be known as the Coal Creek War.

ERIKA: Another war is not what we needed at this time.

Brushy Mountain State Penitentiary

Once the companies realized they would need a standing militia to protect their operations, they decided it would undercut any financial gains made by the convict lease program. Instead, they petitioned the government for a new project: the state's first maximum security prison.

Brushy Mountain State Penitentiary began construction in 1896; naturally, inmates were forced to build the on-site railroad and the original wooden prison. The mine opened before the main building was even finished. By the early 1900s, the facility was vastly overcrowded, and disease spread quickly through the population. Tuberculosis, typhoid fever, and pneumonia were common, but syphilis affected over 75% of the black prisoners alone. There was not much medical care available at the prison. Prisoners were also frequently beaten for underproducing in the mines. Many prisoners died within the walls despite there never being a death row here.

As the prison reached the 1930s, the old buildings were already starting to fall apart. In 1931, they had nearly 1,000 men imprisoned there with facilities for under 700. There were even some comparisons to the work camps of Siberian gulags in Russia.

Tennessee decided to build a new concrete prison and made the prisoners dig out the rocks from a nearby quarry. It was finished by 1934 and included four stories and a huge 18-foot stone wall around the property.

The site remained a prison mine until the late 1960s. A building was built outside of the main walls with room for 100 minimum-security inmates. Most of those housed there were allowed to work in the nearby community of Petros. Many became volunteer firefighters.

Besides these outside rooms, Brushy Mountain was considered the last stop for the worst of the worst convicts. If you were no longer allowed at a lesser prison, you were sent to Brushy.

There was a notorious building on the property called "Death House." It was where the bodies of dead inmates were kept until their families claimed them. If they weren't claimed, they would be taken up the hill and buried at the pauper's cemetery on the hill.

It was also where "The Hole" was, isolating those they felt needed to be separated from the rest of the prisoners. The Death House was demolished in 1957, and D-Block was built on top of it. This would house "the worst of the worst" inmates that had been sent to Brushy.

In 1969, Brushy was reclassified as a maximum-security prison and given the nickname "The End of the Line." This began the most infamous era of the prison. James Earl Ray was transported here after assassinating Martin Luther King Jr. He escaped for a few days with 16 other prisoners but was recaptured in less than two days. He had barely made it two miles.

ERIKA: I bet he was not an avid camper.

MARK: We'll come back to this.

In the early 1970s, the prison was shut down for a few years after the guards went on strike, demanding security improvements. It reopened in 1976 but hadn't been improved much.

In 1981, three inmates stabbed James Earl Ray 22 times. He survived and was moved to a prison in Nashville where he would die six years later.

In 1982, a notorious incident occurred at the prison when seven white inmates captured some guards and used their weapons to attack and kill some of their black rivals.

ERIKA: This place sounds terrible.

MARK: Prisons aren't nice places.

There were more than a few other infamous inmates incarcerated here over its 113 years of operation.

Paul Dennis Reid, the Fast-Food Killer of Nashville, was placed here in 1997 and served time until the Brushy complex closed. Afterward, he was moved to Morgan County Correctional. He had robbed a few

48

Byron "(Low Tax)" Looper was also here for a time. He was a politician who legally changed his middle name to (Low Tax)—parentheses and all. Famously, he ran a negative campaign against Senator Tommy Burks. When he saw he couldn't win, Looper drove to Burks' farm in October of 1998 and shot him in the head. He, too, would later go to Morgan County Correctional after Brushy closed.

> ERIKA: With all this death and horrible suffering, is it any wonder the place is a haunted hot spot? I am not surprised at all that this place is full of ghosts. I am sure there are also some other nasty creatures that go bump in the dark.

In addition to all the dark shadow people often encountered in the halls and negative energy you can find here, there is one ghost we must give a special mention.

Geronimo was a young deer that fell off one of the nearby cliffs and landed in the main yard at Brushy. The inmates managed to nurse it back to health, and they were allowed to keep it as sort of a pet. It was given the name Geronimo due to its jump into the prison yard. It frequently fed on the cigarettes the inmates offered it.

When the prison was closed from 1972 to 1975, the prisoners petitioned to move the deer from the abandoned Brushy site to their new home in Nashville. Geronimo did not do as well in the new prison and attacked an inmate.

49

THE **Dark Side** OF THE **Smoky Mountains**

The deer broke one of its legs shortly thereafter, and the leg had to be amputated. There are no reports of what happened to Geronimo after that. His spirit, however, is sometimes seen wandering the yard of Brushy Mountain.

ERIKA: A ghost deer? Does it have three or four legs?

MARK: The ghost has all four. Good for Geronimo. At least it's not a Not Deer.

ERIKA: You know how I feel about Not Deer!

Brushy was closed and abandoned in 2009 but reopened as a museum sometime later. We're going there for dinner and a paranormal tour.

ERIKA: I'm sorry. We're doing *what?*

MAP OF THE CAPTURE OF THE ESCAPE OF JAMES EARLY RAY AND OTHERS FROM BRUSHY MOUNTAIN PENITENTIARY IN 1977. MAP PROVIDED BY THE KNOX COUNTY HISTORICAL SOCIETY.

ESCAPEES CAPTURED — This map locates the approximate places where authorities recaptured James Earl Ray and five other convicts who fled Tennessee's Brushy Mountain State Prison Firday. The last convict was taken into custody Tuesday. (AP)

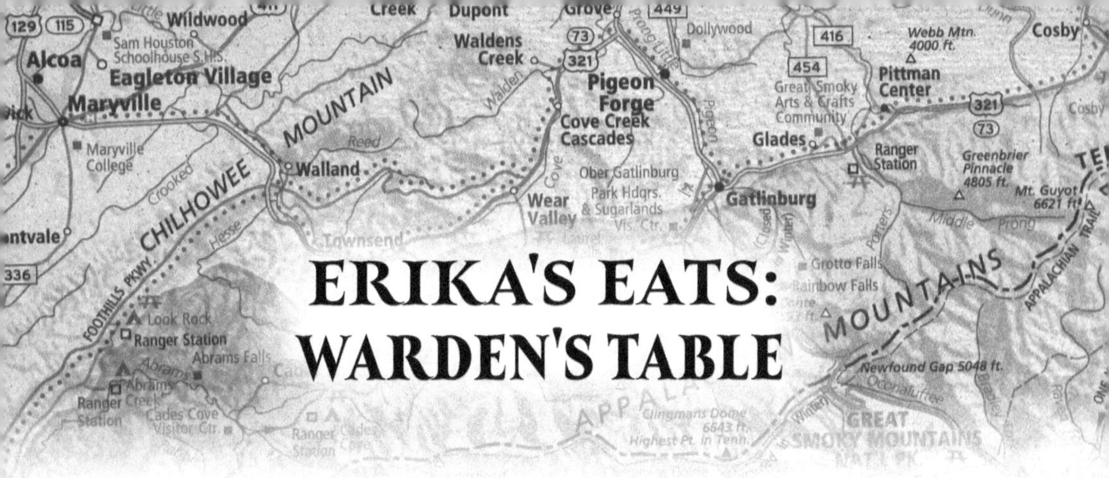

ERIKA'S EATS: WARDEN'S TABLE

The Warden's Table

This is a farm-to-table restaurant on property with a constantly changing menu based on what is available from the nearby farms. Usually, they have some great Southern comfort food served on those old metal cafeteria trays. There is a wonderful distillery for those that might want to enjoy some authentic Tennessee moonshine.

> ERIKA: Fine! Since there is great food and moonshine, I will stay. That is until I see a ghost and then I am *out*.

This was going to be where Hannibal Lecter was imprisoned before he escaped in *The Silence of the Lambs*. This was also where Ray McDeere was housed in John Grisham's *The Firm*. Many authors are inspired by the real-life horror of this place.

> ERIKA: I love that. There is a spookiness that goes with the immensity and dark history of it.

Well, since we're wearing our walking boots, we can join the tour. Remember that it can be chilly here, even in early summer, so bring a coat for the nighttime ghost tour. Jaime Brock still hosts most of the tours here. There are self-guided tours available, but you can rent the place for your own paranormal investigation. For a fee, you can have the place all to yourself.

> ERIKA: NOPE!

MUNCY RABBIT TRAIL: THE BARKLEY MARATHON

I WENT DOWN ONE OF MY "RABBIT TRAILS" WHILE researching this place. We must talk about the Barkley Marathon. Gary "Lazarus Lake" Cantrell and Karl "Raw Dog" Henn heard about the 1977 escape of James Earl Ray. When they saw he had hardly run anywhere in his escape attempt, Cantrell said, "I could do at least 100 miles." And so, the Barkley Marathon was born. Named for Cantrell's longtime neighbor and frequent marathon running companion, Barry Barkley, it had its inaugural run in 1986.

> **ERIKA:** I am going to assume this was a terrible idea.

The race is insanely brutal. Getting into it is also crazy. The Barkley only allows 40 runners, and you have to fill out an essay on "Why I Should be Allowed to Run," pay a $1.60 entrance fee, and complete other strange requirements.

There is no public announcement, and you basically must figure out when to submit your application by contacting previous entrants. Previous entrants who did not finish the race have to provide an additional donation, like shirts, socks, or anything that Cantrell seems to need at the moment. Those who have finished need only bring a pack of Camel cigarettes.

> **ERIKA:** He sounds like he does not have all the fries in his Happy Meal, if you know what I mean?

Racers are given bibs with numbers. Racer number 1 is given to the person Cantrell determines the least likely to finish and is thus "a human sacrifice."

The course consists of around 20 "mile" loops that change distance, elevation, and route constantly. There are no aid stations except water at two points. Runners are allowed to study the map before the race, but once it starts, they can only use their own notes and no GPS or any navigation device.

There is a 60 mile and 100 mile version of this. If you make the 60 miles, you've completed what they call "The Fun Run" version. As of the writing of this book, over 50% of the races have had no finishers. It is considered one of the hardest ultramarathons in the world.

ERIKA: This seems like a very dumb thing to participate in.

The race starts any time on race day from midnight 'til noon. Cantrell blows a conch horn to signal the start within an hour. Then he lights a cigarette at some point thereafter, and that's the signal to start the race. There are 9 to 15 books scattered along the racecourse. The runners must find the books and remove the page corresponding to their bib number to prove they've made the circuit.

If a runner quits, a bugler plays "Taps" upon their return to the start point. As of 2024, Jasmin Paris finished with the 9th book on the 4th lap. That year, more than 30 competitors failed to reach even the first book up a steep climb of two miles.

ERIKA: You are not suggesting we, or any other Traveler, participate in this?

MARK: We should load up on carbs at the Warden's Table before our ghost hunt tonight—just in case Lazarus shows up to start the marathon. I kind of want the number 1 bib just as a souvenir.

ERIKA: I think I will pass on the bib and grab some more moonshine for the tour. Where are we headed after we get the crap scared out of us?

MARK: We're headed out and off back to civilization.

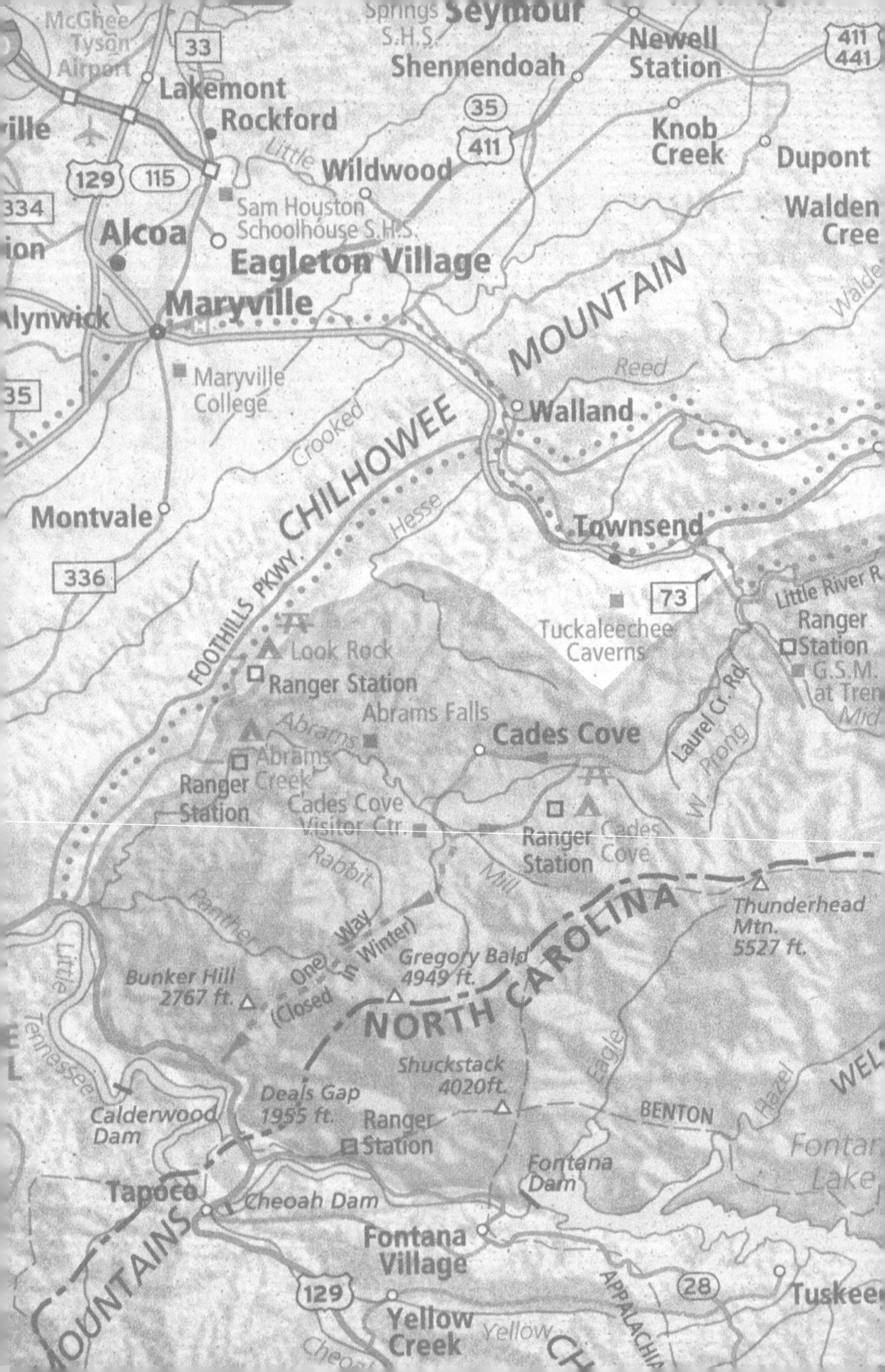

McGhee
Tyson
Airport
Lakemont
Rockford
33
Springs
S.H.S.
Seymour
Shennendoah
35
411
Newell
Station
411
441
Knob
Creek
Dupont
Walden
Cree
ville
129
115
334
Alcoa
Wildwood
Sam Houston
Schoolhouse S.H.S.
Eagleton Village
Maryville
lynwick
ion
35
Maryville
College
Crooked
Little
MOUNTAIN
Reed
Walland
Walde
Montvale
CHILHOWEE
Hesse
Townsend
336
73
Little River R
FOOTHILLS PKWY.
Tuckaleechee
Caverns
Ranger
Station
G.S.M.
at Tren
Midi
Look Rock
Ranger Station
Abrams Falls
Cades Cove
Laurel Cr. Rd.
Abrams
Abrams
Creek
Ranger
Station
Cades Cove
Visitor Ctr.
W. Prong
Ranger
Station
Cades
Cove
Rabbit
Panther
Mill
NORTH CAROLINA
Thunderhead
Mtn.
5527 ft.
Little
One Way
(Closed in Winter)
Gregory Bald
4949 ft.
Bunker Hill
2767 ft.
Tennessee
Eagle
Shuckstack
4020ft.
Hazel
WE
Deals Gap
1955 ft.
Ranger
Station
BENTON
Fontar
Lake
Calderwood
Dam
Fontana
Dam
Tapoco
Cheoah Dam
Fontana
Village
APPALACHI
28
Tuskee
MOUNTAINS
129
Yellow
Creek
Yellow
Cheo
CH

KNOXVILLE, TENNESSEE

KNOXVILLE

Mark: As we head farther into the fringes of the
Smokies, we've got to take a short trip in the
Wayback Machine to understand some of the
history surrounding our next stop: Knoxville.

THIS AREA WAS ORIGINALLY DOMINATED BY NATIVE TRIBES.
There are burial mounds dating back to 1000 B.C. or the Late Woodland
period here. It's noted that Hernando de Soto likely traveled through the
area in 1540 and mentioned a tribe on what is now Bussel Island. The
Cherokee controlled the region by the time European settlers arrived
but had frequent wars with the Creek and Shawnee tribes. The Cherokee
called the area kuwanda'talun'yi, which translates to "Mulberry Place."

Erika: I do love mulberry wine, which is not the point of
this story. Continue.

James White was the first settler in the area in the late 1780s. In less
than a decade, he built a fort and reinforced his settlement. By 1790,
George Washington had named the area the capital of the Southwest
Territory of the fledgling United States of America. The town was founded
and named for George Washington's Secretary of War, Henry Knox.

Erika: Knoxville... That makes sense.

William Blount met with over forty Cherokee chiefs to negotiate for
more lands for the European settlers. The Treaty of Holston was signed
on July 2, 1791. The town set about construction, and a land boom began.

The early history of the town was not unlike the Wild West era,
although it would take over a century for that to start.

The Cherokee had a splinter tribe called the Chickamauga that refused
to recognize the new settlers and would frequently raid the town. At one

point, the Chickamauga allied with another Creek tribe and killed over a dozen of the city's people in an area called Cavet's Station.

> ERIKA: This *is* like the Wild West.

Outlaws and brigands roamed the hillsides around the city proper including the Harpe brothers, who are considered by some to be the earliest documented serial killers in the United States with at least 39 confirmed deaths between them. They were driven out of town after being charged with stealing pigs and horses.

> ERIKA: It is amazing to me that the crime of stealing
> pigs and horses was worse than killing people
> back then.

The Harpe brothers were also suspected in the murder of a man named Johnson, whose body had been found in a nearby river and was covered in urine. His chest had been cut open and filled with stones. This would become the Harpes' signature method of body disposal.

> ERIKA: Wow! That is terrible, gross, and frankly, a lot
> of effort.

The two brothers fled into Kentucky and would later meet their end in 1799 and 1804, respectively. We'll make a note to visit Harpe's Head Road in Kentucky for a future travel book.

> ERIKA: It is located in Dixon, Kentucky. However, not
> part of the Smoky Mountains.

The state of Knoxville was said to have more taverns and tipping houses than grocers.

> ERIKA: I want to say I like the sound of that, but I know
> you're about to ruin it.

According to a 1794 report, the town had no churches and the jail was overcrowded. More land was added to the town and the state joined the Union on June 1, 1796, with Knoxville as the first capitol of the state. By the early 1800s, the town had become a prosperous crossroads on the edge of the Appalachians.

THE BAKER-PETERS HOUSE

IN 1830, DR. HARVEY BAKER BUILT A HOME IN THE CITY. It is at the corner of Kingston Pike and South Peters Road. He became a noted town doctor and a prominent citizen. His home sits on a beautiful farm, and he often treated patients in his own front room. As the Civil War began to develop in the area, Knoxville was a town with divided loyalties. Dr. Baker's son Abner enlisted with the Confederate Army.

> **ERIKA:** I am sure that did not go over well.

Since Knoxville was much less dependent on slavery than the rest of the South, many political leaders in the town were pro-emancipation as early as the 1830s.

> **ERIKA:** Good for them!

In January of 1861, a vote was held to consider secession to join the Confederacy. However, 77% voted against the measure, vowing that the city would stay in the Union. By June of that year, a second vote was held, and while the city remained loyal to the Union, the rest of the state voted in favor of joining the Confederacy.

> **ERIKA:** That is an all too familiar situation.

> **MARK:** The more things change, the more they stay the same.

The city quickly fell to the Union in August of 1863 when the Confederate officer Simon Buckner evacuated Knoxville. History claims that the Union soldiers under General Ambrose Burnside took the town without firing a shot. Except they didn't.

> **ERIKA:** I *was* going to be impressed.

Our dear Dr. Baker was reportedly a Confederate sympathizer—his son being in the Confederate Army after all. There are unconfirmed reports that Dr. Baker was secretly tending to wounded Confederate soldiers in his home. Knoxville's postmaster, William Hall, ran to the Union commander and reported this to the occupying soldiers.

ERIKA: 'Tis true what they say about mailmen: they see all.

A unit of Union troops were sent to the Baker house. There are stories that Dr. Baker was found actively operating on a Confederate soldier. However, this was not the case. The doctor had fled upstairs to barricade himself in his bedroom, and it was there the soldiers fired upon him through the door. Baker was hit and died instantly.

ERIKA: No shots fired, my a**.

Knoxville remained a key Union outpost during the course of the Civil War. General Longstreet led the Confederacy in a siege to try to retake the town in late 1863 but was forced to withdraw after only a few days. The city remained in the Union's hands until the end of the war.

Abner Baker returned home in September of 1865 where he learned of his father's death. He also learned that William Hall had been the one that had turned his father in to the Union authorities. Baker shot and killed Hall in an act of revenge. After being arrested for the murder, several of Hall's friends organized an armed mob to grab Abner from the authorities, and he was lynched.

ERIKA: Does this story have any good parts?

The house passed to George Peters after the Bakers' deaths. Peters and his servants claimed the father and son were not resting peacefully. Plus, there was a more sinister side to the house.

ERIKA: Of course there was.

Dr. Baker was a slave owner, and the slave quarters were in the lowest level of the home. There was a stairway that linked Dr. Baker's bedroom directly to the slave quarters in the basement. There were many tales that Dr. Baker was not a kind master. Though not confirmed, there are rumors of a secret slave graveyard that was once on the property that has been lost to history during the city's expansion.

ERIKA: That is not good. If it is true, I hope it is found.

MARK: There are so many lost cemeteries all over the world. They are generally rediscovered by new constructions.

ERIKA: I know. I've seen that horror movie.

The building is now the home to Finn's Restaurant and Tavern. It is an amazing Irish tavern themed around Finn McCool, a hunter-warrior of Irish folklore.

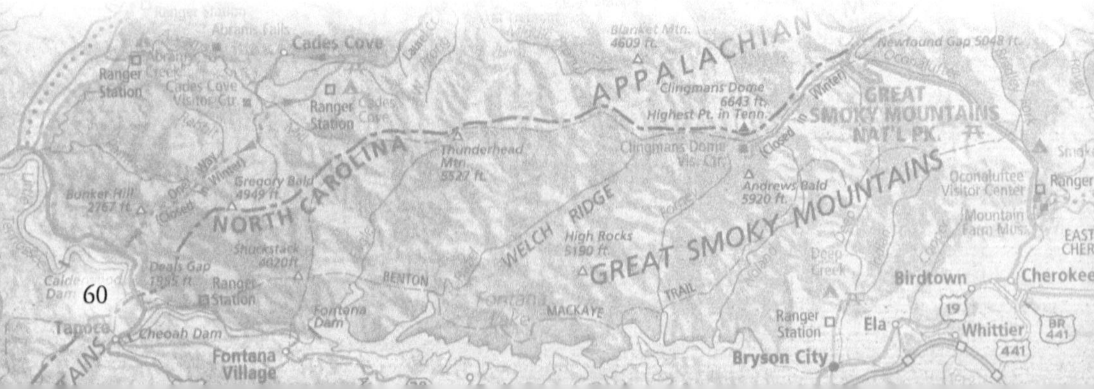

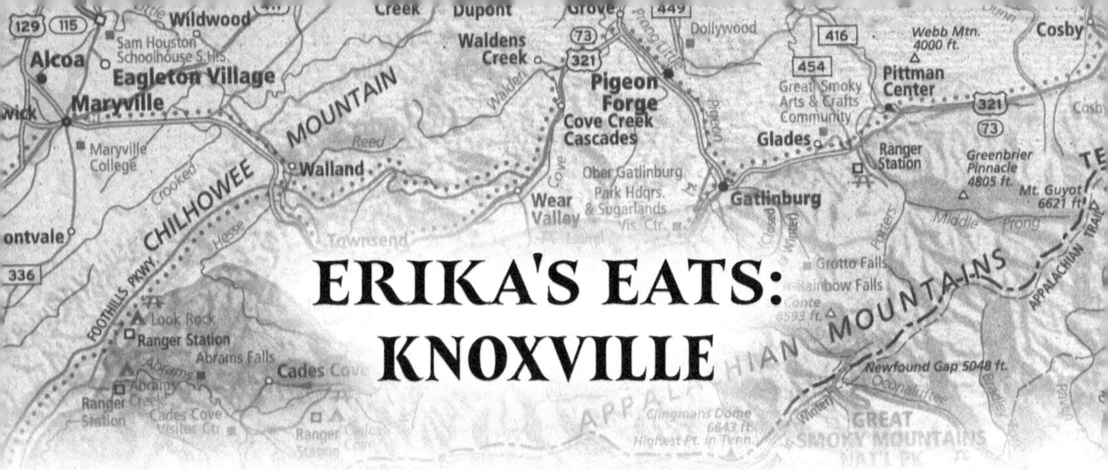

ERIKA'S EATS: KNOXVILLE

Finn's Restaurant and Tavern

Finn's has an amazing menu with some Irish favorites (fish and chips, bangers and mash), and some yummy new takes on Irish cuisine such as the Salmon of Knowledge or the Wings of Kerry in their Guinness BBQ sauce.

I would recommend the Old Abner or two with a toast to "those we know who make poor life choices." Right, Abner?

Speaking of poor life choices, while you are eating here, make sure to look at the old bedroom door. They've moved it down-stairs, and it still has the bullet holes that led to the death of old Dr. Baker.

On a different (and yet just as yummy) note: you can go on a ghost tour of the building from 6:30PM to midnight. Remember to bring a flashlight as they don't allow cell phone lights. Check their website to book your tickets ahead of time.

Not Watson's Kitchen + Bar

This restaurant lived a pre/vious life as a Watson's Department store. The food is made with incredibly fresh ingredients. Mark dove into the Not Yo' Mama's chicken and waffles, and I love spice, so I grabbed The Pretty Hot Burger that was, in fact, pretty hot. Of course, I needed to try their drink menu, chose the Queen Maeve, and felt like royalty afterward.

Farmacy's

The owner of Farmacy's Bettina Hamblin will not disappoint any Travelers with her fun menu. I immediately dove into some of her black & blue fries, and Mark grabbed a "lobstah" roll, which was as delicious as it sounds. Of course, I left room for the limon-cello-white chocolate blueberry bread pudding which was out of this world.

Barrel House Gypsy Circus

This is the place to go if you want a little pep in your step, or you just love cider and mead the way I do. You can't go wrong with some Apple Butter Drifter, but don't just take my word for it. Stop in and grab a crisp, locally made beverage.

Coffee & Chocolate

What is better than coffee and chocolate? NOTHING! This is the place to caffeinate and grab some very yummy treats. I happen to love macarons, so it was a difficult decision between the black-berry vanilla, lavender, London fog… forget it, I want them all. If you find yourself with a similar dilemma, and you want to send cookies my way, I would not be sad.

MARK: Now that we've feasted. We've got one last stop across town.

THE GROUNDS OF OLD GRAY CEMETERY IN KNOXVILLE, TENNESSEE HOUSE THE REMAINS OF MANY OF THE CITY'S MOST FAMOUS FORMER RESIDENTS. PHOTO BY AUTHOR.

OLD GRAY CEMETERY & DARK AGGIE

KNOXVILLE'S DARK HISTORY CONTINUES LONG AFTER THE Civil War.

> **ERIKA:** I would think so since we are standing in the middle of it.

Let's get out of the Wayback Machine for a minute to stretch our legs. I can't think of a more beautiful place than a Victorian era garden that spans over 13 acres of beauty and was added to the National Register of Historic Places in 1996.

> **ERIKA:** What about a Victorian era bar?

I really enjoy walking here at Old Gray Cemetery in the autumn, but it is amazing any time of year. It was named for the English poet Thomas Gray who lived here in the 1700s. He famously wrote, "The paths of glory lead but to the grave."

> **ERIKA:** Poetic and yet creepy. I see we are surrounded by tombstones... Again.

The graveyard is a formally sanctioned arboretum for its diversity of flowers and trees. Old Gray was established in 1850, which was the peak of the garden-cemetery movement that had migrated from Paris. The idea was that cemeteries should be beautiful and invite individuals to visit with a variety of trees and flowers. This graveyard offers way more colors than gray.

> **ERIKA:** This is the second time in the book you have mentioned a cemetery for its beauty. There has to be more...

THE Dark Side OF THE Smoky Mountains

Like all cemeteries and graveyards, there are a myriad of stories told in the stones. One of my favorites involves three stones with the same date of death. I know we just got out of it, but we need to take the Wayback Machine to that fateful day of October 19, 1882.

> **ERIKA:** I see there will be many costume changes for this trip.

Joseph Mabry II was a prominent businessman in 19th century Knoxville. He was in the railroad business and also owned many race-horses. Mabry donated land to the city to establish Market Square in 1853 for the sole purpose of creating a market house for the city; it is still a farmer's market to this day.

> **ERIKA:** Why did we not travel to the market? I could use some fresh wild strawberries.

Mabry II had a son Joseph Mabry III, and though they were well respected in town, it was well known that both men had short tempers and itchy trigger fingers. Mabry II had another son named Will. Will was also quick to anger and had gotten into a gunfight with Constable Don Lusby; the former did not survive. Mabry II was said to have murdered the Constable sometime later in a shootout in retaliation.

> **ERIKA:** Darn it, I should have worn my gunslinger attire for this trip.

Thomas O'Connor owned the Mechanics Bank and Trust on Gay Street. It sat where Clancy's Tavern is now just next to the Tennessee Theater. Mabry II sold O'Connor some land with the stipulation that it would be given to his son Will. Since Will was slain by Lusby in December of 1881, the land wasn't handed over. Mabry II blamed O'Connor for having his son killed to keep the land. He vowed to kill O'Connor himself.

> **ERIKA:** I feel like this won't end well...

According to witnesses, O'Connor waited in the doorway of his bank on the morning of October 19th. He had a shotgun with him as he had heard Mabry II was hunting for him. When O'Connor saw him on the opposite side of the street, he drew his gun and took Mabry II down. When O'Connor reached back into his bank to grab a second shotgun,

Mabry III ran down and shot O'Connor in the chest with his pistol as retribution.

ERIKA: This is like the movie *Tombstone*.

MARK: Oddly, similar in history to the O.K. Corral, I'll admit. We did mention similarities to the Wild West.

O'Connor managed to fire back before dying, and he hit Mabry III in the chest. Within minutes, all three men died in the street. Several witnesses were hit with buckshot from the shotgun blasts.

ERIKA: There is a lesson here about being too close to a gunfight but alas, continue...

Mark Twain would mention this event in his book *Life on the Mississippi*. He wrote that the South is "the highest type of civilization this continent has ever seen," which he followed a footnote describing the Mabry-O'Connor shootout on Gay Street.

ERIKA: Was Mr. Twain being ironic?

MARK: When wasn't he being ironic?

All three men were buried on the same day in Old Gray Cemetery. Mabry II and his son share an obelisk in a corner. Thomas O'Connor is buried on the opposite side.

ERIKA: I wonder if we would have a ghostly shootout in the cemetery if you buried them next to each other?

MARK: The families might have had another shootout at the funerals if they had.

Now, most cemeteries are known to have the occasional spirit. Generally, there is the sense of someone watching and waiting. Perhaps it's simply the feeling of mourning, or that lingering remembrance that causes the

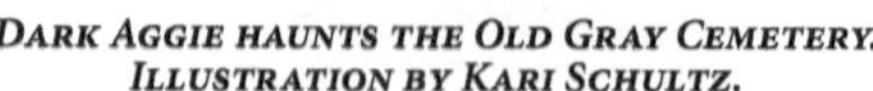

DARK AGGIE HAUNTS THE OLD GRAY CEMETERY.
ILLUSTRATION BY KARI SCHULTZ.

spirits to stay here. Seeing shadows among the over 5,500 graves here is to be expected, but there is something here that is far more unsettling.

ERIKA: Great. You know how much I love "unsettling."

There is an entity said to be latched onto the graveyard. It is called Dark Aggie or sometimes Black Aggie. He is described by witnesses as a cloaked man surrounded by a black mist. Some stories claim he walks among the rows of tombstones, but others claim he floats on his misty, black cloud.

ERIKA: NOPE!

He nearly always appears just before sunset, so there is no need to go into this cemetery after closing time if you are hoping to see him. There are literally hundreds of stories about this figure, but they all generally end with him charging at unwanted visitors and chasing them out of the cemetery.

ERIKA: I don't like the sound of that.

No one is really sure who he is or why he haunts the grounds of Old Gray. There was a story of an old statue that many claimed was his effigy, but it had been removed due to much vandalism of it. That's actually a different Black Aggie up in Baltimore. We'll note it for a future travel.

Paranormal investigators have reported EVPs where the entity claims someone has defiled his grave. Many hear their name whispered behind them with no one there when they turn, but Dark Aggie is then seen out of the corner of their eye some distance away.

There doesn't seem to be a specific spot where he is most often seen, but he appears to be some sort of guardian spirit and reports range all over the grounds.

ERIKA: So, you're saying there is no way to potentially avoid him?

One way to spend some time here after dark and not get arrested (or chased by Dark Aggie) is to come to their movie night hosted by Knoxville Horror. Recently they showed *The Crow* in the graveyard, and they do other events several times a year. I'm looking forward to a future showing of *Return of the Living Dead*. Maybe Dark Aggie can make an appearance?

ERIKA: NOPE! NOPE! NOPE! I am out of here!

MILLENNIUM MANOR

WILLIAM NICHOLSON AND HIS WIFE, EMMA FAIR, BELIEVED the rapture was coming soon. In 1937, at the age of 61, William Nicholson decided to build a home that would be able to withstand the coming Armageddon.

> **ERIKA:** Wonder how that worked out for them?

They moved to Alcoa, Tennessee where he got a job with the Aluminum Company of America and began to work on their castle.

Willam was a staunch believer of Revelations 20:6. He predicted that in 1959 the first resurrection of Christ would occur, and he and the other 144,000 righteous souls would reign for 1,000 years. Thankfully, he completed construction on his castle by 1946 after only nine years of construction, so he had plenty of time to get ready. When the year came and nothing happened, he changed his prediction to 1969. Sadly, neither he nor his wife would live to see if their prediction would come true.

> **ERIKA:** Umm... No one has seen that prediction come true.

Emma died in 1950 at the age of 72 from cancer. William lived another 15 years and died in 1965 at the age of 88. William said on his last trip to the hospital, "If god doesn't intervene soon, I will die."

> **ERIKA:** 88 is a long life.

> **MARK:** We should be so lucky.

The Nicholson family had ten children, but none of them ever lived in the stone castle built by their parents. William never left a will since he believed he was going to be living for a thousand years or more.

> **ERIKA:** I wonder if I can tell my kids the same thing.

Millennium Manor

The castle was abandoned and soon fell into neglect. It was looted and became a local party spot for teenagers and vagrants. The building still stood strong because of the amazing construction by the Nicholsons.

The house was built by hand using levers and ramps to move the stones. There were almost no nails or wood in the building, so there would never be the threat of rust. Nicholson used Roman architecture as his design inspiration. The Arch and Keystone technique is used throughout the house but is very apparent over the doors and windows. The castle was built with stone and cement, its walls over 18 inches thick and floors on top of four feet of stone foundation.

The castle consists of 14 rooms and a two-car garage. It's around 3,000 square feet under a 400-ton roof. A six-story-deep well is also on the property. There is a stone wall surrounding the nearly one acre of the castle and its grounds. It was so solidly built that, during World War II,

A DRONE VIEW OF MILLENIUM MANOR. PHOTO PROVIDED BY MILLENIUM MANOR.

the US Government attempted to buy the castle for $150,000 to use as an armory. Nicholson refused to sell.

Dean Fontaine, a firefighter and historian, purchased the manor in 1995 for $39,000. He was drawn to the house by its unique style and amazed by the idea that it could never burn down. He noted that the structure is so sound that, in 2006, a tornado passed directly over the castle, and he slept through it. Dean and his lovely wife Karen have been working on restoring the manor since their purchase.

> **ERIKA:** I am glad someone decided to take care of it.

> **MARK:** Me too. It's amazing to behold.

Currently, they offer public tours on weekends by appointment only. They also offer educational trips to the castle.

Upstairs includes a gold room that was likely the dining room, but the Fontaines have converted it into a museum, complete with a tribute to the Nicholsons. They have also filled the room with donated medieval weapons.

The Fontaines are still renovating the rooms. They plan to open a coffee house, and they already rent out the building for events like weddings and meetings.

> **ERIKA:** What? No ghosts? Old man Nicolson doesn't hang around shooing off trespassers?

> **ERIKA:** Now it's time to head to bed. We're heading a little farther south of Knoxville to head to yet another castle—all this talk has me yearning for a fairy tale.

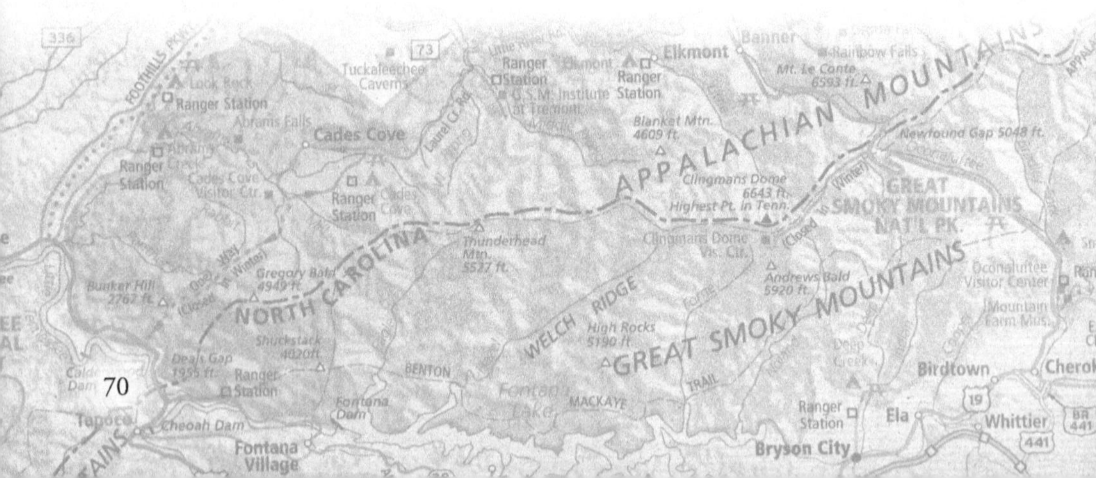

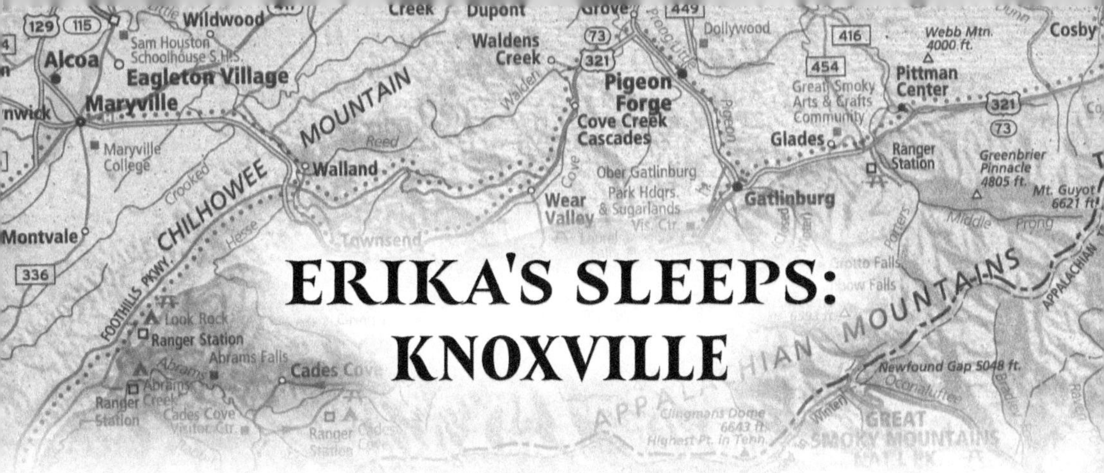

Willamswood Castle

> **ERIKA:** Okay Mark, before I list a few places Travelers can stay in Knoxville, why are we going to a castle?

Willamswood Castle is designed like an old Scottish castle. Which is quite fitting, since the Appalachian hills it is nestled into are the same mountain range as the Scottish Highlands before they did their Brexit from Pangea. The castle is adorned with stained glass windows, ramparts, turrets, and suits of armor. For even more fun, there are secret passageways! Is there a better place for us to sleep tonight?

> **ERIKA:** Is it haunted?

Currently located in the middle of the Ijams Nature Center, it's like walking into another world. Less than 15 minutes to Knoxville but surrounded by 300 acres of nature, it's 4,500 square feet of awesome medieval extravagance. The moving bookcase is my favorite part of the place, but there's also a replica of the Sistine Chapel painted over the four-poster bed in the main bedroom!

Julia Tucker designed the home in the 1990s to honor her late son. Her daughter Judy Roy said her mother had explained it to her this way, "When he died, I decided that I was going to build a castle. He played bagpipes and our family is from Scotland, so Mom took a yellow legal pad out and started sketching. She found a builder and started from there."

Julia grew up in the castle and she noted, "There are a lot of good hidey-holes and secret passageways."

WILLIAMSWOOD CASTLE IS A SIGHT TO BEHOLD. PHOTO PROVIDED BY WILLIAMSWOOD CASTLE.

ERIKA: You still have not mentioned if it is haunted…

Because of the unique amenities, like the aforementioned hidden door in the bookcase, Julia generally provides a tour of the property complete with instructions on how to operate everything before you settle in for the night. There are modern touches like AC/Heat and Wi-Fi, but sadly, there isn't a moat.

It does tend to get booked up quickly but check the website frequently for last-minute openings. The rates are reasonable for what you get as well.

ERIKA: If a castle is not your speed, here are a couple of other locations to rest your head.

Ancient Lore Village

Ever wanted to be in the Lord of the Rings or any fantasy setting? You have to stay in this amazing village. They have themed rooms—my favorite might be the Gremlin Dens—so that you can get some rest after a long day of adventuring. They have amazing food and drinks for all kinds of celebrations. Of course, make your reservations in advance so you get the room you want.

GlampKnox

This is the only way I am willing to sleep in a tent: glamping! You will find yourself getting back to nature in true "Erika won't sleep on the ground" style. This way you can say "I went camping" and still have a great night's sleep!

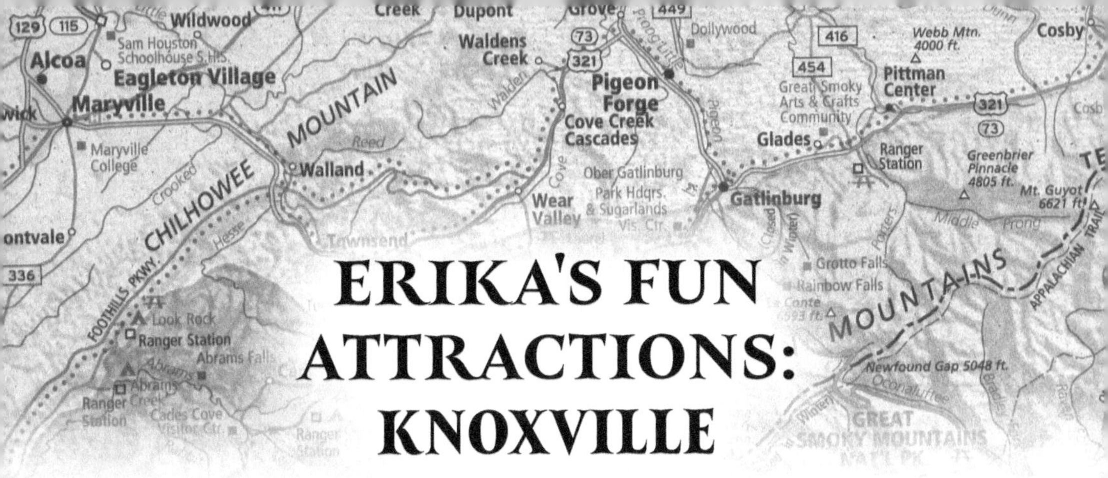

ERIKA'S FUN ATTRACTIONS: KNOXVILLE

IN CASE YOU STILL WANT THE CRAP SCARED OUT OF YOU before bed, head over to one or both of these terrifying attractions. Of course, check their calendar for events before you arrive.

Screamville

These cursed acres have a sinister backstory—get immersed, if you dare. If you love truly terrifying storytelling mixed with monsters and frights, you will love this place. They also have the option of a Camp Getaway, where you can stay… possibly forever.

Frightworks Haunted House

This is a fun haunted house experience, if you love that sort of thing (like Mark). If you are like me, you can wait to see if your friends emerge after all the screaming.

FRIGHTMARE MANOR IS A HAUNTED ATTRACTION HOSTED ANNUALLY WITHIN THE HISTORIC LEXER MANOR. WHERE A FAMILY MASSACRE FACTUALLY OCCURRED IN 1902. PHOTO PROVIDED BY FRIGHTMARE MANOR.

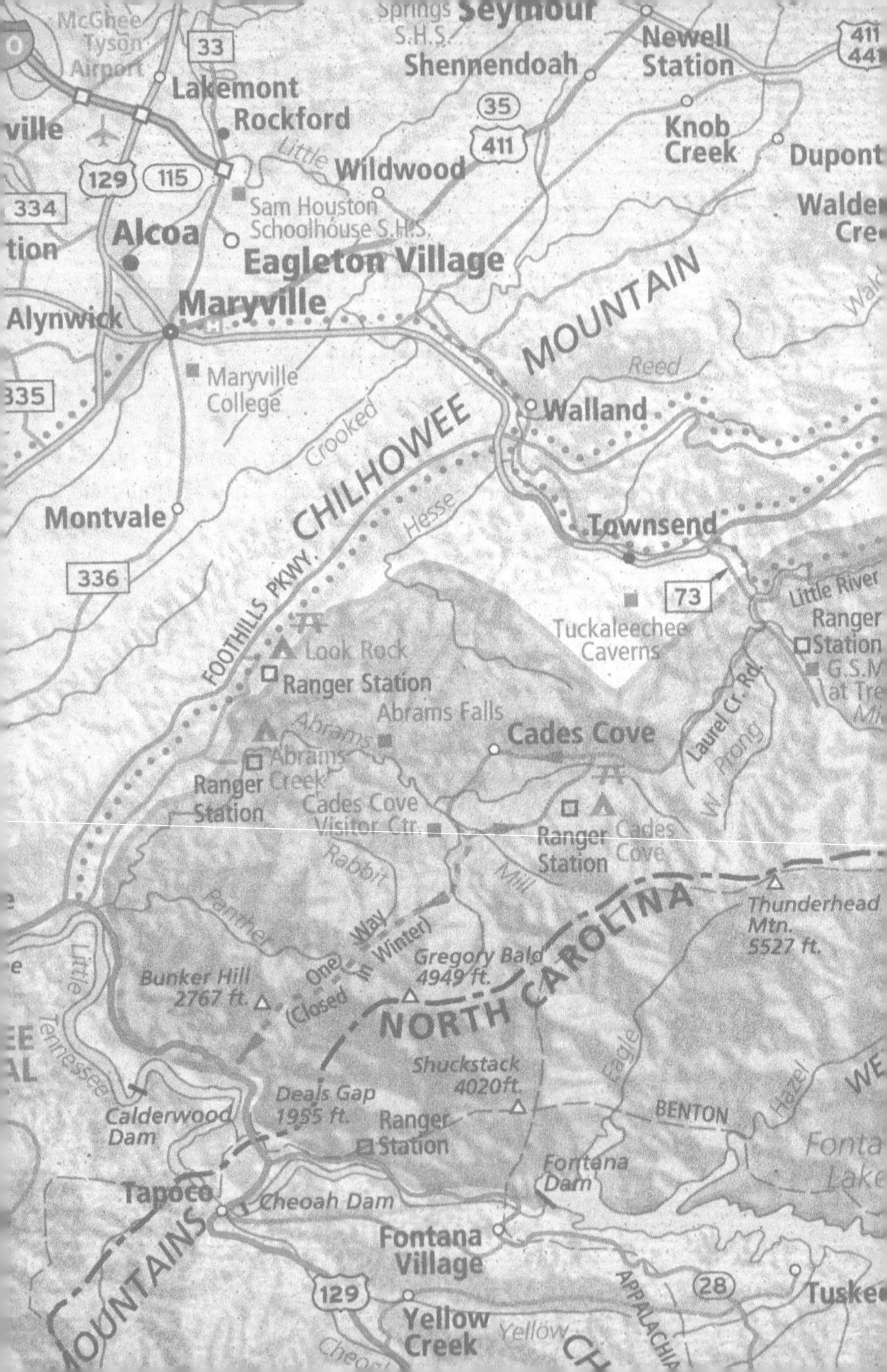

McGhee
Tyson
Airport
Springs
S.H.S.
Seymour
Shennendoah
Newell
Station
411
441
33
Lakemont
Rockford
35
411
Knob
Creek
Dupont
ville
Little
Wildwood
129
115
334
Sam Houston
Schoolhouse S.H.S.
Walden
Cree
Alcoa
tion
Eagleton Village
Maryville
MOUNTAIN
Alynwick
335
Maryville
College
Reed
Crooked
CHILHOWEE
Walland
Montvale
Hesse
Townsend
336
FOOTHILLS PKWY.
73
Little River
Ranger
Station
Tuckaleechee
Caverns
G.S.M.
lat Tre
Mu
Look Rock
Ranger Station
Abrams Falls
Laurel Cr. Rd.
Abrams
Cades Cove
Abrams
Ranger
Station
Creek
Cades Cove
Visitor Ctr.
Ranger
Station
Cades
Cove
W. Prong
Rabbit
Mill
NORTH CAROLINA
Thunderhead
Mtn.
5527 ft.
Panther
One
Way
In Winter)
Gregory Bald
4949 ft.
Little
Bunker Hill
2767 ft.
(Closed
Tennessee
Shuckstack
4020ft.
Eagle
WE
EE
AL
Deals Gap
1955 ft.
Ranger
Station
BENTON
Hazel
Fonta
Calderwood
Dam
Fontana
Dam
Lake
Tapoco
Cheoah Dam
Fontana
Village
MOUNTAINS
129
28
APPALACHIA
Tuske
CH
Yellow
Creek
Yellow
Cheo

SEVIERVILLE, TENNESSEE

SEVIERVILLE

OKAY, WE MADE IT TO THE BUC-EE'S AT THE EXIT TO Sevierville which, at the time of this writing, is the world's largest convenience store in the world at 74,707 square feet. It's worth it just for the clean bathrooms, but I never say no to the triple meat sandwich. We always stop to see if they have Halloween supplies yet and restock the Wayback Machine's snacks.

> **ERIKA:** Perfect timing! Because although it is probably ill- advised, I am taking the Wayback Machine through the amazing rainbow car wash. Let's hope I don't end up lost in time... again.

Well, we don't really need the Wayback Machine for me to tell you that Sevierville was named after the first governor of Tennessee, John Sevier. He was a fierce rival of Andrew Jackson, and they almost had a duel in 1803. John Sevier was governor for six terms. He even served as governor of the area before it was Tennessee.

> **ERIKA:** I love a good duel!

Since the Wayback Machine is all clean, let's go ahead and hop in. The earliest inhabitants of the area, that we know of, were the Natives that were here in the Woodland period around 200 A.D.

The mound builders came around 1200 A.D. and built a village right where the Little Pigeon River and the West Fork meet. There was a burial mound there that was excavated in 1881 and dubbed the McMahan Indian Mound after the farm it was currently on.

> **ERIKA:** Can we say haunted farm? We can!

Of course, the Cherokee dominated this area in the 18th century with many villages along the rivers.

Sevierville

Europeans arrived around this time and began trading with the tribe. Issac Thomas was the most famous of these early traders and exchanged manufactured goods for the animal furs the Cherokee could give him. He was liked and respected by the tribes. He was also the first to collect some of their tales—like Spearfinger.

> **ERIKA:** Why are you bringing her up again? We do not
> need to summon her.

When the first Colonial settlers arrived, the Cherokee quickly saw them as invaders and allied themselves with the British to attack their settlements in the Tennessee Valley. Col. John Sevier launched a punitive series of raids on the Cherokee villages. A peace agreement was reached in 1785 wherein the Cherokee signed away the rights to the county with the Treaty of Dumplin Creek.

> **ERIKA:** I hate that.

> **MARK:** Sadly, that is the way of history. To the victor go
> the spoils.

This area—which is now northeast Tennessee— petitioned to join the fledgling United States as the 14th state in 1785. They called themselves the state of "Franklin" after Bejamin Franklin.

> **ERIKA:** How come we don't have the state of Franklin?
> That would have been amazing!

> **MARK:** There were a bunch of reasons. We don't have
> time to go into all of them right now unless you
> want to go further back in the Wayback Machine.

> **ERIKA:** We'd need more snacks. Continue your story.

The state was denied entry, and the area set up its own nation and court system. John Sevier served as the governor with an annual salary of 1000 deer skins as they had no paper currency. By 1788, North Carolina was granted control of the region and "The Lost State of Franklin" disappeared into history. It wouldn't be until 1796 that the state of Tennessee would be admitted into the Union.

WHEATLANDS PLANTATION

In 1820, the Wheatland Plantation was built on the edge of town. It was constructed by Timothy Chandler who had established this area as his family farm. He was a Revolutionary War veteran. When he passed away in 1819, his son John inherited the farm and began to build the main house. At its peak, the farm covered over 4,600 acres. After the Civil War ended, John Chandler insisted that a large portion of his lands be given to his freed slaves. They formed the Chandler Gap Community, which thrived well into the 20th Century.

> **Erika:** That is very cool.

> **Mark:** There's a good and bad side in every place.

Even though Tennessee would join the Confederacy in 1861, the Smoky Mountain area was mostly pro-Union. Though no major engagements occurred in the area, there were frequent raids from both sides of the conflict.

> **Erika:** I believe that is called a "skirmish."

> **Mark:** A skirmish is when a smaller part of the main force engages separately from the larger force. Raids generally involved looting the local farms and towns for supplies and causing destruction of supply lines.

The Wheatlands was owned by the Chandler family for generations. In 2011, the house was purchased by Richard Parker and John Burns. They aimed to restore the main house and open the property to the public. In their restoration, they discovered some of the plantation's very dark history.

Wheatlands Plantation

ERIKA: Why am I not surprised?

The house itself was built on top of a giant geode. John Chandler was a freemason and decided to incorporate this into the foundation of the house. In further clearing of the land, they discovered that the farm sits on the location of the Battle of Boyd's Creek from 1790. This was where John Sevier attacked a warband of the Cherokee and dumped the casualties in a mass grave. The mound was found when clearing the property. It is estimated that there are at least 28 bodies there.

ERIKA: That is terrible and spooky.

More overgrowth was removed, and the new owners discovered Cedar Spring and the small pond it fed into. There lay a long-abandoned slave cemetery. Archaeologists have studied the area and even found a stone foundation that may have been the original distillery for Wheatlands Whiskey, which was famous down in New Orleans.

ERIKA: I do not love the cemetery, but I do love some whiskey.

WHEATLANDS PLANTATION HOLDS MANY DARK SECRETS. PHOTO PROVIDED BY SEVIERVILLE HISTORICAL SOCIETY.

THE **Dark Side** OF THE **Smoky Mountains**

The new owners discovered there were over 70 recorded deaths in the house, including the last descendant of the Chandler family: Blanche McMahon, who died in 1966. Richard Parker told us, "Of course there are ghosts here. There are ghosts everywhere here."

ERIKA: Of course there are.

Parker leads tours of The Wheatlands every week from Thursday to Sunday. He spoke to us of at least 15 people dying in the master bedroom alone over the years. Two women have died on the main staircase. One died in 1888 of a heart attack while a second fell and broke her neck in 1932.

ERIKA: Why are we here?

MARK: Because we're *Eerie Travels!*

The most famous death, and the source of the most infamous haunting, occurred in 1942. Tim Chandler, one of the last direct familial owners, had gotten drunk and began randomly shooting his pistol throughout the house. His son wound up bludgeoning him to death in order to stop him. Some visitors claim to hear the yelling of a man, thuds, and then a gurgling noise as though the event is being played out over and over.

ERIKA: NOPE!

Noted ghosts include a young girl in a blue dress running up and down the stairs. There are numerous sightings of shadow figures all over the property and grounds. One young tour group member was attacked by what he claimed was a young African American boy who seemed to be dripping wet. He collapsed when the ghost ran through him and, when he was checked by EMS, had symptoms of heat stroke. He had no knowledge of the mansion's past because the tour hadn't even started.

ERIKA: I'm leaving before this tour starts. I am sure it is amazing, but I will wait for you ghost free, with my whiskey, safely *outside.*

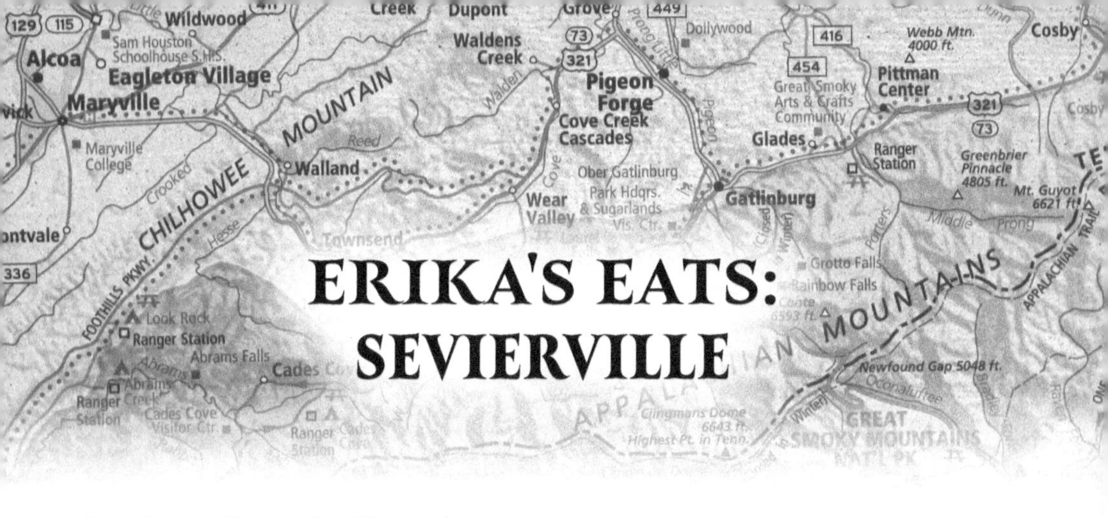

ERIKA'S EATS: SEVIERVILLE

Cookie Dough Monster

You cannot stop in Sevierville without checking out this cookie shop with amazing burgers! As you know, we can load up on sweets, but today's choice is a Fluffernutter shake before we head out to our next stop.

Now that our tour is over, let's head over to our next stop.

MOST TRAVELERS HEAD THROUGH SEVIERVILLE ON THEIR WAY TO VISIT DOLLYWOOD. MANY NEVER SEE THIS ICONIC BRONZE STATUE NEXT TO THE COURTHOUSE. THERE ARE STORIES OF SOME GHOSTLY FIGURE COMING TO WASH IT NIGHTLY. PHOTO BY AUTHOR.

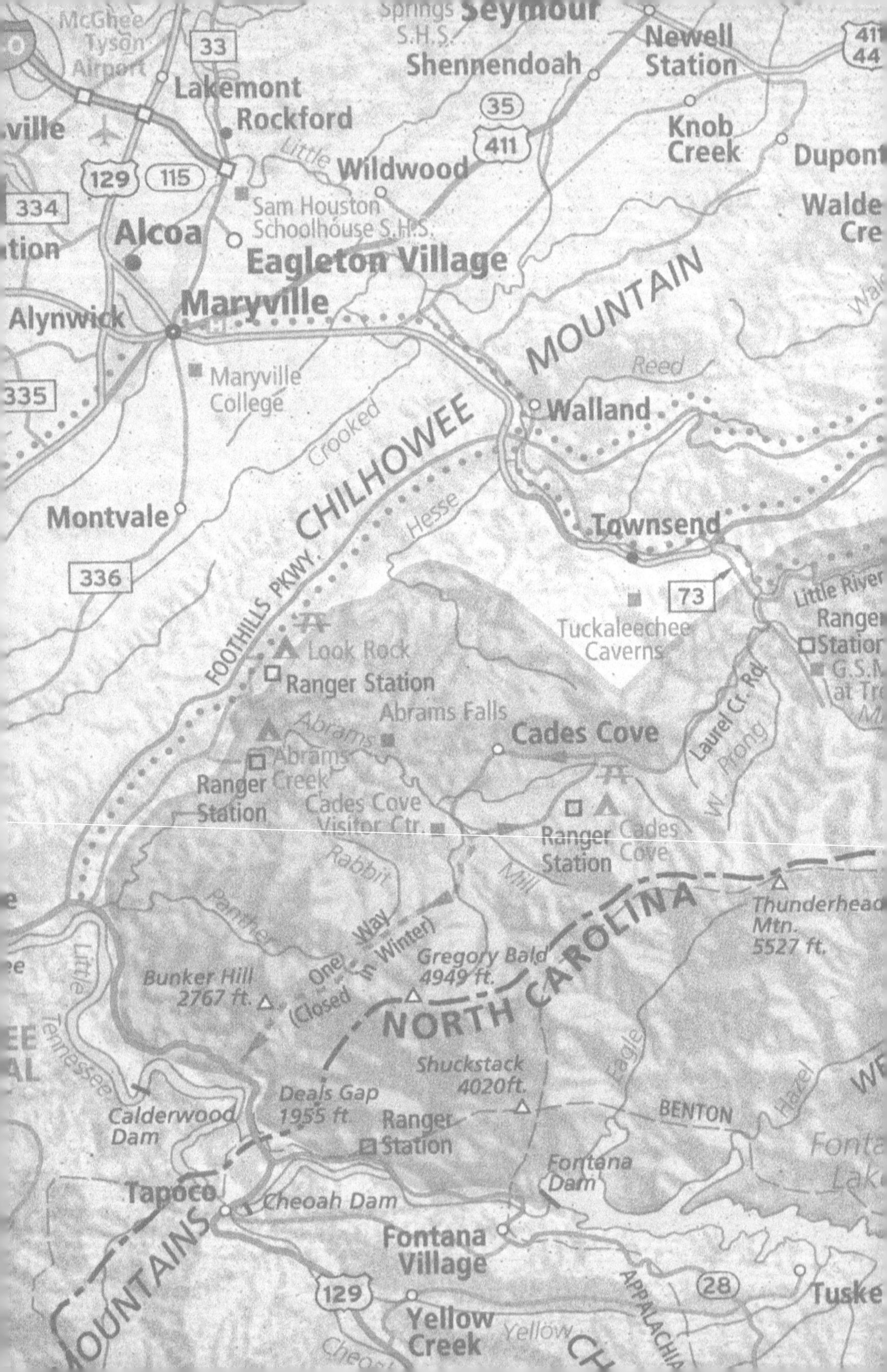

McGhee Tyson Airport
33
Lakemont
Rockford
-ville
129
115
334
Alcoa
-tion
Alynwick
335
Montvale
336
Maryville College
Maryville
Eagleton Village
Sam Houston Schoolhouse S.H.S.
Little
Wildwood
Springs S.H.S.
Seymour
Shennendoah
35
411
411
44
Newell Station
Knob Creek
Dupont
Walde
Cre
Wal
Crooked
CHILHOWEE
MOUNTAIN
Reed
Walland
Hesse
FOOTHILLS PKWY.
Townsend
73
Tuckaleechee Caverns
Little River
Ranger
Station
G.S.M.
at Tr
Mi
Look Rock
Ranger Station
Abrams Falls
Cades Cove
Laurel Cr. Rd.
W. Prong
Abrams
Abrams Creek
Ranger Station
Cades Cove Visitor Ctr.
Ranger Station
Cades Cove
Rabbit
Mill
Panther
One Way (Closed in Winter)
Gregory Bald 4949 ft.
NORTH CAROLINA
Thunderhead Mtn. 5527 ft.
Little
Tennessee
Bunker Hill 2767 ft.
Shuckstack 4020 ft.
Eagle
BENTON
Hazel
WE
Deals Gap 1955 ft.
Ranger Station
Fontana Dam
Fonta
Lak
Calderwood Dam
-EE
-AL
Tapoco
Cheoah Dam
Fontana Village
129
Yellow Creek
Yellow
Cheoa
MOUNTAINS
APPALACHIA
28
Tuske

Townsend, Tennessee

TUCKALEECHEE CAVERNS

OUR NEXT STOP IS JUST OUTSIDE TOWNSEND, TENNESSEE. This area was known by the Cherokee as Tuckaleechee, which translates into "peaceful valley." The area along the Little River was inhabited by the indigenous tribes for generations. It was a fertile hunting ground until the Cherokee were forced out by the European settlers.

> **ERIKA:** I hate that part of history but glad we can learn from it.

> **MARK:** It's sadly not the last we're going to hear about this. Not by a long shot.

In the early 20th century, the Little River Lumber Company opened a railroad to get the lumber from this area down to the tannery in Walland, Tennessee. They formed a town called Townsend. It was named after the founder of the lumber company, Wilson B. Townsend. They would build railroad lines deeper into the Smoky Mountains. The area started having a boom but not of lumber.

> **ERIKA:** That is putting the railway before the product, I would say!

The town of Townsend, and the nearby logging camp of Elkmont, were suddenly building hotels since the railroad was now providing tourists with easy access to the majestic vistas and views in the Smoky Mountains. By the 1930s, the lumber company sold most of the land it owned to the state of Tennessee. This became part of the burgeoning Smoky Mountains National Park. Townsend would be the gateway to the park and the main entrance for some time.

> **ERIKA:** I had no idea.

Tuckaleechee Caverns

Unlike Pigeon Forge, Cherokee, and Gatlinburg, the area around Townsend kept its sleepy, small-town appearance. It has kept its name as "The Peaceful Side of the Smokies." Many prefer this entrance to avoid the attractions and businesses that mark the other gateways into the national park.

ERIKA: A peaceful sleepy town. So, what's dark about it?

While living in Townsend, two young boys discovered a forgotten secret of the mountains. Though, it wasn't a true secret as the Cherokee had used it for shelter and storage and lumber company employees had used it to cool down on hot days. It was on a hot day that the boys supposedly came across the entrance to the Tuckaleechee Caverns.

ERIKA: This sounds like the start to a horror movie.

Bill Vananda and Harry Myers grew up near the entrance to the cavern and even did some minor exploring. As they grew up, they heard stories of Mammoth Cave in Kentucky and Carlsbad Caverns in New Mexico. Their cave was first opened to the public in 1931 by Earl McCampbell, but due to the Great Depression, it closed after only a year. Earl had people go into the cave system with a lantern for the cost of a nickel and were told to "have fun."

ERIKA: Yep... Horror movie.

MARK: They had obviously never seen *The Descent.*

Bill and Harry decided to buy the cavern themselves and work on it. They planned to open it to the public after proper work had been done and have tours. They opened in 1953 with kerosene lamps but were already working on electric lighting, which was completed in 1955.

There are currently a few tour options available at the caverns. Famously billed as "The Greatest Sight Under the Smokies," it is hard to deny its title. Steve Vananda is the current proprietor of the caverns. He is the son of Bill Vananda, one of the founders. He still leads tours here personally.

ERIKA: I thought that was going to go very dark, but it seems like a cool place to come explore.

THE **Dark Side** OF THE **Smoky Mountains**

MARK: Every place is a cool place to explore!

The caverns have typical safety concerns for visitors to natural sites. Floors will likely be wet and uneven. There are many stairs. There are some tight and binding areas to pass through. So, make sure to wear close-toed, comfortable shoes. The tour lasts just over an hour and covers just over a mile and a quarter of caves.

ERIKA: Not too long to feel like a mountain is on top of you.

Though wet, the floors are never truly slippery. The plus side is it is a constant 58 degrees no matter what the surface temperature is like, so it is a great escape from the heat in the summer, and a fun place to warm up when it is snowing in the winter. The paths were built by Steve's father and Myers all those decades ago.

One of the rooms is called "The Big Room." It's a huge cavern nearly 400 feet long, 300 feet wide, and 150 feet tall. That dwarfs even the largest part of Mammoth Cave National Park. The Big Room was accidentally discovered in 1954 by a survey team. It was quickly added to the tour.

TUCKALEECHEE CAVERNS IS HOME TO THE ICONIC SILVER FALLS. PHOTO PROVIDED BY SMOKY MOUNTAIN HISTORICAL SOCIETY.

Tuckaleechee Caverns

Steve said the room could hold a football field. He then showed us just how large it is. He walked toward a stalagmite formation; as he got closer, the stalagmite got bigger. It was like an optical illusion. By the time he reached it, you could see it was nearly 15 feet tall, but it seemed so tiny compared to the vastness of the Big Room.

> **ERIKA:** I prefer a room like this to some of those tight turns back at Rock City.

After crossing a small footbridge next to a formation called Elephant Rock, you'll reach the base of Silver Falls. Steve told us that this is the tallest underground waterfall in the United States, though we thought that honor belonged to Ruby Falls.

> **ERIKA:** Is it bigger than Ruby Falls?

Steve told us, "They love to brag about it. Here's how it actually works." He then went on to explain that Ruby Falls is the highest "uninterrupted underground waterfall" on the East Coast. It falls 145 feet from a ledge into a pond 1200 feet below the earth's surface. Silver Falls goes 210 feet from top to bottom, but it is split into two tiers since there is a pool about halfway down. Either way, it is an incredible sight.

> **ERIKA:** I think Steve was doing math like I do for that one.

> **MARK:** I forget sometimes that you are very good at inventing numbers.

It is said that the Cherokee used the mystical energies that flowed through Silver Falls to bless those that stood in the mist. It could grant luck and prosperity and banish the evil spirits that might be clinging onto a person, so after some of our darker stops, I made this a must visit.

> **ERIKA:** After the trip so far, I do feel the need to banish some evil spirits.

Many parts of the cavern still haven't been fully explored. There's a room past a large underground river that is likely twice as large as The Big Room, but it is partially underwater.

> **ERIKA:** I draw the line at unexplored underwater areas.

THE **Dark Side** OF THE **Smoky Mountains**

There is an explorer tour for more adventurous travelers. That tour goes off the well-trodden paths into some truly unique geological features. On that tour, you are much more likely to encounter the bats and other flora and fauna of the caverns.

ERIKA: I draw the line at bats as well.

MARK: Bats are amazing! Kari will lecture you all about them back on the Wayback Machine.

Again, you'll want to message ahead to make certain that tours are available as they do periodically close for maintenance of the caverns. The Tuckaleechee Caverns are open most days of the year. You can also visit their Davy Crockett Riding Stables, the only National Park authorized riding stables in Cades Cove. It's a neat way to explore the wilderness of the Little River side of the Smokies.

ERIKA: I LOVE horseback riding.

After leaving the caves, we should head to lunch nearby.

THIS IS THE "BEACH AREA" OF TUCKALEECHEE CAVERNS. IT'S JUST ONE OF THE MANY SIGHTS TO BEHOLD UNDER THE SMOKY MOUNTAINS. PHOTO PROVIDED BY TUCKALEECHEE CAVERNS.

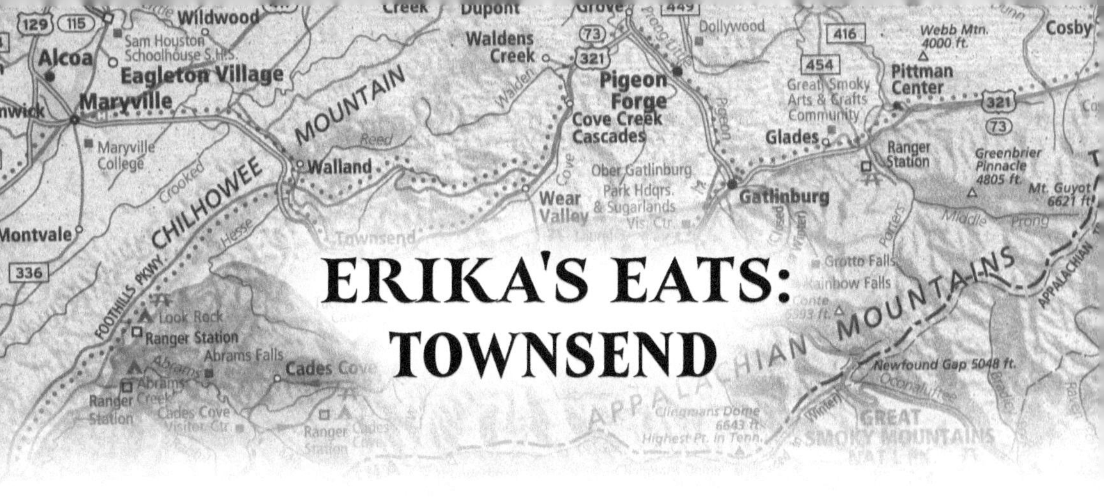

ERIKA'S EATS: TOWNSEND

The Abbey

I think we should hit The Abbey. It's a nice family restaurant located in a former chapel with a great view of the Little River to boot. River tubers can even float up to the outdoor patio there for the Friday night rib special.

Remember to keep your eyes open for the spirit who sometimes comes through the dining room. According to one of the waitresses there, he was even seen several times in broad daylight. Unfortunately, we did not find the history behind the ghost, but they have amazing beer cheese for dipping your pretzel.

MARK: One last thing before we leave Townsend. It is the current home of the Smoky Mountain Bigfoot Festival.

ERIKA: You know I love a good cryptid festival.

Every May, this event brings hundreds of vendors and thousands of guests to Townsend to talk about Sasquatch. There are plenty of sightings of him throughout the Smokies, but we'll get into those later.

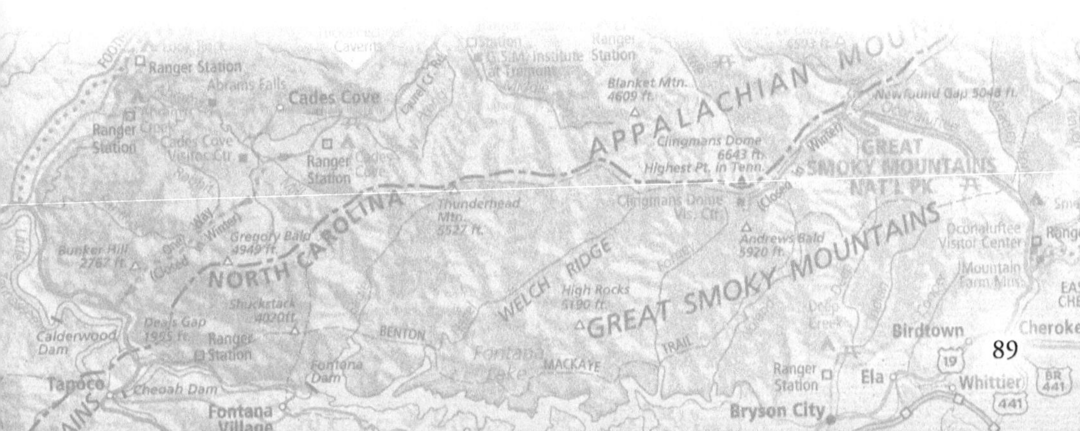

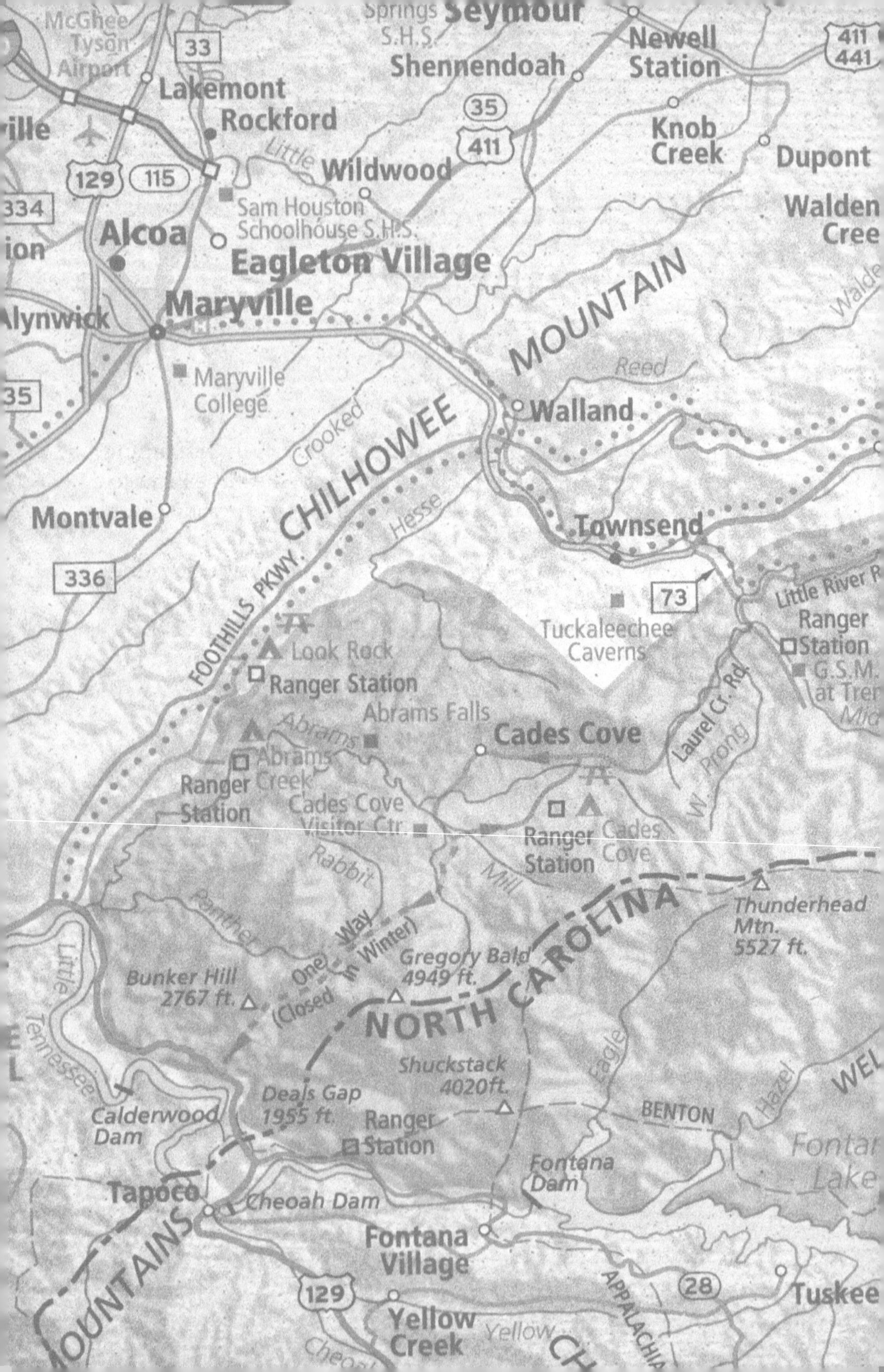

McGhee Tyson Airport
33
Lakemont
Rockford
ville
129
115
334
35
Alcoa
Eagleton Village
Maryville
Alynwick
Little
Wildwood
Sam Houston Schoolhouse S.H.S.
Springs
Seymour
S.H.S.
Shennendoah
35
411
Newell Station
411
441
Knob Creek
Dupont
Walden Cree
Maryville College
Crooked
CHILHOWEE
Hesse
MOUNTAIN
Reed
Walland
Walde
Montvale
336
FOOTHILLS PKWY.
73
Townsend
Tuckaleechee Caverns
Little River R
Ranger Station
G.S.M. at Tren
Mid
Look Rock
Ranger Station
Abrams Falls
Cades Cove
Laurel Cr. Rd.
W. Prong
Abrams
Abrams Creek
Ranger Station
Cades Cove Visitor Ctr.
Ranger Station
Cades Cove
Rabbit
Mill
NORTH CAROLINA
Thunderhead Mtn.
5527 ft.
Panther
One Way (Closed in Winter)
Gregory Bald
4949 ft.
Bunker Hill
2767 ft.
Little
Tennessee
Shuckstack
4020 ft.
Eagle
Hazel
WEL
Deals Gap
1955 ft.
Ranger Station
BENTON
Calderwood Dam
Fontana Dam
Fonta
Lake
Tapoco
Cheoah Dam
MOUNTAINS
Fontana Village
129
Yellow Creek
Yellow
Cheoa
APPALACHIA
28
Tuskee

ELKMONT, TENNESSEE

ELKMONT

WE'RE CLIMBING BACK INTO THE WAYBACK MACHINE again. Elkmont began as a logging camp in the early 1900s when the Little River Company used the area to harvest timber. When the railroad opened up, workers moved into the camp and soon, it turned into a proper small town.

> **ERIKA:** Good thing we cleaned the Wayback Machine out.
> It is getting a lot of use on this trip.

> **MARK:** I'm so glad we stocked up on boiled peanuts.

Right around the time of the first World War, the town transitioned from a logging town into a vacation resort town for the wealthy. The "Appalachian Club" was formed, where the affluent families from Asheville, Knoxville and other cities escaped their lives in the big city to enjoy the beauty of the Smoky Mountains.

Not to be outdone, "The Wonderland Club" started claiming the area as its own. They built even more luxurious hotels and hosted lavish parties. They built the Wonderland Hotel in 1912, which became the center of social life in Elkmont for a time.

In response, the Appalachian Clubhouse was built by the Appalachian Club and hosted dances, recitals, and dinners. The town was booming. More and more families were buying property for summering in the woods.

> **ERIKA:** I am glad we have a club, the *Travelers;* otherwise.
> I would feel left out.

In 1909, however, things in scenic Elkmont took a dramatic turn. The Little River Railroad was bringing logs back into Elkmont for the boom in construction. It was June 30th, and there had been a recent summer storm. As the train approached the town on a sharp curve, the brakeman applied the brakes but greatly underestimated the dampness of the tracks. Plus, due to the eagerness of the buyers, the train was heavily overloaded.

ERIKA: That is not good.

According to the National Park Service historians, the brakes did not have enough traction sand. The passengers and most of the crew were forced to jump to safety. The brakeman and engineer had to stay onboard until the last moment in the hope of minimizing the impending derailment and crash.

ERIKA: That does not sound like a fun job.

The resulting crash was incredible as the train rolled off the embankment. The boilers exploded. The derailed train cars— filled with massive logs— went hurtling into the nearby woods and cabins with incredible force. The train's engineer Gordon "Daddy" Bryson and Charles Jenkins, the brakeman, did not survive the crash.

Instead of deterring traffic to the town, even more tourists flocked to the area to get a glimpse of the wreckage. The tourist boom did not end.

ERIKA: I truly do not understand the slowing down to see the crash mentality.

In 1932, The Smoky Mountain National Park decided to purchase the town of Elkmont to incorporate into the park. The option was given to either sell immediately or take half the money and be given a lifetime lease until the death of the current landowner.

ERIKA: Not really a choice then?

Both the Appalachian and Wonderland Clubs sold out instantly. Most of Elkmont's other landowners chose the lifetime leases. The leases were converted by the government into 20-year leases in 1952. The remaining families were renewed again in 1972. The renewal of the last few surviving families was denied in 1992. The buildings of Elkmont were scheduled to be demolished.

ERIKA: What did the park service say? "You can't have them and neither can anyone else"?

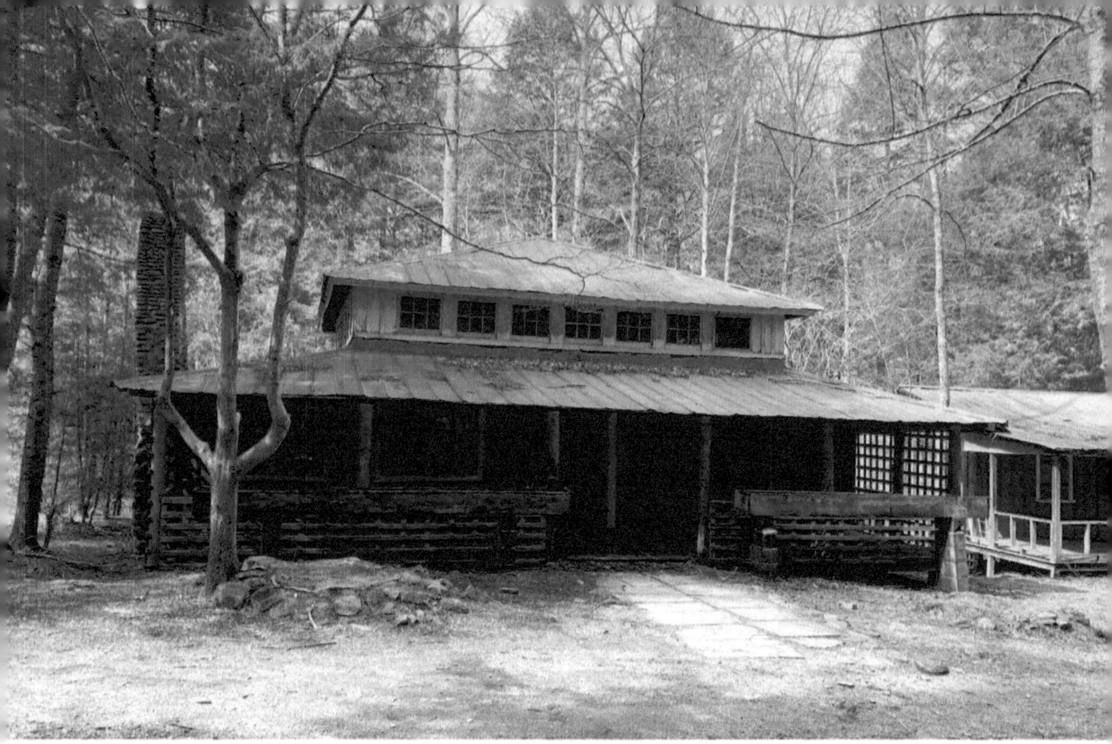

The remains of the town of Elkmont that can be saved are in the process of being restored currently. Photo provided by Great Smoky Mountains National Park.

Mark: Eminent Domain is a powerful thing, and we'll see it used again and again throughout this trip. Sometimes very improperly.

The buildings were saved by the National Register of Historic Places. The National Park Service then had to decide which buildings to preserve. After a study, 18 of the cabins and the Appalachian Clubhouse were scheduled to be saved. They will be refurbished, one by one, until they appear just as they did back in the early days of Elkmont.

Erika: This is a fun place to walk through.

While the other buildings were removed, there are still traces of their existence today. In 1995, a fire damaged the old Wonderland Hotel, and it finally collapsed in 2005. The Appalachian Club lodge has been restored and can be rented out as event space. Several of the cabins have been fully restored, and work is continuing on others slated for refurbishment.

Erika: I like the idea that they kept all this history—even if some of it is a little creepy.

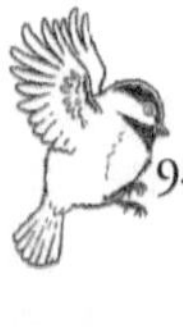

Elkmont

MARK: I love creepy history, so I agree wholeheartedly.

Every year in June, Elkmont attracts thousands of visitors for a natural phenomenon that is very rare in the United States. Photinus carlolinus, also known as the synchronous fireflies, put on an amazing display. During their mating season, these fireflies flash in unison. There is a lottery held by the National Park Service for a chance to view this amazing event.

ERIKA: I LOVE LOVE LOVE fireflies.

MARK: My family always called them lightning bugs.

Elkmont requires a short hike of less than a mile. If you travel either the Little River Trail or the Jakes Creek Trail, you can see the outlying foundations of the older buildings and settlements. The Elkmont Nature Trail is just under a mile loop itself. Reservations are required if you intend to camp at the Elkmont Campground as it is the busiest campground in the Smokies. It is open from April through November.

ERIKA: This was a bit of a drive to get here as well.
(Directions: Drive toward Cades Cove for about seven miles until you see a sign for Elkmont Campground. You'll turn here until you see the ranger station about four miles down the road.

SYNCHRONOUS FIREFLIES ARE AN AMAZING PHENOMENA BEST CAPTURED WITH TIME LAPSE PHOTOGRAPHY. PHOTO PROVIDED BY GREAT SMOKY MOUNTAINS NATIONAL PARK.

THE Dark Side OF THE Smoky Mountains

Take a left at the sign for Elkmont Nature Trail,
where you'll find a parking lot. The lot is within
walking distance of the historic structures
in Elkmont.)

The ghost town is worth the visit for the history, but of course, there are plenty of ghost stories. Mostly, they involve the spirits of Jenkins or "Daddy" Bryson walking the remains of the old rail line. They are reportedly still looking for their missing body parts lost in the great train crash of 1909.

> **ERIKA:** Of course there are ghosts looking for
> body parts.

There are quartz-engraved headstones in the nearby graveyard. Quartz was meant to keep resting spirits interred below ground.

> **ERIKA:** I wonder if that works?

> **MARK:** Ask "Daddy" Bryson when you see him.

There are many infants and children buried here, along with the logging workers that were sometimes victims of tragic accidents. One stone stands out—belonging to Arvile McCarter. It reads, "Sweet peace at last, as we go traveling home…" A peaceful reminder of the past as you stand in the remains of this ghost town in the Smokies.

THE WORK CREW OF THE LITTLE RIVER LUMBER COMPANY STANDING ON THE ELKMONT RAILROAD TRACKS TAKEN SOME TIME BEFORE THAT FATAL TRAIN WRECK OF 1909. PHOTO PROVIDED BY SMOKY MOUNTAIN NATIONAL PARK ARCHIVES.

Cades Cove, Tennessee

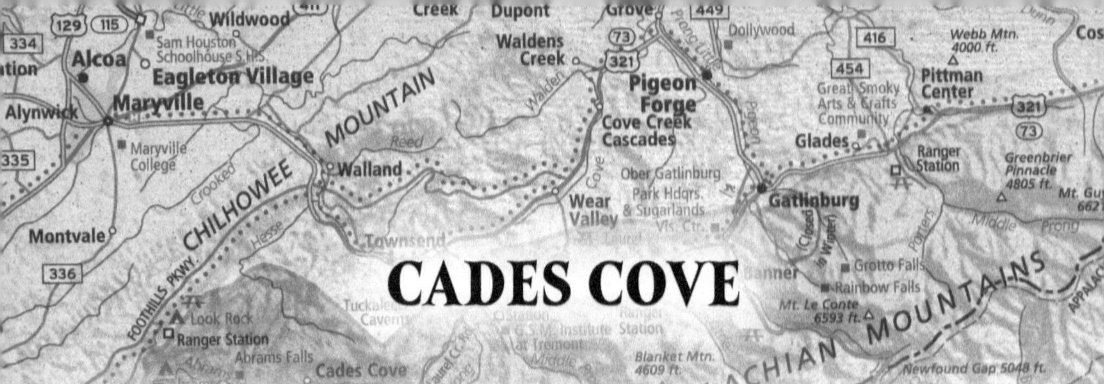

CADES COVE

ONE OF THE MOST VISITED AREAS IN THE GREAT SMOKY Mountains National Park is Cades Cove. It is filled with historic churches, cabins, a gristmill, cemeteries, and more wildlife than many zoos. The Loop Road is always packed with cars full of tourists enjoying the gorgeous mountain views—except on Wednesdays when cars are forbidden.

> **ERIKA:** Wonder what happens on Wednesdays? Or is it Addams family related?

> **MARK:** No. It just fills up with bikers and hikers. Bring your bear spray, just in case.

We must get in the Wayback Machine for a quick trip back to 1820. The Cherokee had been hunting this valley for centuries. Deer, elk, bison, turkeys, and bears were the primary game available. The first European settlers began to arrive and quickly began clearing the land for farming.

By 1850, the population had grown to over 680 people in the valley as the word of the fertile land spread. Numerous children were born as the average household in the area had ten to twelve children at the time. More and more community buildings were constructed, including both Baptist and Methodist churches. Children were taught in farmhouses until schools were built as needed.

Neighbors lived in this area and made community events out of corn husking, molasses making, and gathering chestnuts in the autumn. Marriages would bring the community together. The families would have "weaner cabins" where a young couple could live in privacy for the early days of marriage, but they were still close enough to help with chores and farming.

> **ERIKA:** Interesting part of history. It gives a whole new meaning to "honeymoon phase."

Cades Cove

One young couple was Mavis Estep and her husband Basil. They lived in a two-room cabin right next to the Whistling Branch stream. They lived their life quietly in the Cove, but Mavis had an incredible fear of being struck by lightning. She would be paralyzed with fear during any thunderstorms.

> **ERIKA:** I am also afraid of being struck by lightning—as any smart person should be.

> **MARK:** True, but she took it to extremes.

She had heard of a story about a young lady in the Cove who had been born during a thunderstorm just a generation before her. The girl had always drawn storms around her as if she could beckon them. Mavis herself had been born during a thunderstorm, so this legend strongly affected her. The lady of legend grew into a young woman and married her love.

> **ERIKA:** That is a cool superpower. Like an early version of Storm from the *X-Men*.

On their wedding day, this legendary lady approached the steps of the Baptist church when a bolt of lightning came from a blue sky and struck her dead. Her ghost was said to haunt the graveyard of the church and could be seen as a gown of white lit by blue lightning.

> **ERIKA:** Love the gown, not so much the ghost part.

Mavis was so concerned about this happening to herself that she banned all metal beds and furniture from her home. She even refused to quilt with metal needles. She was an avid quilter, so you can see this was a tough decision for her.

> **ERIKA:** Okay. I am not *that* scared of being struck by lightning.

One of her famous quilts is a patchwork pattern made of pieces of Basil's favorite flannel shirts. She named this quilt "The Cussing Cover" because Basil had been wearing that shirt during their first fight in which she had learned some of Basil's more colorful language.

> **ERIKA:** I am a fan of colorful language.

MARK: You do use a lot of asterisks when adding your commentary.

It was not lightning that would carry Mavis away but a severe illness. It was likely tuberculosis. Mavis struggled for some time and was bed-ridden. She brought Basil forward and gave him permission to remarry after she was gone, as she knew that he—and the farm—would need a strong partner. She did make him promise two things. One, he could never sell any of her quilts. Two, he could never use any of her quilts on any metal beds. Basil agreed, and Mavis passed away shortly afterward.

ERIKA: That is sad.

Less than a year passed before Basil remarried Trulie Jane, a much younger lady living in the Cove. It didn't take long for Trulie to remark about how uncomfortable the old wooden bed was. After much prodding, Basil bought a new metal bed frame for his new young bride.

ERIKA: I sense the breaking of this promise will not end well.

THE PRIMITIVE BAPTIST CHURCH IN CADES COVE. PHOTO BY AUTHOR.

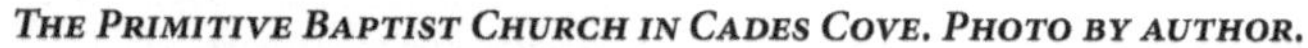

Cades Cove

THE LIGHTNING LADY OF CADES COVE.
ILLUSTRATION BY KARI SCHULTZ.

That winter, on a particularly freezing night, Trulie begged Basil to add one of the quilts to keep warm. Basil had forgotten his promise and agreed. Trulie went and picked up The Cussing Cover, thanks to the warm red flannel patches.

ERIKA: Forgot? I sense a vengeance ghost coming.

Late that night, Trulie startled awake as she saw an angry figure of a woman standing at the foot of their bed. She locked eyes with the figure, and the spectral woman's eyes flared red. The red-eyed woman began to scream. Trulie screamed back and woke Basil as quickly as she could.

By the time Basil awoke, the figure had vanished. He calmed his young bride and told her it must have been a nightmare. After a short while, they both drifted back to sleep.

ERIKA: Oh Basil... You silly man.

A few hours later, Trulie found herself flung out of bed and blinded by a brilliant flash of light. When she regained her vision, she saw her bed had been burnt to cinders, and Basil was dead. The rest of the cabin had been untouched by the freak bolt of lightning. There was no reported storm that evening, just the lone bolt of lightning that had landed on Basil Estep.

ERIKA: Yep... vengeance ghost superpowers.

Trulie sold the cabin and the quilts to one of the Estep daughters. Rumor has it that the quilts are still in the hands of a private collector somewhere in the Smoky Mountains. Though there are variations of this legend, this is the one most commonly reported. No one is quite sure which of the cabins belonged to the Estep family.

ERIKA: Well, since I am not violating the rules set forth by Mavis, I think we are safe to go into them. But I would love to see these quilts.

There are other strange experiences reported in Cades Cove, one being the constant freak thunderstorms reported here. Maybe Mavis is still haunting the area. Maybe the original lightning lady who is lost to legend still lingers near the Primitive Baptist Church. A face is said to occasionally appear on the wall behind a pew in the church. Rangers

Cades Cove

point out there is a strong vein of copper in the area which often draws lightning which may be the source of these legendary Lightning Ladies.

ERIKA: I am rooting for a team of lightning ghosts.

One interesting note about Cades Cove is that there are many grave-yards and cemeteries here. There are 14 noted in census records. Only 11 have been located. There are three cemeteries lost somewhere in Cades Cove.

ERIKA: How do you lose not one but *three* cemeteries?

If you go to Cades Cove yourself, be prepared for frequent stops. The ride is long and can take hours for the loop road, especially if there is a bear jam.

ERIKA: What is a bear jam?

That's a traffic jam where people stop to take pictures of bears and other wildlife that frequent the area. Entrance to the Cove is free, but donations are accepted. There is a $6 parking fee if you plan to wander the trails or scope out any of the churches, cabins, or cemeteries here.

ERIKA: Sounds like a Traveler should bring snacks and
drinks and simply enjoy seeing everything on this
beautiful eleven-mile one-way loop.
Where to next?

YOU NEVER KNOW WHAT AWAITS YOU IN SCENIC CADES COVE. PHOTO PROVIDED BY SMOKY MOUNTAIN NATIONAL PARK ARCHIVES.

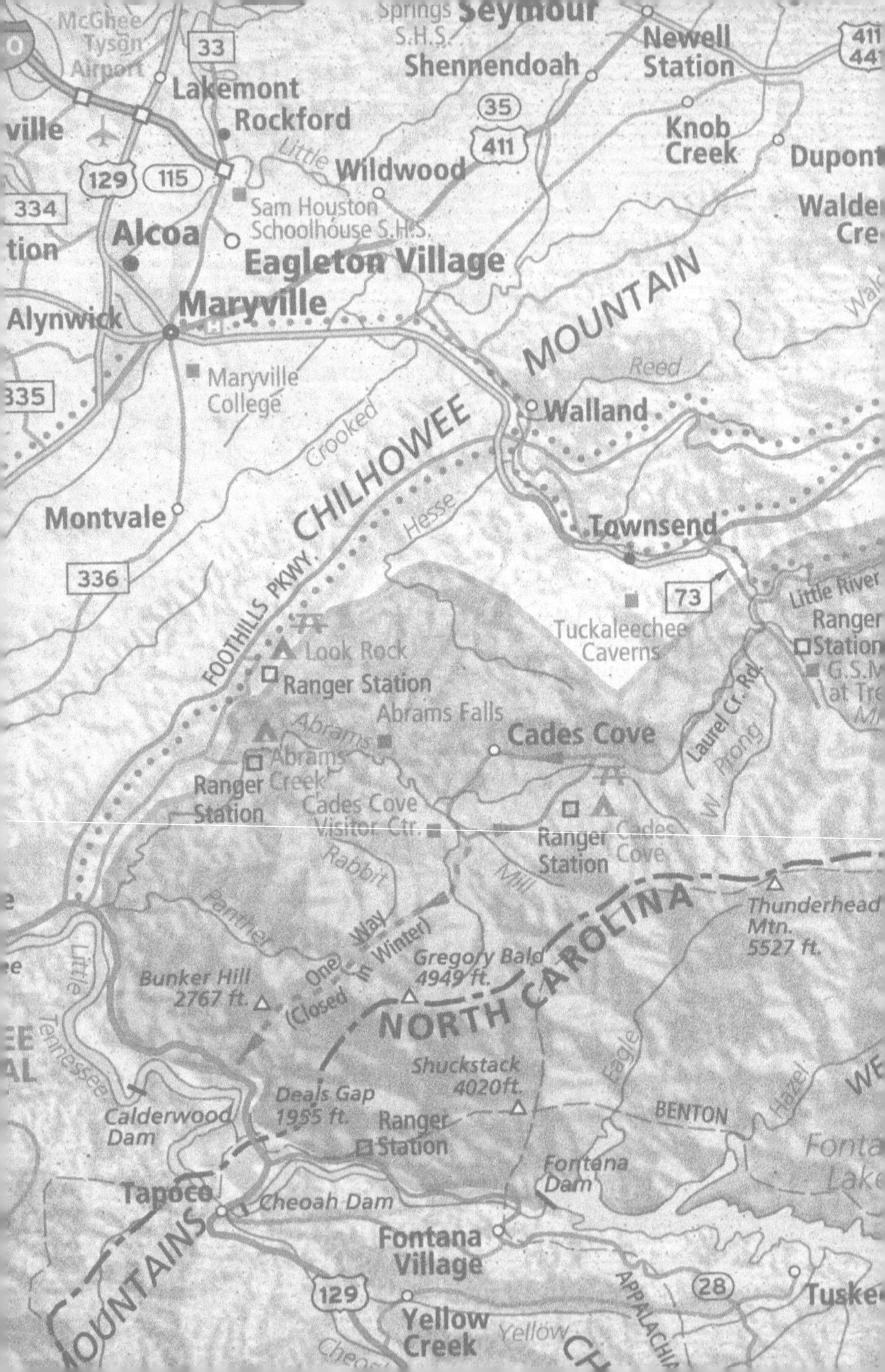

McGhee
Tyson
Airport
Lakemont
Rockford
33
129
115
334
Alcoa
335
tion
Alynwick
Montvale
336
Little
Wildwood
Sam Houston
Schoolhouse S.H.S.
Eagleton Village
Maryville
Maryville
College
Crooked
CHILHOWEE
Hesse
FOOTHILLS PKWY.
Look Rock
Ranger Station
Abrams Falls
Abrams
Abrams
Creek
Ranger
Station
Cades Cove
Visitor Ctr.
Rabbit
Panther
One Way
(Closed in Winter)
Bunker Hill
2767 ft.
Gregory Bald
4949 ft.
NORTH CAROLINA
Shuckstack
4020 ft.
Deals Gap
1955 ft.
Ranger
Station
Little
Tennessee
Calderwood
Dam
Tapoco
Cheoah Dam
MOUNTAINS
Fontana
Village
129
Yellow
Creek
Cheoa
Springs
S.H.S.
Seymour
Shennendoah
Newell
Station
411
444
35
411
Knob
Creek
Dupont
Walder
Cre
MOUNTAIN
Reed
Walland
Townsend
73
Little River
Ranger
Station
G.S.M.
at Tre
M
Tuckaleechee
Caverns
Cades Cove
Laurel Cr. Rd.
W. Prong
Mill
Ranger
Station
Cades
Cove
Thunderhead
Mtn.
5527 ft.
Eagle
BENTON
Hazel
WE
Fonta
Lake
Fontana
Dam
APPALACHIA
28
Tuske
Yellow
CH

PIGEON FORGE, TENNESSEE

PIGEON FORGE

DRIVING INTO PIGEON FORGE IS LIKE DRIVING INTO LAS Vegas without the casinos and being surrounded by beautiful mountains. There are so many roadside attractions and tourist traps, it would take an entire book just to list them all. Though, it wouldn't be an *Eerie Travels* if we didn't get into the history of this area.

ERIKA: Wayback Machine, here we come!

Pigeon Forge was once part of the Great Indian War and Trading Path or the Seneca Trail. Not much is really known about how old this "highway" through the Smoky Mountains truly is. The Seneca Trail was a series of trails broken in by animals traveling between naturally forming salt licks in the region. Elk, bears, mountain lions, and more traveled these trails from Virginia down to Alabama.

The natives of the area would follow these paths as well, eventually widening them. The trails were used for commerce, trade, and communication by the tribes long before Europeans explored the region.

ERIKA: It's a good idea to follow what the animals use
for safe travel. If a 400lb elk can walk it, so can
most humans.

Samuel Wear was a Revolutionary War veteran, and he was one of the first settlers in this area. He built a stockade called "Wear's Fort" at the entrance to a cove here where Walden Creek and the Little Pigeon River met right on the Great Indian Path.

ERIKA: I feel like that seems to be settlers' step one:
make a fort!

It was remote so there was never a huge attack from a war standpoint, but it was a popular target for Cherokee raiders. It is long gone now; however, it was likely where Pigeon Forge City Park is now.

Pigeon Forge

In 1793, Wear's Fort was attacked by the Chickamauga tribe. Wear would retaliate with a punitive march against the nearby tribal village of Tallassee. It would end with the deaths of at least fifteen Cherokee people and the capture of many more. Wear was targeted by the Cherokee thereafter, but he tried to rebuild trust with them after this massacre.

> **ERIKA:** It seems like he kind of deserved to be targeted. He started it with them.

Wear was one of the main emissaries to the Cherokee for establishing treaties in the area. He would still lead battles in territorial disputes for much of the rest of his life. He was a co-founder of the Lost State of Franklin we discussed earlier. Later in life, he would help draft the constitution of the state of Tennessee. Thomas Jefferson even commented that it was the "best written and most in line with the spirit of the United States Constitution" of all those written by the new frontier states.

> **ERIKA:** Good writer, questionable leader?

Wear would even command a regiment in the War of 1812. He died on April 13, 1817, in Sevierville. His monument in the Fort Wear Cemetery reads, "Pioneer, Soldier of four Wars; Colonial, Revolution, Indian, 1812; One of the Heroes of Kings Mountain, and a Founder of the State of Franklin."

> **ERIKA:** I hope we get monuments when we pass.

> **MARK:** I want mine to say, "Here lies Mark Muncy. If not, please contact the caretaker immediately."

So, with all that, the town gets its name from a different early settler. Isaac Love built an Iron Forge on the Little Pigeon River to supply both Wear Fort and the nearby Shields Fort. Shields sat right where Indian Gap Path met the Great Indian Warpath in the Smokies. Its site is where Dollywood stands now. Shields Fort never faced backlash from the natives.

> **ERIKA:** Most likely because they didn't attack the wrong people.

The forge was eventually purchased by John Trotter, who made many modifications including a sawmill. By the mid-1800s, the first health resort opened in the area thanks to Henderson Springs. These were possibly the same health-restoring waters as Silver Falls in Tuckaleechee Caverns.

ERIKA: I never knew how popular these health resorts were back then.

MARK: They still are.

When the Great Smoky Mountains National Park opened in 1934, Pigeon Forge was brought into the spotlight in a big way. By the 1960s, Pigeon Forge was booming. The Robbins Brothers built the first amusement ride by creating the Rebel Railroad. This simulated a ride on a Confederate steam train under attack in the Civil War. It would later be called Goldrush Junction. In 1982, it was bought and turned into Silver Dollar City. Eventually, it became the theme park known as Dollywood.

ERIKA: I feel like Dolly Parton is really who put this place on the map.

MARK: It's always been on the map. Dolly just made it even more popular.

With over 60 million tourists a year coming to the town, it's no wonder that it continues to grow and expand even today. Let's visit some of the spooky—can't miss attractions while we're here.

No visit to Pigeon Forge would be complete without riding the Mystery Mountain Mine roller coaster at Dollywood. Spooky and thrilling with its own theme song. Photo by author.

THE OLD MILL

ONE OF THE MOST PHOTOGRAPHED MILLS IN AMERICA IS right off the main road along the Little Pigeon River. Mordecai Lewis settled here in the late 1700s, and his grandson would build the mill on his land. Isaac Love, Lewis' son-in-law, built the iconic forge here where the town got its name. The families of these two men would shape the early days of the town.

Isaac's sons constructed the Lewis Mill, named after their grandfather. They would end up selling to John Trotter sometime later. During the Civil War, Trotter would set up a secret location on the second floor to help make uniforms for the Union. He even made a hospital on the third floor for wounded Union soldiers, despite being in a Confederate state.

ERIKA: This seems to be a theme in our travels.

The mill was destroyed twice by floods, once in 1875 and again in 1920. Both times, the mill was rebuilt. In 1933, at the height of the Great Depression, the mill fell to the bank and was bought by the Stout family. In 1952, it became known officially as The Old Mill. The original grinding stone, the last remaining piece of the mill constructed in 1830, was replaced in 1977.

ERIKA: Now I am looking up what a grinding stone is.

MARK: Now you're getting the hang of things.

In 1995, The Old Mill joins forces with the neighboring Cornflour Restaurant to become the Old Mill Restaurant. It is still there today. The restaurant offers country cooking with great views of the Little Pigeon River.

ERIKA: You get free banana nut muffins with breakfast and corn fritters for lunch and dinner. Yum!

The Old Mill is a fine restaurant with a haunted past on the Pigeon River. Photo by author.

There are supposedly several spirits that haunt the Old Mill and its neighboring dining establishment. The main room of the mill is haunted by the spirit of potter Douglas Ferguson who often visited the mill to grab clay for his nearby studio. He has been seen several times wearing his striped apron and walking through the guest area.

ERIKA: Of course, you waited 'til we sat down to eat to mention it's haunted, Mark.

Another apparition famously appeared during a wedding reception at the Old Mill Restaurant on the top floor. During the dessert course, a shadow figure appeared to come up the stairs, turn, and walk right through the tables. It disappeared in an instant. The witnesses all claimed to smell gunpowder as it vanished in a plume of black and red smoke. This was in 1999.

ERIKA: Oh, a ghost that smells like war.

There are guided tours available at the Historic Old Mill every Tuesday through Saturday for most of the year. At the time of this writing, Emmitt has been guiding the tour for nearly 50 years. Tell him *Eerie Travels* sent you.

CASTLE OF CHAOS

UP FIRST IS THE CASTLE OF CHAOS IN THE HOLLYWOOD Wax Museum Entertainment Center. There are a few attractions within the Castle of note. First up is the titular Hollywood Wax Museum where you can see some amazing waxwork figures of history's greatest celebrities.

> **ERIKA:** Like the monument, I wonder if they'll make wax figures of us.

> **MARK:** I love the *Waxworks* movies.

There's also Hannah's Maze of Mirrors which is an astounding, carnival-like experience on another level.

> **ERIKA:** Apparently, you need to rescue a princess here. What fun!

> **MARK:** It's all fun and games until you fight a dragon.

There's also a great year-round haunted attraction called Outbreak: Dread the Undead. The haunt includes live actors and animatronics.

> **ERIKA:** Why is it *always* a laboratory releasing zombies?

Finally, there is the Castle of Chaos. This is a motion simulator ride where you also have a light gun. You'll wear 3D glasses and start by targeting zombie clowns—it goes downhill from there. It's an amazing, immersive experience and well worth your time.

> **ERIKA:** Shooting zombies might be one of my favorite sports that is not really a sport. Travelers, post your score and tag us. I wanna know who is best!

ALCATRAZ EAST

IF YOU ARE A FAN OF TRUE CRIME AT ALL, THEN ALCATRAZ East Crime Museum is a must stop. This museum is over 25,000 square feet of some of the greatest collections of criminal memorabilia in history. With a revolving collection of exhibits, there is always something new to see here.

> **ERIKA:** SO EXCITED!!!

The main gallery features exhibits from the golden age of pirates to the gunslingers of the Wild West, including the bloodstained floorboards of the cabin where Jesse James was killed.

> **ERIKA:** I have been to the Jessie James festival in Northfield, MN, but that is for another book.

Other exhibits include items from notorious serial killers like Ted Bundy and John Wayne Gacy. There are artifacts from Sing Sing and Alcatraz as well. They even have a gallery of infamous getaway cars including the white Ford Bronco used in the infamous O. J. Simpson low speed chase.

> **ERIKA:** Wow! That is amazing. It used to be in Washington DC, correct?

> **MARK:** Yeah, this whole collection used to be in the National Museum of Crime and Punishment before it closed there. Now you can see it all here!

You'll go through all the stages of a criminal investigation and see artifacts from famous lawmen like Elliot Ness and Buford Pusser. You can also learn about jobs in Forensic Science and Case Law. There is just so much history here for the enthusiast.

ERIKA: I have to say I am blown away. This is a really cool stop and totally one of the creepiest things I have ever seen. Humans can be more monstrous than monsters.

ALCATRAZ EAST IS HOME TO AN AMAZING COLLECTION OF TRUE CRIME MEMORABILIA. MAKING IT A MUST VISIT IN PIGEON FORGE. PHOTO BY AUTHOR.

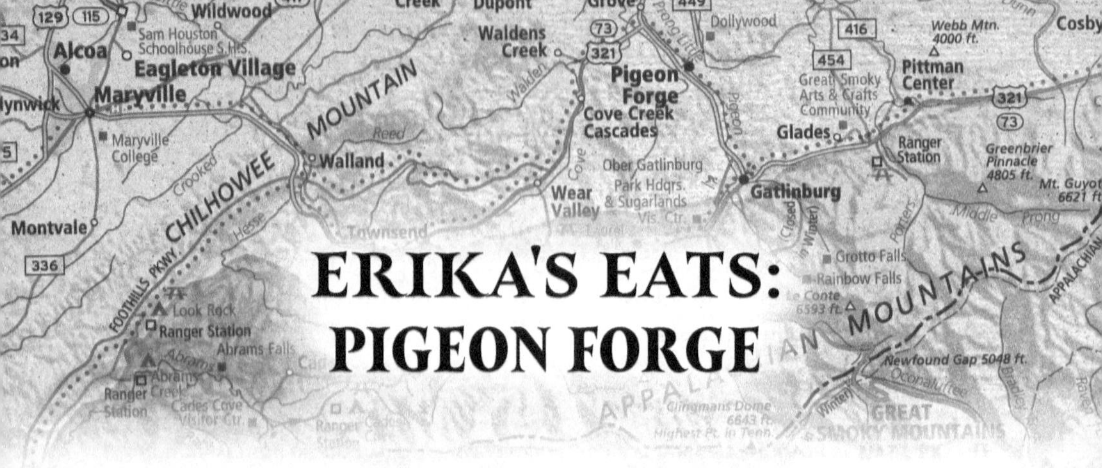

I HAVE TO SAY THERE ARE WAY TOO MANY AMAZING
places to eat in Pigeon Forge. But here are a few favorites:

The Yard: Milkshake Bar

Okay, milkshake fans, hold on to your butts! The Yard is where you can get a real milkshake! I have two words for you: THE UNICORN—milk chocolate ice cream, spots of pink vanilla rolled in rainbow sprinkles, and finally, two marshmallow ears and a unicorn horn covered in sprinkles. They have a ton of choices to satisfy every sweet tooth, including Kari's favorite, the Cookie Monster.

Mel's Classic Diner

Who doesn't love a classic diner where you can get an amazing stack of pancakes or a six-scoop banana split for breakfast? This diner will transport you in time without all the muss and fuss of the Wayback Machine.

Pirates Dinner Show

You can't visit Pigeon Forge without stopping by a dinner show. Since this is my Eats List, I chose the pirate show. Who doesn't love action adventure while eating their four-course feast? They even have gluten free options for peeps like me! This is a family-friendly show.

Hatfield's & Mccoy's Dinner Show

Mark prefers this hillbilly-themed dinner show. Sure, The Hatfield & McCoy feud was in Kentucky and West Virginia for the most part, but that doesn't mean you can't enjoy a fun show with all you can eat fried chicken. Another Pigeon Forge tradition.

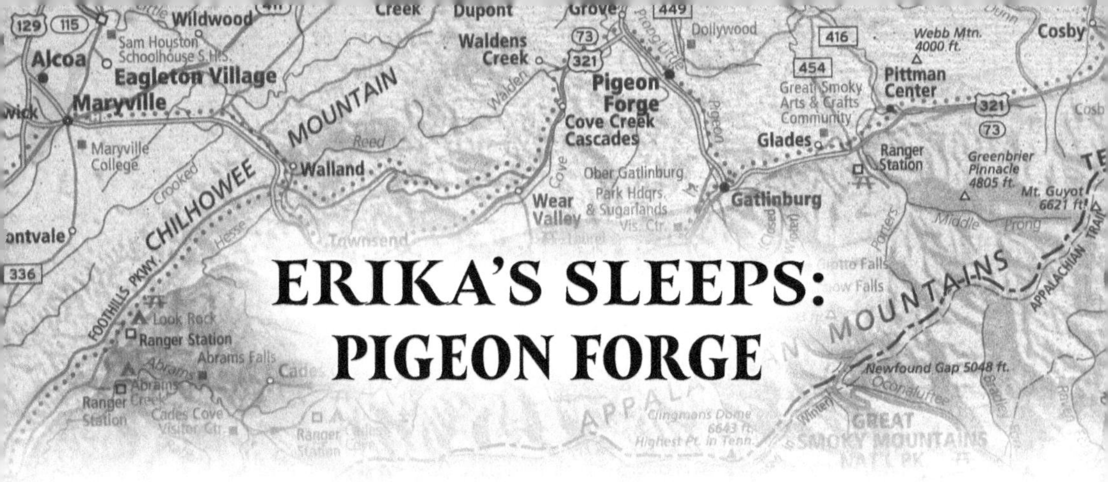

ERIKA'S SLEEPS: PIGEON FORGE

Affordable Cabins in the Smokies

What better place to stay in the mountains than at a cabin? You can search *"Cabins in the Smokey Moutains"* to book the right cabin for your group of Travelers. Make sure you book in advance.

The Inn at Christmas Place

Do you love Christmas time? Some people get as excited about the Christmas season as Mark and I do about Halloween. If this is you, this is a can't-miss stay. There is something for every holiday itch you could want to scratch!

The Family Inn

To bed down for the evening, Mark was going to suggest we stay at the Family Inn. This hotel has a legendary haunted room where one of the cleaning ladies was slain in the early 1980s. This kindly spirit is said to watch over guests, but she appears as a shadow that can be startling to unsuspecting hotel patrons. Just know that she means no harm and is said to keep the hotel safe from any future unpleasantness. Sadly, at the time of this writing, it was closed for renovations with no definitive reopen date scheduled.

ERIKA: YAY! Creepy hotel avoided... for now.

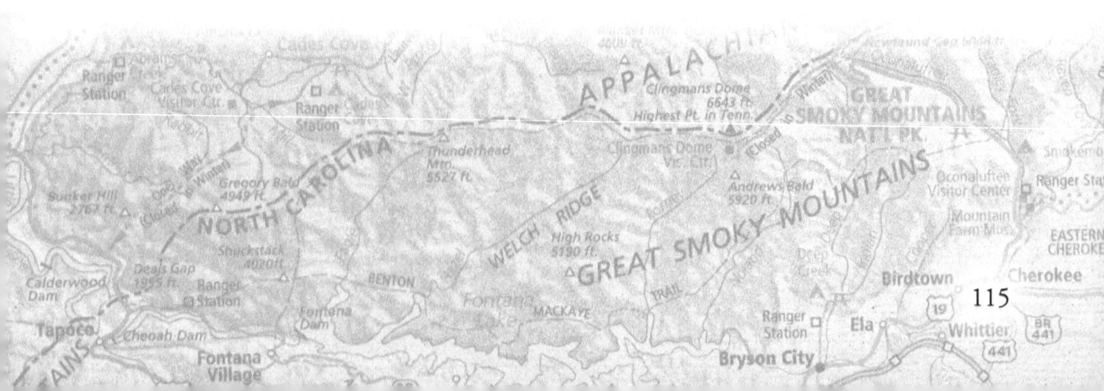

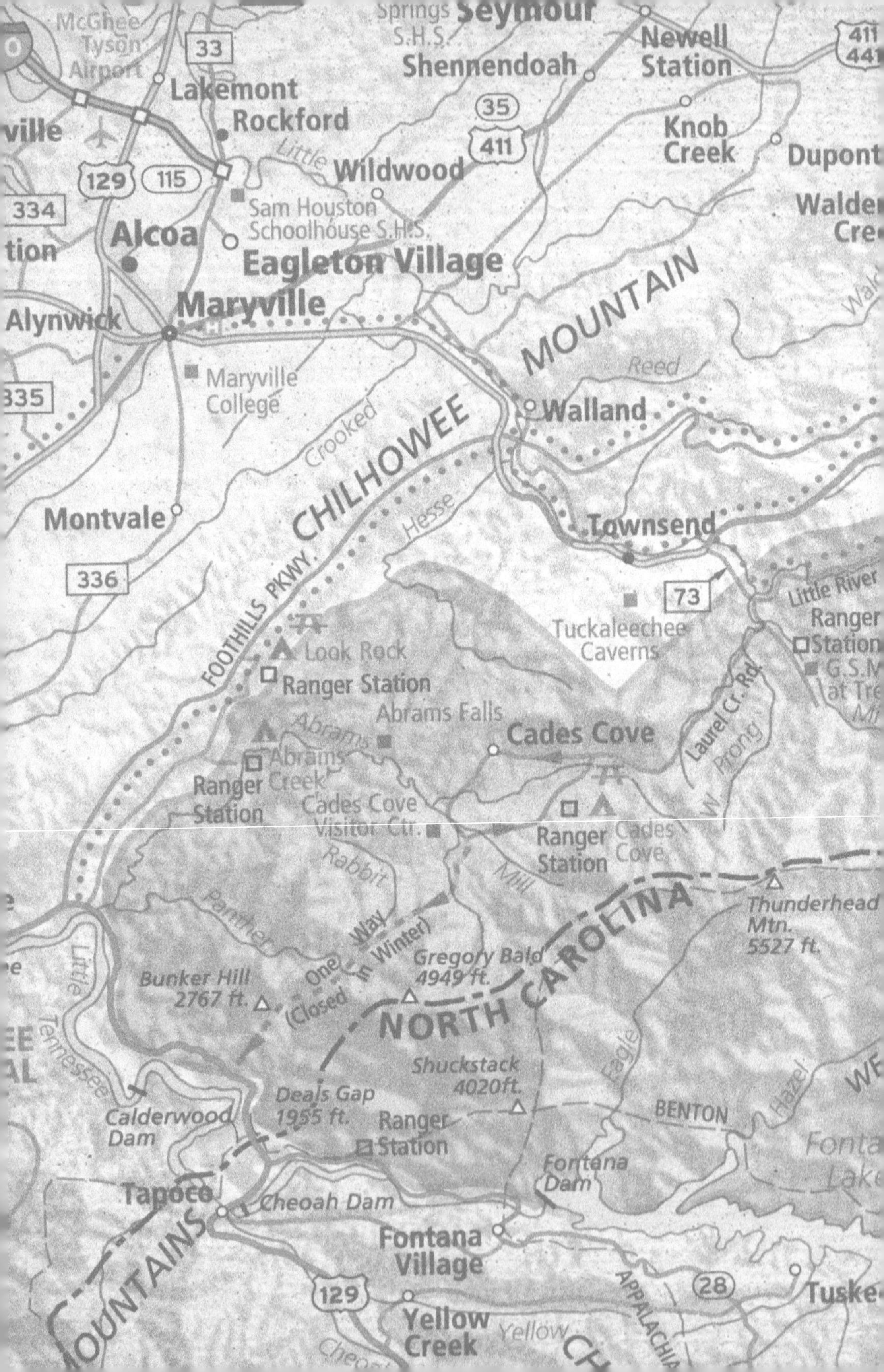

McGhee Tyson Airport
Springs
Seymour
S.H.S.
Newell Station
411 441
33
Shennendoah
ville
Lakemont
Rockford
35
Knob Creek
Dupont
411
129 115
Little
Wildwood
Walden Cree
334
Sam Houston
Schoolhouse S.H.S.
Alcoa
Walde
tion
Eagleton Village
Maryville
Alynwick
335
Maryville College
Crooked
CHILHOWEE
Reed
Walland
Hesse
Montvale
Townsend
336
FOOTHILLS PKWY.
73
Little River
Ranger Station
Tuckaleechee Caverns
G.S.M. at Tre Mi
Look Rock
Ranger Station
Abrams Falls
Laurel Cr. Rd.
Abrams
Cades Cove
Abrams Creek
Ranger Station
Cades Cove Visitor Ctr.
W. Prong
Ranger Station
Cades Cove
Rabbit
Mill
Panther
NORTH CAROLINA
Thunderhead Mtn.
5527 ft.
Little
Tennessee
One Way (Closed in Winter)
Gregory Bald
4949 ft.
Bunker Hill
2767 ft.
Eagle
EE
AL
Shuckstack
4020 ft.
Deals Gap
1955 ft.
Ranger Station
BENTON
Hazel
WE
Fonta
Lake
Calderwood Dam
Fontana Dam
Tapoco
Cheoah Dam
MOUNTAINS
Fontana Village
APPALACHIA
28
Tuske
129
Yellow Creek
Yellow
Cheo

Gatlinburg, Tennessee

GATLINBURG

A short drive from Pigeon Forge is what many con-sider to be the heart of the Smoky Mountains: the city of Gatlinburg, Tennessee.

> **ERIKA:** Can we take a break from the Wayback Machine please? There have been a lot of costume changes on this trip.

> **MARK:** Well, if you insist. However, there is a funny story about how the town got its name.

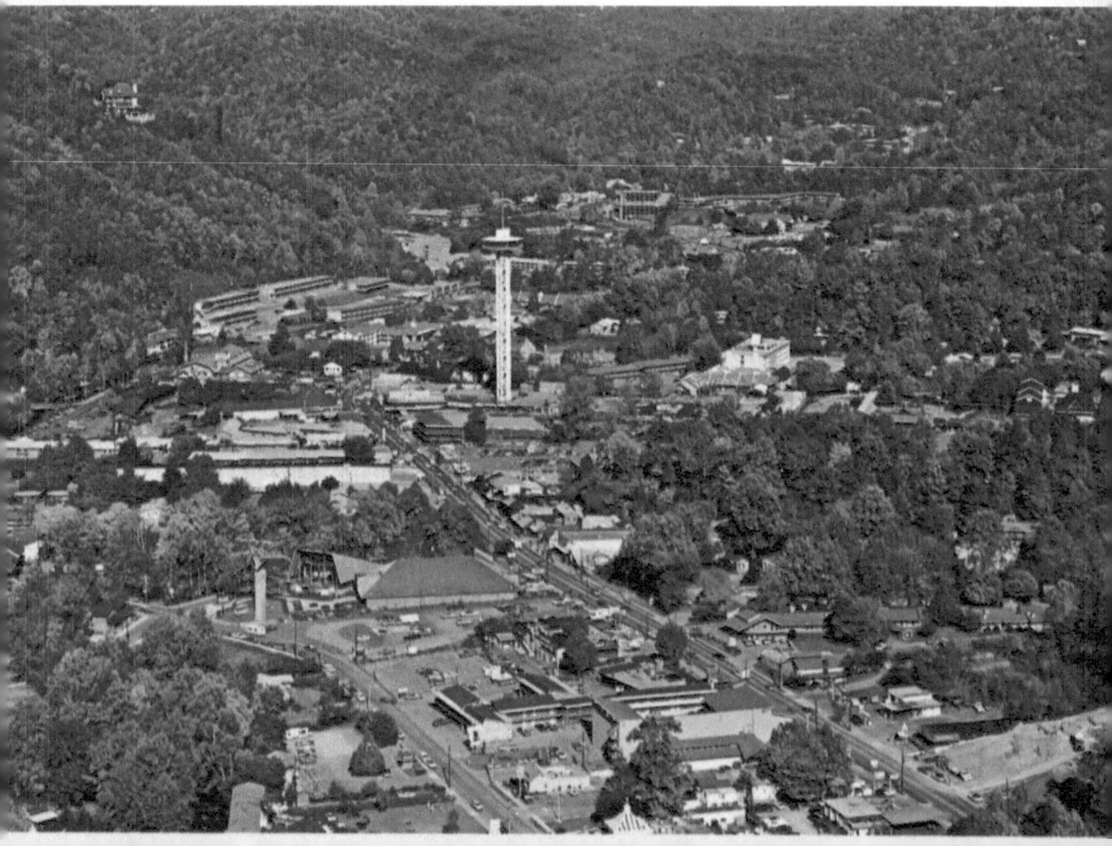

THE OGLE CABIN

THE FIRST EUROPEAN TO SETTLE IN THIS AREA WAS William Ogle. He started building the first true homestead in the area in 1802. Previously, it had been part of the Indian Path through the mountains. He cut down a bunch of logs for his cabin before going home to his family in South Carolina to tell them about the "Land of Paradise" he had found. He kept going on about the white oaks that filled the area. Sadly, he died before ever returning. It wouldn't be for four more years that his widow and her family would come to the land he had mapped for them.

There they found his hewn lumber, and so they finished his cabin and settled in the area. The family would live there over 100 years, not leaving it until 1910. The Ogle family kept their farm until 1921. The cabin was used as a hospital for some time in the early 1920s before becoming a museum in the late 1920s.

ERIKA: This story had Wayback Machine all over it.

Noah Ogle founded a general store in the area where now sits The Shops at 715 Parkway. The store itself was later moved to the new intersection of River Road and Elkmont Highway. This store was huge and supplied the entire town for decades. It was torn down in the 1970s to make room for the Mountain Mall.

ERIKA: It is interesting how we tend to tear down buildings versus restoring them. I hope that is a trend that changes.

In 1854, the town was called White Oak Flats, and many families had residences along the hollows and streams in the valley. Radford C. Gatlin opened a second general store to compete with the Ogle store. Gatlin was a well-known preacher who also established the Gatlinite Baptist Church in town. When the town needed a post office, it was decided that it would

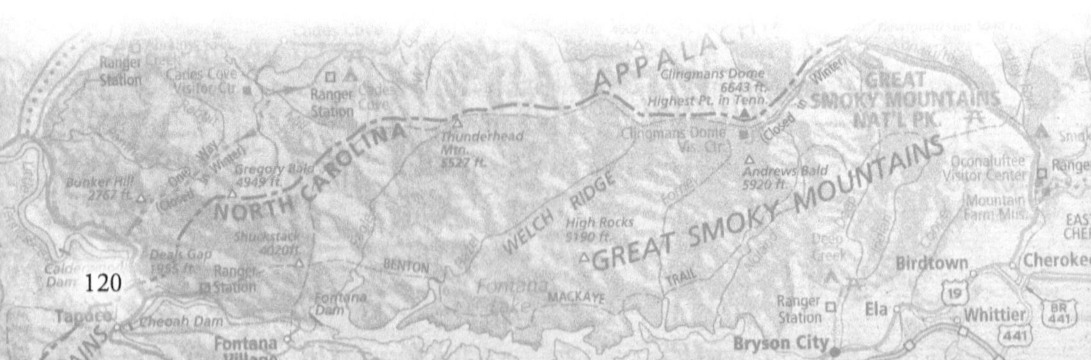

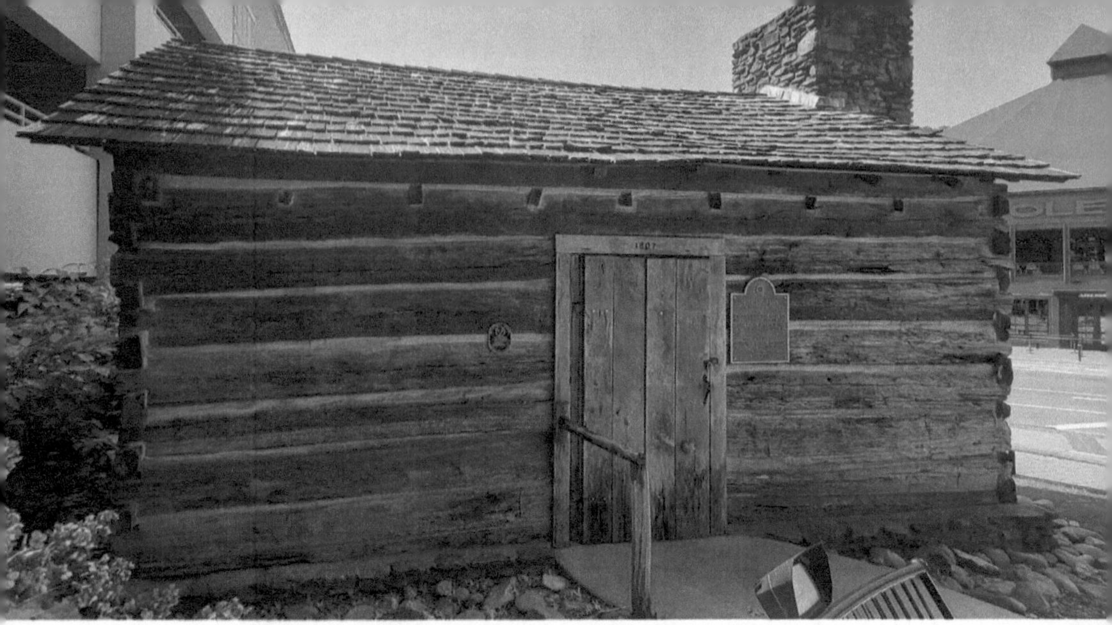

The Ogle Cabin sits in the heart of downtown Gatlinburg, right off 441. Photo by author.

open inside Gatlin's shop as there was no room at the Ogle store. White Oaks was now called Gatlinburg.

Of course, Gatlin and the Ogles did not get along. It did not help that Gatlin was a Democrat who supported the Confederacy in the Civil War. The Ogles were Republicans supporting the cause of the Union. No one really knows how bad things got, but Gatlin was eventually forced to leave his store and the town that bore his name. The name did stay.

> **Erika:** It's interesting that they threw out the man but kept the name. I wonder if the sign was too expensive to replace.

The Ogle cabin was moved from its original site to the site of Gatlinburg's first church building which had been lost over time. The cabin is still there today and is open as a museum just around the corner from Ripley's Aquarium of the Smokies.

WHITE OAK FLATS CEMETERY

THERE ARE SEVERAL CEMETERIES NEAR GATLINBURG, BUT this one is a true hidden gem. Just behind the shopping area called The Village, there's a short hike up the hill to the sign for White Oak Flats Cemetery. Established in 1830, you'll find many famous names from town, including some of the Ogle family.

ERIKA: More cemeteries and a hike?

MARK: Worth it!

Wiley Oakley, the Roamin' Man of the Mountains, is buried here. He was a famous traveler who shared his love of the Smoky Mountains with world famous figures, including Franklin Roosevelt, Henry Ford, and John D. Rockefeller. He was a hugely popular storyteller on the radio. He was known for being the "Will Rogers of the South."

ERIKA: So, kind of like you, huh?

MARK: I wish.

Wiley's most famous story involved his love, Rebecca. He was so smitten that they ran to the preacher to get married late one night. The preacher refused to hold the ceremony at such a late hour. Wiley and Rebecca pleaded at the door. The preacher finally had them slip money and paperwork under the door and married them without ever opening the door. Wiley would joke that they "got hitched by an invisible preacher man!" Rebecca is buried in White Oak Flats next to Wiley.

ERIKA: At least they are together for whatever happens after we kick it here on Earth.

THE **Dark Side** OF THE **Smoky Mountains**

There are around 4,000 graves here. About 1,000 of them are unmarked and unknown. It is theorized that those unknown graves are responsible for many of the spectral encounters. There have been numerous shadow figures reported here and even a lady in white. She may be linked to our next stop. With so many unmarked graves, it is difficult to place who the spirits might be.

ERIKA: Then let's go, huh? No need to have any wandering spirits join us.

WHITE OAK FLATS CEMETERY IS A FREQUENT STOP FOR GHOST TOURS IN GATLINBURG FOR GOOD REASON. PHOTO BY AUTHOR.

GREENBRIAR RESTAURANT

LOCATED A SHORT DRIVE FROM THE CEMETERY, AND JUST off Gatlinburg's main drag, lies the Greenbriar Restaurant. It is currently known for its hand-cut, dry-aged steaks. One of the finest dining experiences available in Gatlinburg, they host the Greenbriar Whiskey Society there on the third Thursday of every month. Not to be outdone, the Greenbriar Women of Wine event is on the first Thursday of every month.

> **ERIKA:** I'm glad we made a reservation as anyone trying
> to come here should.

The Greenbriar is decorated like a speakeasy with a cozy cabin twist. It was once a lodge in the 1930s, catering to the wealthy hunters and travelers visiting the town. It also housed many events.

> **ERIKA:** I'm down to having a tomahawk ribeye dinner
> and then grabbing one of their signature drinks,
> The Lydia. I'll top it off with a cigar from their
> amazing selection while sitting on the deck.

> **MARK:** I'll join you. Their steaks are legendary.

This is where another Lady in White tale begins.

> **ERIKA:** Of course it is...

She is only known as Lydia. She was young, in love, and engaged to a young man in town. On the day of her wedding, she left the lodge dressed in her wedding gown and waited at the church for her love. Sadly, he never arrived. Lydia waited for hours but slowly made her way back to the lodge. The next part of the story is taken from the Greenbriar Restaurants' menu:

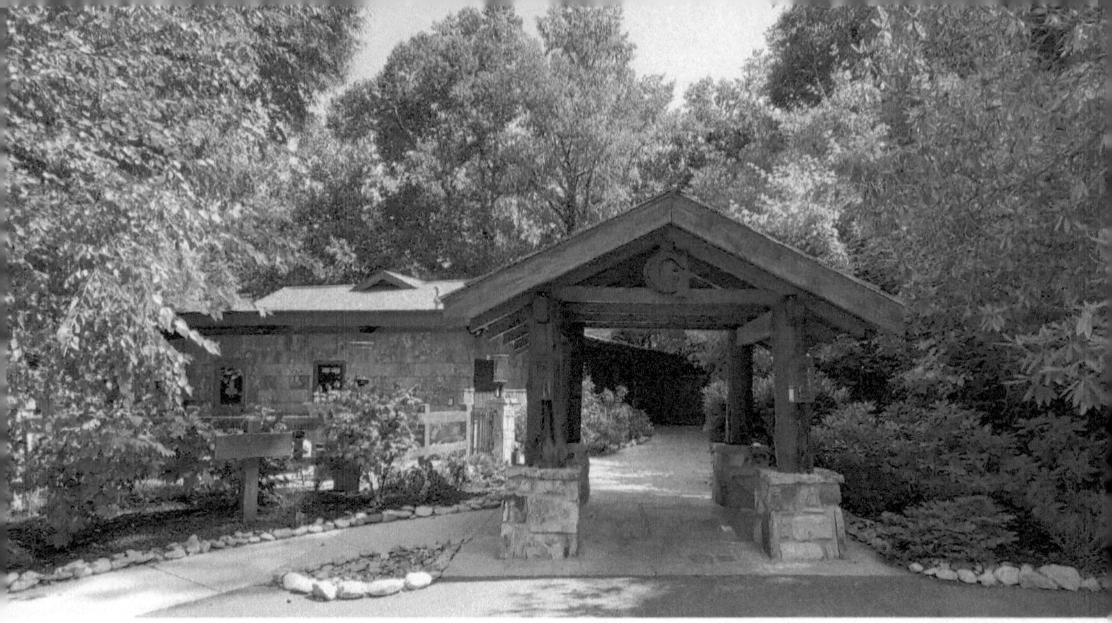

The Greenbriar Restaurant is haunted by a Lady in White. Photo by author.

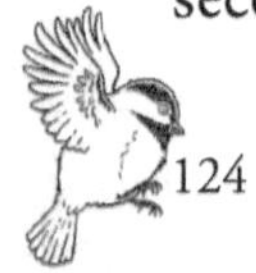

"Unable to overcome her anger and frustration at being jilted, she climbed the stairs to the second-floor landing. She threw a rope over the rafter beam and hung herself.

"Several days after Lydia's death, her love was found dead in the Smokies, mauled to death by a big mountain cat."

Erika: I do not like this story at all.

Now there are several variations of this story. In one, the poor man was killed before the wedding by the beast. Her ghost is said to wander from the restaurant to the White Oaks Cemetery, where he is buried in one of the unmarked graves.

Another version said that their relationship was unrequited; to seek revenge, she took the form of a cat and slayed the young man herself. There are others who say it was the Wampus Cat of the Cherokee that had heard of Lydia's heartache and killed the man in her name. We'll talk about the Wampus Cat a bit more later.

Erika: I love the Wampus Cat!

There are many stories of people seeing Lydia's ghost ever since that fateful night. Recent sightings include seeing her up on Greenbriar's second floor, looking down at diners. The East Tennessee Paranormal

Greenbriar Restaurant

Research Society once did an investigation here and found some very strange photographic anomalies and EVPs.

ERIKA: Okay, I am glad I grabbed a drink to hear this, but knowing it's named after her makes it a bit creepy.

The restaurant is open in the evening on Tuesday through Sunday. Hours do vary by season so call ahead for reservations. They have many seasonal menu options as well. Let them know you'd like a table that has a good view of the second-floor landing. Be sure to say "hello" to Lydia.

THE WHISKEY BAR AT THE GREENBRIER RESTAURANT HAS QUITE THE EXTENSIVE SELECTION OF FINE SPIRITS FOR TASTING WITH THE LOCAL GHOST. PHOTO BY AUTHOR.

THE FAIRY HOUSE

OUR NEXT STOP IS ANOTHER BRIEF HIKE OFF THE MAIN drag. There are two ways to get to this location. The well-known path is to take the Twin Creeks Trail which is a 4.5-mile hike along the historic Voorheis Estate, which has *nothing* to do with Jason Voorhees of Crystal Lake fame. This is a great trail full of history and scenic sites away from the crowds of Gatlinburg.

> **ERIKA:** Why would you bring up Jason Voorhees?

> **MARK:** Why wouldn't I?

There is, however, a much easier way to get to the Fairy House. Just drive up and park at Mynatt Park.

> **ERIKA:** That is good because now I'm freaked out about a guy with a machete and a hockey mask.

Walk a tad up Cherokee Orchard Road to the Twin Creeks Science Center. On slow days, you can park at the Science Center if you let them know it's just to see the Fairy House. There's no real trail to the house, but enough people walk this way that it's easy to see during certain times of the year.

> **ERIKA:** And no threat of a hockey mask–wearing killer finding you in the woods.

Walk the fence line of the Science Center behind the barn, and you'll see the path heading up to the Fairy House. It is not prohibited to go this way due to the Twin Creeks Trail being so close, but be respectful if the Science Center is having an event.

> **ERIKA:** I am excited to see where fairies live.

The Fairy House was, sadly, not built by the Fae, but it sure looks like it might have been. It was built for the Voorheis Estate as their pump house for a spring on the property. The crawling vines, along with the nearby waterfall, give the building its fanciful name. It is most definitely worth the short hike. Standing there, I would not be surprised to find some fairies coming out of the nearby stone works.

ERIKA: Well, at least there is a chance for Fae. Just make sure you don't take any home with you, Travelers!

THE FAIRY HOUSE IS A HIDDEN TREASURE IN GATLINBURG. PHOTO BY AUTHOR.

THE MYSTERIOUS MANSION

Opened in the 1980s, Gatlinburg's Mysterious Mansion is a truly awesome year-round haunted house attraction. Inside, there are three stories of secret passages and winding staircases. Live actors have plenty of time to scare you. It is updated every October with a higher scare level on weekends with more actors and thrills.

> **Mark:** There is no touching from the actors, so even you are safe to visit, Erika.

> **Erika:** I am not worried about actors touching me. I am worried they will jump out, and I will end up touching them ... with my fist. Anyway, is this place also haunted?

That said, there are a couple of legends of true hauntings in the mansion. One story involves a little girl who fell off the balcony of the neighboring hotel. Her spirit is sometimes reported just outside the mansion, pointing up at the balcony from whence she fell. Visitors will mention what a great actor she is to those inside the haunt. The haunters inform them that they have hired no such little girl.

> **Erika:** Now I don't want to wait outside either...

The other spirit is a dark cloaked figure that walks throughout the maze. Many of the actors assume it to be someone coming to relieve them, then it simply vanishes. Visitors to the mansion often talk about the menacing cloaked figure that followed them all the way through the haunt when no actor was there to do it. No one knows who this spirit is. He is thought to be attached to a real haunted object that is used to decorate the attraction. Sadly, no one is sure what object it is exactly.

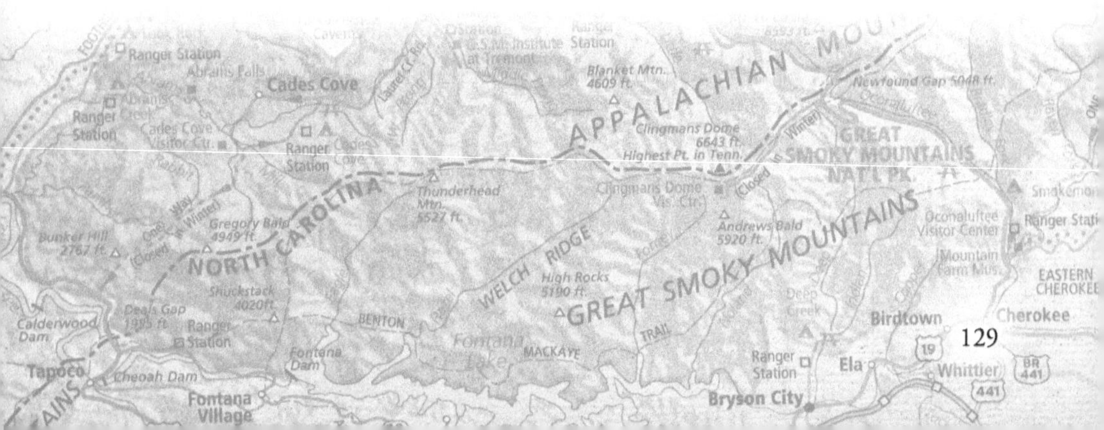

GATLINBURG'S MYSTERIOUS MANSION HAS BEEN IN OPERATION FOR DECADES AND IS OPEN ALL YEAR. PHOTO BY AUTHOR.

ERIKA: Wow, it is not safe inside or outside for me. Please tell me that's all of them.

There is some talk of a Lady in Gray who may be the spirit of a former owner, but most employees wouldn't openly discuss her. Witnesses simply say she moves through walls and is sometimes seen moving props and furniture. All these stories only add to the mystery of the mansion.

ERIKA: NOPE! Too many ghosties for my taste.

Any way you look at it, the Mysterious Mansion is well worth the price of admission and is a fun, family-owned attraction. Check ahead to make sure of their operating hours before your visit.

RIPLEY'S BELIEVE IT OR NOT, THE AQUARIUM, AND HAUNTED ADVENTURE

THERE ARE A FEW RIPLEY'S ATTRACTIONS IN THE TOWN OF Gatlinburg. All three are well worth exploring. Robert Ripley is a well-deserved hero of all of us at *Eerie Travels* as, in his lifetime, he traveled to over 200 countries in search of strange and wonderful oddities. He would bring tales home, or better yet, the items and people themselves.

> **ERIKA:** He sounds like you: bringing home weird things your kiddos hate.

> **MARK:** Is that why they never visit?

Every *Ripley's Believe It or Not* Odditorium has a rotating collection of artifacts that have been gathered for over a century. The Gatlinburg location was recently remodeled and is always worth a visit. Optical illusions, themed galleries, and a wide variety of odd and unusual artifacts make this a must-stop. It is wheelchair and stroller friendly.

> **ERIKA:** I am sure some of the oddities have "things" attached to them.

> **MARK:** Very likely. I'll have to take you to their warehouse in Orlando one day.

> **ERIKA:** NOPE!

Ripley's Aquarium of the Smokies has more creatures than there are people that live in Gatlinburg. That's no real feat as less than 5,000 people live in the city itself. The millions of tourists do outnumber the creatures here, but it certainly seems like they might not. With over 10,000 exotic sea creatures and over 350 individual species, it's two floors of amazing sights.

ERIKA: Any ghost fish here?

There is also a Ripley's Mirror Maze, a Moving 5D Theater, Mini Golf, and a Guiness World Records Museum as well. But we're going to visit Ripley's Haunted Adventure. This is a 10 to 15-minute haunted house set in an old casket company.

ERIKA: I think I might go play mini golf. Meet you outside?

You start in an old mine shaft elevator that takes you to the upper floor. From there, you must find your way out. This is a well-designed haunt with a huge design budget—and it shows. There are some amazing effects and usually well-trained actors within. Well worth the price of a bundle admission with the other Ripley's themed attractions.

RIPLEY'S HAUNTED ADVENTURE IS OPEN YEAR ROUND RIGHT OFF GATLINBURG'S MAIN STREET. PHOTO BY AUTHOR.

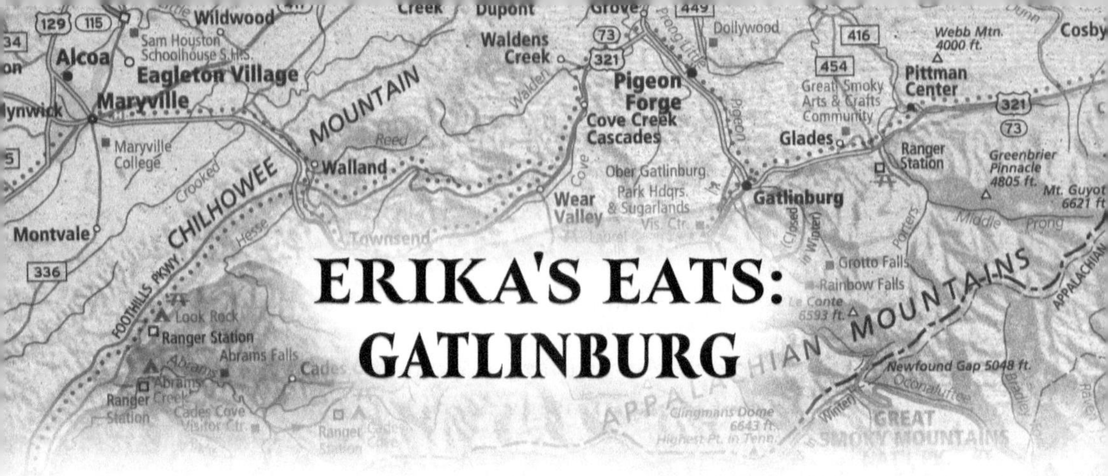

ERIKA'S EATS: GATLINBURG

You can, of course, eat at The Greenbriar Restaurant we mentioned above, but here are a couple of other fun options.

Tennessee Jed's

Do you love good sandwiches? I do! Sometimes, you need to simply grab a quick sandwich, and this is the place to do it. I know Mark loves fried baloney, but I will take a perfect BLT anytime. So, if you are out and about on your adventure, stop here for a delicious bite to eat.

Clifftop Restaurant at Anakeesta

Okay, so this one might be on top off a mountain, but it doesn't just offer an amazing view. You can go on rides and zipline through the mountains. Since I like to keep my feet on the ground, I will munch away on some blue cheese chips and grab a drink at The Bar at the Top of the World.

Anakeesta is an amazingly themed place on top of the mountain that is like walking into a fantasy realm right out of Tolkien or Dungeons and Dragons. The views from the top of the mountain here are breathtaking and well worth the price of admission and your time.

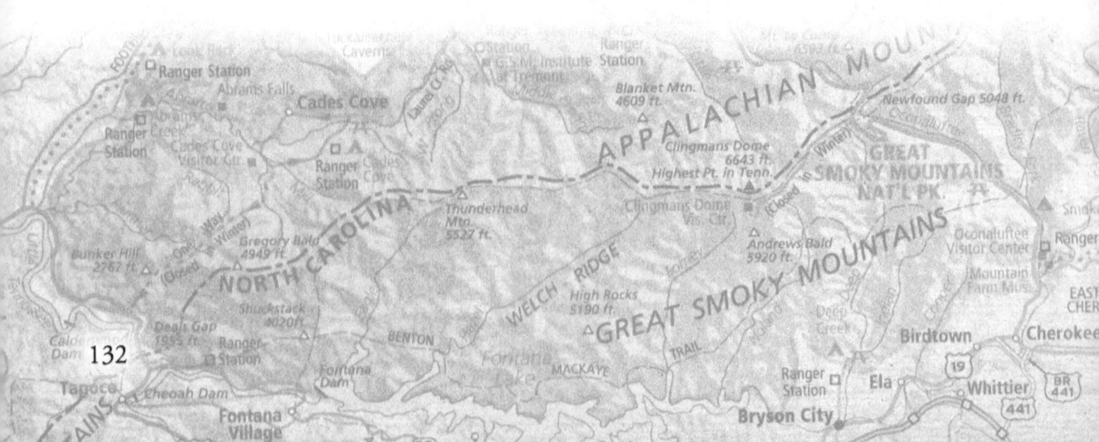

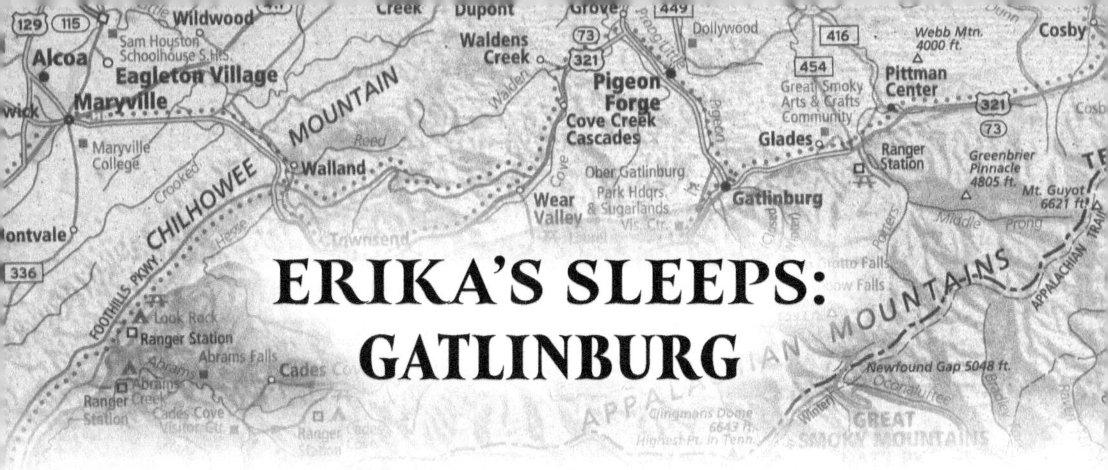

ERIKA'S SLEEPS: GATLINBURG

AFTER ALL OF THAT, WE JUST NEED A SUITABLY HAUNTED location to stay tonight. Thankfully, we have several options available to us.

Garden Plaza Hotel

In July of 1980, two teenaged girls were found dead at the Holiday Inn in Gatlinburg. One girl was found murdered in a stairwell leading to the roof. Her friend was found just a few hours later in her room, lying on the floor next to the bed. Both had been strangled. They were on vacation from Crestwood, Kentucky and were about to start their senior year of high school. The girls had been seen with a local drifter at a lounge earlier in the evening. He was arrested the following day.

There are a few story variants, but the true crime reports do say both girls were staying on the fourth floor in separate rooms. Reports of paranormal activity center on room 413. People who stayed in the room complained of screams and odd smells. Supposedly, a dark shadow is often seen in the room.

The Holiday Inn was renamed the Garden Plaza Hotel. With the name change came more ghostly stories. There is a poltergeist in the kitchen who is said to be an employee named Alvin. There was a story of a scout leader that murdered his troop on the seventh floor, but it was never corroborated. The hotel operated for years until it was recently demolished. It has been replaced by a Hampton Inn. It's unknown if any of the ghosts have moved into the new building.

Rocky River Motel

Rocky River Motel was originally built as the Rocky Waters Motor Inn. In 1934, it was constructed to accommodate the tourists visiting the recently founded Great Smoky Mountain National Park. The hotel has only been owned by only two families since opening day. Originally built by the Lawson family, it is now owned by the Patel family. For generations, this hotel has been an exceptional place to stay. Each room has a private balcony overlooking the Cliff Branch Creek. The balconies are right over the water so you can hear the rushing creek all night.

The hotel has had many visitors in its nearly 90 years of operation. Many have spent extended stays here. Many have also reported strange things happening in the hotel.

One noted story is from someone who stayed at the motel for several weeks. They said that they frequently noticed the clock on their wall running counterclockwise. They would then see strange orbs of light coming from the balcony and flying through the wall on the far side of the room.

Another guest reported that they saw a strange figure that looked vaguely like a woman crawling out of and into their bathroom "just like *The Ring* movie." They later told us they never truly felt alone in the room.

There are no reports of any dark history specifically happening at the hotel. In fact, the hotel was recently renovated into a full 4-star luxury resort. Now called The Historic Rocky Waters Inn, it truly is a remarkable hotel with full-service amenities. There have been no recent reports of any paranormal activity since the renovation.

Other ideas... with fewer ghosts.

I know that not everyone wants to have a spooky night like Mark. I would recommend looking up some of the truly amazing cabin experiences you can have on Airbnb and Vrbo. There are simply too many to list, though you'll certainly find a gem waiting for you.

The Great Smoky Mountains National Park

THE NATIONAL PARK

PRESIDENT CALVIN COOLIDGE SIGNED A BILL IN MAY OF 1926 that established The Great Smoky Mountains National Park along with the Shenandoah National Park. The Department of the Interior was tasked with purchasing and maintaining 150,000 acres of land. Over a thousand landowners were displaced once the park was established. They left behind their farms, schools, churches, and more. The park now contains the largest collection of historic log buildings east of the Mississippi River.

> **ERIKA:** I want to say something about it being taken to begin with, but I am going to let you tell the story.

> **MARK:** It does seem like history is repeating itself.

This was not the first time the government forced out the people of this area. When European settlers reached this area in the late 1700s, they found themselves in the land of the Cherokee. This tribe had permanent towns, farms, and an extensive network of trails between their settlements in the area. We'll be discussing their plight again shortly. For now, know that this area has an extremely bloody history dating back to September of 1776.

> **ERIKA:** Exactly!

Native Americans are reported to have been hunting in these mountains for over 14,000 years. There have been many artifacts found dating back as far as 8000 B.C. Settlements were likely established around the early 1000 B.C. era; ceramics and other evidence of agriculture were discovered alongside ancient animal migration paths just inside the park's boundaries.

In 1904, a travel writer and librarian named Horace Kephart came to the Smokies for health reasons. He had heard of the recuperative powers of the mountain climate. He saw the lumber industry destroying the mountains and the lives of the people trying to move to the mountains for their health.

> **ERIKA:** He is not wrong.

Kephart wrote a book titled *Our Southern Highlanders: A Narrative of Adventure in the Southern Appalachians and a Study of Life Among the Mountaineers.* In the book, he described the daily life and culture of the people living in the Smoky Mountains. It was the first time an author had explored this topic in a widely published book. Kephart advocated the creation of a National Park. He would also go on to map large portions of the Appalachian Trail through the Smokies.

> **ERIKA:** He sounds like an unsung hero.

Kephart died on April 2, 1931 in an automobile accident. Three years later, the Great Smoky Mountains National Park would be officially dedicated.

> **ERIKA:** I am sorry he did not get to see what he helped to create. Maybe his ghost wanders and watches?

> **MARK:** I thought you didn't want any more ghosts.

During the 1930s, the Civilian Conservation Corps began building the infrastructure to the park after the land was acquired. They would build trails along those ancient paths that winnowed their way through the mountains and valleys and construct watchtowers on the mountain peaks and campground facilities all over the park.

> **ERIKA:** Sounds like epic camping. Most likely with bears and Bigfoot!

On September 2, 1940, President Franklin D. Roosevelt came to the park. At Newfound Gap, he gave a speech to a large crowd:

> "We used up or destroyed much of our natural heritage just because that heritage was so bountiful. We slashed our forests, we used our soils, we encouraged floods, we overconcentrated our wealth, we disregarded our

THE **Dark Side** OF THE **Smoky Mountains**

unemployed—all of this so greatly that we were brought rather suddenly to face the fact that unless we gave the thought to the lives of our children and grandchildren, they would no longer be able to live and to improve upon our American way of life.

"The winds that blow through the wide sky in these mountains, the winds that sweep from Canada to Mexico, from the Pacific to the Atlantic—have always blown on free men. We are free today. If we join together now—men and women and children—to face the common menace as a united people, we shall be free tomorrow. So, to the free people of America, I dedicate this Park."

It is now the most visited park in the United States. In 2010, the park noted for the first time it had reached over 20 million visitors in a year.

ERIKA: So glad they did preserve this place. It is so beautiful.

PRESIDENT FRANKLIN D. ROOSEVELT PRESIDES OVER THE OFFICIAL OPENING OF THE GREAT SMOKY MOUNTAINS NATIONAL PARK IN THIS HEADLINE FROM THE ASHEVILLE CITIZEN TIMES ON SEPT 3, 1940. HEADLINE CLIPPING PROVIDED BY SMOKY MOUNTAIN NATIONAL PARK ARCHIVES.

LUCY OF ROARING FORK AND THE PLACE OF A THOUSAND DRIPS

ERIKA: A thousand drips? Who counted?

IF YOU'VE COME TO THE SMOKIES, YOU'LL WANT TO SEE some of that magnificent nature that was saved by the creation of the National Park. For those that want a place to visit that doesn't require much of a hike, then we're going to head for a waterfall anyone can get to, even those with limited mobility. Time to go see a unique seasonal waterfall.

ERIKA: Yay! I love short hikes.

Drive on the one-way road called the Roaring Fork Motor Nature Trail. It circles the park and goes along the Roaring Fork River for a time. The whole trail is about 5.5 miles long but takes about an hour to drive, much like the Cades Cove Loop. This road does close in the winter. Turn at traffic light #8 right off the main parkway in Gatlinburg. Follow Historic Nature Trail Road 'til you enter The Great Smoky Mountains National Park proper. Just past the Rainbow Falls Trail Head, you'll find Roaring Fork Road, which is cars only.

ERIKA: A drive and a hike.

Along the Roaring Fork Motor Nature Trail, you'll be able to see historic cabins, natural beauty, and of course, gorgeous waterfalls. If you have a large truck or an RV, you can't do the trail due to its narrow lanes. Consider a rental car.

THE **Dark Side** OF THE **Smoky Mountains**

ERIKA: That explains your crazy driving. I'm going to keep
my eyes closed.

Down the trail, you'll come across the Bud Ogle Homestead; they sell trail guides and books about the trail here. They'll have even more details about some of the historic buildings you'll see along Roaring Forks.

Before we head to the falls, we must keep our eyes open for one of the most famous ghosts in the Smokies. This is a classic tale.

ERIKA: I knew there was a ghost! To the
Wayback Machine!

The year is 1909, and the valley is filled with several families, including the Ogles, the Jaspers, and the Gilberts. No one knows which family Lucy belonged to, but she was a very pretty girl and was well loved by everyone in the Roaring Fork community and in the town of Gatlinburg. Everyone knew she would be courted by every eligible bachelor in the Smokies.

The valley was very rural, and it would be another quarter of a century before electric lights would come to the area. Lucy loved to stay up late reading by candlelight. One day while hiking in the woods, she tripped

ROARING FORK HAS MANY CABINS LIKE THIS ONE. NO ONE IS TRULY SURE WHICH ONE WAS THE HOME OF THE GHOST OF LUCY. PHOTO BY AUTHOR.

and sprained her ankle. After making it home, she was forced to spend days in bed reading.

> **ERIKA:** Reading in bed sounds like a perfect lazy
> afternoon.

MARK: My favorite way to spend a day.

A handsome gentleman named Foster happened upon her in the woods a short while later. She was still limping, so he offered to give her a ride home on his horse. He was worried she might be ill as her skin was very hot as she climbed up behind him. He took her to the cabins near the road, and she thanked him. She quickly limped off into the cove.

The next day, he decided to go visit her parents and ask to court her. When he asked around about Lucy, the townsfolk told him to head to the new cabin down the road. There, he approached the cabin and the man working outside of it.

He introduced himself and asked about Lucy. Foster was convinced she must have been ill to be so warm and not concerned by the wintery air. Her hands had been downright hot to the touch as she had held onto him.

"Our dear Lucy is no longer with us," said the father with tears in his eyes. "You are also not the first rider to come to our cabin seeking to court her this year."

> **ERIKA:** What???

Foster was convinced that the father was covering for the daughter or simply trying to scare him away. Then he noticed how newly built the cabin was. He remarked on it, hoping to avoid being chased off or possibly shot by an overprotective father.

"It is new," the father explained. "We had it built last year after the old cabin burned down with poor Lucy inside. She had been reading in bed with a sprained ankle. The candle fell over and spread from book to bed, and with her hurt, she…"

He said no more and walked Foster over to her tombstone under a White Pine tree. There upon it was a lit candle.

"We don't know how or why the candles keep burning and appearing here," said the father. "She must still be with us yet."

THE PLACE OF A THOUSAND DRIPS IS A BEAUTIFUL SPOT TO SEE ON THE ROARING FORK LOOP. PHOTO BY AUTHOR.

ERIKA: Wait, there was a candle on the grave? Just *burning*? NOPE!

That story has been told time and time again here. No one is quite sure where her stone or cabin was located. Her spirit is seen as a young lady, usually with a limp. She's evolved with the times and asks for rides as a hitchhiking ghost. While descriptions sometimes differ, she is often seen wearing a white top and jeans, though her feet are bare. Once in your vehicle, you will feel the heat coming off of her and the faint smell of a campfire or a candle.

ERIKA: That is fun. A ghost who is a fashionista.

She tends to vanish quickly if too many questions are asked of her. Calling her by name is a sure way to get her to disappear in a flash, leaving only the lingering smell and sense of warmth.

ERIKA: Well, I love that she is warm. Most ghosts are cold, so that is a surprise.

Back on the trail, it's a slow drive to our next stop. It should take about an hour unless you want to stop at all the scenic locations. Then plan for about a three-hour tour. Toward the end of the trail is The Place of a Thousand Drips.

Lucy of Roaring Fork and The Place of a Thousand Drips

This waterfall is so amazingly unique that it only occurs occasionally. It is a very low flowing fall, so it is always heavier just after a nice rain. Rain is more common in the early spring and late fall so plan accordingly, but it is visible much of the year. The stream cascades down over 30 feet of rocks. The rocks have formed an incredible set of formations due to water slowly sculpting them over many years. The carvings look almost manmade, but they simply show how amazing nature can be.

Look out for plenty of people stopping at marker 15 near the end of the trail. If you stay in the car, you can see the falls on the left side. The driver's side will have a great view. Watch out for photographers and other visitors trying to get a great shot. The pros say to use long exposure to enhance the appearance of the low flowing water over the rocks, particularly if you come on a dry day.

Moss-covered rocks, draped with lacy water, make this a truly spectacular view. It's an unforgettable waterfall that should be added to any trip to the Smokies. Say "Hi" to Lucy if you see her.

BALES CEMETERY IS ON THE BASKINS CREEK TRAIL JUST OFF THE ROARING FORK MOTOR TRAIL. IT IS A SHORT HIKE FROM THE EPHRAIM BALES CABIN. MANY BELIEVE ONE OF THE UNMARKED GRAVES HERE IS LUCY'S. PHOTO PROVIDED BY SMOKY MOUNTAIN NATIONAL PARK ARCHIVES.

RAINBOW FALLS

IF YOU WANT A CLASSICALLY IMPRESSIVE WATERFALL, THEN Rainbow Falls is the tallest single-drop waterfall in the national park. The water cascades 80 feet over a sheer cliff face, rushing over the rock formations at the bottom of the magnificent drop.

ERIKA: I heard that Rainbow Falls is considered romantic.

The hike to Rainbow Falls is about 5.5 miles and goes up about 1,500 feet. It is not recommended for young children, and everyone must wear comfortable hiking shoes. Plan for about a five-hour hike there and back from the parking area. The trail beyond is for expert hikers and goes another four miles to the peak of Mount Le Conte. Pack lots of snacks and water.

ERIKA: That is a hike, but it is very worth it!

Be careful if you do head to the falls. Don't climb on the rocks! While it is tempting to get that perfect shot, several deaths have occurred in recent years and serious injuries occur on a regular basis. People don't realize how slippery the algae make the rocks at Rainbow Falls. Plus, you are a long way from medical help.

RAINBOW FALLS IS WORTH THE HIKE. WATCH YOUR STEP AS IT IS VERY SLIPPERY. PHOTO PROVIDED BY GREAT SMOKY MOUNTAINS NATIONAL PARK.

WHALEY-BIG GREENBRIAR AND OWNBY LONGBRANCH CEMETERIES

THE OWNBY AND THE WHALEY CLANS WERE SOME OF THE first families to settle the Greenbriar area in the northern part of the Great Smoky Mountains. Sometimes called Big Greenbriar, this area is on the opposite side of the park from Cades Cove and Elkmont, which is confusingly referred to as Little Greenbriar.

ERIKA: I bet that can be confusing.

MARK: Especially when researching the history of the Smokies.

The Whaley family lost the land three times due to eminent domain. The first was when the National Park Service bought their land in Greenbriar for the creation of the Great Smoky Mountains. A short while later, the Tennessee Valley Authority purchased their land for the construction of Norris Dam. Finally, their land at Oak Ridge was purchased for the Manhattan Project.

ERIKA: Wow! Those are some amazing reasons.

MARK: I don't think they were pleased any of those times.

This area contains the largest concentration of rock walls and old chimneys in the Smokies. The National Park Service preserved these as a representation of pioneer life in Appalachia. There's a long trail hike to the John Messer Barn along the Porters Creek Trail. This is an easier trail but still not for the faint of heart. There are numerous waterfalls and even the remains of the 1920s steam train resting at the bed of Injun Creek, a misspelling of Engine Creek, where the Elmont train crash occurred.

There are plenty of timber rattlesnakes as well as bear sightings in the area, so be careful.

ERIKA: I think I might skip the snakes and bears.

The first of our stops is the Whaley-Big Greenbriar Cemetery. It's a short hike off the Porters Creek Scenic Loop. There is a second cemetery called the Friendship Cemetery about a half-mile onward for more adventurous souls. This first cemetery, however, is reportedly the home of a Grim.

ERIKA: A Grim? What the heck is that?

There is a spectral large black dog that is said to guard the cemetery. Common in England and Scotland, there was a custom in the 19th century to bury a dog under the cornerstone of a church so that its ghost might serve as a guardian spirit for the graveyard. This cemetery has numerous sightings of such a creature, often mistaken for a black bear, which do frequently roam these woods. However, when witnesses look closer, they see it is an unusually large canine guarding the cemetery grounds. Its howl reminds them of a mournful wolf. It is noted for having deep red eyes and tends to vanish into the shadows of the stones.

ERIKA: That sounds terrifying.

Back in the car, it's just a short drive to the Porters Creek Trail Trailhead at the end of Greenbriar Road. It's only a short—but slightly steep— hike to the Ownby Cemetery. The tombstones here are a mixture of well-kept stones and some that have long lost their inscriptions and definition. The grave of note is Mary Whaley, an infant who was born and died on Aug 11, 1909. The grave is said to be visited often by a lady in white.

ERIKA: I love a good Lady in White ghost.

We're going to turn around, but if you want to adventure down the trail, you can continue onward to the John Messer barn, which was built around 1875. Just behind the barn is the Smoky Mountains Hiking Club Cabin that was built in the mid-1930s, thanks to a special permit. The trail continues to another Brushy Mountain (not the one from Tennessee earlier) with several waterfalls but is very tricky unless you are an experienced hiker.

ERIKA: Then I will pass on that hike. Where to next?

CHIMNEY TOPS

WHILE THE CHIMNEY TOPS TRAIL IS LIKELY THE MOST popular trail in the Smokies, due to its short length and spectacular view, we can only recommend it for those ready for a workout. It goes up nearly 1,400 feet in just under two miles, so it is a steep climb. Bring plenty of water.

ERIKA: And snacks!

At the time of this writing, the final section of the trail is closed to all public use. That includes the rocky ridge often called the "backside of the Chimneys," and the summit is not accessible. The area was severely damaged by fire, and it is not safe for visitors. Many people ignore the warnings and have had to be removed by rescue parties after serious injuries. There has been at least one fatality as well.

ERIKA: Travelers, please do not be "that" person who violates the rules.

Be careful in any of your hikes throughout the Great Smoky Mountains National Park. Enjoy the magnificence of nature, the deep history, and keep your eyes open for the spirits of the mountains.

THE VIEW OF CHIMNEY TOPS IS ONE OF THE GRANDEST IN THE SMOKY MOUNTAINS. PHOTO PROVIDED BY GREAT SMOKY MOUNTAINS NATIONAL PARK.

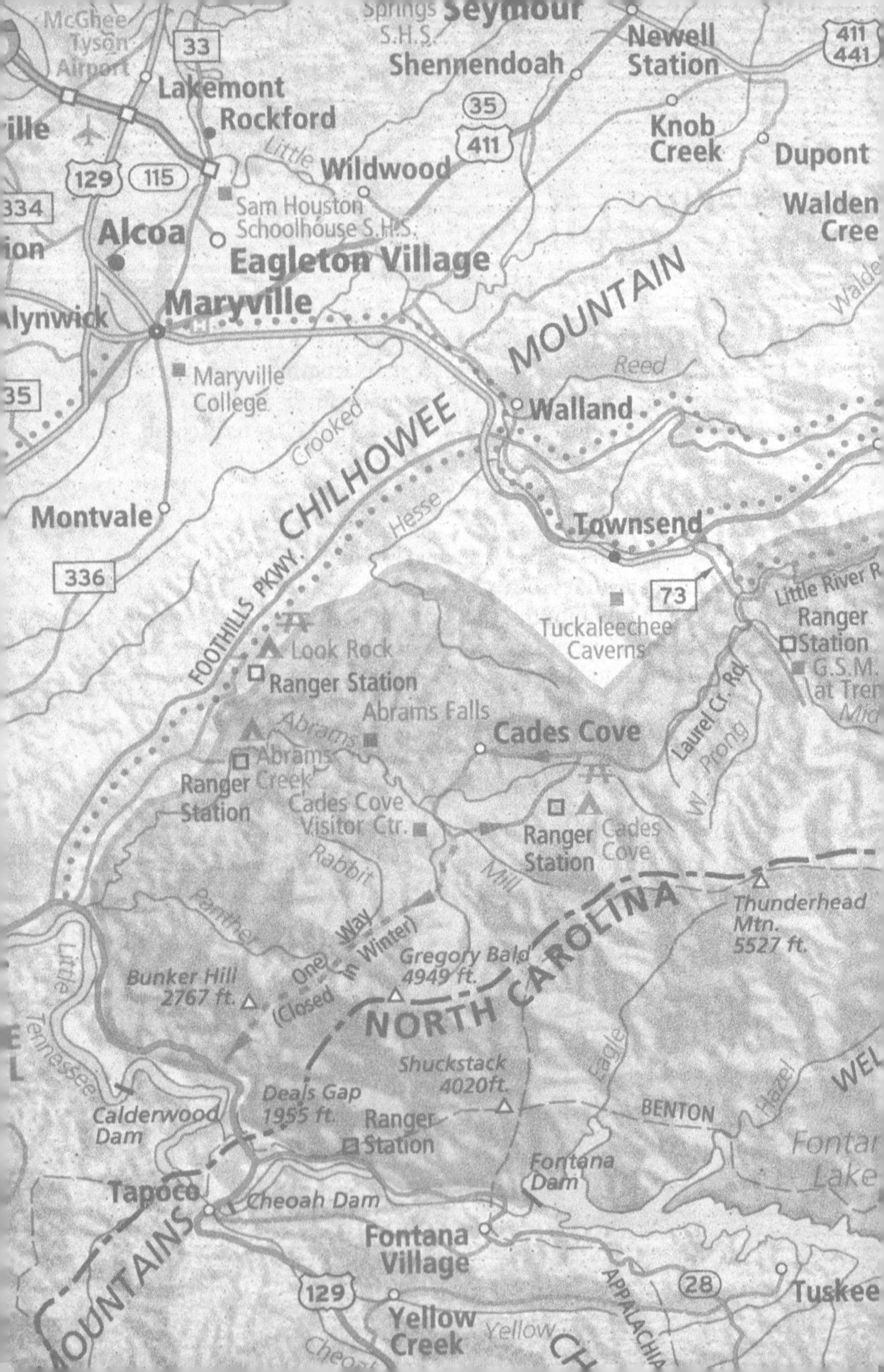

McGhee
Tyson
Airport
33
Lakemont
Rockford
Little
Wildwood
129
115
334
Alcoa
Sam Houston
Schoolhouse S.H.S.
Eagleton Village
Maryville
lynwick
Springs
S.H.S.
Seymour
Shennendoah
Newell
Station
35
411
Knob
Creek
411
441
Dupont
Walden
Cree
ille
ion
35
Maryville
College
Crooked
CHILHOWEE
MOUNTAIN
Reed
Walland
Walde
Montvale
Hesse
Townsend
336
FOOTHILLS PKWY.
73
Little River R
Ranger
Station
G.S.M.
at Tre
Mi
Look Rock
Ranger Station
Abrams Falls
Tuckaleechee
Caverns
Abrams
Abrams
Creek
Ranger
Station
Cades Cove
Visitor Ctr.
Cades Cove
Laurel Cr. Rd.
W. Prong
Ranger
Station
Cades
Cove
Rabbit
Mill
NORTH CAROLINA
Thunderhead
Mtn.
5527 ft.
Panther
One Way
(Closed in Winter)
Gregory Bald
4949 ft.
Bunker Hill
2767 ft.
Little
Tennessee
Shuckstack
4020 ft.
Eagle
BENTON
Hazel
WE
Fon
Lake
Deals Gap
1955 ft.
Ranger
Station
Calderwood
Dam
Fontana
Dam
Tapoco
Cheoah Dam
Fontana
Village
Appalachia
28
Tuskee
MOUNTAINS
129
Yellow
Creek
Yellow
Cheoa
L

Cherokee, North Carolina

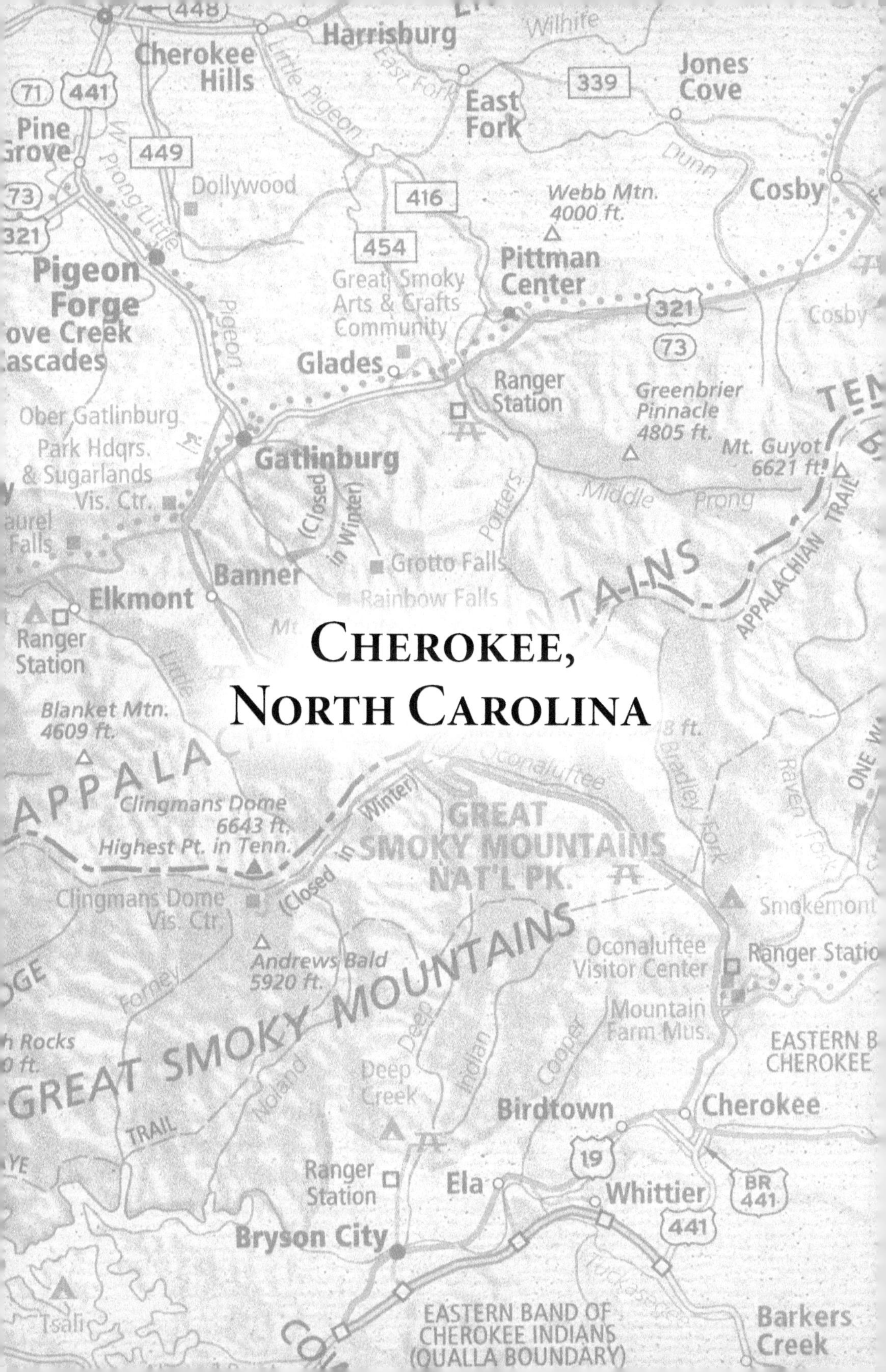

CHEROKEE

I CANNOT DO JUSTICE TO THE HISTORY OF THE CHEROKEE people in just a small chapter of our book. Their lineage constituted the largest politically integrated tribe at the time of the European colonization of the Americas. They are estimated to have controlled over 40,000 square miles of the Appalachian Mountains in what is now northern Georgia up through South Carolina, North Carolina, and Tennessee.

During Spanish exploration of the area, the Cherokee claimed these mountains had seen many battles and wars as they settled them. The Cherokee were divided into seven clans including Long Hair, Blue, Wolf, Wild Potato, Deer, Bird, and Paint. Each had a semi-democratic political structure under two chiefs, a Peace Chief and a War Chief, both of whom served as leaders when needed. Towns were divided into Red Towns and White Towns

As with all the Indigenous Peoples of North America, know that they were treated badly by every government that tried to claim their lands. By 1759, the British began indiscriminate destruction of native towns including the Cherokee, whom they were allied with. In 1773, the Cherokee and Creek tribes exchanged a portion of their land in the Treaty of Augusta, ceding more than two million acres.

After 1800, the Cherokee assimilated slightly to the American settler culture. They adopted colonial methods of farming, weaving, and home-building. The syllabary system of writing was developed in 1821 by Sequoyah, a Cherokee that had been with the U.S. Army in the Creek War. This allowed the entire tribe to become literate within a short time. In 1828, *The Cherokee Phoenix* became the Native American's first newspaper.

ERIKA: That is very awesome.

Sadly, gold was discovered on Cherokee land in Georgia in the 1830s. Even though the Supreme Court sided with the tribe after being forced to sign the Treaty of New Echota, ceding all their land East of the Mississippi, President Andrew Jackson refused to honor their decision. He passed the Indian Removal act of 1830.

Cherokee

The Trail of Tears took place during the fall and winter of 1838 and 1839, respectively. Although funds had been procured for this, it was badly mismanaged, and the inadequate supplies led to terrible suffering. The trail cost the tribes everything. Over 4,000 died on the 116-day forced march to Oklahoma. New challenges began immediately with the Osage and Cherokee who were already there after the treaty of 1817.

Before the Trail of Tears, a unique group of Cherokee, the Oconaluftee, secured permission to stay in North Carolina with the help of a lawyer named William H. Thomas. He had a large amount of business with the tribe, so fought hard to keep himself successful and the tribe protected for over 30 years.

To avoid losing their protected status, the Oconaluftee reluctantly assisted in the search for Cherokee Nation Indians that had fled into the Smokies to avoid relocation. One of those in hiding was Tsali, a hero to many Cherokee for his resistance to the Indian Removal Act. He had caused the deaths of many soldiers. To prevent retaliation, Tsali agreed to surrender and face his execution. Due to his sacrifice, many others still hiding were able to settle with the Oconaluftee in western North Carolina. Thus began the Eastern Band of Cherokee.

Today, there are over 10,000 members of the Eastern Tribe, and most live on the Cherokee Indian Reservation, also known as the "Qualla Boundary." The communities are all in the western portion of the North Carolina range of the Smoky Mountains. Unlike most other reservations in the United States, this one is entirely open to visitors and tourists. In fact, tourism is the most profitable industry for the local economy of the tribe.

Hotels, a casino, restaurants, campgrounds, shops, and even amusement attractions flourish around the town of Cherokee. Museums here help preserve and interpret the history and culture of the Cherokee people. Culturally, traditional crafts and skills have blended with modern lifestyles in the city. The speaking of the Cherokee language has also seen a remarkable resurgence in recent years.

"Unto These Hills" has been performed for decades. It is the third oldest historical outdoor drama in the United States. Photo by author.

ERIKA: It is an amazing place to visit, and there is so much to do here!

You can't miss the renowned outdoor drama *Unto These Hills*. Since July 1, 1950, this play tells the story of the formation of the Eastern Band of the Cherokee from their early years through the Trail of Tears. It is a seasonal show from May through August most years. It is very emotional and has striking imagery throughout.

Usually in the fall, the theater here also does a haunted trail based on Cherokee legendary creatures. A recent one was based on the dreaded Raven Mocker. This is a shapeshifting creature that feeds on the life force of the dying. They take the shape of giant ravens and caw while draining the very essence of life from their victims. The haunted trail immerses you in the folklore and legend of the chosen theme for the year.

Visit the Museum of the Cherokee People to be immersed in the culture and language of the Cherokee. If you plan your visit ahead of time, you might meet one of the amazing storytellers there and be allowed to engage with the Cherokee's rich oral history tradition. One of the storytellers told me, "To the Cherokee, the supernatural is just natural." Then he spoke of the Moon-Eyed People.

ERIKA: I need a snack before we go down another trail.

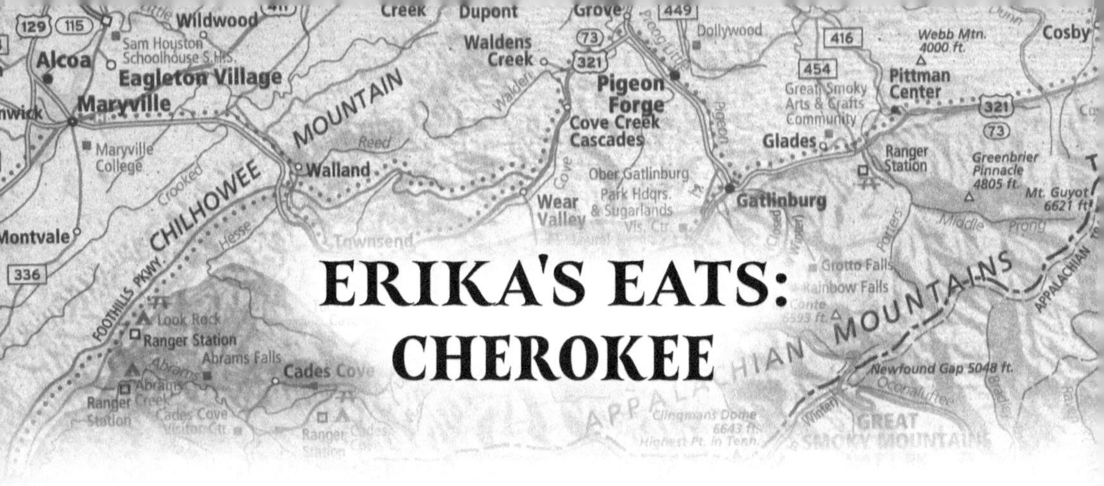

ERIKA'S EATS: CHEROKEE

THERE ARE SO MANY FUN RESTAURANTS IN CHEROKEE. I am going to highlight a couple we loved.

Native Brews Taphouse

Besides having great house-made beer, it has some very indulgent items on the menu including fried Oreos. This is another place where Mark can grab his fried baloney sandwich, and I can get a Warrior Burger with jalapeno pimento cheese. SO AMAZING! Also, several of the waitstaff have told us of a shadow figure that comes out at night, so when they are closing, they are never alone!

Qualla Java Café

The Qualla Java Cafe is just what we caffeine addicts need. Grab a dark chocolate frappe like me or an iced tea like Mark, and you can put it in a souvenir travel cup to take on the road with you.

VINTAGE POSTCARD OF THE TOWN OF CHEROKEE FROM THE LATE 1950S. PHOTO PROVIDED BY THE CHEROKEE HERITAGE SOCIETY.

THE MOON-EYED PEOPLE

The Cherokee storyteller told of a strange race of people that predated his people in the Smoky Mountains. These weren't preternatural beings like the Nunnehi but pale-skinned humans with bearded faces and large blue or gray eyes. They were described as being very short with small round bodies. Their eyes were so bright and sensitive to light that they would only come out at night. Thus, the name "Moon-Eyed" People.

Erika: They sound almost cute.

According to Cherokee history, their eyes were so sensitive to light that even a full moon was too strong for them, and they had to flee to caves or their low-lying forts of logs and wood. The Cherokee say that the Creek tribe came up from the South and invaded the territory of the Moon-Eyed People. Their lands apparently stretched from the Little Tennessee River all the way north to what Kentucky is now. They were even reported to have some stone forts along their borders.

Erika: It is interesting that they pushed out these people.

Mark: The theme keeps repeating itself here.

The Creek would strike on the nights of the full moon to drive the Moon-Eyed People from their forts and caves. The pale-skinned people were too weak to fight back and were driven deeper into the caves or west, depending on which path was safest for them.

The Cherokee were said to have warred with the remaining tribe of Moon-Eyed folk. This was detailed by botanist Benjamin Burton in his book from 1797. He said, "The Cherokee tell us that when they first arrived in the country in which they inhabit they found it possessed by certain 'moon-eyed-people,' who could not see in the daytime. These wretches they expelled."

The Moon-Eyed People

Early historians and early documentarians of the Cherokee collected these stories. In 1902, James Mooney noted that the Moon-Eyed People were white and possibly albino. In 1782, John Sevier, the early first governor of Tennessee, visited a site in northern Georgia called Fort Mountain. There, he met a 90-year-old Cherokee chief named Oconostota who told him a story he had learned from his own ancestors. The tale involved a fort being built by white men from "across the great water." Oconostota said that these men "crossed the great water and landed first near the mouth of the Alabama River near Mobile." Possibly the Moon-Eyed People came from elsewhere.

There is a Welsh myth that has blended with the Moon-Eyed People story, thanks to that story from Oconostota and John Sevier.

Prince Madoc ab Owain Gwynedd was a famous Welsh explorer that may have beaten Columbus and even Leif Erikson to America. In 1170, young Prince Madoc, fleeing internal conflict in Wales, set sail westward. If true, this story would make him the true first European explorer to reach the continent of North America.

What's intriguing is this legend traveled across the ocean from Wales and blended into the oral histories of the Native American tribes. Several details are interwoven with the Welsh stories saying he traveled to a far-off land, building castles and forts. He tried to avoid conflict with the indigenous population by intermarriage but, ultimately, was driven into caves. Survivors of his expedition returned to tell his tale back in Wales.

THE **Dark Side** OF THE **Smoky Mountains**

MARK: It is a common tactic used for thousands of years
by people from all over the world.

Some early European explorers reportedly encountered Native American tribes with distinctly European features including beards, red hair, and blue eyes. These "Welsh Indians" supposedly spoke a language similar enough to Welsh that it allowed for early communication between the natives and the explorers.

Even more curious is the fact that the Cherokee of the Ohio Valley area far to the north also speak of the Moon-Eyed People. Here, native historians link them to the mound builders dating as early as 500 B.C. The mystery around these early people is substantiated in many ways throughout North America, yet we have no idea who they were or where they went.

ERIKA: Do you think they are still around somewhere?

MARK: Maybe those folks exploring the cave systems
might stumble on something. Again, I'm not
watching *The Descent* again while we're
traveling around here.

THIS SERPENTINE WALL OF ROCKS IS SAID TO HAVE BEEN CONSTRUCTED BY THE MOON EYED PEOPLE ACCORDING TO THE CHEROKEE. IT IS LOCATED ATOP FORT MOUNTAIN STATE PARK IN NORTH GEORGIA. PHOTO PROVIDED BY THE BLUE RIDGE HISTORICAL SOCIETY.

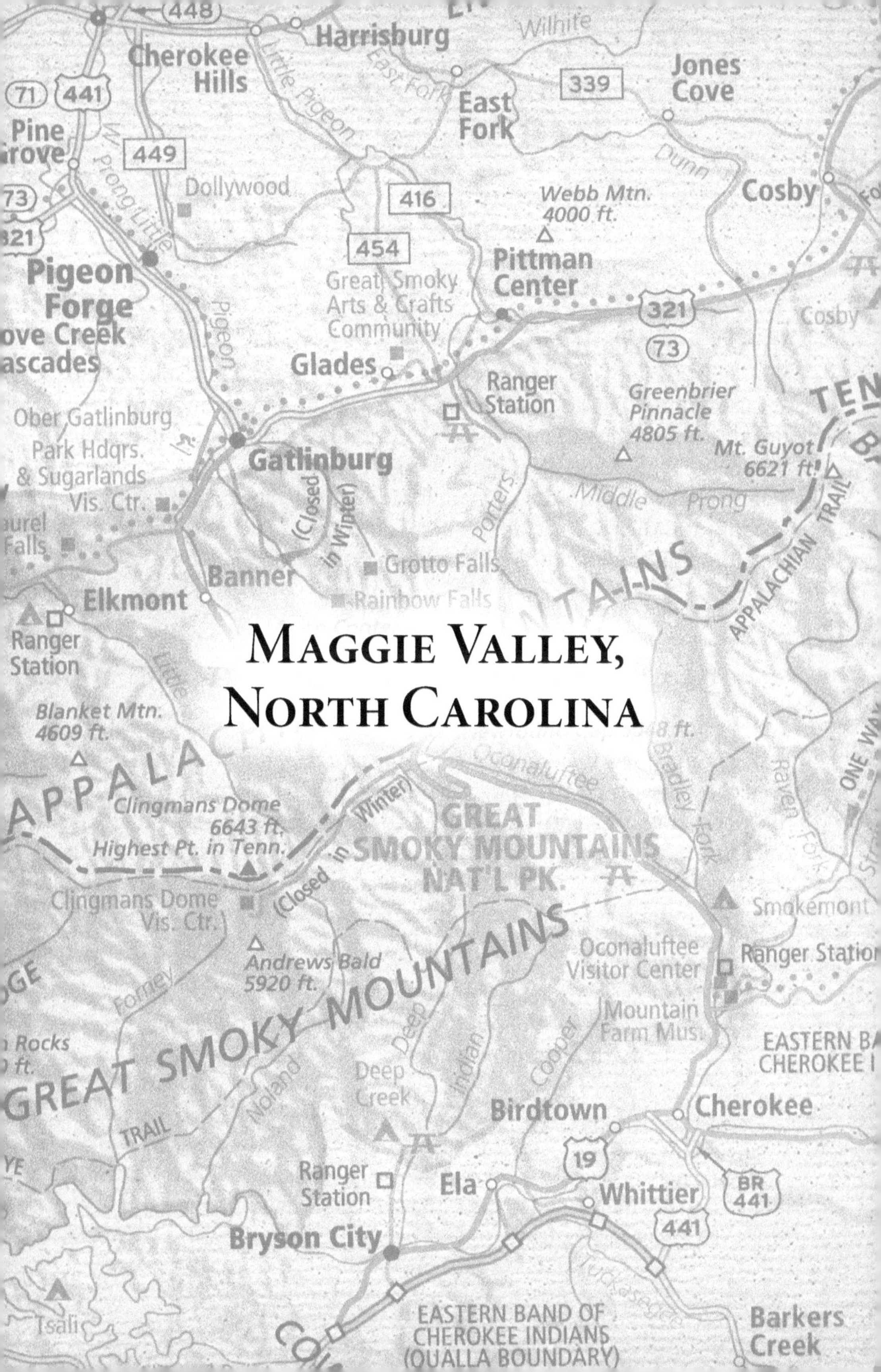

Maggie Valley, North Carolina

MAGGIE VALLEY

AS WITH EVERY AREA WE'VE TRAVELED, THE FIRST DOCU-
mented inhabitants of this area are the Cherokee. The Cherokee speak
of a great flood that drove their people deeper into the mountains. They
already knew of the great cunning of Dilsdohdi, Anglicized as Aganunitsi
or "The Water Spider." The Spider brought fire to the world when all the
other Great Animal Spirits had failed. He succeeded by making a bowl of
webbing and carrying the flames across the water. This marked the cunning jumping spiders with red hair on their backs forever after.

> **ERIKA:** We do love spiders!

> **MARK:** Kari and you can have all the spiders. I'll stick with
> the ghosts and other monsters.

Aganunitsi saw the flood waters rising and the poor Cherokee in dire
need of escape. The Water Spider made a giant web to help the tribe climb
the mountains and steered them safely to what is now Maggie Valley. The
Cherokee revere Dilsdohdi as a symbol of resourcefulness and seek its
blessings. Cherokee storytellers make certain to inform listeners, "This
is not the water spider that looks like a mosquito, but the other one, with
black downy hair and red stripes on her body."

> **MARK:** Kari was happy to point out this is likely *Phidippus
> johnsoni*, the red-backed jumping spider endemic
> to the Cherokee lands.

> **ERIKA:** Kari is the expert on such things. I agree!

While here, the Cherokee created several trails from where Asheville
is now and into their lands to the west. These now make up the main roads
of US-19 and US-276. They stayed here until forced out by European

settlers, as is the story so often repeated in these mountains. The first settler came in 1785 and began to grow corn on his plot of land.

ERIKA: Corn, huh?

MARK: Still the most common crop of the area.

The community wasn't even considered a town for over a century. In the early 1800s, a hunter named Henry Plott came to the valley with his hunting dogs. These dogs would be bred here for generations. In 1989, the Plott Hound would be designated as North Carolina's State Dog.

ERIKA: They are cute and look a little like my dog Tali
with brindle coloring.

It wouldn't be until 1904 when John Sidney Setzer grew tired of traveling miles for his mail and petitioned for a post office. He even offered up his home to serve as the post office. He was told he'd need to have several months of records to be accepted.

ERIKA: I love that inconvenience caused a change.

Using his parlor as a makeshift post office, he kept diligent records. At the end of six months, he resubmitted, and they accepted but on the one condition that he had to give the post office a name. He submitted several names, but they were already taken. He then submitted the name Jonathan Creek (for the creek that ran through his property) and the names of his three daughters. They accepted his daughter Maggie as the new name of the settlement post office.

ERIKA: Wow! Just send in a list of names?

MARK: It's still like that today.

Maggie Mae Setzer was so embarrassed when she heard the news that she ran away to hide in the cabin she had been born in. Eventually she grew accustomed to it and grew into a young lady and a fixture of the now-growing settlement. At the age of 17, blonde, blue-eyed Maggie married Ira Pylant of Nashville, and she moved away to Texas. She would return to visit many times before dying at the age of 88 in 1979.

THE **Dark Side** OF THE **Smoky Mountains**

ERIKA: But I have seen Maggie. She's not a ghost, is she?

It's not her ghost who is sometimes seen around the valley. There are community members selected to be Miss Maggie every few years. This town mascot is often seen walking the streets of the town and waving to the tourists as they head through town on their way to Soco Gap and its spectacular waterfalls or back to Cherokee or Bryson City.

THIS POSTCARD FROM THE MID-1960S SHOWS MAGGIE MOUNTAIN CRAFTS IN MAGGIE VALLEY. THE SHOP IS STILL THERE AND STILL FEATURES UNIQUE GIFTS AND THE INCREDIBLY DELICIOUS AUNT MAGGIE'S HOMEMADE FUDGE. PROVIDED BY THE MAGGIE VALLEY HISTORICAL SOCIETY.

GHOST TOWN IN THE SKY

GHOST TOWN IN THE SKY, WHICH WOULD LATER BECOME Ghost Town Village, was an extremely popular Wild West themed amusement park in the heart of Maggie Valley. R. B. Coburn heard about a local shepherd named Dan Carpenter. The legend goes that Dan lost a sheep somewhere up Buck Mountain and could hear its cries. R. B. and Dan went up the mountain and searched but never found the cave entrance despite being able to hear the bleating sheep somewhere underground.

ERIKA: Ghost sheep?

MARK: Yet another lost cavern.

R. B. dreamed up the idea to build a mountain cavern experience and bought the land from Carpenter. He built Wild West Village and figured the caverns would bring in the tourists in droves. The cavern portion was never built, and the property frequently had to be rebuilt as the ground would often collapse.

ERIKA: That sounds like an omen.

It was opened on May 1, 1961 and became a huge success. The mountaintop locale was only accessible by a ski-lift or an incline railroad. At its peak, over 600,000 people would attend the theme park over a season.

ERIKA: That is a lot of people.

The park was divided into several "towns" that were themed to different aspects of the American Wild West. "Old West Town" was the heart of the park with a couple of saloons, a schoolhouse, bank, and jail. Over the years, several rides and rollercoasters would open. It's hard to believe it didn't open a haunted house until 2009.

ERIKA: That was primed for a haunted house!

GHOST TOWN IN THE SKY SITS ABANDONED. PHOTO PROVIDED BY MAGGIE VALLEY HISTORICAL SOCIETY.

With frequent stunt actors having gun fights at the park, one name is revered above all others: The Apache Kid. Jim Jumper, a full-blooded Cherokee, began as a stunt fall in one of the earliest shows at the park. His fall was so great, R. B. Coburn famously said, "Don't let him go back down the mountain again. He stays here. He's my gunfighter." The Apache Kid became a fixture of the park's many daily gunfights.

> **ERIKA:** These stunt actors who do these shows daily
> are amazing.

Sadly, the park had a gradual decline and eventually closed its doors permanently at the end of the 2009 season. There have been numerous attempts to reopen it, but a lengthy legal battle after the death of one of the recent owners has pretty much doomed the site.

> **ERIKA:** That is sad. I bet it could be reopened as
> something very cool.

> **MARK:** Several attempts have been made. Nothing
> serious has come about yet.

This has not deterred urban explorers from climbing up the hill and revisiting the old abandoned theme park. This is highly illegal, and

Ghost Town in the Sky

security is tighter than they realize. Many have been arrested for trespassing in the old Ghost Town in the Sky.

ERIKA: Travelers, again, please follow the rules!

If you would like to visit, the base of the mountain is an open lot, and there are some artifacts, including a stagecoach and the original incline railroad cars. To visit the top, you must petition for a tour coordinated by Haywood County Tourism and the current owners. This is no mean feat; it's unlikely to be granted without a really good reason to visit and document the remnants of the old attraction.

THE LONG ABANDONED RED DEVIL ROLLER COASTER WILL LIKELY NEVER RUN AGAIN HERE AT GHOST TOWN IN THE SKY. PHOTO PROVIDED BY SMOKY MOUNTAIN TOURS.

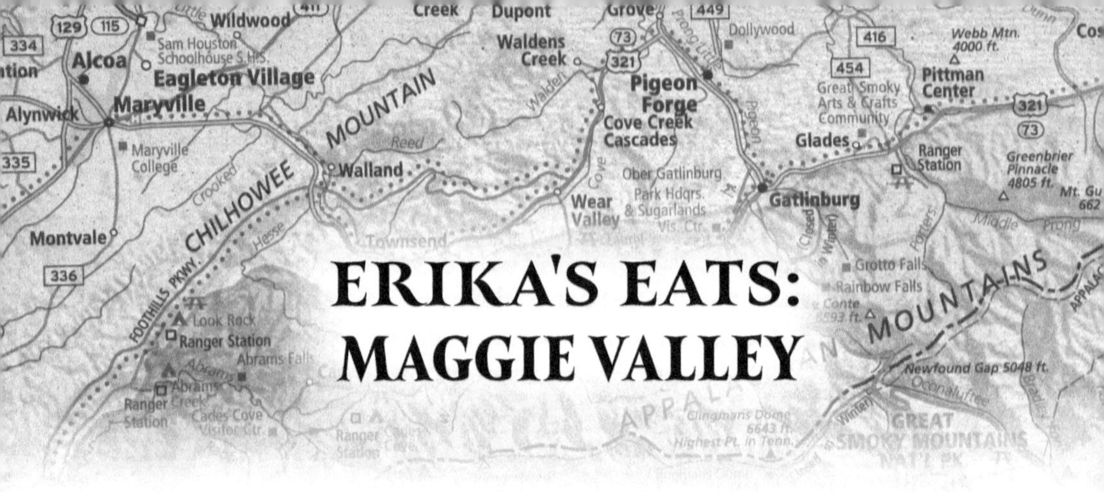

ERIKA'S EATS: MAGGIE VALLEY

Joey's Pancake House

Right across the street is the iconic Joey's Pancake House, which first opened in 1966. Get there early and enjoy one of the best breakfasts you can find in the Smokies. While there, keep your eyes open for a kind figure who will ask you how you are enjoying your morning. This is supposedly the spirit of Joey O'Keefe, the founder of the restaurant. He passed away in 2001 but likes to make sure his customers are always happy and full.

It is not fancy, but the pancakes and other breakfast options are out of this world good. There is usually a wait, but it's worth it.

Caffeine and Chaos

What can I say about a place that has caffeine and stuffed shakes? YES, PLEASE! This is a fun place to grab a yummy treat to share like a Celebration Bowl, containing 12 scoops of ice cream, three toppings, and whipped cream. I dare you to try to finish it all!

Maggie Valley is a great skiing destination and has seen a resurgence in tourism. It is an amazing place to vacation to get away and see nature. It has fun shops and many amazing places to eat and explore. It is a favorite spot for bikers in the spring and summer.

LAKE JUNALUSKA

IN THE VALLEY NEIGHBORING MAGGIE, LAKE JUNALUSKA is considered one of the most peaceful and tranquil lakes in the state. It is renowned as a place to center oneself and seek solace.

That said, there is a creature that lives in the waters. It may be a legendary Tatzelwurm, a lake monster straight from Swiss folklore. In Switzerland, the creature is sometimes called a Stollwurm or "tunnel-dragon." They are described as being seven feet long and four or five feet in width. It has four legs like a salamander and its head has feline features—a true "cat fish."

The one seen in Lake Junaluska has been reported several times since the early 1980s. Tourists relaxing at the lakeside say that the creature usually spits water at them when it comes ashore. One story involved a couple of fishermen who thought it was the largest hellbender they'd ever seen, only to be rebuffed when they reported it, due to their description of its size and furry, cat-like face.

ERIKA: I love the idea of a fuzzy cat monster. MEOW!

The hellbender salamander is a species of giant salamander native to the area. They do have four short legs and a long body but rarely leave the water and never grow to more than three feet from snout to tail. According to the Threatened Species Report in 2022, "The hellbender faces an array of challenges that jeopardize its habitat and overall well-being. These challenges include habitat degradation, habitat modifications, pollution, and the looming threat of emerging diseases. The conservation of this species is of paramount importance to ensure its continued existence in the wild."

While the hellbender is a possible candidate for the Lake Junaluska serpent, it doesn't seem likely. This creature has been seen numerous times by people that are familiar with hellbenders, and they know this

Lake Junaluska

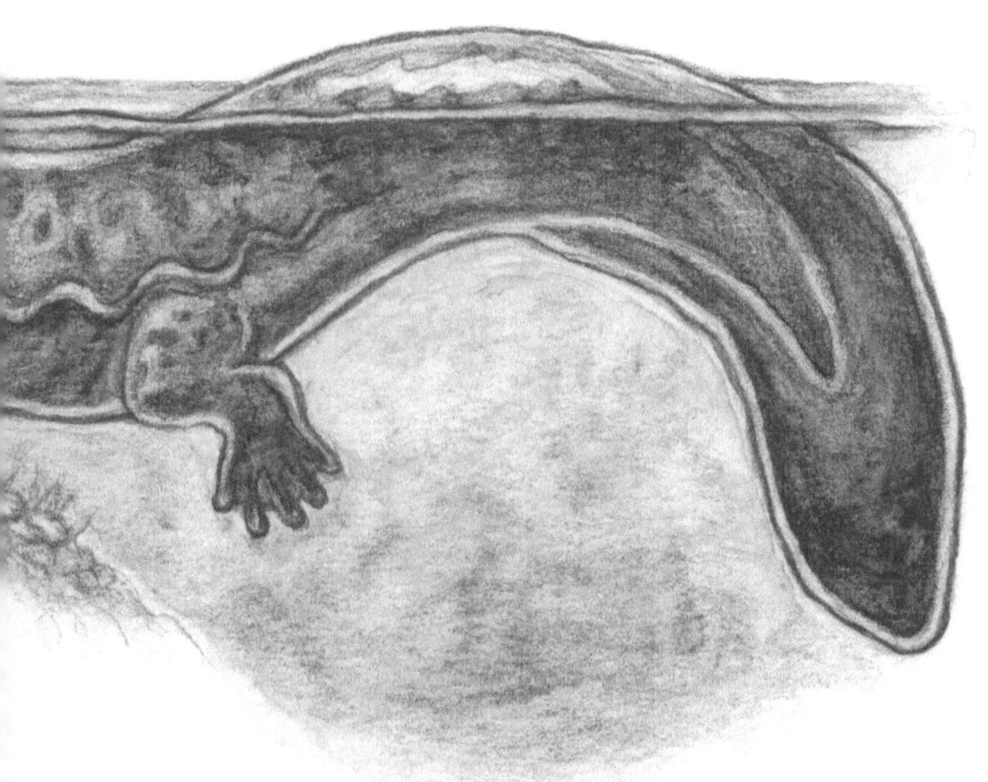

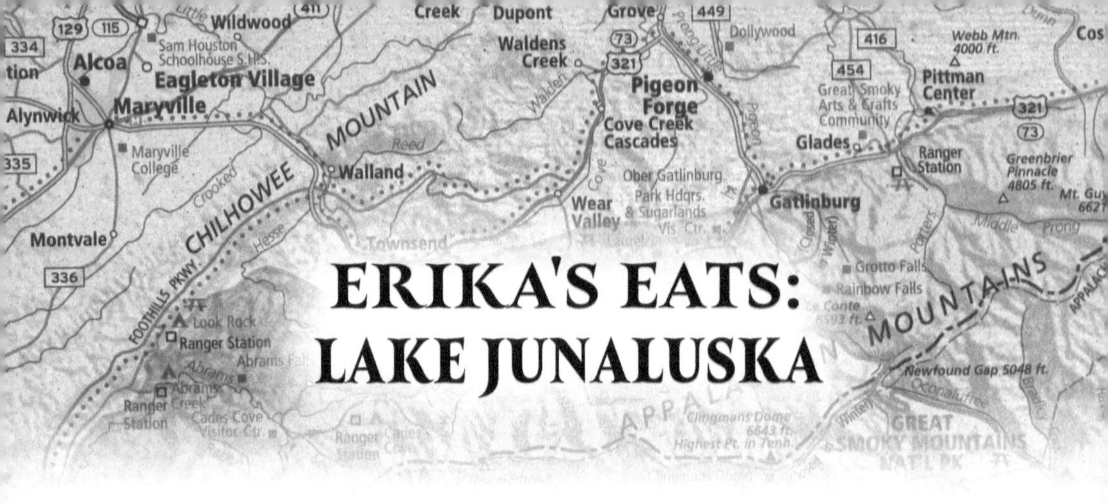

ERIKA'S EATS:
LAKE JUNALUSKA

Crepe & Custard

This postcard from the mid-1960s shows Maggie Mountain Crafts in Maggie Valley. The shop is still there and still features unique gifts and the incredibly delicious Aunt Maggie's homemade fudge. Provided by the Maggie Valley Historical Society.

THIS POSTCARD DEPICTS THE FAMOUS CHEROKEE BOAT TOUR OF LAKE JUNALUSKA. THEY ARE STILL OFFERING TOURS ON THE CHEROKEE IV BOAT TODAY. PROVIDED BY THE MACON COUNTY HISTORICAL SOCIETY.

LJ-31   CHEROKEE BOAT THE SECOND ON LAKE JUNALUSKA, N.C.

The Roadways

THE ROADS THROUGH THE SMOKIES

THE GREAT SMOKY MOUNTAINS ARE FILLED WITH SCENIC drives; it's one of the easiest ways to see the majesty of these amazing mountains. You can travel from town to town while taking in the scenery. Some of the main roads to sightsee on include Clingmans Dome Road, Newfound Gap Road, and the Cades Cove Loop and Roaring Fork Nature Trail.

There are some general rules for the roads here in the mountains. First, plan ahead! Some of these roads don't have many bathrooms or food facilities. Most have spotty GPS and cell service, thanks to the mountains. Always check road conditions before setting off.

> **ERIKA:** Travelers, we are emphasizing these rules for a reason!

> **MARK:** Stay safe!

Watch for wildlife! There are many animals out here, so be careful of bears, elk, deer, and the smaller critters. Ensure you are driving at safe speeds and keep your distance.

Be respectful of the protected natural areas. Leave no trace and dispose of trash properly. Stay on designated roads and trails. Do not disturb anything!

Lastly, make sure to stop and get out of your vehicle when the opportunity arises. There are plenty of designated parking areas, picnic locations, and visitor centers. Hiking some of the short trails and stopping at some of the scenic overlooks will stay with you long after you've left the mountains behind.

TAIL OF THE DRAGON GHOSTRIDERS

STARTING AT FOOTHILLS PARKWAY AND US-129 IN Chilhowee, Tennessee and ending in Deals Gap, North Carolina, the Tail of the Dragon is an incredibly adventurous drive. It's 11 miles with over 318 curves snaking through the Smokies. While there are no scenic overlooks once you start the loop, there is a great stop at Deals Gap Motorcycle Resort when you complete the loop.

ERIKA: Deals has the best t-shirts!

Tail of the Dragon is popular with many bikers as it is considered a great challenge to complete the world-famous road. It's also fun for drivers looking for a twisty-turning adventure. The drive has many notoriously named turns including Copperhead Corner, Rockslide Corner, The Wall, The Gravity Cavity, and Shaw Grave Gap. Many of these turns have professional photographers stationed there taking pictures of your vehicle as you pass them. You can purchase these off the advertised websites later.

ERIKA: That is really cool. Action shots!

MARK: Maybe we can get a picture of the Wayback Machine on it.

The road is infamous for its dangerous turns; there are many injuries and fatalities along the Tail of the Dragon every year as people push their luck. The turn at The Whip by Chilhowee Lake has claimed several lives. One spirit is said to still ride the turn, trying to perfect it.

ERIKA: So, like Ghost Rider?

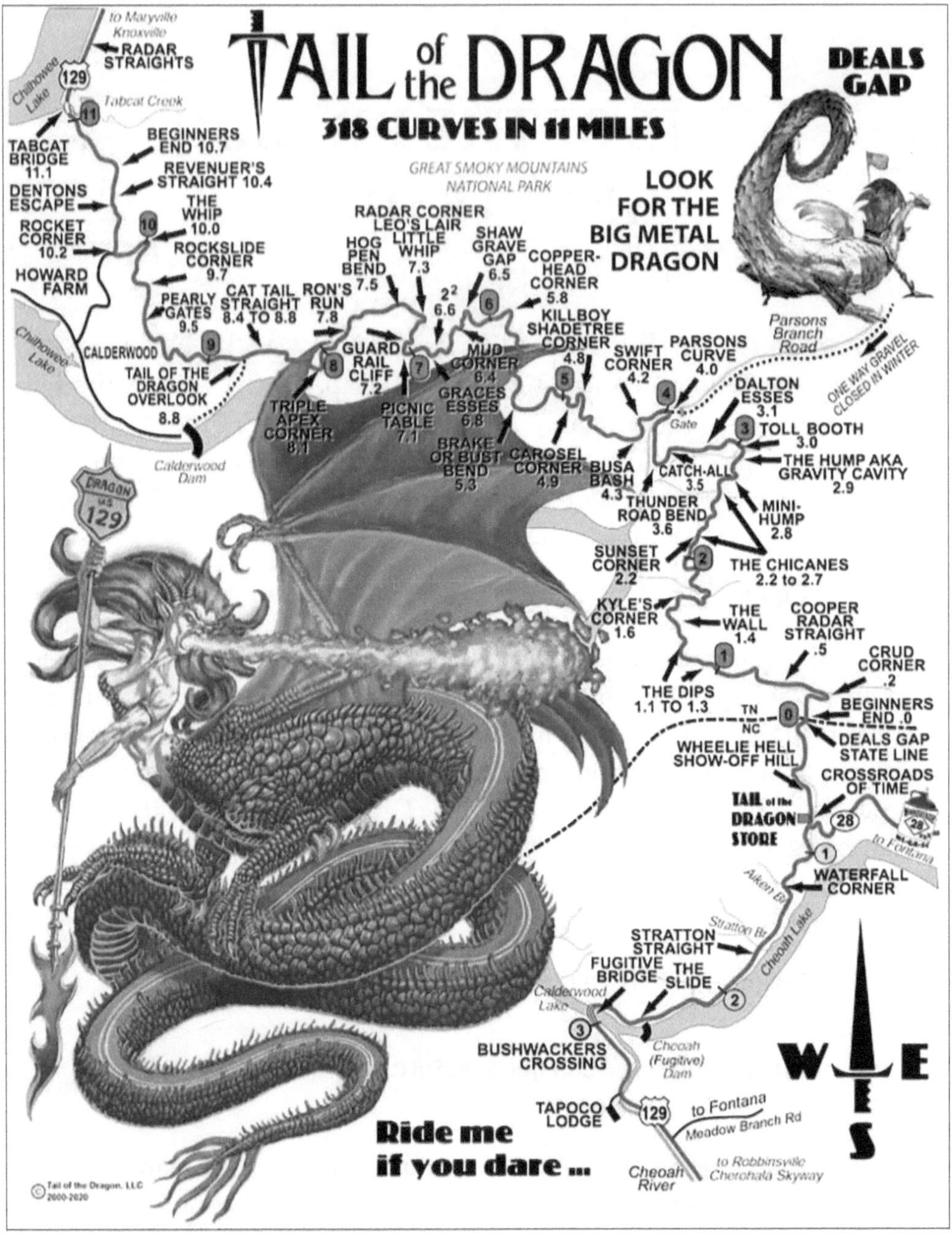

TAIL of DRAGON
DEALS GAP
318 CURVES IN 11 MILES
GREAT SMOKY MOUNTAINS NATIONAL PARK
LOOK FOR THE BIG METAL DRAGON
to Maryville Knoxville
RADAR STRAIGHTS
Chilhowee Lake
129
Tabcat Creek
11
TABCAT BRIDGE 11.1
DENTONS ESCAPE
ROCKET CORNER 10.2
HOWARD FARM
BEGINNERS END 10.7
REVENUER'S STRAIGHT 10.4
THE WHIP 10.0
ROCKSLIDE CORNER 9.7
10
PEARLY GATES 9.5
CAT TAIL STRAIGHT 8.4 TO 8.8
RON'S RUN 7.8
Chilhowee Lake
CALDERWOOD
9
TAIL OF THE DRAGON OVERLOOK 8.8
Calderwood Dam
DRAGON US 129
RADAR CORNER
LEO'S LAIR
HOG PEN BEND 7.5
LITTLE WHIP 7.3
SHAW GRAVE GAP 6.5
COPPER-HEAD CORNER 5.8
2² 6.6
6
KILLBOY SHADETREE CORNER
GUARD RAIL CLIFF 7.2
TRIPLE APEX CORNER 8.1
8
7
PICNIC TABLE 7.1
MUD CORNER 6.4
GRACES ESSES 6.8
4.8
5
SWIFT CORNER 4.2
PARSONS CURVE 4.0
Parsons Branch Road
ONE WAY GRAVEL CLOSED IN WINTER
4
Gate
DALTON ESSES 3.1
3
TOLL BOOTH 3.0
THE HUMP AKA GRAVITY CAVITY 2.9
BRAKE OR BUST BEND 5.3
CAROSEL CORNER 4.9
BUSA BASH 4.3
CATCH-ALL 3.5
THUNDER ROAD BEND 3.6
MINI-HUMP 2.8
SUNSET CORNER 2.2
2
THE CHICANES 2.2 to 2.7
KYLE'S CORNER 1.6
THE WALL 1.4
COOPER RADAR STRAIGHT .5
1
CRUD CORNER .2
THE DIPS 1.1 TO 1.3
TN NC
0
BEGINNERS END .0
DEALS GAP STATE LINE
WHEELIE HELL SHOW-OFF HILL
CROSSROADS OF TIME
TAIL of the DRAGON STORE
28
28
to Fontana
1
WATERFALL CORNER
Aiken Br
Cheoah Lake
Stratton Br
STRATTON STRAIGHT
FUGITIVE BRIDGE
THE SLIDE
2
Calderwood Lake
3
Cheoah (Fugitive) Dam
BUSHWACKERS CROSSING
TAPOCO LODGE
129
to Fontana
Meadow Branch Rd
Cheoah River
to Robbinsville Cherohala Skyway
W E N S
Ride me if you dare ...
Tail of the Dragon, LLC
2000-2020

Tail of the Dragon Ghostriders

MARK: Johnny Blaze, Danny Ketch, or Robbie
Reyes for you?

ERIKA: Nicholas Cage!

MARK: Why did I ask?

Like something out of a comic book, this phantom motorcycle has been reported by numerous drivers as trying to cut the sharp turn and riding straight off the side of the road. The bike looks like something from the late 1960s, and the rider seems to be laughing. A few have even said the rider's helmet hides a skull head. The vehicle is all black. There are some reports saying he drives all the way from Guard Rail Cliff a couple of miles away.

ERIKA: That would freak me out and be incredibly cool at
the same time.

The Dragon A.K.A US-129 is definitely worth the drive—just keep your wits and drive safely. Report any sightings of the Ghost Rider to the gang at the Tail of the Dragon Store. It's right after Wheelie Hell Show Off-Hill.

THIS METAL STATUE MARKS THE SOUTHERN END OF THE TAIL OF THE DRAGON AT THE DEALS GAP STORE. PHOTO BY AUTHOR

FONTANA DAM

FOR DECADES, THE TENNESSEE VALLEY AUTHORITY wanted to build a hydroelectric dam in the Fontana area. The land was owned by the Aluminum Company of America in the late 1930s, and they weren't really interested in selling. With the storm clouds of war brewing in Europe, defense department officials began to see this area as a secure spot for the war industry.

> **ERIKA:** Of course it is.

The Fontana project started just four months before the Japanese attacked Pearl Harbor. Only three weeks after December 7, 1941, the first trucks began the long trek into the wilderness to start the construction of what would become the largest dam east of the Rockies. It would be built in record time.

The Alcoa aluminum plants were turned to military use and provided power from the new dam. The nearby Oak Ridge became a top-secret weapons laboratory. A rumored base called Big Hole on the far side of Asheville would also be powered by this amazing dam. These would also be the locations associated with the Manhattan Project's early days.

> **ERIKA:** Cool projects. But I am sure not everything
> went smoothly.

Flooding over 10,230 acres, the dam created a 30-mile-long lake with over 238 miles of shoreline. Many more thousands of acres of its feeder streams became incorporated into the Great Smoky Mountains National Park. Another nearly 70,000 acres were taken by the Tennessee Valley Authority for use in the building and maintenance of the Fontana Dam. In all, over 1,300 families were displaced and over 2,000 graves had to be removed and reinterred.

Fontana Dam

ERIKA: Moving that many dead people seems like it would
be a horrible idea.

While the TVA stated that most of the removed structures were little more than shacks and old pioneer homesteads, some claim there were many significant town buildings that were burned by the TVA workers. Many families still hate the dam, and the goodwill of the war effort was little consolation.

ERIKA: Understandable. If I were them, I think I would
hate it too.

The government agreed to build a new road to the more remote locations that were not flooded by the dam. This would reconnect some people to their ancestral family land and graveyards that could only be reached by boat. Unfortunately, this road would never be completed. More on it later.

FONTANA DAM IS KNOWN AS "THE MIRACLE IN THE MOUNTAINS." PHOTO BY AUTHOR.

THE **Dark Side** OF THE **Smoky Mountains**

ERIKA: A little mystery sandwich in our travels.

MARK: Well, it's farther away since the road was never built. We'll get there. We just have to go the long way around.

After decades of dispute, the government finally paid a large settlement to most of the families affected by Fontana, and emotions began to cool. The area around the dam is known for its pristine forest and natural beauty. The visitor's center is located there as an unmissable stop. It is even on the Appalachian Trail as it crosses the dam.

ERIKA: Okay, but where is the *eerie* part of these travels? I was expecting angry "my grave was moved" ghosts.

Instead of ghosts, we have one of our favorite cryptids. There are numerous sightings of the Smoky Mountain's Bigfoot along the shoreline here. It is often seen coming out of the tree line and darting quickly back into the ridges that dot the lake. There are so many sightings there that it has been marked as an active point of interest by several local hunting teams and the Big Foot Research Organization.

ERIKA: Not surprised. This is a perfect location for our tall friends.

The Bigfoot here have gray coloring to their fur. It is so often commented on that many speculate that they have adapted a natural winter camouflage. The natives in this area once referred to the "Old Gray Man of the Woods." It is thought they might be referring to a family of Sasquatch that live somewhere in the vicinity.

The nearby Fontana Village Resort and Marina offers camping sites, cabins, and even rooms at its mountain lodge. There is the amazing Wildwood Grill here as well as the Mountainview Bistro for food options. The Fontana General Store and the Fontana Ice Cream Parlor are also there for necessary Bigfoot hunting supplies.

ERIKA: Ice cream is a necessary supply for a Bigfoot hunt!

Fontana Dam

The Fontana Dam churned out 228,000 kilowatts of power when it started up way back in 1945. It powered those vital aluminum factories 45 miles away in Alcoa that were churning out military aircraft for World War II.

The sight of the dam itself is very astounding. Shortly after it began operation, French existentialist philosopher Jean-Paul Sarte came to Fontana on a wartime press junket. He was amazed by the dam and the city that seemed to have appeared out of nowhere in this wilderness. He called it "The Miracle in the Wilderness." It still astonishes visitors to this day.

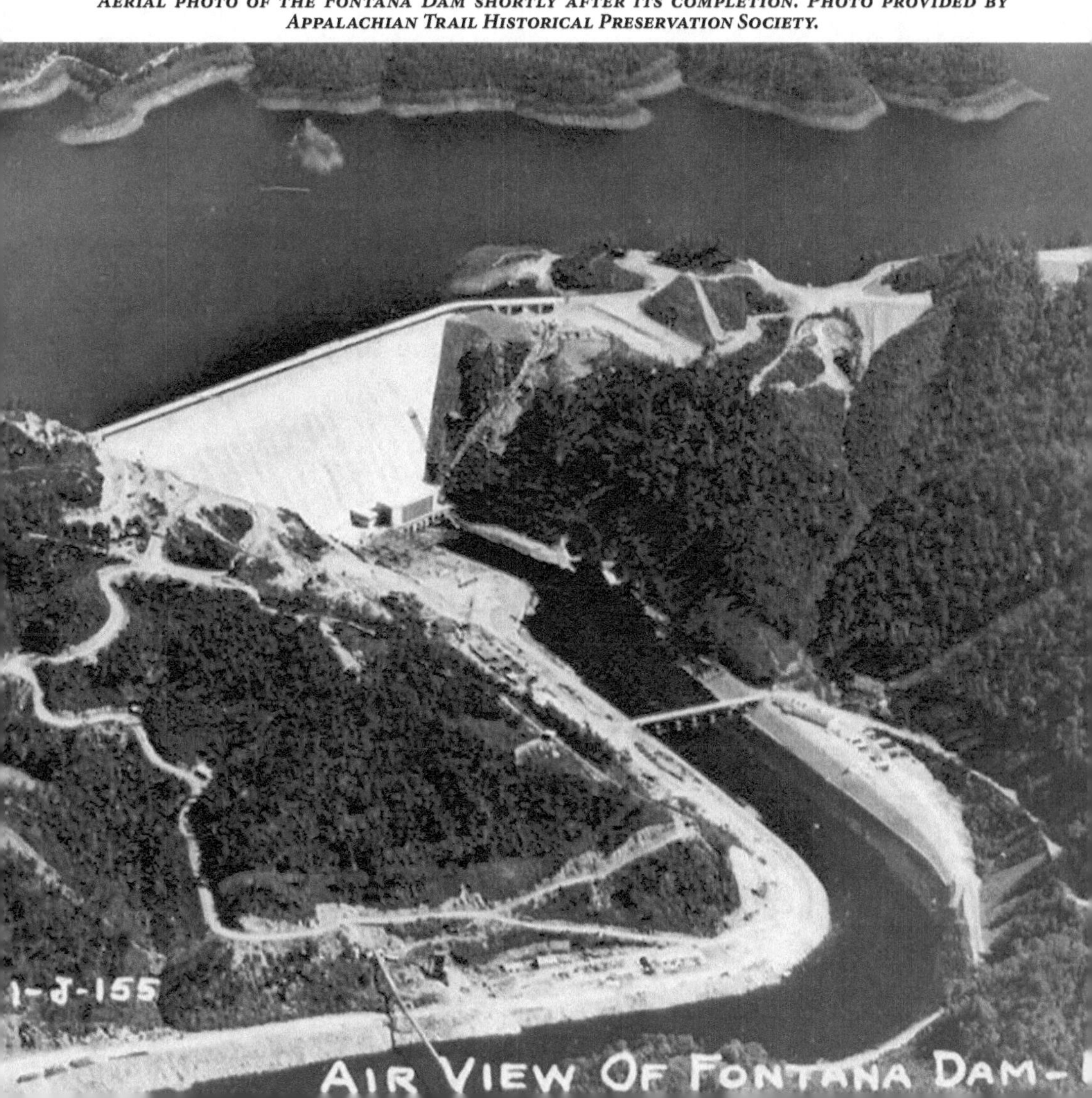

AERIAL PHOTO OF THE FONTANA DAM SHORTLY AFTER ITS COMPLETION. PHOTO PROVIDED BY APPALACHIAN TRAIL HISTORICAL PRESERVATION SOCIETY.

NOLAND CREEK LIGHT

WORTH GETTING OUT OF THE CAR FOR A BIT IS A LEGEND trip near the Dam.

The Noland Creek Trail is a nine-mile-long historic trail and is considered a moderate to strenuous hike near the Fontana Dam. There are over 200 cemeteries along the length of the trail. The are many ruins of old settlements from before the foundation of the Great Smoky Mountains and Nantahala National Forest. Lake Fontana along this trail was also a known haunt of Spearfinger back in the times of the natives.

ERIKA: Hold on to your livers, Travelers!

There's a legend of a settler who died searching for his daughter in the hills surrounding this trail. To make amends for not finding her, his light is said to appear to those who get lost after straying off the trail. The legend says that his light will guide you back to safety. There are others who say he's a similar phenomenon to the lights seen from the Thomas Divide Overlook or those at Brown Mountain.

ERIKA: This is the first time we should actually follow the lights.

THE THOMAS DIVIDE OVERLOOK IS A MUST VISIT FOR THOSE LOOKING FOR THE GHOST LIGHTS OR POSSIBLE UFOs. PHOTO PROVIDED BY GREAT SMOKY MOUNTAINS NATIONAL PARK.

THE BLUE RIDGE PARKWAY AND THE DEVIL'S COURTHOUSE

WHILE NOT OFFICIALLY A PART OF THE SMOKY MOUNTAINS, the Blue Ridge Parkway is one of the most scenic drives in the Smokies. The Parkway extends from Cherokee, North Carolina all the way up to Blue Ridge, Virginia where it connects with Virginia's Skyline Drive. It is full of amazing views throughout the entirety.

While weaving its way along some of the highest ridges in Western North Carolina, it passes through several tunnels. It goes by many scenic overlooks filled with wildlife, wildflowers, and waterfalls. There are the remains of numerous historic buildings and several hiking trails with parking spots as well.

> **ERIKA:** Make sure you take it slowly, so you don't miss an amazing place to stop.

If you think back to long before the parkway and long before roads existed, the Cherokee hunted around these mountains for generations. The Cherokee spoke of a terrifying figure called Tsul'Kalu; in English, he is called Judaculla. He is spoken of as having lived in a place called Tsunegun'yi, a haunted land. It is thought that his cave lies in this mountain. Near here somewhere is the entrance to his haunted halls.

> **ERIKA:** So, he is terrifying and has a haunted cave... NOPE!

We're not done with Judacalla just yet, but we'll get back to his story later. Here on the Blue Ridge Parkway, there's a very popular overlook with a large parking area that looks out at Tsunegun'yi. It's referred to by the name given by early European explorers who heard the stories of the giant Tsul'Kalu and his tormenting of the Cherokee people. They knew he had to be the Devil himself.

ERIKA: That seems like a general term they used for
nearly every creature.

MARK: I can't count how many places named after the
Devil or Hell that I've been to.

This overlook is called The Devil's Courthouse. It looks over a towering mountain with a bare cliff face. This is where Tsul'Kalu, also known as Judacalla, also known as The Devil, held his court. He would determine if your soul was worthy of life or should be thrown from the mountain.

ERIKA: He seems super judgy. Also, maybe a small fine
instead of getting thrown off the mountain?

Today, there is a trail to the top of the Devil's Courthouse, a dizzying 5,720 feet at the summit. It is short but very steep and only for those strong of health. The scenery is beautiful but stay on the trail as there are many rare, high-altitude plants that call this trail home. Do not stray and accidentally damage them. These plants date back to the glacial period, so be extra careful.

ERIKA: You don't want to end up being thrown off
the mountain.

The Blue Ridge Parkway and The Devil's Courthouse

The view at the top is extraordinary, and on a clear day, you can see mountains from North Carolina, South Carolina, Georgia, and Tennessee. The drops here are quite far and would certainly be fatal—one more reason to be careful and stay within the overlook walls. Climb the Devil's Courthouse at your own risk.

THE GIANT HEAD OF MOUNT LE CONTE

FOR THOSE ADVENTUROUS TRAVELERS THAT MADE THE hike to the Devil's Courthouse, there's one more hike to consider.

The third highest point in the Great Smoky Mountains is a bucket list stop for climbers. Many hike for 10 to 15 miles and climb over 3,000 feet off the Parkway to Le Conte Lodge. There, after months of preparation, they finally arrive and are disappointed. There are no scenic views, no incredible vistas! What was the point? Well, there's a little more hiking to get to those, but the lodge is a great place to stop and rest.

ERIKA: I like the "rest" part of that.

The lodge itself was commissioned in 1925, long before the Smoky Mountains National Park was even considered. There are still ten cabins there that you can reserve to give you a place to rest. The dining hall is open most days for even the day hikers to get some of their famous hot chocolate and no-bake cookies.

ERIKA: Hot chocolate and cookies? I am in!

High Top, which is the summit, is just a short distance away, but again, it is shrouded by trees most of the year, making it not much to photograph. Hikers tend to pile rocks here to make the peak a little bit taller, but please leave no trace and don't stack rocks.

ERIKA: Be a hiking ninja.

Apollo Ridge isn't far from the lodge, and it is where the views start to pay off. It got its name from the lodge employees in the 60s and 70s that used to take hikers here to watch Apollo moon mission launches. It offers a spectacular view of Newfound Gap and Kuwohi, formerly known as

The Giant Head of Mount Le Conte

STONE HEAD OF MOUNT LECONTE. ILLUSTRATION BY KARI SCHULTZ.

Clingmans Dome. It's a great place to watch the sunrise, especially in the fall or winter.

ERIKA: Especially with hot chocolate and cookies!

Myrtle Point is not far, and you can see Brushy Mountain and more of Kuwohi. In May, you can see the Sand Myrtle in bloom, which gives the point its name. Head from there to what many consider to be the best view in the Smokies: Cliff Tops.

ERIKA: This part of our travels suddenly has a lot more
walking. So, what is Cliff Tops?

Cliff Tops is a giant rocky outcrop usually called Sunset Rock. It is a very popular spot and usually not as secluded as you would think. However, the sunset here is spectacular. From Cliff Tops, you can see Kuwohi, Thunderhead, Chimney Tops, Balsam Point, and even some of Ski Mountain. "If I could only have one vista in the Smokies, this one would be it!" said one hiker.

ERIKA: I feel that the *eerie* part of this is about to pop up.

It is also where the Cherokee's Stone Head, or Stone Face, was supposedly born. He was formed out of the very rocks on the top of Mount Le Conte. He would roll down the mountainside and gather up more stone as he hunted for the livers he craves so much. It would be in the valley below where he first encountered his rival Spearfinger.

ERIKA: What is it with all the liver eating? Hannibal
Lecter would be jealous.

Stone Head returns up Mount Le Conte in the winter to slumber and sleeps somewhere in an undiscovered cave. The Cherokee state that he no longer goes up to the peak as he fears retribution from the Thunderbirds for being too close to the heavens. So up at the peak, you should be safe from him.

ERIKA: What about the Thunderbirds? Are we safe
from them?

MARK: They are the good guys.

Balsam, North Carolina

BALSAM

The Balsam Mountains aren't technically the Smoky Mountains but are a part of the parent range of the Blue Ridge Mountains of western North Carolina. There's a great valley here among the mountain tops that, itself, is over 5,000 feet in elevation above sea level. Its name is Graveyard Fields. It's a very popular destination for hikers along the Blue Ridge Parkway.

> **Erika:** Why would anyone want to go to the Graveyard Fields?

> **Mark:** I think any *eerie traveler* worth their salt would love to go to any Graveyard Fields.

The valley's unusual monicker comes from a time when a windstorm came across the valley and uprooted most of the trees. The stumps were quickly covered with moss and lichen and made the area resemble an overgrown graveyard. After the area was heavily logged, some major forest fires swept through the valley. The soil was heated so much it was practically sterilized. Plants, trees, and shrubs are just now returning to the area. It is quite stunning in the fall.

> **Erika:** Well, that is a bit less scary than I thought.

The sign post marks the location of the Graveyard Fields of the Balsam Mountains. Photo by author.

BALSAM MOUNTAIN INN

Let's take a quick trip in the Wayback Machine to 1908. Two brothers-in-laws, named Joseph Kenney and Walter Christy, traveled to the area of western North Carolina to start their own business. They both loved the great outdoors and decided to build a boarding house in the mountains to attract those of like-minded persuasion.

> **Erika:** That sounds like a good idea.

> **Mark:** As we've noticed, it's worked like a charm around here.

They saw the Smoky Mountain Railroad was going to be coming through, so they built the Balsam Mountain Springs Hotel nearby. It was massive with one hundred rooms, most with porches to observe the scenic vistas. Fine dining, fishing, hunting expeditions, and more were offered to their guests.

Balsam Gap station was a huge success at this time, and it only helped the hotel prosper. Many guests stayed entire summers, and this made the brothers very successful. The hotel became known as "The Grand Old Lady." She was named for her beauty as well as that of the world-class view from her veranda.

> **Erika:** This sounds like a great story—which means it is about to go off the rails.

The Great Depression came, and times got lean. The hotel survived but was nearly a shell by the late 1970s. In the 1980s, it was empty and in need of repair. While hiking in the Balsams, Merrily Teasley had come across the hotel and purchased the property. She began to restore it and reopened the first two floors in 1991. She slowly opened the third floor while restoration continued.

Erika: That is good. I love it when a wonderful place is restored.

In 2017, another investor took over. Marzena Wyszynska updated the hotel with heating, electrical work, and new plumbing. It reopened again in April 2018. It was renamed the Grand Old Lady Hotel in January of 2019.

Erika: I think they couldn't have picked a better name.

Sadly, the pandemic hit shortly after opening, and the hotel was forced to close again. As of this writing, the inn has reopened again under the stewardship of Rodney and Lorraine Conrad. The community has rallied behind them to help restore the hotel which is once again Balsam Mountain Inn.

Erika: So, when do the ghosts come into play?

Most of the haunted stories of the building come from Wyszynska's time as the owner. Her first night as owner, she slept in the inn but felt her sheets ripped off her by an invisible force. She hired a priest to come in and bless the property. This seemed to intensify the haunting rather than pacify it. She teamed up with local paranormal investigators, who told her the ghosts were merely confused by all the renovations and were not a threat.

Erika: NOPE! That is an aggressive ghost.

Instead of further attempts to remove the ghosts, she began to welcome them. She would post signs in known haunted rooms and encourage guests to journalize their experiences. Many guests reported shadow

190

figures, whispers, strange giggling, doors slamming, and other typical poltergeist-like activities like moving objects and strange knocking.

ERIKA: I do not like any of that.

The most famous ghost here is known as "The Sheriff." He is often seen in room 205. According to investigators, he was shot in a dispute outside the hotel in 1928. He was brought to room 205, where he bled to death. His name and that of the perpetrator are unknown, but his spirit has been seen here more than any other in the hotel. Apparently, he likes the ladies as he makes his presence known to women far more than men.

ERIKA: Getting hit on by a spirit is an interesting way to spend an evening.

Just before the closing of the hotel in 2021, during the pandemic of 2020, a paranormal team led by Kane Hodder of Jason Voorhees fame came to document some of the strange occurrences. Having the hotel to themselves makes the movie they filmed intriguing viewing. *Balsam* was filmed entirely in and around the hotel, and it is highly recommended viewing.

ERIKA: That might be the most epic ghost hunt ever. I will be watching *Balsam* in my not haunted hotel room.

MARK: I'll be watching *Jason X* for Kane's incredible performance as my favorite hockey masked killer.

The Conard family are still restoring the Balsam Inn. At the time of this writing, up to 50 of the rooms are open at various times of the year. Building back is going to take time. The Spirits of the Inn Bar and their Coffee Shop are open most days and worth a visit. They frequently have folk events to help raise funds to restore the Grand Old Lady of Balsam to her former glory. Make sure to say "hi" to the Sheriff in 205.

ERIKA: Or just give him some money and leave with the hope that he doesn't follow you home.

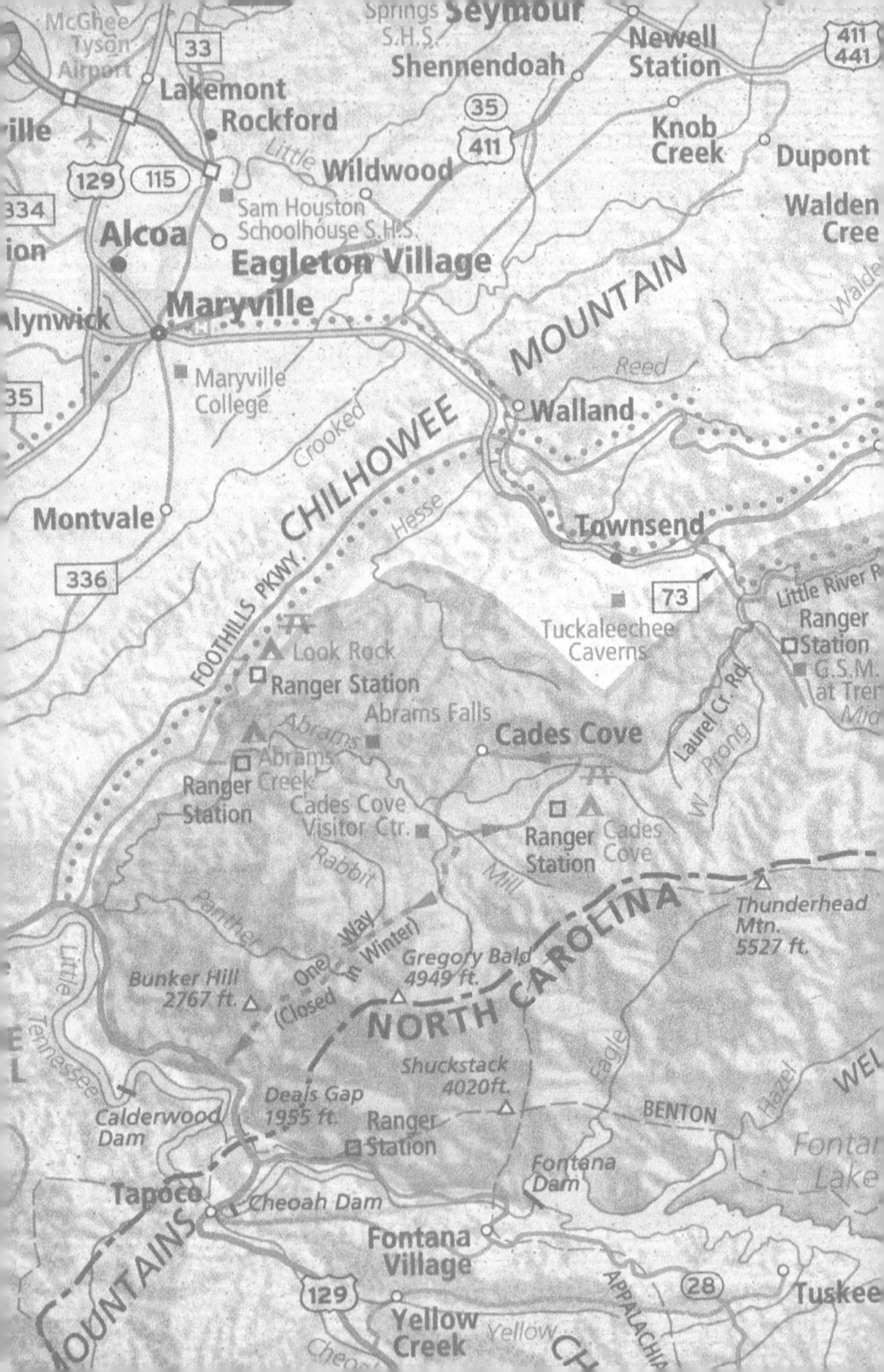

McGhee Tyson Airport
33
ille
Lakemont
Rockford
129
115
334
Alcoa
35
Alynwick
Maryville
Eagleton Village
Little
Wildwood
Sam Houston Schoolhouse S.H.S.
Springs S.H.S.
Seymour
Shennendoah
35
411
Newell Station
411 441
Knob Creek
Dupont
Walden Cree
Walde
MOUNTAIN
Reed
Maryville College
Crooked
CHILHOWEE
Walland
Montvale
Hesse
Townsend
336
73
Little River R
Ranger Station
G.S.M. at Tren
FOOTHILLS PKWY.
Tuckaleechee Caverns
Mio
Look Rock
Ranger Station
Abrams Falls
Cades Cove
Laurel Cr. Rd.
Abrams
Abrams Creek
Ranger Station
Cades Cove Visitor Ctr.
Ranger Station
Cades Cove
W. Prong
Rabbit
Mill
NORTH CAROLINA
Thunderhead Mtn. 5527 ft.
Panther
One Way (Closed in Winter)
Gregory Bald 4949 ft.
Little
Tennessee
Bunker Hill 2767 ft.
Shuckstack 4020ft.
Eagle
BENTON
Hazel
WE
Fonta
Lake
Deals Gap 1955 ft.
Ranger Station
Calderwood Dam
Fontana Dam
L
Tapoco
Cheoah Dam
Fontana Village
APPALACHIA
28
Tuskee
MOUNTAINS
129
Yellow Creek
Cheoa
Yellow
CH

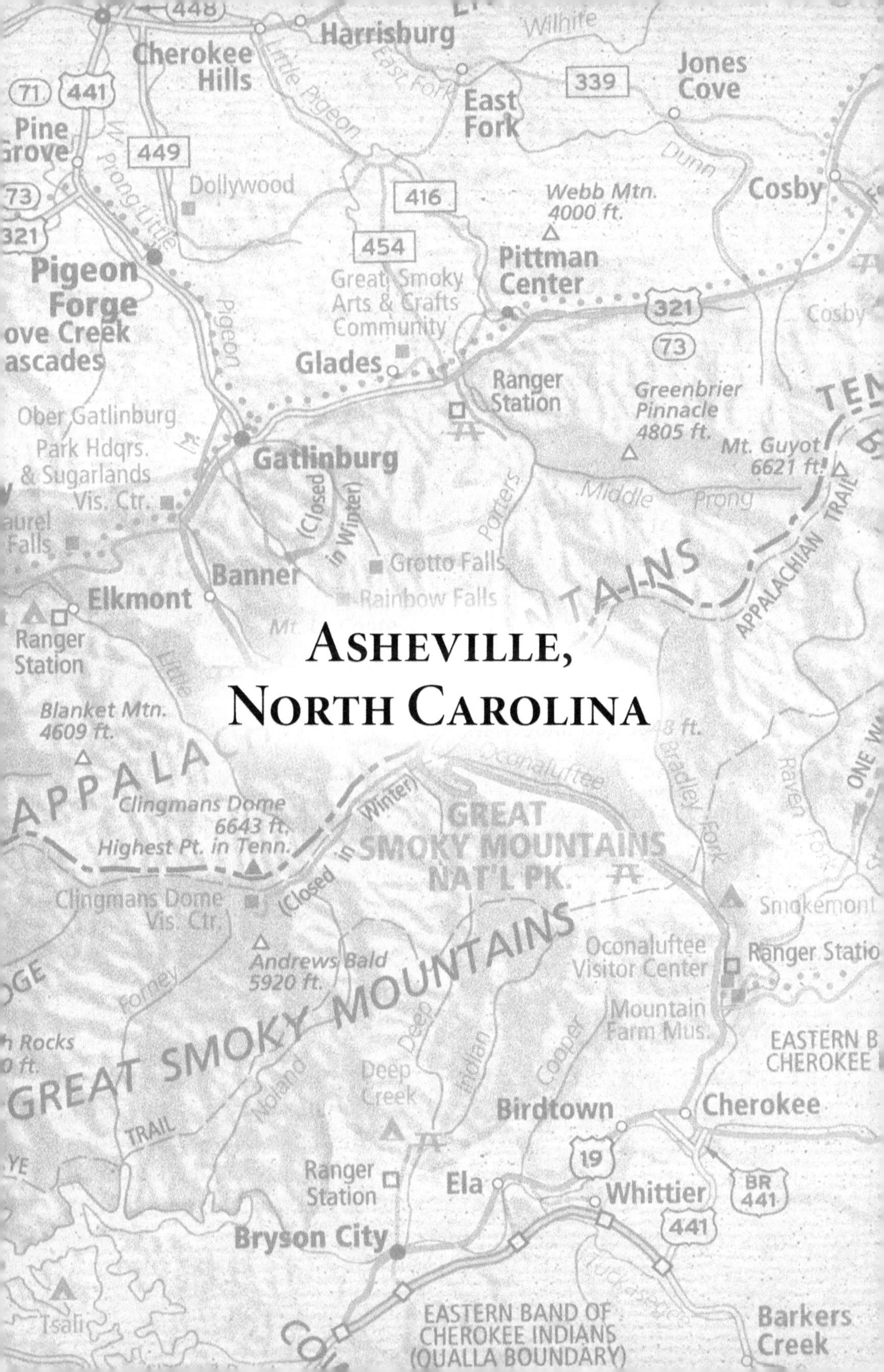

Asheville, North Carolina

ASHEVILLE

ORIGINALLY KNOWN AS MORRISTOWN WHEN IT WAS founded in 1794. Asheville gets its name from Samuel Ashe, the governor of North Carolina, when it was fully incorporated in 1797. It didn't become a city until 1882, after the arrival of the railroad. In 1889, George Vanderbilt helped draw people to the city when he constructed Biltmore; we will talk more about him later.

> **ERIKA:** I feel like we are going to need the Wayback Machine. I will load it up with more snacks.

> **MARK:** Hopefully, we can find another boiled peanut stand somewhere around here.

When the Great Depression hit, Asheville's banks went into bankruptcy. The town itself refused to file bankruptcy and, instead, worked to clear up its debts which did not happen until the late 1970s. The plus side was that Asheville dodged the urban renewal era of most cities in the 1950s and 60s. This meant most of its historic buildings were never replaced. This gives the town a huge boost, now that we realize the true value of historic locations.

> **ERIKA:** That is very cool of the city to do because the buildings are so unique.

It also may be why the town is one of the most haunted cities in the United States. While Savannah and St. Augustine get a lot of fame, Asheville has a huge number of haunted locations. Many spiritualists believe this area has a huge number of vortexes from combinations of ley line conjunctions and the limestone bedrock underneath, thus the large amount of preternatural energy in the city.

Asheville

One fun tradition in Asheville is sadly no longer with us. We'll have to get in the Wayback Machine and go back to October in the early 2000s. In 2006, the Asheville Zombie Walk started as a flash mob. Hundreds showed up after a Myspace recruitment drive. Over the years, it grew into a huge event. It garnered national attention when Vice President candidate Sarah Palin made an appearance in Asheville on the same day as the Zombie Walk. It was quietly discontinued in 2017 and, as of this writing, has not returned from the grave.

FLYER FOR THE LAST ZOMBIE WALK IN ASHEVILLE AT THE TIME OF THIS WRITING. HOPEFULLY IT MIGHT RETURN FROM THE GRAVE SOMEDAY. PROVIDED BY BUNCOMBE COUNTY HISTORICAL SOCIETY.

CHURCH OF THE REDEEMER

BUILT IN 1886, THE CHURCH OF THE REDEEMER IS A HIS-toric Romanesque Episcopal church in the Woodfin neighborhood of Asheville. The church itself has two notable Tiffany glass windows. It was built as the family chapel for a neighboring mansion, though the mansion has since burned down.

ERIKA: I feel like this is about to get spooky!

The graveyard at the back of the church has a long set of sloped stairs. A "Lady in White" spirit is often seen coming down those stairs and walking past the church onto Riverside Drive. She crosses the road and vanishes as she heads toward the French Broad River. No one knows who she is or her story. Some suspect that she is a member of the family that lived in the mansion, but records here are spotty at best.

ERIKA: Yep. It got spooky!

A recent sighting occurred when an Uber driver was picking up a passenger at the church. While waiting for his passenger to come out of the church, he saw the apparition.

"At first I thought there must have been a wedding at the church that day," wrote Ken Holland. "It was a warm March morning, and the flowers were in bloom everywhere. I was on my phone to let the passenger who was attending the service know I had arrived. No one had left the church just yet, but then I looked up and saw her. She looked like she was just walking and looking at the flowers as she strolled right down in front of me and right across the road. I was glad no one was driving by as she didn't even look as she crossed the road. I went to roll down my window to see if she was okay. Then, as soon as she crossed the street, she vanished. I freaked out!

"My rider arrived just a moment later while I was still stunned in astonishment. She hadn't seen [the apparition] and said there was no wedding that day. I swear I still see her face sometimes when I go to sleep. I didn't tell anybody for years until I heard someone mention her on a ghost tour my friend and I were on."

ERIKA: NOPE!

THE STEPS TO THE CHURCH OF THE REDEEMER IS WHERE A GHOSTLY LADY IN WHITE IS SPOTTED OVER AND OVER AGAIN. PHOTO BY AUTHOR.

CRAGGY PRISON

ORIGINALLY BUILT IN 1924, THE OLD CRAGGY PRISON WAS one of 61 prisons constructed to house criminals that would be used to help build roads. As it hits its one hundredth birthday, this once medium-security prison looks like an abandoned piece of history, but it is neither empty nor abandoned.

The prisoners housed here were mostly convicted of low-grade felonies like theft and assault. They were assigned work details with the Department of Transportation to help do minor roadwork like filling potholes, painting lanes, or picking up litter. Typically, they needed minimal supervision from the correctional officers.

> **ERIKA:** Sounds like a productive plan.

In 1987, Old Craggy Prison was closed as a new prison was built shortly down the road. By 1989, all the prisoners had been moved to the New Craggy Prison, and the place was mostly abandoned. The laundry building at the facility remained open and run by prisoners. It is still used to this day while the rest of the prison lies vacant.

> **ERIKA:** I am now waiting for the spooky part of
> this story...

Now fenced off due to the unsafe conditions inside the deteriorating main buildings, no one is quite sure of the fate of Old Craggy Prison. Some want it restored and open for tours like Brushy Mountain. Others want it to be bulldozed as it is prime real estate.

> **ERIKA:** How is it "prime real estate" if it's next
> to a prison?

> **MARK:** Because there's a beautiful river behind it.

The prison is not currently open for tours, but it is unlawfully visited by urban explorers. There are an average of 10 to 20 arrests per year of trespassers on the property. The spirits here can be seen on the old grounds so there is no need to go where it is illegal to do so.

> **ERIKA:** So, going there might make you a "resident" of the prison?

The apparitions seen the most are darting shadows that linger low to the ground. Often dismissed as rats or other vermin, they tend to look more like balls of shadow, running from dark corner to dark corner. Sometimes, they even float like dark orbs going from window to window—even outside the upper floors.

> **ERIKA:** I do not like this.

Descriptions are remarkably like the shadow spheres reported in some parts of Appalachia. They tend to gather around places with negative emotions and are even said to be aggressive when approached. One more reason not to trespass at Old Craggy Prison! Best to take pictures from well outside the fence line. After all, it is still an active correctional facility.

The only dark presence here that may take you away is the police.

FLETCHER SCHOOL OF DANCE

THE ASHEVILLE BALLET GUILD WAS FOUNDED IN 1964. IT was originally the Fletcher School of Dance. It is North Carolina's oldest non-profit ballet company. They offer classes and even a lecture series on dance appreciation for the community. Dance is all about expression of the soul through every leap and twirl.

ERIKA: I took ballet when I was younger.

The building itself is non descript, but during renovations in the early 1990s, the construction workers noted odd things happening to their equipment. Devices like saws and heavy tools would be moved after locking up for the night. Electronic equipment would shut off even though the power was still on. One worker mentioned he saw a shadowy figure come over to a workbench and turn off the circular saw as his partner was running it.

ERIKA: Sounds like the resident spirit was not happy with the changes.

After renovation, the school reopened, and there were no reports of strange activity for some time. However, in 2017, it seemed to return for a period during a holiday practice class. Several cast members training for the upcoming ballet pageant reported feeling very uneasy and a strange shadow figure watching them from offstage. After the sighting, practice was canceled for the day.

ERIKA: Maybe it didn't like the show? Guardian dance teacher?

Again, there is no further documentation or reason for this activity. It just simply seems to come and go.

Fletcher School of Dance

BEALE AND PEGGY FLETCHER WERE VERY POPULAR ON THE VAUDEVILLE CIRCUIT. THEY FOUNDED THE FLETCHER SCHOOL OF DANCE. AUTHOR'S NOTE: SADLY, THE SCHOOL BUILDING ITSELF WAS LOST IN THE DAMAGE OF HURRICANE HELENE, THEIR LEGACY LIVES ON THROUGH THE ASHEVILLE BALLET.

BEAVER LAKE

Located in the gorgeous North Asheville neigh-borhood is Beaver Lake. It's a must visit for spectacular sunsets and bird-watching. Although it is privately owned, the trail along the perimeter of the lake is open to the public. There are rules listed near the boat launch as it is private property. For those with a canine friend along, no pets are allowed on the trail.

> **Erika:** The pups will have to stay out, but it is very beautiful.

There is a small dam at the corner of Merrimon and Glen Falls. It is a beautiful site along the trail. However, several people have seen a young man who looks like he's wearing clothes from the 1970s walking along the top of the dam. As people shout at him, he waves, jumps into the water, and is never seen again. Numerous police reports and park warden reports have documented these sightings as a potential drowning or suicide. Sadly, there were many true suicides here over the years. Apparently, this man is the residual spirit of one of them.

> **Erika:** That is sad. But Travelers, if you see him, wave hello.

Another "Lady in White" is also seen nearby, looking down into the water. Perhaps she, too, is one of the many who lost their lives in Beaver Lake.

> **Erika:** NOPE! Too many ghosts. Where to next?

THE NAKED GHOST OF CRAVEN STREET BRIDGE

The French Broad River snakes through Asheville. Just south of where I-240 crosses the river on the western edge of the city, a group of boys decided to go swimming in the early 20th century. There had been some storms upriver which, unbeknownst to the boys, created a quick undercurrent.

Erika: I don't like where this is heading.

They dove into the water and laughed and played. They did not realize that they were drifting down the river much quicker than normal. They noticed when they approached the bridge at Craven Street that rapids had formed around the bridge pylons. They began to panic, but it only intensified when they realized one of their number was missing.

Erika: Oh no!

The boys searched for their friend underwater. They called for him from the shoreline. One of the kids ran to get help. A search party was quickly formed as the word spread, and boats with lanterns began to search for the missing young man. By sunrise, the search was called off. Boats were sent to dredge the river, but they never found the body.

Erika: That is very sad.

Now, travelers say when they cross the bridge, a naked boy crosses in front of them. When they yell out to him, he runs on as if oblivious to their calls. When one witness claimed she was able to catch up to him, he simply vanished into thin air. The naked ghost of Craven Street bridge is even seen in the winter, prompting many more reports, fearing for the child's safety. The ghost, however, doesn't seem to be bothered by the cold.

THE **Dark Side** OF THE Smoky Mountains

ERIKA: Travelers, remember that this is an active bridge. You can park next to it to get a good look but be careful. We do not need any more naked ghosts!

CRAVEN STREET BRIDGE CROSSES THE FRENCH BROAD RIVER AS IT WINDS ITS WAY THROUGH ASHEVILLE. PHOTO BY AUTHOR.

(THE OMNI) GROVE PARK INN

FIRST OPENING IN 1913, THE GROVE PARK INN WAS BUILT by Edwin Wiley Grove. He had made a small fortune by selling a malarial preventative called Grove's Tasteless Chill Tonic. As malaria was an extremely common disease at that time in the southern United States, this was a popular seller. Grove himself suffered from a chronic cough and moved to Asheville on his doctor's orders. Asheville was hugely popular and, at the time, full of health resorts. Grove saw the popularity of the area and decided to build his own inn to serve Asheville.

ERIKA: Did the tonic work?

MARK: Apparently, a little bit. Throw enough medicinal herbs into something, and it might break a fever.

Some guests of the inn over the years have included George Gershwin, Harry Houdini, President Barrack Obama, and F. Scott Fitzgerald. It was built to be one of the finest hotels ever constructed. It is known for elegance and charm. It's a strikingly beautiful location and well worth a visit. Now the Omni Grove Park Inn, you can enjoy fine dining, events, a world class golf course, and more.

ERIKA: It looks like a castle.

One spirit here, however, is almost as famous as the hotel itself. The Pink Lady has been seen here for going on a century now. She is thought to be the spirit of a young lady who fell from a fifth-floor balcony in the early 1920s. Though there are no records of her death, her spirit is well documented.

ERIKA: Pink Lady reminds me of the movie *Grease*.

THE **Dark Side** OF THE **Smoky Mountains**

She usually appears as either a pink mist or as a lady in a flowing pink ball gown. She mostly appears to children staying at the hotel. She seems to have a strange fondness for those that are ill. One noted case involved a doctor staying at the inn in the 1940s. He left a note with the staff during check-out to make certain that they thanked the lady in the pink dress that his children had enjoyed playing with during their stay.

ERIKA: Is she a nice spirit or a mean spirit?

Though mostly a harmless spirit, she has been blamed by the staff for electrical issues and even some rearranged furniture. In room 545, she reportedly wakes up guests by tickling their feet. Employees of the Grove Park Inn seem to treat her as another attraction as she has never hurt anyone and seems to just be a doorway into history.

THE OMNI GROVE PARK INN IS HAUNTED BY THE SPIRIT OF THE PINK LADY. PHOTO BY THE AUTHOR.

HELL'S HALF ACRE

WILL HARRIS WAS A CRIMINAL OF THE WORST CALIBER. HE had been arrested for everything from assault and burglary to murder of a police officer. He escaped prison numerous times. He also escaped from a chain gang in Charlotte, North Carolina.

The city of Charlotte hired its first black detective, Van Griffin, to chase him. The detective caught him and booked him into the county jail. Harris escaped quickly, and Detective Griffin caught him again. This time, he was sent to prison in Raleigh.

Once there, Harris began plotting another escape. This time, he escaped from yet another chain gang and hid in a wagon load of bricks. He was tired of being caught by Griffin, so he fled to Asheville to look for an old girlfriend named Mollie Maxwell.

Harris made it to town on November 12, 1906. The next day, he spent $35 buying a nice suit, a bottle of bourbon, and a .303 rifle. He went to Mollie's sister's home. Pearl Maxwell lived in an African-American community known at the time as "Hell's Half-Acre" or "The Devil's Half Acre." It was a segregated portion of Asheville.

Pearl told Harris that Mollie had moved to Hendersonville about 20 miles away. Harris decided that it was too far, and maybe Pearl should be his new girl. She told him she was already Toney Johnson's girl. He said he'd stay and talk to Toney. He spent the day drinking and getting ready for a fight. When Johnson came home at 11 p.m., he got just that.

ERIKA: So, he thought that he could "fight" Toney and that would make Pearl want to be with him?

MARK: We did say he was the worst caliber. Also, we didn't say he was a good people person.

Johnson ran to two police officers, Captain John Page and Officer Charles Blackstock. He told them Harris was armed and dangerous and had his girl Pearl. He told them Harris claimed to be the Devil himself, and he kept waving around a gun.

ERIKA: Toney is a smart man.

As they approached the building to confront the armed man, Harris opened fire through the door and took down Officer Blackstock. He also wounded Captain Page in the arm. He then escaped out of the back of the building.

ERIKA: Wonder if they knew how good he was at escaping?

He walked into the center of the community and began to open fire on anyone standing there. He wound up killing a shopkeeper named Benjamin Addison, Walter Corpening who was walking home from his job, and Tom Neil who was just sitting on his porch. He then shot a dog in a nearby alley.

ERIKA: This guy is a terrible person.

Captain Page went and got backup. He and another officer named James Bailey got into a heated shootout with Harris. The battle reportedly lasted over ten minutes. Bailey was killed, but Harris was wounded. Harris turned and fled, but Page was unable to catch him.

ERIKA: WOW!

Hell's Half Acre

A group of 300 angry townspeople descended on the police station and started their own manhunt. It took two days, but a bloodhound named Biscuit Eater led a railroad agent named Frank Jordan to a barn in the town of Fletcher about eight miles away. There, they located Harris.

ERIKA: Biscuit Eater is a hero! Also, I love that name.

MARK: I knew you would. He is a good boy!

There, 100 men opened fire and over 500 rounds were shot. Harris's body was badly mangled with over 100 bullet wounds. The mob brought his body back to Asheville for display. The City of Asheville said the killing spree was over and banned the sale of alcohol for a time to avoid any further incidents of drunken violence. The odd thing is Will Harris's body mysteriously vanished after it was removed from public display.

ERIKA: Even his body escaped?! Wow!

SENSATIONAL HEADLINES DESCRIBING THE CARNAGE DURING THE WILL HARRIS RAMPAGE. – ASHEVILLE CITIZEN TIMES, NOVEMBER 14, 1906. (SHOULD WE SAY SOMETHING ABOUT HOW WE DO NOT AGREE WITH THIS?)

BRAVE CITY OFFICERS FALL DEAD ON ST

EGRO RUNS AMUCK ON ASHEVILLE'S STREETS, KILLIN PATROLMEN BLACKSTOCK AND BAILEY AND WOUNDIN CAPTAIN PAGE; ONE NEGRO KILLED AND TWO WOUNDE

nd Who Proclaimed Himself As "Will Harris of Charlotte" Starts Out On Death Dealing Tour With Murderous Rifle of the Deadly "Savage" Pattern.

TENSE EXCITEMENT RUNS THROUGH GATHERING CROWDS

eville Hardware Company's Store Forced Open By Authorities to Arm Pursuers of the Murder-er--Member of Company Later Appears and Distributes Arms.

THEIR FAMILIES.

Mr. Charles R. Blackstock leaves a wife and four children His wife is quite ill and her physician fears the effect of the shock. Mr. Blackstock was a native of this county and lived at 49 Charlotte street.

Mr. J. W. Bailey was a native of Madison but has made his home in Asheville for a number of years at 173 South Main street. He leaves a wife and child, a boy about 2 years of age.

Both Mr. Bailey and Mr. Blackstock had been on the police force for a long time and ranked among the first as efficient officers, both having fine records.

ammunition in the store, and others, impatient at the long delay, hastened on the man hunt. On all sides could be heard men saying, "On for another Ku-Klux. That's what we need." And had a Ben Cameron arisen from the crowd and given the old war cry of the klan hundreds would have fol-

GENERAL SEARCH T BE MADE TOD.

Chief Bernard telephoned this ning to all the surrounding which could be reached, telling authorities to look out for Harris, nishing as accurate a description possible.

Begining at daybreak this morn every available man will be used search of the entire mountainside far as possible clear to Wilm Chief Bernard said he could use e man who would volunteer.

was the woodyard which he opera He was known as a worthy and spectable man, living in a peace manner. He was shot just inside grocery door. The bullet penetr the brain through the right eye, p ing out through his head.

Fire Bell Tolled.

Immediately after the extent of damage became known, Chief Bern caused the fire bell to be tolled riot call, but he could not arm crowds which gathered in answer, murderer was armed with a rifle had shown himself to be a dead while a few pistols were the ar ment of the entire crowd.

After repeated requests Chief

Thomas Wolfe, the writer, lived a short distance away. He was inspired by this to write the short story "The Child by Tiger" to recount this tragic and infamous incident.

ERIKA: You can still find this online if you want to read it.

That section of Eagle Street is said to have numerous ghosts associated with this killing spree. Many have seen a police officer wearing a 1920s era outfit running down the street as if in pursuit of someone. A large black shadow figure is seen marching down the street and turning into an alleyway where it vanishes. A phantom dog howl can be heard often where no dog is seen.

ERIKA: NOPE! I am out. Where to next?

MARK: Not just yet.

There's one last odd bit about this story that drives conspiracy theorists and historians crazy. There is a rumor that the body the posse brought back was not Will Harris. The theory is that they were so stymied by his escape that they killed some poor look-alike and mangled his body. That would explain the quick disappearance of the body before someone looked too closely.

Will Harris may have eluded the long arm of the law yet again. There were witnesses who swore they had seen him a few months later in New Orleans, Louisiana. There he had been observed getting into yet another gunfight, and this time he was shot dead. Though this has never been corroborated by any official channels, it adds one more layer to an already terrible story.

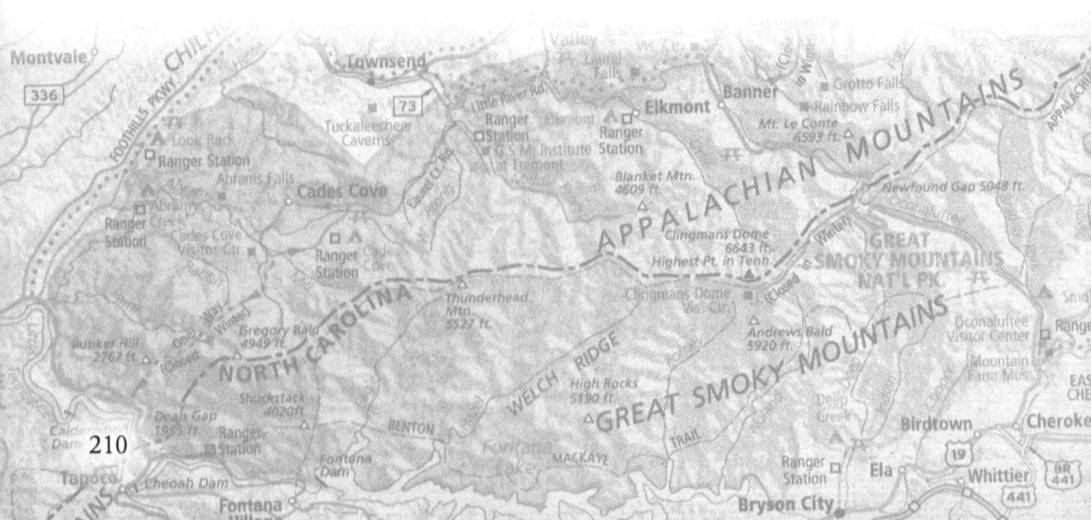

HIGHLAND HOSPITAL

ORIGINALLY FOUNDED AS DR. CARROLL'S SANATORIUM IN 1904 by Dr. Robert S. Carroll, the Highland Hospital was relocated in 1909 and renamed in 1912. Dr. Carroll had given Duke University his hospital and treatment program for addiction and mental/nervous disorders. His program was based primarily on diet, exercise, and occupational therapy. It attracted patients from all over the world to Asheville.

In April of 1936, Zelda Fitzgerald checked herself into Highland Hospital for the first time. The famous novelist, then estranged from her husband F. Scott Fitzgerald, had several bouts of what was called "nervous exhaustion" and had been hearing voices. Her novel *Save Me the Waltz* was nearly autobiographical and had been written during her stay at the Henry Phipps Psychiatric Clinic just outside of Baltimore a few years prior.

> **ERIKA:** Wow! She is also the inspiration for Daisy in *The Great Gatsby* — Beau's (our producer and editor) favorite book.

She stayed for several years at Highland but eventually returned to her home in Alabama. She would return to Highland a few more times for short visits over the next couple of decades. In November of 1947, she came for what would be her final stay.

> **ERIKA:** I don't like the word "final."

Dr. Carroll had some questionable practices. These included electroshock and insulin therapy. He also liked to hire "cured" patients. One of these patients-turned-staff members was Willie Mae Hall, a night supervisor at the hospital. Hall reportedly liked to give a double sedative to those patients she did not like. Additionally, she would lock their bedroom doors in the Central Hall dormitory overnight.

NINE WOMEN BURNED TO DEATH IN FIRE AT HIGHLAND HOSPITAL

(Continued From Page One)

seriously ill, sleeping patients when driven back by heat and smoke.

Patients who escaped the building were clad in flimsy night garments. It was a chilly night with the mercury hovering in the mid-40s.

Nurses quickly huddled the rescued patients into another building where some sat quietly discussing the fire and others yelled hysterically.

Police rescue squads, assisted by Miss Ellen Heiser, anethesist at Norburn hospital, worked over Mrs. Hipps and Mrs. Kennedy two hours before abandoning efforts to revive them. Dr. P. R. Terry, Buncombe county coroner, said both women died of asphyxiation.

Extra Equipment Used

All city fire equipment was rushed to the burning structure as well as pumping trucks from Biltmore and Enka. Off-duty firemen were alerted and special crews aided in the fight. More than 40 firemen continued to pour water on the ruins all night and two lines of hose were playing on the smouldering debris throughout the morning. The first body to be recovered from the ruins was found at 8:18 a.m. It was charred beyond recognition. A second body was uncovered at 10:15 and from a diamond ring and wedding ring hospital authorities identified it as that of Mrs. Doering.

Chief Fitzgerald halted the search for other bodies upon the advice of A. M. DeBruhl, city building inspector. The inspector said that the stone walls apparently were in no immediate danger of collapsing but that the section in which the bodies of the other victims were known to be buried was dangerously weak.

Charles W. Dermid, director of

although several had to be assisted down the stairs. Those overcome by smoke were carried out.

The women on the upper floors behaved "admirably," he said. There was little hysteria and once rescuers reached a patient she responded immediately to all sugestions, he added.

He expressed the belief that the victims were asphyxiated before flames reached them and that none died from burns.

The building was one of four units of the mental hospital which is operated as a psychiatric unit of the Duke university hospital at Durham. It is located on Zillicoa avenue, about three miles from the heart of the city.

Highland hospital was started in August 1904 a, a tiny institution on Haywood street and developed to the point where in 1944, when it was taken over by Duke university, its replacement value was estimated at $700,000 with 12 buildings, 80 patients and 109 workers. It is situated on a tract of 50 acres with an additional 400 acres of mountain woodland five miles away.

The institution's founder, Dr. Robert S. Carroll served as medical director until his retirement Jan. 1, 1945, when he was succeeded by Dr. Basil T. Bennett, psychiatrist.

Long in Leadership

Long recognized as one of the world's foremost psychiatrists, Dr. Carroll founded the hospital 44 years ago as Carroll's sanitarium. In 1912 the name was changed to Highland hospital and in 1939 Dr. Carroll donated it to Duke for operation as a unit of the university's department of neuropsychiatry.

In March of last year friends of the hospital were notified of plans

Night is illuminated by worst fire disaster in Asheville history.

MRS. FITZGERALD HAD BEEN HERE FOR A MONTH

NEW YORK, March 11.—(UP)— Mrs. F. Scott Fitzgerald had been ill for some years but went to the Highland hospital for nervous diseases only a month ago from the home of her 85-year-old mother, Mrs. Anthony Sayre in Montgomery, Ala.

The dead woman's daughter, Mrs. S. J. Lanahan, who lives here, said interment would be in Rockville, Md., where the author is buried and where his family originates.

Mrs. Fitzgerald was 48 and a writer in her own right. She wrote one novel "Save Me the Waltz" and many short stories for such magazines as the Saturday Evening Post and the American Mercury. She collaborated with her husband on

MITCHELL **HAYNES**

HEROES AT FIRE—These two Biltmore high

NEWSPAPER ARTICLE ABOUT THE FIRE AT HIGHLANDS HOSPITAL AND THE DEATH OF ZELDA FITZGERALD. ASHEVILLE TIMES, MARCH 11, 1948.

On March 10, 1948, Hall cut all the phone lines and started a fire in the kitchen of the main building. It spread rapidly to every floor due to the dumbwaiter shaft. The hospital staff and local firefighters did everything they could to fight the blaze. Nine female patients who had been sedated and locked in their rooms died from the fire. One was only able to be identified by her charred slipper beneath her body. It was Zelda Fitzgerald.

The property was owned by Duke University until the 1980s. It was sold and is now a recovery home for teens and young adults. While only direct family members of patients are allowed to visit the private facility, the neighborhood was once the hospital campus.

Zelda was known to take frequent walks during her time as a patient at Highland Hospital. Her spirit is still seen wandering the neighborhood

Highland Hospital

around Highland Park. She is dressed in a robe, and many approach her thinking she is a lost elderly lady. If approached, she will seem to be hearing a conversation from beyond. One witness reported she seemed to be trying to remember her name when he asked her for it. Then she simply faded away in front of them.

ERIKA: So even outside it isn't safe. Back in the car.
Where to next?

A PHOTOGRAPH OF F. SCOTT FITZGERALD AND HIS WIFE ZELDA FITGERALD IN HAPPIER TIMES. PHOTO PROVIDED BY THE BUNCOMBE COUNTY HISTORICAL SOCIETY.

WANETA STREET

ACCORDING TO LOCAL GHOST TOURS, TWO WOMEN WERE tragically beaten to death on Waneta Street in the 1920s. The murder mystery was never solved. While we could find no trace of the crime or the original reporting, this story has been repeated often due to the apparition that appears here.

ERIKA: So, it is local folklore?

MARK: That's a good way to describe it.

The ghost of the murderer is said to stalk Waneta Street at night. He is seen wearing a long black coat and carrying a pipe or large stick. He often approaches lone walkers along the road.

ERIKA: An armed ghost? I don't want to meet him.

Most of the tours in the area talk about this haunting, but with limited information, it's tough to pin down the origin or even the sad, forgotten victims.

ASHEVILLE WAS A MAZE OF ROADS IN THE 1920S AS THE TOWN WAS BOOMING. CRIME WAS A TROUBLING ISSUE FOR THE TOWN. PHOTO PROVIDED BY THE BUNCOMBE COUNTY HISTORICAL SOCIETY.

RIVERSIDE CEMETERY

RIVERSIDE **C**EMETERY IS HOME TO OVER 13,000 GRAVES. Many notable figures from history are buried here, including several congressmen, senators, and governors. William Sydney Porter, known more famously as O. Henry, was buried here in 1910. Thomas Wolfe is interred here, and. his grave is often adorned with pens, pencils, and tribute letters from writers. Lillian Clement lies here. She was the first woman to be elected to state legislature in the South.

There are numerous soldiers here. Of note, 18 German POWs from World War I are buried here. The memorial to them denotes that they died of typhoid fever while imprisoned at the nearby Hot Springs internment camp from 1917-1919. A powerful quote from the German poet Johann Wolfgang von Goethe is inscribed on the monument in both German and English. It reads:

> *"Nicht grossern vorteil vusst'ichzu nennen*
>
> *Als des'Feindes Verdienst erkennen.*
>
> *No greater gain for the human spirit*
>
> *Than a sense of our foeman's merit."*

As hauntingly beautiful as the cemetery is, the ghosts frequently seen here are an anomaly that defies history. A ghostly brigade of Confederate soldiers is often seen marching through the grounds. The 1865 Battle of Asheville did not occur here, and there were very few casualties, yet the spirits of the past echo here amongst the tombstones. No one knows exactly why.

ERIKA: Maybe it's ghosts pretending to be soldiers?

MARK: Or maybe ghosts of reenactors?

WWI POW memorial at Riverside Cemetery. Photo by author.

MERRIMON AND BROADWAY

JAMES SNEAD AND JAMES HENRY FROM TENNESSEE WERE convicted of horse theft in 1835. The men admitted to lives of sin, gambling, and drinking. They said they did not steal Elsberry Holcombe's horse, however. They insisted they had won it fair and square in a poker game.

> ERIKA: So, they were found guilty of stealing a horse they didn't actually steal, but did other terrible things they were not convicted of? Sounds like karma got them.

Both men had been tried and convicted two weeks prior to their hanging. The only witness for the prosecution was the plaintiff Holcombe. He said that the men had pretended to be strangers and invited him to their roadside camp with fire and drink. Then the two men played cards, but Holcombe refused to participate. Henry bet Holcombe's mare in the game and lost. Holcombe refused to let Snead take his horse, but Snead pulled a knife on him. The two men rode off, and Holcombe reported the crime to the police in Asheville.

> ERIKA: Seems like something they would do.

When they were hung on May 29, 1835, the trap door of the gallows did not operate properly and only opened partway. The men slid down slightly and began to strangle. When the door finally opened, it was not enough of a fall to break their necks. The men slowly died of strangulation in front of the thousands of witnesses who had gathered for the hanging.

> ERIKA: Yikes! That is terrible.

Merrimon and Broadway no longer truly intersect thanks to all the interstate on-ramps and off-ramps that now populate the area. It is now near the Asheville Botanical Gardens. The roadways in this area are

THE **Dark Side** OF THE **Smoky Mountains**

avoided by the homeless. They have reported that, in the early morning hours, you can hear the sounds of horse hooves, the gallows door, and choking and gurgling. Sensitive individuals have even claimed an inability to gain proper oxygen along with a feeling of lightheadedness.

ERIKA: Eww. We should move to the next location.

X MARKS THE SPOT OF THE APPROXIMATE LOCATION OF THE GALLOWS NOW WHERE MERRIMON AND BROADWAY INTERSECT. MAP PROVIDED BY THE BUNCOMBE COUNTY HISTORICAL SOCIETY.

BATTERY PARK HOTEL

IT'S NOW AN APARTMENT BUILDING, BUT 1 BATTERY PARK AVENUE was once the famous Battery Park Hotel. In 1936, a young girl named Helen Clevenger was visiting Asheville from New York with her uncle. Her parents were teachers and chemists and practiced the Bahá'í faith. I n the Old South, this was looked down upon because the Bahá'í believed in equality for all races.

> **ERIKA:** Into the Wayback Machine we go!

On July 16, 1936, at around 1a.m., there was a terrible thunderstorm in Asheville. William Clevenger was awakened by a loud clap of thunder. He worried about his niece in the next room but didn't immediately get up to check on her due to the hour. He slept through the rest of the storm.

> **ERIKA:** I feel like he should have checked on her.

The next morning, he went to check on her when she hadn't woken him with her usual cry of, "Uncle Billy!" When he opened the door to her room, he found his niece lying in a pool of blood with a bullet wound to her head and strange slashes on her face. The autopsy would say she died of a .32 caliber bullet. Her Bahá'í ring was noted in all the police reports and, later, in nearly every newspaper article pertaining to the murder.

> **ERIKA:** So, it was a gunshot and not thunder. He should have checked on her.

On July 23, after pressure from all over the world, as the murder had made international headlines, the police were forced to make an arrest. After interviewing several men, they arrested a young black night janitor named Martin Moore for the crime. According to the police, Moore confessed to the crime. He was sentenced to die in the North Carolina gas chamber in December of that same year.

YOUNG N. Y. WOMAN SHOT THROUGH CHEST AND STABBED IN FACE

Killing Heat Adds Hourly To U. S. Toll

CHICAGO, July 16. — (UP) — Killing heat persisting in scattered sections of the three great valleys of the middle west added hourly today to its already tremendous death and property toll.

Deaths from the heat which spread across the nation 12 days ago edged past 3,500. Damage to crops mounted to $500,000,000 with no signs of stopping there.

Black clouds poured draughts of cooling air across 14 drought-ridden prairie states but left a dozen more

Pajama-Clad Body Of 19-Year-Old Helen Clevenger Found By Uncle.

HAD BEEN HERE 2 DAYS

Niece Of State College Professors; Clues Sought In Mystery Case.

Clad in striped green pajamas, the body of Miss Helen Clevenger, pretty 19-year-old daughter of J. F. Clevenger, of Great Kills, Staten Island, New York, was found dead in her room at the Battery Park hotel this morning at 8:30 o'clock.

An examination by physicians dis-

HEADLINES DESCRIBING THE MURDER OF HELEN CLEVENGER AT THE BATTERY PARK HOTEL. ASHEVILLE TIMES, JULY 16, 1936.

ERIKA: I do not believe he "confessed."

They needed a scapegoat. Martin Moore said that he had been beaten for days and that was the only reason he had confessed. Per his later statements, he thought he was only confessing to sneaking into her room to commit a robbery. Nothing had been stolen from her if this had truly been a robbery gone wrong.

ERIKA: I hate hearing stories like this.

True Detective magazine had a full dramatization of the story in their October issue a short while later. The sheriff's office even approved a radio drama of the case which would air in 1937.

ERIKA: True crime always fascinates people.

There are numerous theories as to who the true killer might have been. Some blame the manager's nephew who disappeared after the murder. Locals speculated about German violinist Mark Wollner who had given a false alibi. He was a well-known womanizer and had been a suspect in other murders. A witness outside the hotel said he saw someone jump from a lower roof on the night of the murder. Wollner was noted to have a severe limp at his questioning.

ERIKA: He seems like a better suspect.

Booker T. Sherrill was another employee of the hotel. He was off that fateful evening but was good friends with young Martin. He noted in an interview, "Every Thursday night, sometimes twice during that night, I'll have a dream where Martin comes to me and says the same thing in every dream, 'I didn't kill 'em Books. He killed all of them.' That went on for at least two years."

ERIKA: Wow! His spirit was trying to help.

No one lives in room 224 for long at the Battery Park Senior Apartments, or so the stories say. No one has said what is exactly the issue with the room, but they almost always demand to be moved after a short while. While not the only ghost story in the building, it is certainly the most famous.

ERIKA: Seems like there are many reasons for the spirits
to be restless.

Babe Ruth, George Vanderbilt, and many others of note stayed in the hotel before its renovation into apartments. Various other crimes and atrocities were reported in the hotel over its decades of operation. Is it any wonder there are several lingering spirits here? One spirit of note is a man who was reportedly also murdered in the former hotel. He is often seen in the pantry area in the main kitchen.

ERIKA: Wonder if he adds a little ghost seasoning
to the food?

As for the spirit of Helen Clevenger, she seems to be a permanent resident of the Old Battery Park Hotel. She is not seen in room 224 but is seen wandering the halls, particularly on dark and stormy nights.

ERIKA: Because her killer was never caught!

THE OLD BATTERY PARK HOTEL IS NOW THE BATTERY PARK SENIOR APARTMENTS FOR THOSE OF 62 YEARS OF AGE OR OLDER. IT WAS RECENTLY RENOVATED. TOURS CAN BE ARRANGED BUT BE RESPECTFUL OF THE RESIDENTS. PHOTO BY AUTHOR.

BASILICA OF ST. LAWERENCE

ONE OF THE MOST RECOGNIZABLE BUILDINGS IN ASHEVILLE is the Basilica of St. Lawrence. It was designed by the architect Rafael Guastavino, who retired to Asheville after originally coming from Spain. He made many famous buildings throughout North Carolina, including the Duke Chapel in Durham and the Motley Memorial in Chapel Hill. The main dome of the Basilica is one of the largest free-standing domes in North America.

ERIKA: The building is amazing!

Sadly, Guastavino never lived to see the completion of this building. He passed away during its construction. His last request was to have himself interred in the walls of the Basilica, which he considered to be his masterpiece. He also asked to have room for his wife and daughter when they passed at a later date. His body was placed in the wall while construction continued. His wife and daughter, however, wouldn't be allowed to be laid to rest there as laws changed before they passed to not allow burials on private property. They were both eventually buried in the cemetery nearby.

ERIKA: I bet his spirit isn't happy about that at all.

Guastavino's architectural system is seen to this day in many American landmarks including Carnegie Hall, Grand Central Station in New York, and Grant's Tomb.

The church is open from Tuesdays to Fridays for tours. Many on the tour note that they have seen an almost transparent apparition of a man, a woman, and a young lady walking the halls. They often stop to look at the various statues of saints in the Catholic Church. Sometimes, they admire the various stained-glass windows that adorn the Basilica. Witnesses identified the figures as those of Guastavino and his wife and daughter.

THE **Dark Side** OF THE **Smoky Mountains**

ERIKA: I am glad they are together now.

Another spirit is seen in the left chapel, which is known as the Chapel of Our Lady. It is here that a priestly figure is seen greeting invisible passersby. His appearance is usually followed by poltergeist activity, including flickering lights and doors opening or closing.

ERIKA: NOPE! I am good with walking ghosts but *not* when they move stuff.

Whether you are religious or not, it is a beautiful building and well worth a visit while in Asheville.

THE IMPRESSIVE ARCHITECTURE OF THE BASILICA OF ST. LAWRENCE. PHOTO BY AUTHOR.

CHURCH STREET

CONTINUING THE RELIGIOUS THEME, CHURCH STREET IS so named as it houses three of Asheville's oldest churches. Asheville had been billed for a long time as a city of great healing and crisp, clean mountain air. All the health resorts and spas certainly drew people to the burgeoning city in those early days of the 20th century. Though, in 1918, the Spanish influenza came to town and proved the town could offer no respite from its ravages.

> **ERIKA:** There is so much about these healing clinics and locations I didn't know.

> **MARK:** It's like this book is educational. Sorry.

Before the construction of the churches here, this road was where the many victims of the flu outbreak were buried in unmarked graves. The city had simply run out of coffins, and the mortuaries were flooded with decomposing bodies. They eventually paved over the area, and beneath the concrete foundations of the buildings here lie thousands upon thousands of bones.

> **ERIKA:** I don't like that idea at all.

The most notable apparition that haunts this street is called the Black Abbot or the Dark Sister. He or she is a dark shadow figure that resembles someone wearing priestly garb or perhaps a nun's robe. The figure wanders up and down the street, seemingly performing blessings. It is considered the most documented haunting in Asheville and is included on nearly every ghost tour.

> **ERIKA:** It's probably keeping the rest of the spirits in the unmarked graves at bay.

THE JACKSON BUILDING

BUILT IN 1924, THE JACKSON BUILDING, DESIGNED BY noted architect Ronald Greene, was western North Carolina's first skyscraper. History alone makes it worth a visit, but there is more to this building than meets the eye, even with its Gothic castle peak complete with stone grotesques jutting out of the building's face.

> **ERIKA:** It is amazing to look at. This is where I would film that Asheville *Ghostbusters* movie!

Originally, this building site was the home of W.O. Wolfe's stonecutting business; notably, Wolfe was the father of author Thomas Wolfe. Monuments at the base of the building include a half-finished tombstone. The shop was mentioned in Wolfe's *Look Homeward Angel*. There is a second monument with bronze carving tools and an inscription from the book on it.

"He would find his father in the workroom… using the heavy wooden mallet with delicate care, as he guided the chisel through the mazes of an inscription… As Eugene saw him, he felt that this was no ordinary craftsman but a master."

THIS PHOTO SHOWS HOW BUSY ASHEVILLE WAS BEFORE THE GREAT DEPRESSION. THE STEEPLES OF CHURCH STREET CAN BE SEEN BEHIND SOME OF THE BUSTLE OF MAIN STREET. PHOTO PROVIDED BY THE BUNCOMBE COUNTY HISTORICAL SOCIETY.

The Jackson Building

ERIKA: It is amazing how they used to carve stone.

MARK: Many artisans still use this hand carving technique today.

The monuments are in a series of concentric circles at the base of the Jackson Building. Many say this bullseye marks the spot where a man jumped to his death from the top floor after the Stock Market Crash of 1929. There are at least two more suicides reported in that same period of time.

ERIKA: Yikes!

Famously, Fredrick M. Messler was a real estate tycoon who, on April 5, 1930, went to the eighth floor and used a Spanish revolver to end his life. He was suffering from an undisclosed illness that was likely to kill him; the real estate market at the time only seemed to hasten his decision to commit suicide.

Messler's office was on the sixth floor, and his spirit is often seen pacing back and forth. Supposedly, the spirit of L.B. Jackson himself is seen checking on his impressive skyscraper and the improvements built into it. He apparently marvels at the modern amenities added to the building before vanishing into nothingness.

ERIKA: At least he is proud of the changes and isn't angry.

OUTSIDE THE JACKSON BUILDING STANDS THE MEMORIAL MARKER FOR THOMAS WOLFE'S FATHER IN THE BULLSEYE DESIGN ON THE SIDEWALK. PHOTO BY AUTHOR.

CHICKEN ALLEY

AS YOU APPROACH THE CHICKEN ALLEY, KEEP AN EYE around a foot off the ground for a display of fairy storefronts built into the walls. You'll know you are close to a magical place when you see them.

> **ERIKA:** I love them so much! It is a whole fairy community here.

Molly Must is a local artist and the creator of many of the large murals that adorn Asheville. She created a prominent mural of a rooster that marks the entrance to Chicken Alley. It's a small and very narrow alley near downtown Asheville named for the large number of chickens that would flock there in the city's early days.

> **ERIKA:** I love the thought of a bunch of chickens hanging out.

The spirit seen most often is that of Dr. Jamie Smith. Dr. Smith had a distinctive dress style, wearing a wide-brimmed black fedora hat and a long black duster coat. He always carried a medicine bag in one hand and walked with a silver pommeled cane in his other hand. He often walked to Chicken Alley to visit his favorite bar, Broadway's Tavern.

> **ERIKA:** Is he a good ghost or a bad ghost?

At the turn of the century, the town was a bit bawdy. The men working the nearby logging camps and mills would come to the town on weekends looking for a good time. This kept the bars and brothels of the area open late. Dr. Smith seemed to enjoy the free-wheeling nature of the town. The rumor was that most of his money came from treating the various social diseases of those partaking in these good times.

> **ERIKA:** He was a nice doctor then.

Chicken Alley

In 1902, Dr. Smith went into Broadway's Tavern in Chicken Alley. He was immediately drawn into a large bar fight. He tried to break it up, but he was stabbed in the heart by one of the participants and died instantly. His killer was never brought to justice. The bar burned down almost exactly a year after that night.

ERIKA: Wow! That is not good.

Ever since that fateful evening, there have been many sightings of Dr. Jamie Smith still walking the alley late at night. His wide hat and long coat are unmistakable. Often, he is seen carrying his medicine bag. People even report hearing the tip of the cane tapping on the street as he walks by. There are some who say he even stops to lean over and pet a ghostly chicken wandering under the mural that marks the alley's entrance.

ERIKA: Aww, he is still looking out for the people *and* chickens! Sounds like a fun ghost.

CHICKEN ALLEY IS MARKED BY AN AMAZING MURAL CREATED BY ARTIST MOLLY MUST. PHOTO BY AUTHOR.

ASHEVILLE PINBALL MUSEUM

WHILE NOT TRADITIONALLY HAUNTED, THIS MUSEUM LETS visitors play over 70 pinball machines and video games from the golden age of arcades to modern new releases. While there is only a small fee to play all you want, you'll want to keep your eyes open for an unusual guest.

ERIKA: I love pinball!

MARK: Time to cue up Rush's "Tom Sawyer" on my Zune.

ERIKA: I can't believe you still use that thing.

An anonymous employee told us that he frequently sees a strange figure beside the *Bally Wizard* pinball machine. The figure appears to be in clothes from the late 1970s and may be waiting for the employee to turn on the machine first thing in the morning. When approached, he raises his arms and backs away, disappearing into the wall beside the machine.

ERIKA: A disco era ghost!

MARK: Disco will never die!

No one knows who he is or why he's there. Another employee verified the apparition's reported appearance and said he almost looked like a photograph with bell bottom jeans and an unbuttoned shiny white shirt. Even without the spiritual presence, this museum is a great way to visit the past without a Wayback Machine.

ERIKA: I will even play here with the cool ghost!

MARK: Groovy!

ONE OF THESE MACHINES IN ASHEVILLE'S PINBALL MUSEUM IS REPORTEDLY HAUNTED. PHOTO BY AUTHOR.

SUPERMAN
YACHT CLUB
SPACE RIDERS
ATARI / 1978

ASHEVILLE MYSTERY MUSEUM

THERE ARE HUNDREDS UPON HUNDREDS OF GHOST STORIES and legends surrounding Asheville. Most have been well-documented by best-selling author Joshua P. Warren. He currently owns a collection of oddities and artifacts in the Asheville Mystery Museum.

ERIKA: This place sounds creepy!

The museum is only able to be visited as a part of the Haunted Asheville Ghost Tour. The tour begins behind the Asheville Masonic Temple on Broadway, and the museum is housed in the basement. It contains some must-see items from indigenous artifacts to modern ghost hunting equipment.

THE SIGN FOR ASHEVILLE'S MYSTERY MUSEUM. PHOTO BY AUTHOR.

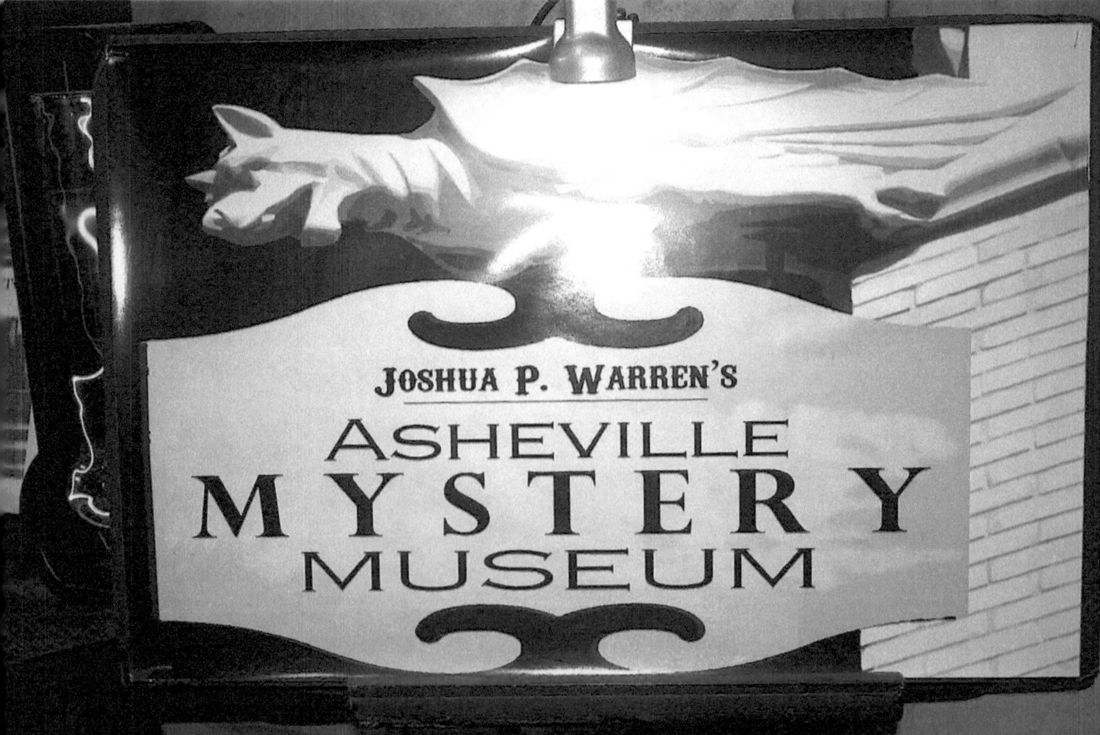

HELEN'S BRIDGE

ASK ANYONE IN ASHEVILLE WHERE THE MOST HAUNTED location in the city is, and they'll likely say Helen's Bridge. Thomas Wolfe mentions walking under the bridge in his book *Look Homeward, Angel*. The arched bridge crosses College Road on Beaucatcher Mountain. Built in 1908, it led to the reconstructed Tudor-style home of John Evans Brown known as Zelandia.

The house and bridge were constructed by Brown after he spent several years in California and New Zealand during their Gold Rush periods. He had the bridge built with nearby quarried stones to provide access to his new home. He lived there for some time with his wife. After his wife passed away, he moved away from what the locals referred to as "The Castle of the Mountain."

In 1977, Zelandia was listed in the National Register of Historic Places. The mansion itself is only visitable by invitation as it is private property. The mansion is reportedly not haunted in any way. However, the bridge is home to an infamous spirit.

ERIKA: I am surprised the mansion isn't haunted.

The bridge gets its name from a woman named Helen. There are several versions of her legend, and none of them can be verified. One story is that she moved to Asheville with her infant daughter, looking to start a new life as she had lost her husband in a war. While cooking, a large fire broke out, and she was unable to reach her daughter. While firefighters were able to save Helen, the loss of her child proved too much. Depressed, she wandered up to the bridge and hung herself from one of the support posts.

ERIKA: That is terrible.

Another version of the story is that she was living at the mansion and having an affair with one of the members of the staff. When he refused to

accept their offspring as his own, she ended her life by hanging. No matter what version of the story you wish to believe, sightings of her spirit at the bridge are well-documented.

ERIKA: Sounds like she met a terrible end.

Helen's Bridge is a frequent stop for paranormal enthusiasts and is mentioned on every ghost tour in town. Visitors to the bridge say that, sometimes, Helen will even talk to them. She'll speak to them of the tragedy of losing a child before disappearing without a trace.

ERIKA: NOPE!

The story goes that if you call her name three times while under or on the bridge, Helen will appear. Many witnesses say they have car trouble while visiting the remote bridge—batteries draining, stalled engines, and other issues are constantly reported.

ERIKA: Why is it always saying the name of the ghost three times?

MARK: Traditionally, it is because it mocks the Holy Trinity. Ritual and intention are everything.

Other apparitions are reported near the bridge as well. One paranormal team encountered what they described as strange "monster-like figures" coming out of the brush on the sides of the bridge. One group even reported being physically attacked by unseen forces that had been somehow drawn to all the spiritual activity on the bridge.

ERIKA: I have to say that this place has the most negative energy I have felt so far. It seems like something nasty has taken up residence here.

MARK: It appears that Helen's spirit is no longer alone.

For now, though, it's finally time to hit the most famous haunted location in Asheville.

THE INFAMOUS HELEN'S BRIDGE.
PHOTO BY AUTHOR.

THE BILTMORE ESTATE

THE ESTATE WAS ORIGINALLY BUILT AS A VACATION HOME for George Washington Vanderbilt after a visit with his mother in 1886. George was one of the heirs to the Vanderbilt industrial fortune. He purchased 125,000 acres and began construction on his 26th birthday. It would become the largest privately owned home in America.

ERIKA: Wow! This place is huge!

MARK: It's bigger than some of the towns we've visited.

Vanderbilt spent a large portion of his inheritance building the large estate. He had to build a private railway into Asheville in order to bring in his family and guests so that they would visit. Though the city has grown and is much closer now; at the time, Biltmore was quite a distance from the city proper.

There are dozens upon dozens of books about the history of the estate and the house. Now open to the public, the mansion, winery, and gardens make it one of the largest tourist destinations in North Carolina. It has been featured in numerous movies including *Being There* with Peter Sellers and *The Private Eyes* with Tim Conway and Don Knotts.

ERIKA: I am sure there are some spirits here.

There are many ghost stories around the estate. The most popular story involves George Vanderbilt himself. During his life, Vanderbilt had amassed an impressive library. He would devote much of his time to perusing the various rare volumes he had acquired over the years. His habit was to retreat to the library whenever a storm came. His spirit is often seen as a shadow figure in the library whenever storm clouds gather near the property.

ERIKA: Interesting... Summoned by storms.

His wife Edith's spirit is often heard in the library calling his name. It's as though he's lost himself in studying or reading, and she is asking him to return to their guests.

ERIKA: I love that.

There are many other stories of phantom laughter, strange music, and voices echoing through the estate's halls and passages. There are even stories of water splashing and sounds of a party emanating from the long empty indoor swimming pool. The Vanderbilts may be proof that while you can't take it with you, you can still enjoy a luxurious lifestyle even when you are no longer alive.

ERIKA: I think I need to hit the winery before running into any of the ghosts here.

There are dozens and dozens of books about the Vanderbilts and Biltmore Mansion. You can pick one of them up in the gift shop here, if you want to know more. Don't forget to visit the awesome "Halloween Room" with its amazing murals.

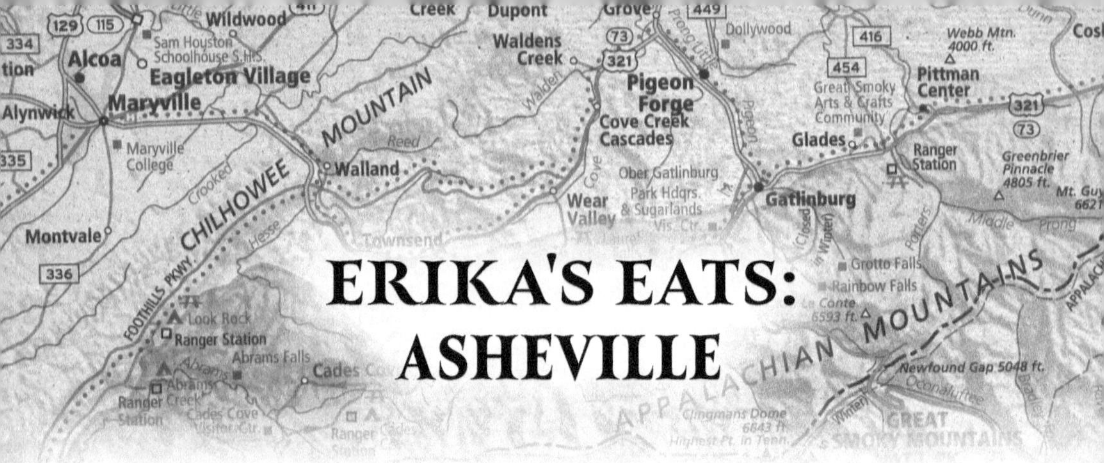

THERE ARE SO MANY AMAZINGLY FUN FOOD AND DRINK stops in Asheville. Make sure you do your own exploring, but I decided to list a few of my favorites.

Rosabees

This wonderfully fun restaurant brings Hawaiian food and desserts to Asheville. It s warehouse-like atmosphere is just what I needed. I grabbed a MonkeyPod Mai Tai along with a Loco Moco, which is my favorite brunch fare. It's a traditional Hawaiian dish of rice, hamburger, eggs with a delicious gravy. Mark dove into the Biscuit Sando because of the grilled Spam! Whatever your tummy is wanting, it can find it here.

Daddy Mac's Down Home Dive

Do you want yummy food late at night? This is the place. Mark and I had to start with The Craving: waffle fries piled high with just tons of toppings like chili and cheese. Then I dove into the Cowboy Frito salad in a jar. Mark grabbed Uncle Cecil's Wing King Board (he had to take some back to the hotel because his eyes were WAY bigger than his tummy). Of course, I wouldn't be in travel mode without trying one of their amazing top shelf blackberry margaritas!

Babettes: A New Orleans Coffeehouse

You know I love my coffee as much as I love avoiding ghosts. First and foremost, they have beignets! These are some of my favorite treats, and they have a churro version that is to *die* for (but not literally, we don't need more ghosts in Asheville). Also, they have chicory coffee, and if you have never had it before, you must try it. Mark isn't a coffee drinker, so he grabbed a freshly squeezed lemonade and tea (His default drink is an Arnold Palmer). They have a full menu so go and explore!

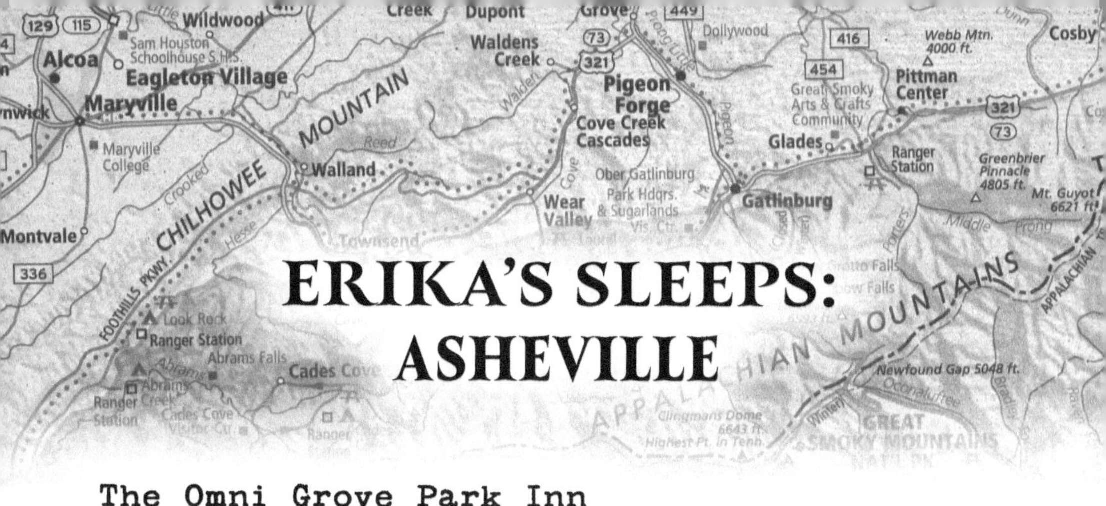

ERIKA'S SLEEPS: ASHEVILLE

The Omni Grove Park Inn

Mentioned above. You might be able to meet the ghost in the pink dress.

The Princess Anne Hotel

This is an upscale option in an old historic house. After your long journey so far, it is a luxurious place to put your feet up. With so much history, who knows if you will be alone during your stay?

The Earth and Sky Dwellings in Asheville

Hold on to your hats, Travelers. No matter what kind of Traveler (or nerd) you are, you *have* to stay in one of these amazing cabins. An Airbnb in Asheville has created unique experiences in their mountain-top cabins. It doesn't matter if you want just a normal cabin experience, or if you want to be in a Harry Potter Quidditch tent (like me!), or even if you have a dream of sleeping the night in a Hobbit hole (like Mark), this is the place for you! I cannot recommend this experience enough, but make sure you book ahead!

POSTCARD SHOWING THE PRINCESS ANNE HOTEL IN THE 1940S. CARD PROVIDED BY THE BUNCOMBE COUNTY HISTORICAL SOCIETY.

ERIKA'S EXTRA STOPS: ASHEVILLE

Earth Magick

I don't know about you, but I think it is very important to recharge after going to all of these spooky places. The Earth Magick store is located in downtown Asheville, and you can get all the cleansing sage and crystals to recharge for your journey ahead. Make sure to let them know you are a Traveler and grab some amethyst for the road!

The Great Escape Room

I love an escape room! These are super fun to do with a couple of friends or a big group. If you are staying the night in Asheville, why not lock yourself in a little space, figure out the clues, and hopefully get out before the time is up? They have rooms of varying difficulties, and some are quite spooky!

YOU CAN FIND ALL YOUR MAGICAL NEEDS IN EARTH MAGICK IN DOWNTOWN ASHEVILLE. PHOTO BY AUTHOR.

WAYNESVILLE, NORTH CAROLINA

LAST SHOT MEMORIAL

WE MUST TAKE A SLIGHT DETOUR IN TIME AND SPACE WITH the Wayback Machine.

> **ERIKA:** As if we haven't been in-and-out of the Wayback Machine this whole time!

We are traveling to July 6, 1781, to one of the last major battles of the American Revolutionary War near the Green Spring Plantation in Virginia. This would be one of the last major battles before the siege of Yorktown. British and American forces were marching all over the Southern Colonies at this time. No one knew where the next battle would occur.

Marquis de Lafayette was shadowing General Cornwallis's British troops who had recently left North Carolina into Virginia. Cornwallis was intending to meet with Benedict Arnold to get reinforcements from the main British army. On that July morning, Lafayette met with a small force of Continentals under the command of General Anthony Wayne.

The ensuing battle was nearly a complete loss for the Revolutionary forces. Lafayette was trying to lead his men out of Cornwallis's trap. Wayne, seeing the collapse, knew there was no time to withdraw his own men. To save the rest of the army, he had his severely outnumbered men make a bayonet charge into the British center. It delayed Cornwallis's advance, and Lafayette was able to marshal reinforcements with George Washington, which would lead to the decisive Battle of Yorktown.

> **ERIKA:** That seems like a bold move.

The crazed charge, and other strange battlefield tactics, earned General Anthony Wayne a promotion to brigadier general and the nick-name of "Mad" Anthony Wayne. Some couldn't decide if it was heroic or foolhardy. The *New Jersey Gazette* had this to say about the general: "Madness—Mad Anthony, by God, I never knew such a piece of work

Last Shot Memorial

heard of—about eight hundred troops opposed to five or six thousand veterans on their own ground."

One soldier in this battle was Colonel Robert Love. He was given some land in North Carolina for his service in the Revolutionary War. In 1809, he donated a large portion of that land for a courthouse and a public square to help found the city of Waynesville, named for his famed commanding officer.

ERIKA: That was super nice of him.

A short time later, Waynesville played a significant role in another war. The news of Robert E. Lee's surrender at Appomattox a month prior traveled very slowly to the Southern states at the end of the Civil War. In early May of 1865, Confederate troops known as Thomas's Legion had a skirmish in Waynesville with Union soldiers led by Lieutenant Colonel William Bartlett. Thomas's Legion was made primarily of Cherokee and mountain men. They had been a thorn in the Union's side throughout the war with constant raids of towns and supply lines in the Smoky Mountains.

ERIKA: I love the phrase "thorn in my side." Cutting off supplies would do that.

THE LAST PHOTO OF THOMAS'S LEGION IN WAYNESVILLE. PHOTO PROVIDED BY HAYWOOD COUNTY HISTORICAL SOCIETY.

The skirmish, known as the Battle of Waynesville, was over in less than a day, and a truce was quickly called. The date of this altercation is hazy as both sides reported different dates. The exact date of the surrender of Thomas's Legion shortly afterward is not even definitively known. It is said they were told they could keep their guns as long as they went home, and in exchange, the Union would not plunder the city.

> **ERIKA:** Interesting arrangement. I'm not sure if one like
> that would be made in the present day.

Though not the true last fight of the Civil War, this became the popular opinion, and a monument was placed here to mark the "last shot" of the Civil War. Less than two years after his surrender, Thomas himself was declared insane and committed to a mental asylum in Asheville. "As mad as General Wayne himself," spoke one local paper of his committal. He was likely suffering from Alzheimer's.

> **ERIKA:** It is sad that the disease was not understood at
> that time.

There is a historical Civil War tour in Waynesville that will tell you so much more about the town's place in the War Between the States. While they do not visit the monument as it currently sits between two houses on private property, it can be visited as long as you are respectful of the two adjoining properties.

Today, the town is known for the Haywood Arts Regional Theater, where another "Lady in White" is often seen during musical performances.

> **ERIKA:** You know I love a good Lady in White! But I don't
> think I'll be visiting the Theater now.

The Folkmoot center here hosts many events spotlighting the area's cultural heritage through folk music and dance. In July every year, they host the Folkmoot USA State International Festival of North Carolina. Performers with authentic and reproduced costumes present representations of their heritage during the two-week celebration.

In the center, keep your eyes open for the spirit of a model who died after a photo shoot in the building. Not much is known about her, except that she was so distraught from some sort of embarrassment that she ran out into the street and was hit by a car. Her crying is often heard echoing through the center when it's supposed to be unoccupied.

> **ERIKA:** NOPE! I am out.

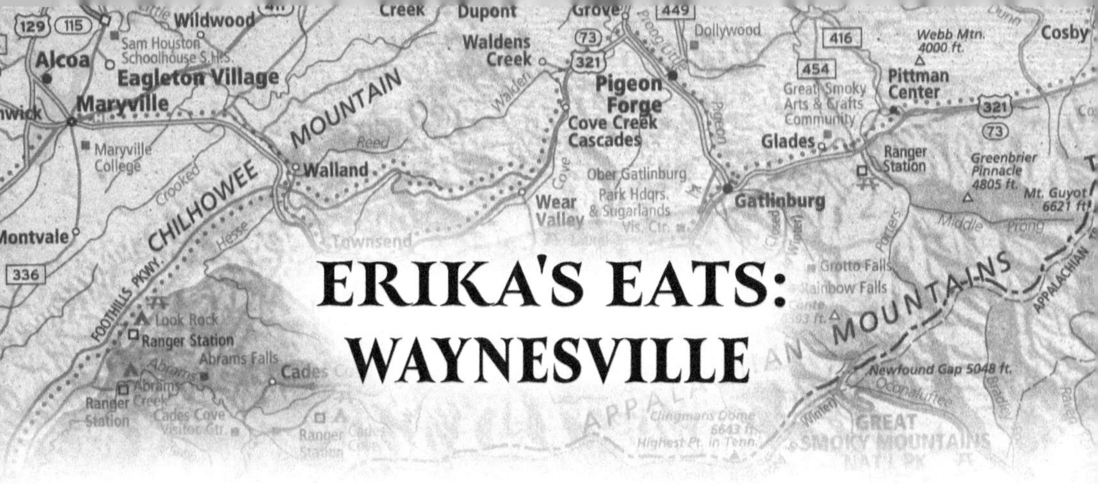

ERIKA'S EATS: WAYNESVILLE

The Scotsman Public House

This amazingly fun Scottish bar will not disappoint. Located in a building that used to be a Masonic Lodge, it is now a wonderful place to grab a shepherd's pie (my favorite) or fish 'n chips (Mark's favorite). If you are wondering if something otherworldly is watching, you should grab a signature cocktail like Lucy's Fur Coat. After a couple, you'll hopefully forget you are not alone.

A ghostly mason in what looks like a ceremonial robe is often seen at closing time. Many of the pub's staff have seen it, but no one has any idea who it could be.

Smoky Mountain Roasters

Need a pick-me-up? You can grab a locally roasted coffee with any flavoring you can imagine here. The menu is way too long to even hint at, but if you want to try my favorite… well, you'll still have a long list. Caffeine abounds here, so you'll certainly find your new favorite!

Boojum Brewery Taproom

This place is a nod to my favorite Bigfoot legend. You'll find a fun menu, amazing drinks, and a great place to grab a souvenir t-shirt. They have fun events and live music if you are in the mood. Be sure to try one of the craft beers from the Boojum Brewing Company.

MARK: Funny you mentioned the Boojum. Let's head to Sylva and delve into the story behind this legendary figure.

ERIKA: Let me finish my Hounds of Helles beer (or two), and I would love to!

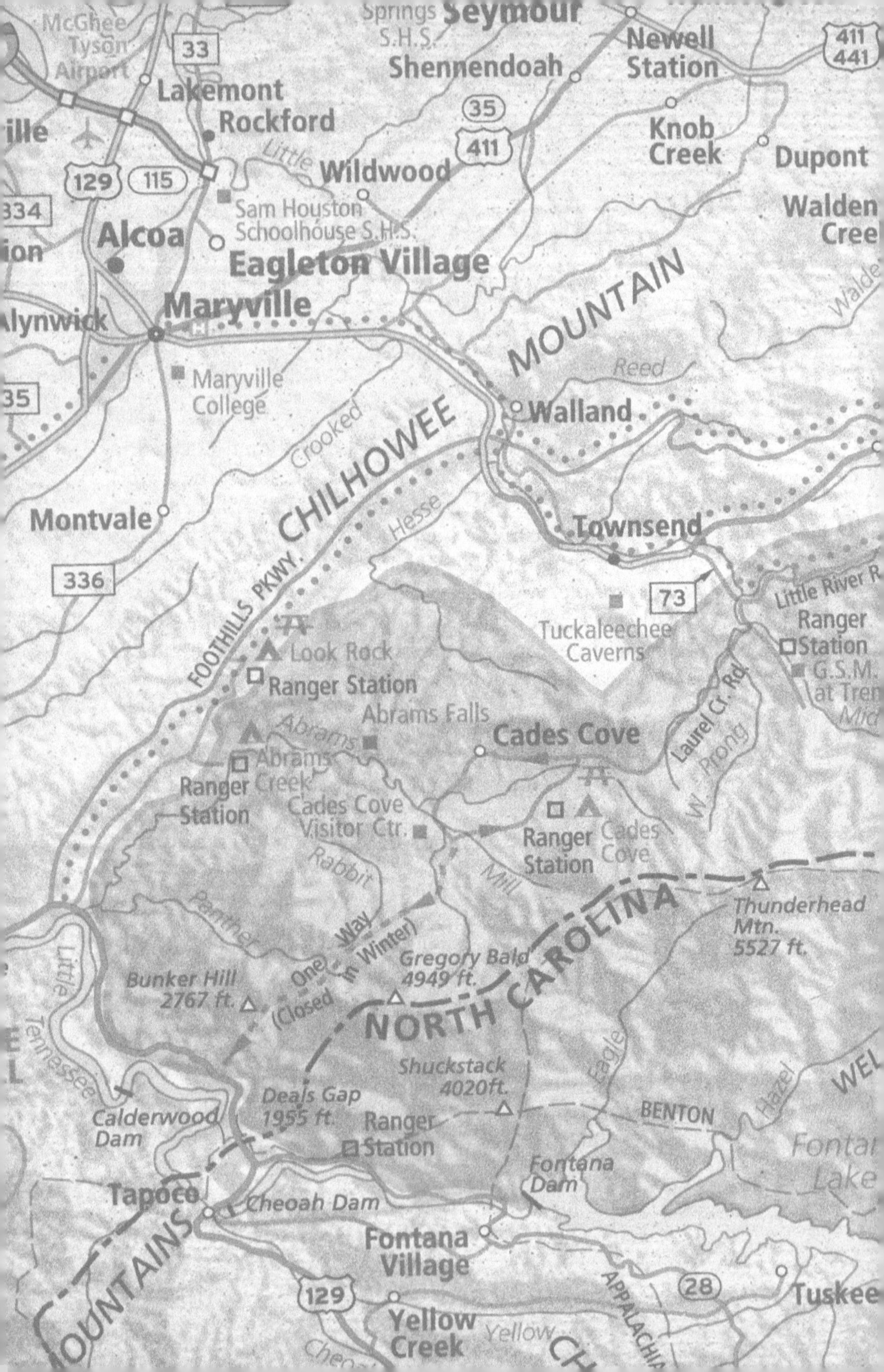

McGhee Tyson Airport
33
Lakemont
Rockford
Little
Wildwood
129
115
Sam Houston Schoolhouse S.H.S.
334
Alcoa
Eagleton Village
Maryville
alynwick
35
Maryville College
Crooked
336
Montvale
CHILHOWEE
FOOTHILLS PKWY.
Hesse
Springs
Seymour
S.H.S.
Shennendoah
35
411
Newell Station
411
441
Knob Creek
Dupont
Walden Cree
MOUNTAIN
Reed
Walland
Townsend
Walde
73
Little River R
Ranger Station
G.S.M. at Tren Mid
Tuckaleechee Caverns
Look Rock
Ranger Station
Abrams Falls
Cades Cove
Laurel Cr. Rd.
W. Prong
Abrams
Abrams Creek
Ranger Station
Cades Cove Visitor Ctr.
Ranger Station
Cades Cove
Rabbit
Mill
Panther
Way
One
(Closed in Winter)
Gregory Bald
4949 ft.
NORTH CAROLINA
Thunderhead Mtn.
5527 ft.
Bunker Hill
2767 ft.
Little
Tennessee
Shuckstack
4020ft.
Eagle
Hazel
WEL
Deals Gap
1955 ft.
Ranger Station
BENTON
Fonta
Lake
Calderwood Dam
Fontana Dam
Tapoco
Cheoah Dam
Fontana Village
L
MOUNTAINS
129
APPALACHI
28
Tuskee
Yellow Creek
Yellow
Cheo

SYLVA, NORTH CAROLINA

SYLVA

SYLVA IS A TOWN OF MANY MYSTERIES.

The white former courthouse looms over Main Street. The town claims it once held the mighty Dills Falls, a giant 249-foot waterfall in the town limits, but it was destroyed to build a bypass.

> **ERIKA:** This sounds like something Douglas Adams would write in *The Hitchhikers Guide to the Galaxy*.

Except the falls were only 40 feet tall and were *never* destroyed. The town supposedly got its name from a strange Danish handyman that lived there for a few months. But now it's been discovered that he wasn't Danish—rather, he was likely Portuguese—and his name wasn't even Sylva but Selvey.

> **ERIKA:** This story is getting confusing.

> **MARK:** That's a good summary about a lot of history.

It's a town full of legends and stories. There are stories of ghostly figures that march through the town's main street. There are tales of a ghost who haunts the second floor of the old Jackson County Courthouse, which is now the Jackson County Public Library. Just like the stories about the town, none of them seem to have any true historical basis. The town is full of mysteries.

> **ERIKA:** And ghosts, it seems.

BOOJUM

THERE IS ONE STORY THAT DATES TO THE EARLY DAYS OF the mountain's settlements near where the town sits today. It involves a young girl, a farmer's daughter, a "Wild Man," gems, and moonshine. I think that should get your attention.

ERIKA: Keep going. It's my favorite!

The story usually takes place in the Balsam mountains, even Haywood County where the Boojum Brewery is located. However, it appears that this story occurs much closer to Blackrock Mountain and the unique giant boulder there.

The most well-known version of this story is often told about the lost Eagle's Nest Hotel in Waynesville. After its opening, guests would hear strange noises coming from underneath the hotel. They could hear a strange stomping and other evil noises. They called it the "Boojum." The creature had somehow buried a horde of gems beneath the hotel's foundation. The guests demanded that the hotel owner do something about it!

ERIKA: Do something about the noises or the gems?

Supposedly, a young girl named Annie saw the creature, who was covered in hair except for his lean face, which was etched by loneliness. Unlike other women he had watched from afar, Annie didn't run. She fell in love and moved to the mountains to be with the Boojum.

ERIKA: This sounds almost like a *Beauty and the Beast* fairy tale.

They lived happily for some time as he polished gems and brought her gifts. They would call out to each other by hooting like an owl or screeching like a wildcat. Apparently, this is where the term "hootenanny" comes from. It's a derivation of "Hootin' Annie."

THE **Dark Side** OF THE **Smoky Mountains**

One day, the Boojum disappeared, and Annie couldn't find him. She was convinced the owner of the Eagle's Nest had taken her Boojum. To retaliate, she burned the hotel to the ground. Her howl can still be heard there to this day, though the hotel is long gone.

There's another version that far predates it. This one takes place on what is now Blackrock Mountain and Pinnacle Park. What was once a watershed for the town of Sylva is now a strenuous hiking trail.

According to this iteration of the story, the Boojum was well known in these hills. He hunted for precious gems in the caves of the Balsam, Blue Ridge, and Smoky Mountains.

He was around seven feet tall, covered head-to-toe in a coat of gray fur, and even had a small tail. He was thought to be quite gentle, and most early settlers and even the Cherokee weren't scared of him. In fact, many traded with him. He would give them pelts and animals in exchange for worked gems and jewelry. He had even taken to wearing a floppy felt hat the miners had given him so that he wouldn't be mistaken for a bear.

He did still love a young lady. She wasn't a farmer's daughter though. She was the daughter of a Cherokee chief. The princess was forbidden from marrying the "Wild Man" as he had no tribe and could bring little to such a marriage. The Boojum was undeterred, and he sought to buy her hand with gems. The chief said it would take a thousand times more gems than he had when he first asked for her hand.

The Boojum knew that there were miners pulling up more precious stones in the hills; early settlers had flooded into the area hoping for gold but were very pleased with the rubies and other precious stones they found

Boojum

**THE BOOJUM PLANS TO USE MOONSHINE TO GET GEMS.
ILLUSTRATION BY KARI SCHULTZ.**

instead. He knew it would take a lifetime of trading to gather enough to win his princess, but he came up with a plan.

The Boojum had learned that the miners loved to drink large jugs of moonshine. After their long days of working in the mines and caves, they would store their gems in large sacks before taking them to town. They would then buy moonshine and supplies and return up into the mountains. With this in mind, the Boojum began to scheme.

ERIKA: This is going to be amazing. I can tell!

The Boojum grabbed moonshine jugs from the nearby stills and took them to the miners, saving them from having to make the trip to town. He was so large he could carry many jugs at once. When the miners got drunk and eventually fell asleep, he would fill the empty jugs with gems and take them back down the mountain and to the Cherokee chief. The plan worked like a charm.

ERIKA: Brilliant!

He was allowed to take the hand of his princess, and they lived happily ever after in the woods of Blackrock Mountain. Their children are supposedly the gray haired "White Thangs" or light-furred Bigfoot that are seen in the Smoky Mountains to this day. If you go to Pinnacle Park and take that strenuous hike up Blackrock Mountain, about a half mile up, you will find a giant rock with a fissure down the middle. It stands out on the trail. This is supposedly a marker of the edge of the Boojum's territory.

ERIKA: I have to say I like the second story more than the first. Also, we keep hearing those rumors about the White Thangs. I wonder if they still hunt for gems?

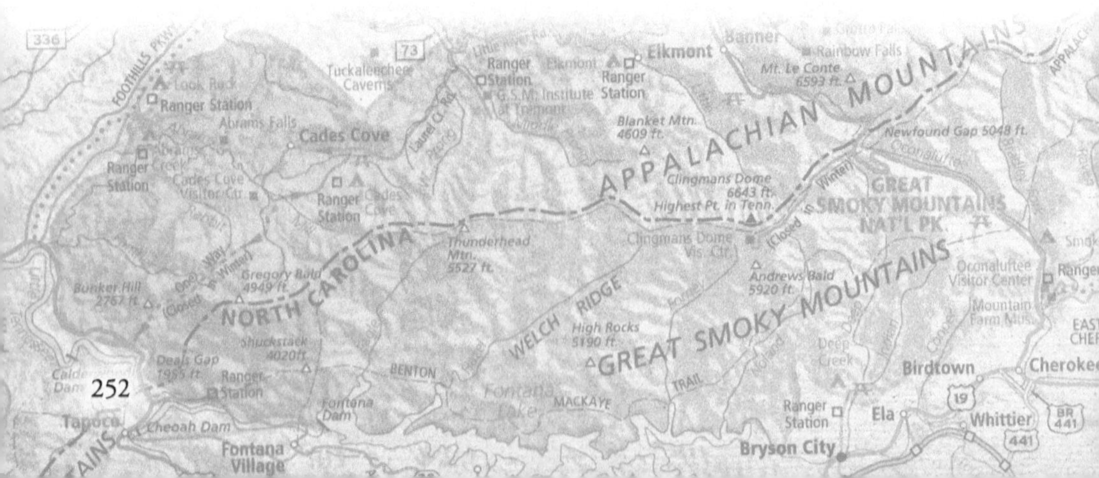

CATAMOUNT

IN 2011, THE U.S. FISH AND WILDLIFE SERVICE REMOVED the eastern cougar subspecies of *felis concolor* cougar from the Federal List of Threatened and Endangered Wildlife. They said it was to correct an anomaly that listed the species despite it having likely gone extinct many decades before the Endangered Species Act had even been drafted. The last official sighting was in 1938.

ERIKA: There is actually an old film of this creature!

Oddly enough, the catamount has a new name in the area around Sylva: the Ghost Cat. There have been numerous sightings in the area, especially in the last few years. Some describe it as a panther; others say it looks like the largest bobcat they've ever seen. One report even calls it by the infamous moniker of the Wampus Cat.

ERIKA: Do you think the spirits of catamounts turn into Wampus Cats?

MARK: Unlikely. The Wampus Cat has a unique origin story. We'll get to it in a minute.

The government agency says these sightings are most likely cougars that have traveled a great distance, like one that was tracked from South Dakota to Connecticut in 2011. Other sightings are likely bobcats that have been misidentified or possibly even a long-traveling Florida panther. They might even be simply wild big cats that have been released or escaped from captivity.

ERIKA: I think they have a less fun explanation.

These anomalous sightings are called ABCs or Alien Big Cats. This is similar to the acronym UFO for Unidentified Flying Object or UAP for

The Catamount statue in the snow from Western Carolina University. While not an accurate depiction it is the most well known. Photo provided by Western North Carolina University Alumni Association.

Unidentified Aerial Phenomena. This has led to some possibly exaggerated stories, with the creature having six legs or a third eye. There are also stories of sabertoothed tigers trailing hikers in the area.

> **ERIKA:** Wow! I think they would be more likely to eat the hikers.

The catamount may be extinct, but the sightings and witnesses say otherwise. If it is a Wampus Cat, then it's a whole other ballgame.

> **ERIKA:** Agreed! Can we discuss the Wampus Cat now?

The Wampus Cat was once a beautiful Cherokee woman who wanted to experience a pre-hunt ceremony like the ones her husband attended. Women were forbidden from seeing these sacred rites. Her curiosity overwhelmed her, and she decided she must know the secrets of the medicine man.

> **ERIKA:** She was determined. I like that.

She wrapped herself in a cougar pelt and crept near the sacred circle in the woods where the men had gathered to receive blessings before their next hunt. She inched closer and closer to take in every detail of the ritual

Catamount

THE WAMPUS CAT IS MENTIONED MANY TIMES IN THE LEGENDS OF THE APPALACHIAN MOUNTAINS. ILLUSTRATION BY KARI SCHULTZ.

until she was spotted. The shaman cursed her: the cougar skin became her own flesh, and she would never be allowed to live among humans again.

ERIKA: I do not love that.

The Cherokee storytellers say she still roams the woods to this day, forever wandering the Appalachian Mountains. She kills and eats livestock, game, and even attacks people since she can never rejoin society. Whenever strange cat noises mixed with humanlike cries echo through the hills, it is said that the Wampus Cat is on the prowl again.

ERIKA: So, she hunts hikers?

MARK: It might explain some of the thousands of missing hikers that disappear every year.

WESTERN CAROLINA UNIVERSITY RECENTLY UNVEILED THEIR NEW CATAMOUNT STATUE. IT IS MUCH MORE SAVAGE THAN THE ORIGINAL STATUE AND HAS EYES THAT GLOW FIERCELY. PHOTO BY AUTHOR.

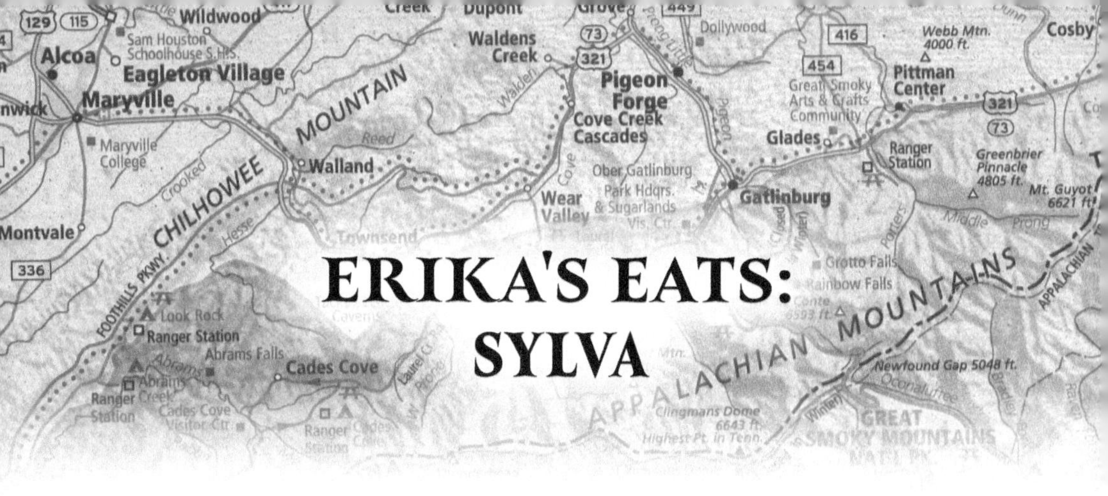

ERIKA'S EATS: SYLVA

Lucy in the Rye

This is a fun breakfast/lunch restaurant located in a row of shops on Main St. in Sylva. Besides the amazing breakfast and baked goods, I personally love their benedicts. It is also part of the walkway for a couple of local ghosts. One of them is said to be a Confederate soldier—at least the top part of him. So, you might have an extra ghostly guest at your breakfast table.

> **VALERIE:** My favorite place to eat when I visit Mark and Erika. OH! And I drew an "Appalachian Mermaid" that's on their wall!

City Lights Cafe

If you need to grab a caffeinated drink or a yummy sandwich, this might be the place. Of course, the café is also attached to an amazing bookstore with a resident cat. Although there are not many stories of spooky spirits, it is a fun place to relax and browse while enjoying a cinnamon sugar latte.

THE CITY LIGHTS CAFÉ HAS EXCELLENT TREATS WITH AN AMAZING BOOKSTORE UPSTAIRS. PHOTO BY AUTHOR.

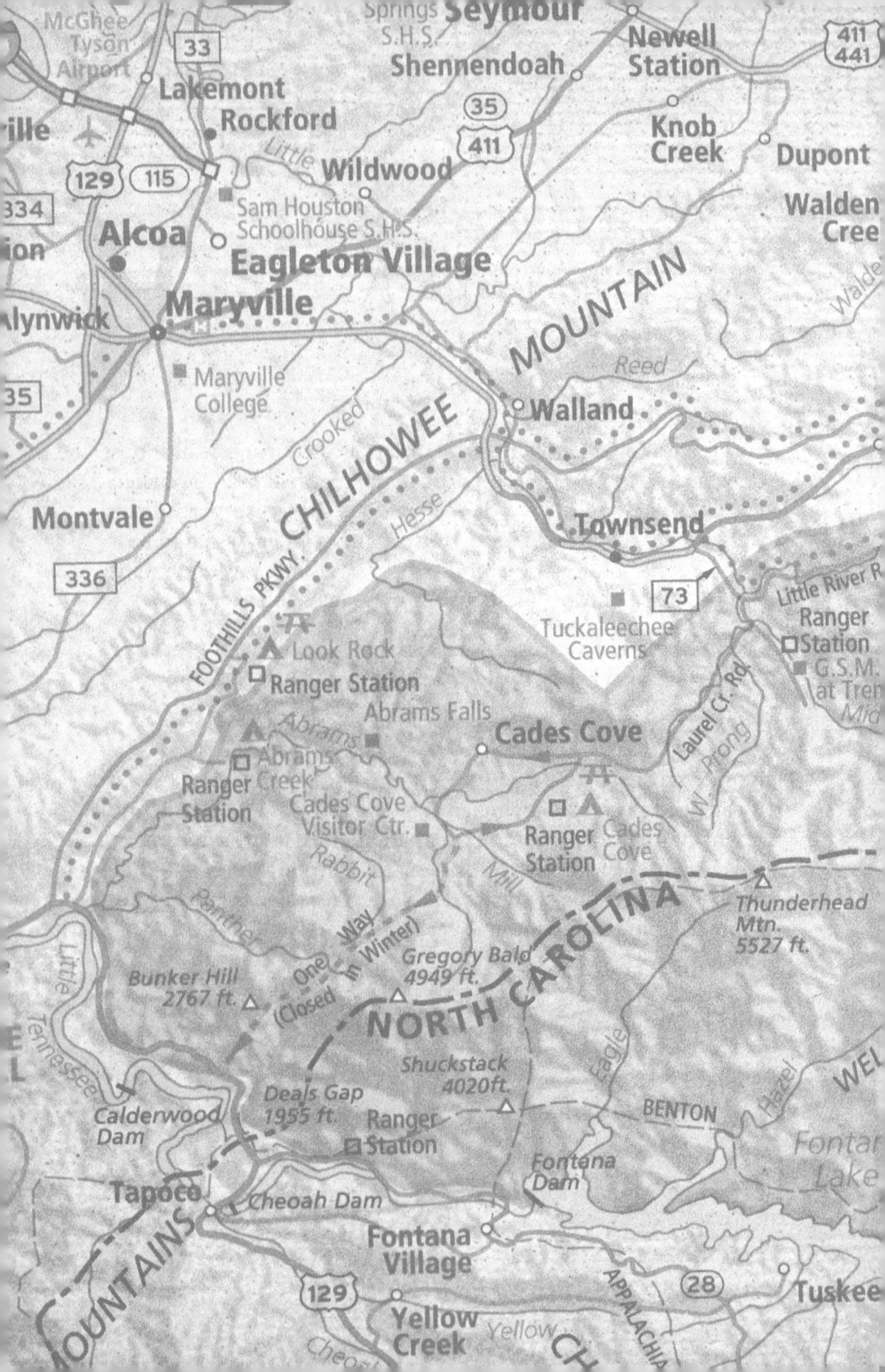

McGhee
Tyson
Airport
ville
Lakemont
Rockford
33
129 115
334
Alcoa
35
lynwick
Eagleton Village
Maryville
Little
Wildwood
Sam Houston
Schoolhouse S.H.S.
Springs
S.H.S.
Seymour
Shennendoah
35
411
Newell
Station
Knob
Creek
Dupont
411
441
Walden
Cree
Walde
Maryville
College
Montvale
336
Crooked
CHILHOWEE
Hesse
MOUNTAIN
Reed
Walland
Townsend
73
Little River R
Ranger
Station
G.S.M.
at Tren
Mid
FOOTHILLS PKWY.
Look Rock
Ranger Station
Abrams Falls
Abrams
Abrams
Creek
Ranger
Station
Cades Cove
Visitor Ctr.
Tuckaleechee
Caverns
Cades Cove
Ranger
Station
Cades
Cove
Laurel Cr. Rd.
W. Prong
NORTH CAROLINA
Thunderhead
Mtn.
5527 ft.
Rabbit
Mill
Panther
Little
Tennessee
One Way
(Closed in Winter)
Bunker Hill
2767 ft.
Gregory Bald
4949 ft.
Shuckstack
4020 ft.
Eagle
BENTON
Hazel
WE
Fonta
Lake
Calderwood
Dam
Deals Gap
1955 ft.
Ranger
Station
Fontana
Dam
Tapoco
Cheoah Dam
Fontana
Village
MOUNTAINS
129
Yellow
Creek
Cheoa
Yellow
APPALACHIA
28
CH
Tuskee
L

Cullowhee, North Carolina

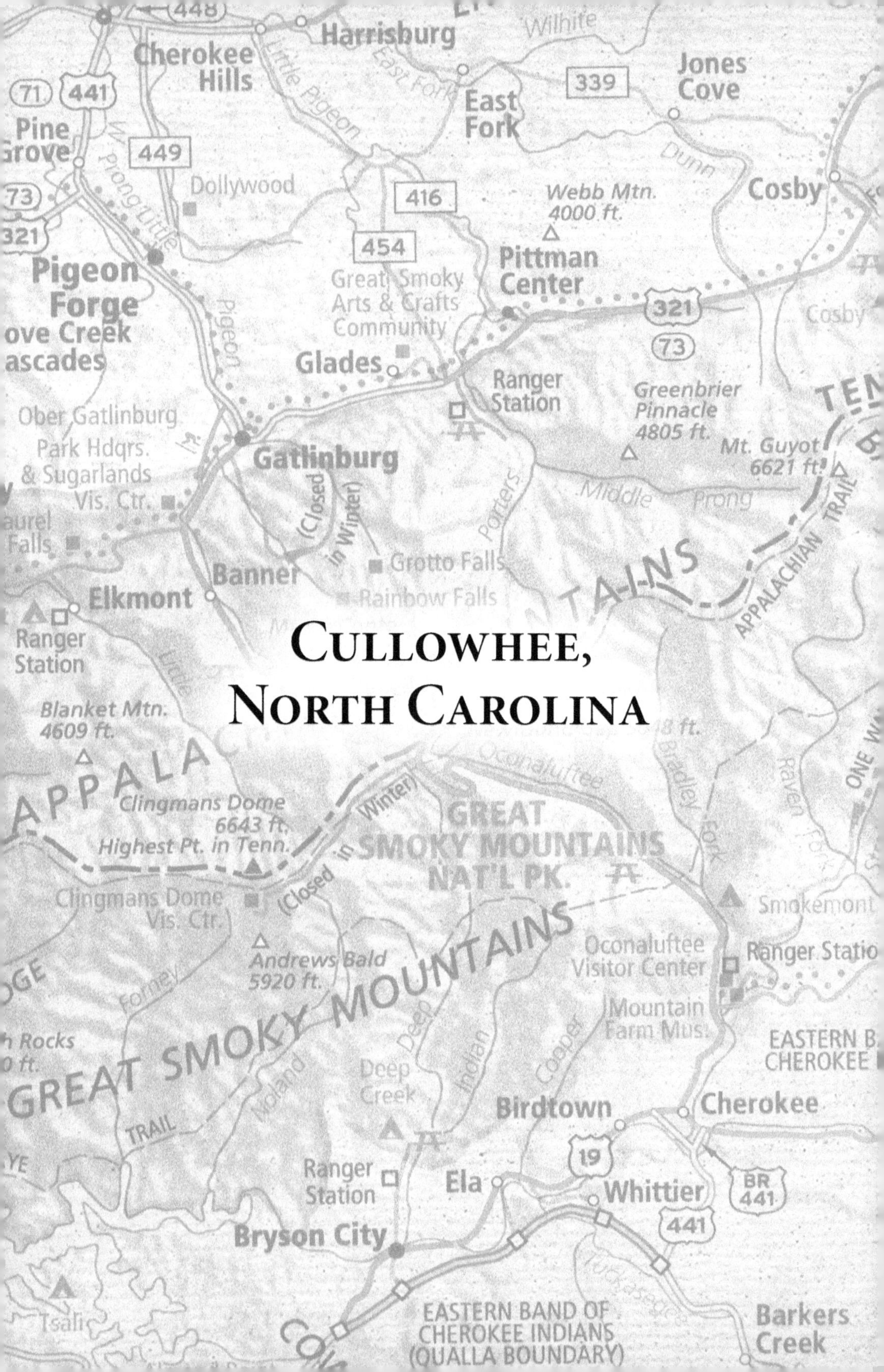

CULLOWHEE

DEPENDING ON WHO YOU ASK, THE WORD "CULLOWHEE" IS either a Cherokee word meaning "Valley of the Lillies" or an anglicized version of the Muskogee-Creek tribe's word "Corra-hi," which means "the Place of the Corra People." In the late 18th century, the European settlers noted the valley's extremely fertile land.

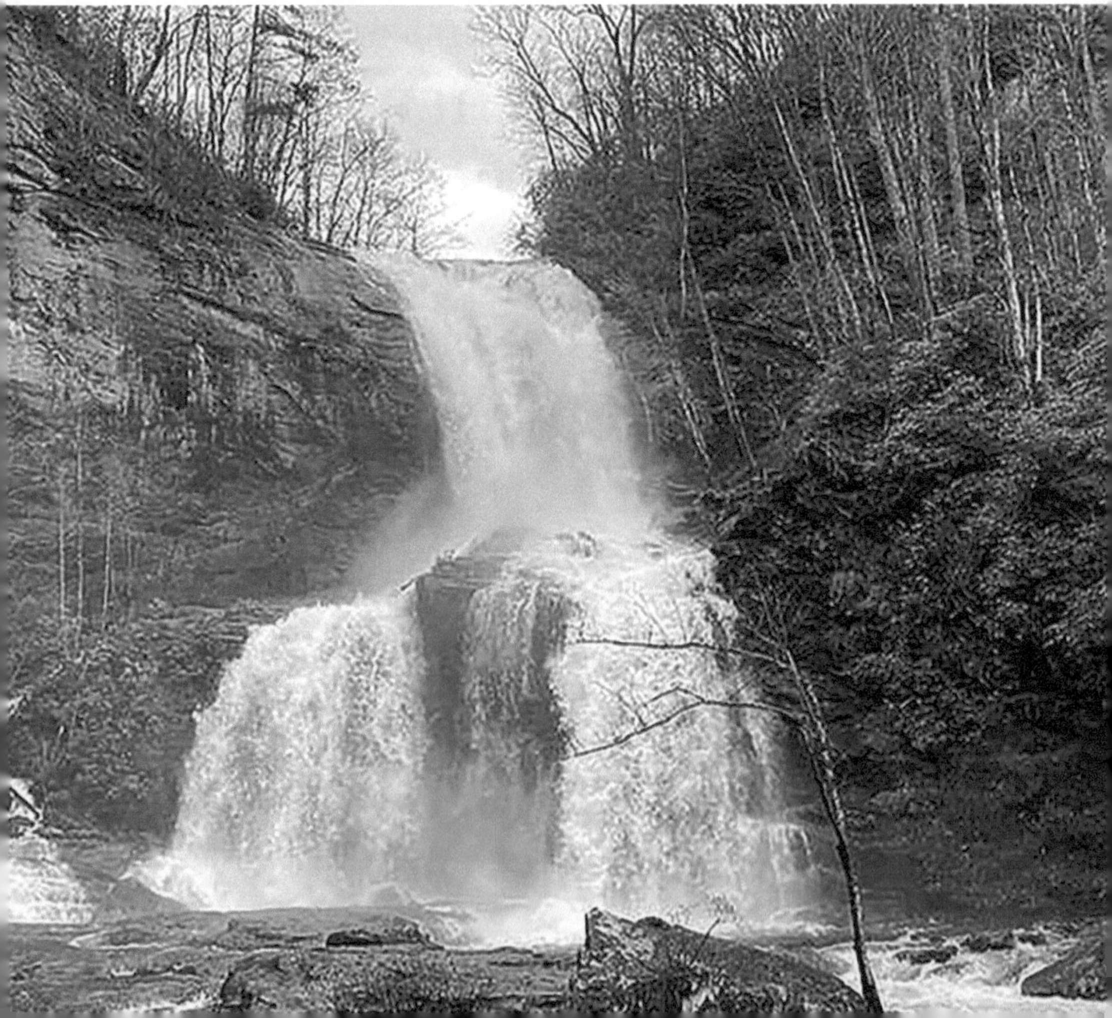

WESTERN CAROLINA UNIVERSITY

Western Carolina University was established in 1889 as a high school called Cullowhee Academy. Robert Lee Madison founded the school to train teachers and create educational opportunities for all Western North Carolina as it was booming at the time with mines, farming, and even early tourism.

The buildings themselves were built on several ancestral Cherokee mounds. The Killian Building, opened in 1966, was placed on a bulldozed mound site that had been cleared out a decade before its construction. In the 1800s, the mound was supposedly examined by researchers working for the WCU's Office of Public Relations and was cleared as having no burial objects.

> **Erika:** I feel like they said they checked, but people don't always do a good job.

> **Mark:** Especially if it was inconvenient to find something where they wanted to build.

The Killian Building is now said to be cursed by the desecration of what was once likely a sacred mound. Students report odd feelings of dread in the building. There have been a large number of reported health scares, with many students and staff reporting panic attacks over the years. It has an infamously bad reputation.

> **Erika:** See, taking shortcuts isn't good!

The Scott Residence Hall is known to have a haunted 8th floor. The history here is tragic; in the early 1990s, a young student lost her battle with depression. She hung herself in the east wing of Scott Hall. For several years, the floor was completely closed off, which led many to believe

THE **Dark Side** OF THE **Smoky Mountains**

her spirit couldn't leave the building. To this day, bathroom lights will flicker, and doors open and shut on their own. Water in the women's restroom often turns on when no one is there. Phantom footsteps echo through the halls.

ERIKA: That is tragic.

Students say that Harril Residence Hall has a haunted 5th floor. Here is another sad tale: a young girl died of an asthma attack while her boyfriend was spending the night. She suffocated in her sleep before she could be saved. The boy was thought to have committed some foul act but was eventually cleared of any wrongdoing. The 5th floor is now haunted by her spirit with many reports of poltergeist activity. Elevators act strangely on this level, sometimes not opening and returning straight to the bottom floor. Others have reported a shadow figure and feelings of being watched.

ERIKA: I feel like this campus has way more ghosts than students.

THIS VINTAGE PHOTOGRAPH SHOWS THE EARLY BUILDINGS OF WESTERN NORTH CAROLINA UNIVERSITY FROM AROUND 1920. PHOTO PROVIDED BY SPECIAL COLLECTIONS AT WESTERN NORTH CAROLINA UNIVERSITY.

Western Carolina University

The most famous haunted building here is the Moore building. There are many rumors and urban legends surrounding the 3rd floor of Moore. The story behind the legends is yet another tragedy of a young lady on campus. A young education major was murdered in the mid-1960s by a local resident. She had apparently spurned his romantic advances. The man was ultimately convicted but sentenced to only a few years at Broughton Hospital in Morganton due to family connections in local government.

> **ERIKA:** I hate that. She didn't really get justice.

Since 1917, the Moore Building has been used for many different things. It is currently closed and will likely reopen in 2025 after undergoing extensive renovations. Originally built as a women's dormitory, it also served as an infirmary in the 1930s—complete with a morgue in the basement. In the 1970s, it served as a male dormitory. In the late 1980s, it became the Nursing, Health, and Human Science Facility until closing in 2012 for the aforementioned renovations.

On campus, you can hear many rumors of tragedies in Moore Hall. In addition to the young woman's spirit there, a teacher was supposedly murdered in the building sometime in the 1980s. Another woman may have been slain there in the 1920s. The common denominator in all these stories is the 3rd floor.

> **ERIKA:** Seems like the building needs spiritual cleansing.

George Frizell, a WCU alum and Head of Special Collections at Hunter Library, says all these stories are just rumors. He's heard them all and found no documented records of any of them. He notes how similar the stories are to other reported hauntings at schools all over the world.

> **ERIKA:** A college official denied something that might deter students? I would say that is surprising, but we all know it's not.

Quincy Thomas, a former student, says that the rumors may not be true, but his time there was certainly haunted.

"I used to be a part of a paranormal team that went all over Western North Carolina to haunted locations like Helen's Bridge, Balsam Mountain Inn, The Road to Nowhere, etc.," Thomas said. "They all have this eerie energy around them. None of that compared to the bad feelings in Moore

THE **Dark Side** OF THE **Smoky Mountains**

Hall, Scott Hall, and the Killian Building at WCU. We've got so many EVPs [Electronic Voice Phenomena], echoing footsteps, and strange lights from investigations in those buildings when they were empty of everyone but us. There's certainly more going on in Moore than they want us to know."

Students and visitors to the campus are asked to keep an open mind and open eyes. Also, be mindful of the Cherokee history that once called this area home.

ERIKA: Okay. I am ready to leave this spooky campus. Where to next?

WESTERN CAROLINA UNIVERSITY TODAY USES THE CATAMOUNT AS THEIR MASCOT. THE MANY GHOST STORIES HERE HAVE NO HISTORICAL BACKGROUND, YET THEY PERSIST. PHOTO PROVIDED BY WESTERN CAROLINA UNIVERSITY ARCHIVES.

JUDACULLA ROCK

There are a ton of Cherokee stories of Tsul`kälû´, who inhabited these hills long before the Cherokee came to the Smoky Mountains. It is said that his name means "he has them slanting." Supposedly, this refers to his eyes. He was said to be seven feet tall and had 14 fingers and toes with 7 on each hand and foot. In some tales, he is covered in a red hair like a Bigfoot or a Wild Man.

> **ERIKA:** 14 fingers? He sounds like he would be good at basketball.

The stone of Judaculla Rock earned its name from the legendary creature's anglicized name. There are those that say it was carved by Tsul`kälû´ as a map of the area and game hunting rules for the early peoples of the valley. There is another story that Tsul`kälû´ jumped down, and his feet made the strange impressions on the huge rock when he landed. Some theorize that it's a map of the stars and towns in the area, demarking the realm the Tsul`kälû´ ruled.

> **ERIKA:** I think I love the star map idea most of all!

There are other strange coincidences when you combine stories of Tsul`kälû´ and the Moon-Eyed People. The stories align with the fact that there were two other stones at some point; one was buried in a mining accident and the other is supposedly buried in a nearby quarry, according to reports from early settlers, though it was never fully excavated.

> **ERIKA:** So, we might only have part of the map?

> **MARK:** It's like a jigsaw with missing pieces. I hope we find those other rocks someday.

THE **Dark Side** OF THE **Smoky Mountains**

In a limited dig, archaeologists from Western Carolina University found quarrying tools dating the large soapstone to between 3000 B.C. and 200 B.C. Sadly, Judaculla Rock is quickly eroding, which makes it difficult to study. There are several signs here depicting the history of the rock and some of the Cherokee stories. Steps are being taken to help prevent erosion; currently, there is a viewing platform with interpretive signs.

ERIKA: It is a fun place to visit, and there is a little free library right next to it.

MARK: We all love those little free libraries!

To the Cherokee, the petroglyphs mark the trail from the old townhouse at Cullowhee "Tsul`kälû´s Place" and Tsul`kälû´s reported home on Tanasee Bald, also known as Tsunegûñyĭ. Those who theorize it is a map point to the locations of several towns and former mounds, which are marked on the rock with spiral patterns. Others try to point out the Cherokee had no written language at this point. Owl Goingback, author and friend of the podcast, likes to point out that "it's always a white man who says that."

ERIKA: I love Owl! His *Crota* monster is terrifying though.

JUDACULLA ROCK IS COVERED WITH PICTOGRAPHS THAT HAVE NEVER BEEN TRANSLATED. SADLY, THEY ARE FADING AWAY. PHOTO BY AUTHOR.

Judaculla Rock

Similar soapstone boulders have been found in western North Carolina and northern Georgia. Brinley Rock, Track Rock, and Sprayberry Rock are all still being studied, but none have the sheer number of markings as this stone. In fact, no stone east of the Mississippi has this many petroglyphs.

One tale of the rock states that Tsul`kälû´ claimed a bride among the Cherokee, and he took her with him to the Spirit World. Her brother and mother wanted to see her again, so they came to Cullowhee. There, they fasted for seven days outside of a cave where the sister lived with Tsul`kälû´ and the other Nunnehi. Unfortunately, the brother did not fast on the last day and ate some meat. This angered Tsul`kälû´ so much that he slew the brother. His bride was so distraught she asked to return home through where Judaculla Rock is now.

ERIKA: Did he let her go?

Tsul`kälû´ decided on a compromise. He would not give up his bride, but faithful warriors and the women of the earthly tribe would be welcomed into the spirit world upon following the instructions he placed on the stone with lightning. Other Cherokee traditions mark the rock as a place of honor and use it as a focus for several rituals through the turning of the year. Many even spend seven days fasting at the rock hoping to enter the spirit world.

ERIKA: That is awesome!

There are other theories that the rock is an etching of the Battle of Taliwa, where the Cherokee defeated the Creek tribe in 1755. Some archaeologists believe it is from a pre-historic tribe who lived here near the end of the last Ice Age. No one really knows.

ERIKA: Where is science in all of this?

MARK: Soap stone and the carvings are impossible to
date with our current technology. Archaeology
has sadly never been an exact science.

THE **Dark Side** OF THE **Smoky Mountains**

The rock has also been the site of numerous "initiation" rituals for students at Western Carolina State University. There are stories of strange sounds emanating from the rock after dark. Several ghost-like apparitions have been seen here on many occasions. Along with a nearby cemetery, it has a well-earned spiritual reputation. It is well worth the visit to see an ancient piece of history that may bear the markings of a wrathful god of the Cherokee. Visit soon before erosion smoothes away the remaining pictographs.

THIS POSTCARD SHOWS HOW DETAILED JUDACULLA ROCK LOOKED BEFORE THE ELEMENTS TRULY STARTED TAKING THEIR TOLL. CARD PROVIDED BY THE JACKSON COUNTY HISTORICAL SOCIETY.

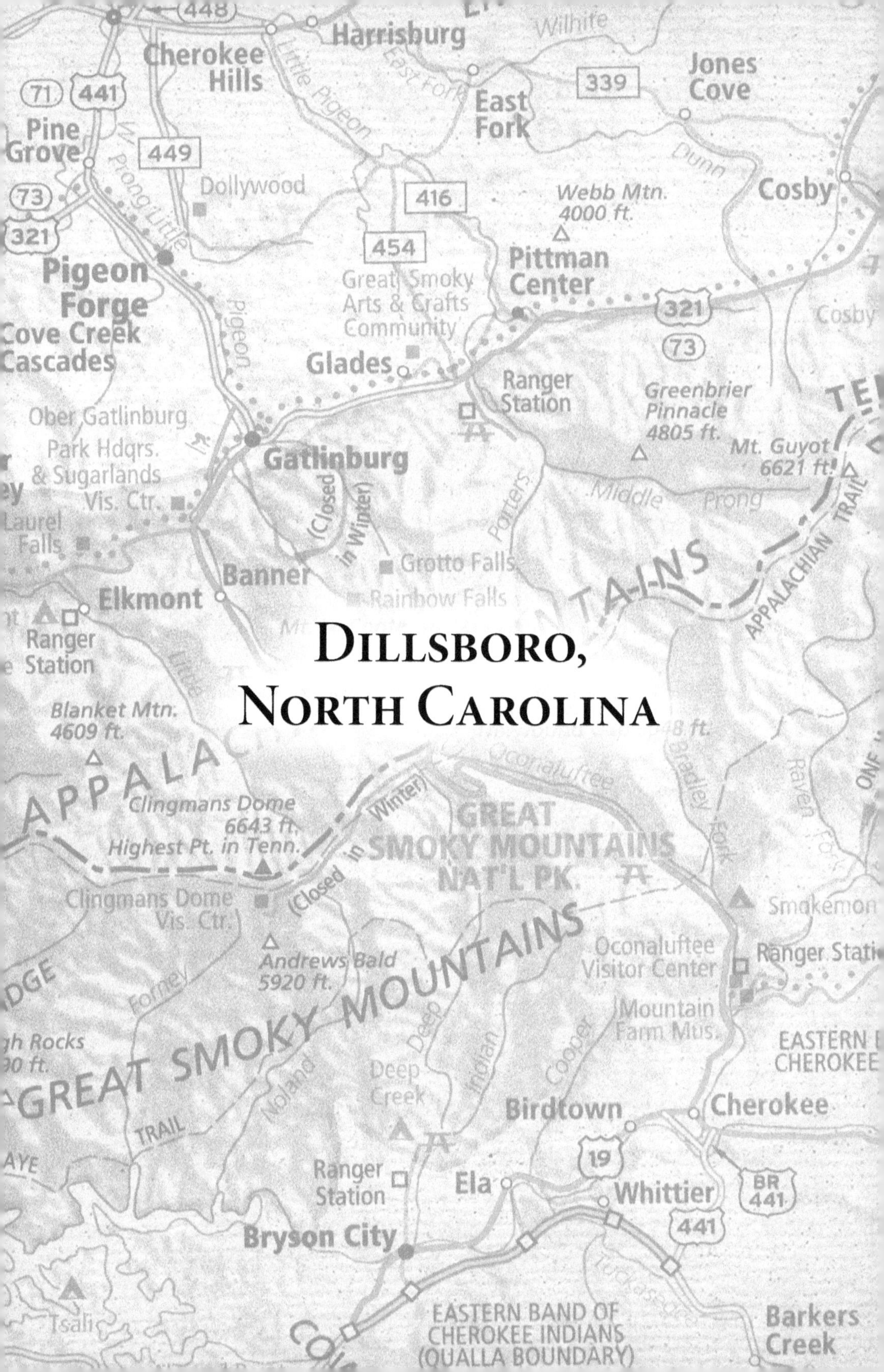

448
Harrisburg
Wilhite
Jones Cove
339
71 441
Cherokee Hills
East Fork
East Fork
Cosby
Pine Grove
449
Dollywood
416
Webb Mtn. 4000 ft.
Dunn
Cosby
73
454
Great Smoky Arts & Crafts Community
Pittman Center
321
321
Pigeon Forge
Pigeon
73
Cove Creek Cascades
Glades
Ranger Station
Greenbrier Pinnacle 4805 ft.
TENN
Ober Gatlinburg
Park Hdqrs. & Sugarlands Vis. Ctr.
Gatlinburg
Middle
Prong
Mt. Guyot 6621 ft.
Laurel Falls
(Closed in Winter)
Porters
MOUNTAINS
APPALACHIAN TRAIL
Banner
Grotto Falls
Rainbow Falls
Elkmont
Ranger Station
Blanket Mtn. 4609 ft.
DILLSBORO, NORTH CAROLINA
Oconaluftee
Bradley
Raven Fork
ONE
APPALA
Clingmans Dome 6643 ft.
Highest Pt. in Tenn.
(Closed in Winter)
GREAT SMOKY MOUNTAINS NAT'L PK.
Clingmans Dome Vis. Ctr.
Andrews Bald 5920 ft.
GREAT SMOKY MOUNTAINS
Oconaluftee Visitor Center
Smokemont
Ranger Station
RIDGE
Forney
Mountain Farm Mus.
gh Rocks 90 ft.
Deep Creek
Indian
Cooper
EASTERN CHEROKEE
GREAT SMOKY MOUNTAINS
TRAIL
Noland
Deep Creek
Birdtown
Cherokee
AYE
Ranger Station
Ela
19
Tsali
Bryson City
Whittier
441
BR 441
EASTERN BAND OF CHEROKEE INDIANS (QUALLA BOUNDARY)
Barkers Creek

DILLSBORO

THE TOWN OF DILLSBORO WAS ORIGINALLY CALLED NEW Webster. In 1889, the state allowed it to change its name to Dillsboro after William Allen Dills, who had let the town use his farmland to build their basic infrastructure. The Dills house is still there and is now called the Riverwood Shops. It overlooks both Scott's Creek and the Tuckasegee River. The home was the town's first post office.

There's a legend here in Dillsboro that's been repeated so much that we must include it here. Sadly, it doesn't hold up under the brutal eye of history.

ERIKA: So, it's a campfire tale?

THE SIGN FOR HISTORIC DILLSBORO SITS ACROSS FROM THE WONDERFUL WHISTLE STOP INN, A GREAT BED AND BREAKFAST. PHOTO PROVIDED BY DILLSBORO CHAMBER OF COMMERCE.

JARETT HOUSE VAMPIRE

THIS STORY GOES LIKE THIS. IN THE SPRING OF 1788, THE Alfort family moved to Dillsboro. T There were rumors that the Alforts were descended from European royalty. Dr. Alfort bought land by the river and built an impressive colonial home; he even opened an office and pharmacy in the front rooms of the house.

The townspeople were very happy that a doctor had arrived, but it was odd he would set up shop in such a rural community. Several prominent citizens went to the doctor but died mysteriously afterward. Rumors and accusations flew about Dr. Alfort, but the local minister calmed the people.

That fall, the minister's young daughter was found dead in her bed with puncture marks in her throat. The minister's wife swore she saw a dark form hovering over her daughter, but she had been paralyzed with fear and unable to stop the attack. The town formed a posse to hunt for the vampire in their midst but found nothing.

ERIKA: I love a good European vampire!

The town was plagued by frequent reports of a large, dark flying shape. One night, a young boy from over the hill came to tell his grandfather that something was attacking his family. The townsfolk formed a posse again and found the boy's parents and two sisters dead with strange marks on their necks. The black form was seen retreating over the hill. They chased it to the Alfort house.

ERIKA: This sounds like one of the Universal
Monster movies.

Dr. Alfort met the mob assembled at his door but refused to let the men inside. The sheriff arrived, and they dragged the doctor away and tied him to a nearby tree. Inside, they discovered that the upstairs bedrooms were empty. In the basement, however, they found three coffins, and Mrs. Alfort was sleeping in one of them.

THE JARRETT HOUSE IS CURRENTLY UNDER RENOVATION AND HOPES TO REOPEN SOON.
PHOTO BY AUTHOR.

The sheriff and minister proclaimed the Alfort family to be vampires. The young son was never found, but the doctor and his wife were hanged and burned inside the house.

ERIKA: That is not how you typically kill vampires.

MARK: Did I say this makes sense?

The land the house was on is where the Jarrett House now stands. There are a few issues with this legend. Firstly, Dillsboro wasn't a town or even the name of the settlement here in 1788. There are obviously some modern vampire horror elements thrown in, like puncture marks. That is often the case with these oral history stories.

The other thing is that the Jarret House was built shortly after the founding of the city in 1884 by W.A. Dills, the founder of Dillsboro. There are no records of any other house ever being there. The Jarret House was originally the Mount Beulah Hotel and built to accommodate the growing number of railroad guests. It was in operation for over a century. Its famous dessert was Jarret House vinegar pie which is tastier than it sounds.

ERIKA: I hope so. Vinegar pie sounds terrible.

272

Jarett House Vampire

Recently, the house fell victim to the declining economy and was sent to the auction block in 2020. As of the time of this writing, it was purchased and is undergoing renovations. There are supposedly several ghosts that haunt the building. Its dark reputation is perhaps emboldened by the rumor that the missing Alfort son might still be lingering in the area, or maybe it's just another tall tale of the Appalachian Mountains.

ERIKA: When it reopens, I'm sure you'll want to see if there are any spirits still in residence.

AN HISTORIC PAINTING OF THE JARRET HOUSE HANGS IN THE LOBBY. PHOTO PROVIDED BY THE DILLSBORO CHAMBER OF COMMERCE.

COWEE TUNNEL

JUST OUTSIDE OF DILLSBORO, RESTING ON THE HORSESHOE bend of the Tuckasegee River, lies a haunted train tunnel with a very tragic history. This track is the home to ghosts who date back a century or more.

ERIKA: Are we getting back into the Wayback Machine?

MARK: You called it. You're getting good at this.

In 1882, the Western North Carolina Railroad was trying to shorten the bend of the railroad at the horseshoe turn in the river. They decided to build the Cowee Tunnel. Experienced rail workers were hard to find, so they rented convicts from the nearby prisons. Hundreds of prisoners were brought in and forced to live in stockades along the Tuckasegee River. Many were from Brushy Mountain, and others were from Old Craggy Prisons.

ERIKA: I didn't know you could "rent" convicts.

MARK: Haven't you been paying attention? That's what all those prisons we've visited have done.

Most of the prisoners were young Black men, imprisoned for petty crimes, and others were, of course, wrongfully convicted. A young WNC railroad worker named Will Sandlin watched these prisoners be treated almost as badly as they'd been during the slave trade just a couple of decades earlier.

ERIKA: I hate to hear that.

On the morning of December 30, 1882, guard Fleet Foster ordered his chain gang onto a ferry to cross the river and work on the bridge.

Cowee Tunnel

According to Sandlin, his gang housed some of the more dangerous criminals in the camp, so they wore extra heavy chains on their ankles. Shortly after embarking, the ferry began to take on water toward the end of the boat.

ERIKA: I don't like where this is going.

The men quickly moved to the prow, and the sudden motion nearly stood the boat high on one end. As a result, the boat instantly capsized. The men, weighed down by their chains, were dragged quickly to the bottom of the river. In all, 19 convicts' bodies were found days after in the freezing cold river.

ERIKA: That is horrible.

The convicts' ages ranged from 15 to 55 years of age at the time of their deaths. The 19 men, who were all African American, were buried in a mass grave on a ridgeline near the tunnel. Their names were Alexander Adams, Nelson Bowser, Orren Brooks, Moses Brown, Albert Cowan, Lewis Davis, David Dozier, Charles Eason, James Fisher, Jim McCallum, Thomas Miller, John Newsom, Robert Robinson, George Rush, Jerry

HISTORIC PHOTO OUT OF COWEE TUNNEL FROM AROUND 1890 A FEW YEARS AFTER OPENING. PHOTO COURTESY OF SPECIAL COLLECTIONS AT WESTERN NORTH CAROLINA UNIVERSITY.

EIGHTEEN CONVICTS DROWNED.

A Flat Boat Sinks With Them in the Tuckaseegee River.

Raleigh News-Observer.

A few days since we published an account of the trip of Governor Jarvis to the Western North Carolina Railroad, and gave an account of the operations at the Cowee tunnel, which is near the bank of the Tuckaseegee River, in Jackson county. On that section of the road are employed about 200 convicts. Yesterday Lieutenant-Governor James L. Robinson, who came down from his home in Macon county, brought the news of a horrible disaster at the crossing of the Tuckaseegee River, the news of which he received from Mr. W. B. Troy, the officer in charge of convicts on the Western North Carolina Railroad.

It appears that the camp of the convicts, that is, the stockade in which they

NEWSPAPER COVERAGE OF THE DISASTER WHILE DIGGING THE COWEE TUNNEL. RALEIGH NEWS-OBSERVER JANUARY 8, 1883.

Cowee Tunnel

Smith, George Tice, Allen Tillman, Sampson Ward, and John Whitfield. Their graves remain unmarked.

ERIKA: It might be good for the state to at least put a plaque to commemorate them.

MARK: There's a historical highway marker, but that's it.

The guard, Foster Fleet, nearly drowned, but one of the convicts named Anderson Drake came to his aid and saved his life. The man dragged Fleet to the shore and then got him up the bank to safety. Some reports on the Cowee Tunnel Disaster claim it was another convict named Samuel Pickett that did the rescue. There are two stories that claim the savior was later beaten or pardoned. Either way, it appears there was a cover up to shift blame.

The Cowee Tunnel has been plagued by tragedy since the death of those 19 men. There have been cave-ins, derailments, and more. Stories claim the seepage in the tunnel are the tears of the dead men buried in the hillside. Others say the tunnel was cursed by the convict that had been beaten, even though his heroism saved his guard. Either way, it is filled with an odd sense of foreboding.

ERIKA: Sounds like not all those people are at rest.

Some people come to the tunnel on foot to see it in person, but it is on private property, and trespassing is a crime. Besides, it is nearly 700 feet in length, narrow, and extremely dangerous. There's a much better way to see it, but we'll have to go to nearby Bryson City for that.

ERIKA: I have a feeling we get to go on a train!

THOUGH NOT THE COWEE TUNNEL 19, THEY WOULD HAVE LOOKED VERY SIMILAR TO THESE INCARCERATED LABORERS THAT WERE ALSO WORKING ON THE WESTERN NORTH CAROLINA RAILROAD FROM 1890. PHOTOGRAPH PROVIDED BY HUNTER LIBRARY SPECIAL COLLECTIONS, WESTERN CAROLINA UNIVERSITY.

ERIKA'S EATS: DILLSBORO

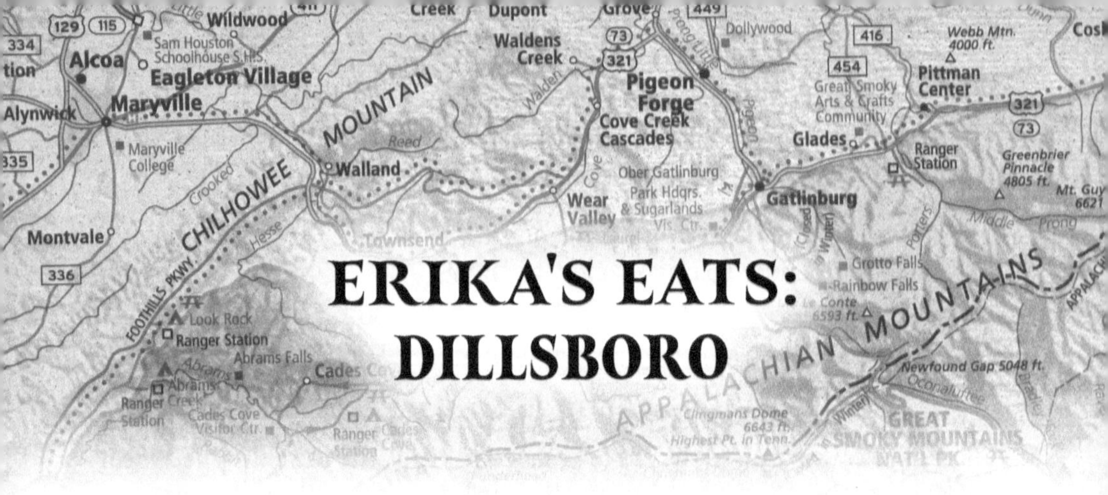

Foragers Canteen

This is an amazing farm-to-table restaurant located in the old train station in Dillsboro. As we know, many people have passed through, and there might be a few spirits still hanging around. I love the pecan-crusted trout, and Mark will definitely dive into the piggy's in a basket. Their fries are topped with pulled pork, beer cheese, and candied bacon.

Innovation Station

Right next door to Foragers, you can grab a local IPA or cider and look out into the cute city of Dillsboro alongside the train track. I love a Noble Tart cherry cider myself.

Forager's Canteen is a frequent stop for the Great Smoky Mountain Railroad. Photo provided by Forager's Canteen.

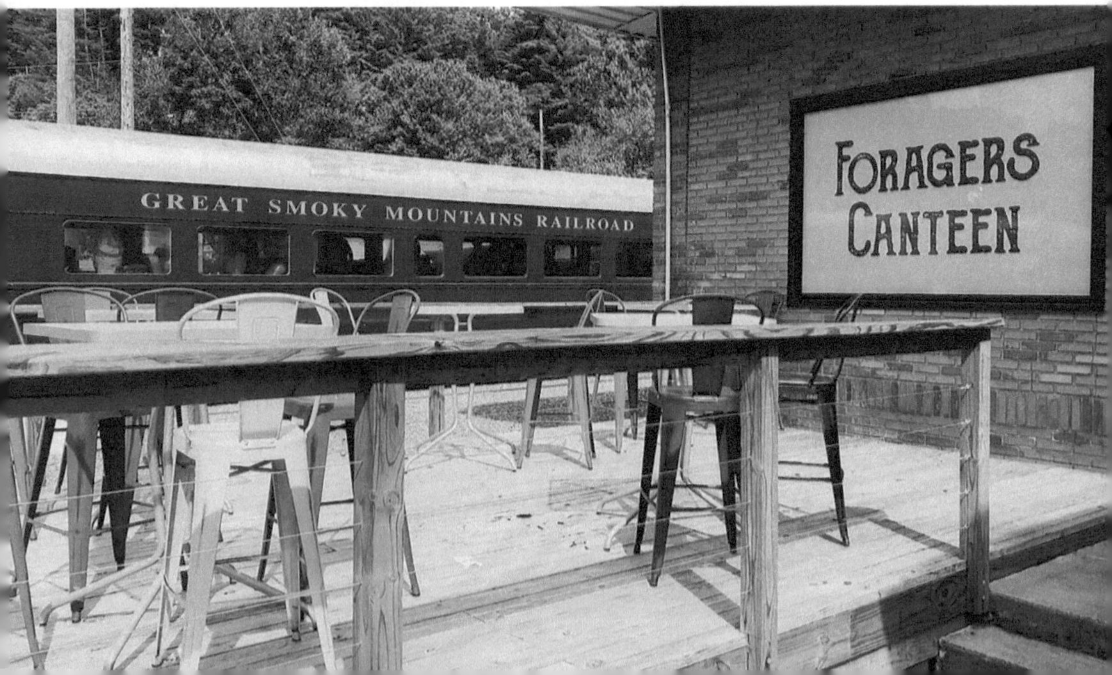

Bryson City, North Carolina

BRYSON CITY

ORIGINALLY, THE VILLAGE OF KITUWA WAS LOCATED HERE alongside the Tuckasegee River. Indigenous cultures have lived in this area for an estimated 14,000 years. Kituwa was the oldest Cherokee village and often called "mother town." The mound where the suspected council house may have been located is just outside of Bryson City. You see it as you head out toward the nearby town of Franklin.

In 1567, a chief from Kituwa met with some of the early Spanish explorers to the area; this meeting was documented by explorer Juan Pardo. During the Revolutionary War, many of the Cherokee allied with the British, so American soldiers burned out Kituwa in 1776. The Cherokee still consider the site sacred and are part of the conservation efforts there today.

THIS ANGELIC GRAVE MARKER ON THE NEARBY HILL LOOKS OUT OVER BRYSON CITY BELOW. PHOTO BY AUTHOR.

GREAT SMOKY MOUNTAINS RAILROAD

THERE WERE SEVERAL DIFFERENT RAIL LINES LOCATED here. The Great Smoky Mountains Railroad (GSMR) started with the Murphy Branch of the Western North Carolina Railroad which ran folks through the western parts of North Carolina and Eastern Tennessee. As the automobile became more and more popular, the railway lines in the area began slowly closing down. They would make their last full freight run in 1985.

> **ERIKA:** I think people sometimes forget that trains are still a huge part of moving goods and people in this country.

The state of North Carolina decided to purchase the tracks of the Dillsboro to Murphy line and began to restore them. In 1988, the GSMR was formed, and the first scenic train rides began. Today, more than 200,000 passengers enjoy this train annually.

> **ERIKA:** I am one of them.

There are several excursions along the GSMR lines. They vary in length from four-hour treks to full-day trips. They often have themed days like *Polar Express* rides in the winter. The Tuckasegee River Excursion is the one that will take you through the haunted Cowee Tunnel. You will also pass the staged train crash from the Harrison Ford and Tommy Lee Jones movie *The Fugitive*. Pieces of that train and the prisoner bus are still right next to the track there.

> **ERIKA:** It is neat to see it because I love that movie.

> **MARK:** The famous dam scene was filmed at Fontana Dam.

The Great Smoky Mountains Railroad is an amazing way to experience the grandeur of the Smokies. Photo provided by The Great Smoky Mountains Railroad.

ERIKA: Tommy Lee Jones and Harrison Ford!

One engineer, who worked the line when it was still active in the 1940s, spoke of a shadowy figure that stood near the tracks on the Judson to Bryson City run. The figure would inevitably vanish into the woods nearby. He thought he had imagined it until another engineer asked about seeing a similar thing at the exact same location. They learned that a man had been struck by the train and died there in the 1920s. The dark shape is still seen at that same spot by some of the current engineers.

ERIKA: NOPE!

A travel tip: avoid the enclosed cars in the summer as it gets stifling hot. Enjoy the open-air cars. In the wintertime, do the opposite. Fall is when you will find the most spectacular views of the Smoky Mountains' autumn foliage. There are some food options on some of the routes, but it is best to eat up ahead of time in case they sell out.

ERIKA: There is also a fun popcorn shop nearby called Pop-N-Jacks if you want to stock up before getting on the train. I did!

The remains of the staged train wreck from the 1993 movie The Fugitive can still be seen as you ride the Great Smoky Mountains Railroad. Photo provided by The Great Smoky Mountains Railroad.

ILLINOIS
SOUTH
90

FRYEMONT INN

THANKS TO THE BOOM OF TOURISTS INTO BRYSON CITY due to the Southern Railroad, Amos and Lillian Frye, both prominent attorneys in Asheville, decided to build their dream hotel here in the Smokies. They hired Richard Sharp Smith, who was the supervising architect for the Biltmore House in Asheville.

> **ERIKA:** This is going to get spooky, isn't it?

It was during the great Chestnut Blight in the early 1920s that the hotel was built. Many of the trees used to create the hotel are no longer able to be used in construction. Smith also hired local artisans and many Cherokee stone masons to build the fireplaces and adornments in the hotel. The sum of these unique features made this inn truly a marvel. The hotel finally opened in 1923.

Amos and Lillian's original home is located next door and is now called the Randolph House. It is still owned by descendants of the Frye family. The hotel itself is now owned by the Brown family, and they have been running the place for decades.

Several paranormal teams have told us of encountering a strange presence at the Fryemont. One historical haunting of the place was the ghost of Amos Frye himself. His spirit is typically seen in room 216.

> **ERIKA:** I feel a Wayback trip coming up. I'm grabbing my popcorn!

In the early 1930s, a couple were staying for the season at the hotel. They'd been there many times. The father had been an engineer for the Alcoa Company and was looking to help acquire land for the future Fontana Dam. Fontana Village had not yet been built, so they were staying at the inn.

They often hung out with Amos and Lillian Frye and became close friends. They would often play games and dine together. They always

stayed in room 216. At the end of the season, they returned to their home in Atlanta but kept in touch with the Frye family.

ERIKA: That all seems normal.

In 1947, the couple returned one more time to the Fryemont Inn. Again, they requested room 216. Lillian was still running the hotel with the help of her daughter Lois Randolph. She was overjoyed the couple had returned after such a long time.

After checking in, the couple quickly retired for the evening as it had been a long trip. The wife was awakened in the middle of the night by her husband, who was frantically throwing all their unpacked items back into their suitcases.

ERIKA: Ummm... that seems weird.

The following account is retold on the Fryemont website:
"Wake up! We're leaving!" he exclaimed.
The wife asked what was going on. What had happened?
"I just woke up, and Amos Frye was standing at the foot of our bed," he said.
Amos had been dead for 12 years at that point.
The woman later told the innkeepers, "You have to understand, my husband was an engineer. He didn't believe in ghosts. But he refused to

ever again step foot in the Fryemont Inn."

ERIKA: I am with him on that! NOPE!

The current owners have no personal encounters to speak of but are glad to retell the tale to any guests. They are even open to ghost hunters who might want to rent the hotel off-season for their own investigations.

ONE OF THE COMFORTABLE ROOMS IN THE HAUNTED FRYEMONT INN. PHOTO PROVIDED BY THE FRYEMONT INN.

THE ROAD TO NOWHERE

THE BUILDING OF FONTANA DAM DESTROYED MANY SET-tled places in the valleys near Bryson City. One town completely submerged was Judson. Another town that had to be razed was Proctor. It was named for Moses and Patience Proctor, two of the first European settlers in the valley.

> **ERIKA:** Wow! I think it is incredible that an entire town was just gone.

> **MARK:** With the recent flooding disasters, some towns are simply no longer there not too far from here. At least these folks had warning.

As you leave Bryson City, there's one stretch of road marked by a warning sign. It reads, "Welcome to The Road to No-Where: A Broken Promise! 1943-? No more wilderness."

> **ERIKA:** That sounds ominous.

If you follow the road for several miles, it eventually stops just before a long, dark tunnel. The road, as the name suggests, goes nowhere. It ends just past the tunnel at the mountain wall. There are hiking trails that continue onward, but the road just stops.

> **ERIKA:** Why is that?

The trails continue on to the old ghost town of Proctor, now deep in the woods of the Smoky Mountains. The town of Judson, however, was completely flooded, but the tops of the buildings can be seen when the lake runs low. Many of the families displaced by the dam now call Bryson City their home.

> **ERIKA:** But why does the road just *stop?*

THE **Dark Side** OF THE **Smoky Mountains**

To allow these families access to the old cities, ancestral homes, and cemeteries, the Tennessee Valley Authority promised to build the road from Bryson City all the way to Deals Gap. Unfortunately, only those six miles and the tunnel were completed before construction was halted in the 1970s. The families never forgot and fought for decades. In 2018, a $52 million dollar settlement was made with the families.

ERIKA: That is terrible. It seems like completing the road might have been a better idea.

Karen Marcus, a psychologist in her 60s who has five generations of ancestors whose gravesites are now only accessible by arduous hiking trails, says, "The promise was not a financial settlement. The promise was to build the road. The promise will never be kept."

She also says there are no ghosts there. "There's no ghostly whatever. It's just an eerie feeling in that long tunnel as you walk to a dead place, not a place of the dead."

ERIKA: That place is creepy!

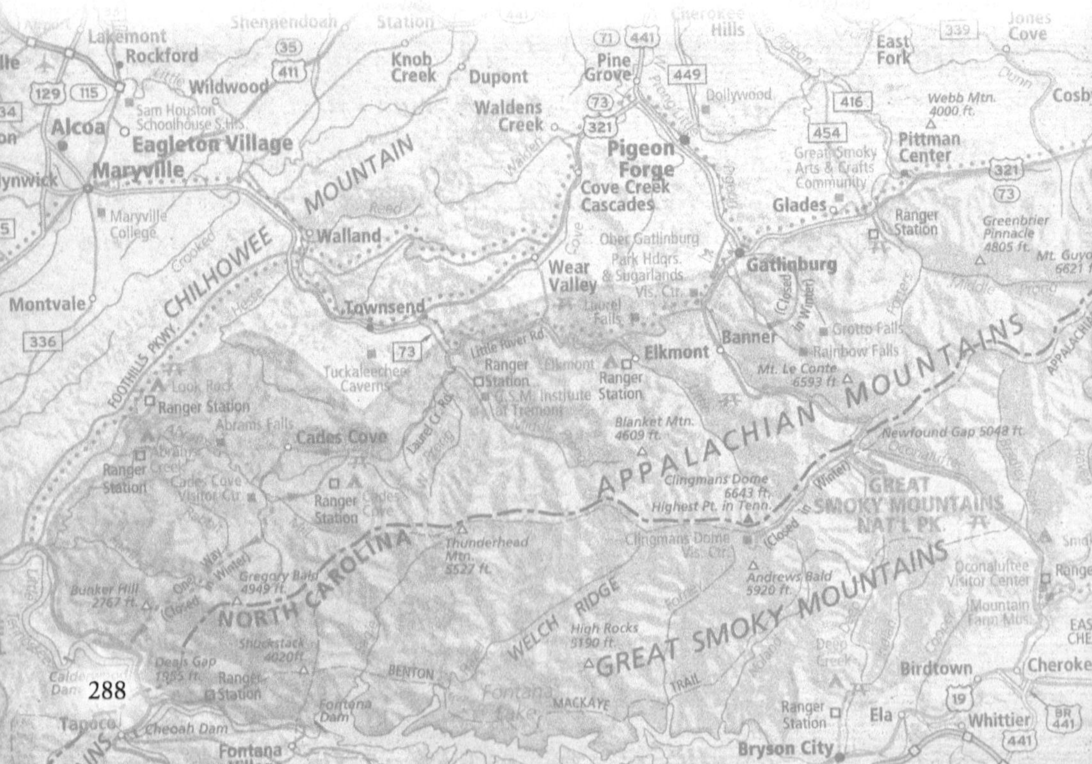

Franklin, North Carolina

FRANKLIN

THE TOWN OF FRANKLIN, NORTH CAROLINA IS KNOWN AS the Gem Capital of the World. It is in the heart of the Blue Ridge Mountains and the foothills of the Great Smoky Mountains and surrounded by the Nantahala National Forest. The Cherokee word "Nantahala" means "Land of the Noonday Sun." It's an appropriate name for a forest filled with so many gorges and hills; the sun only reaches some areas when directly overhead.

Spanish explorers came here under the Conquistador Hernando De Soto in 1540 seeking gold. They came across the Cherokee natives who had a sophisticated culture and an organized tribal government. The Spanish visited again and again, not finding gold, but remarked in journals of the strange gems and stones the natives seemed to gather in droves.

> **ERIKA:** I love shiny objects! I know rubies were in large supply!

Today, the town is a popular stop along the Appalachian Trail for hikers. The Bartram Trail also travels alongside the town of Franklin.

NIKWASI MOUND

THIS MOUNTAIN TOWN WAS ONCE NIKWASI, A MAJOR TRADE hub of the Cherokee as noted by the Spanish. The Nikwasi Mound has stood in this spot in the town of Franklin for thousands of years. It has never been excavated, so its exact build date is completely unknown. The Cherokee name of "Nikwasi" means "The Center." That name shows how much this area meant and still means to the people here.

ERIKA: Is a mound usually where people are buried?

MARK: Not always. Many times, they are built to mark places of significance. Middens amongst the Florida tribes were simply garbage piles. We think, anyway.

As the European nations started competing for the lands here, they formed alliances with the Cherokee. The British came here in 1730, and Sir Alexander Cuming called a council at the round house that stood on Nikwasi Mound. He won their allegiance to the British king and took some of their men back to England including Attakullakulla, known as The Little Carpenter, who would later become one of the greatest Cherokee chiefs in history.

ERIKA: This story is starting off nicely, but I feel like that will change.

The British kept up a trading network with the Cherokee for some time. The Cherokee even sided with the British during the French and Indian War. In 1760, the encroachment of British colonies turned feelings against the alliance, and two years of war raged in what is now Macon County including Nikwasi. Several major battles took place here with losses on both sides.

THE **Dark Side** OF THE **Smoky Mountains**

ERIKA: Interesting.

MARK: Remember, the Nûññĕ'hĭ also reportedly revered
      this mound.

In 1775, William Bartram would be the first traveler to describe the area with exceptional detail. Bartram had been born in Philadelphia in 1739, and his father John Bartram was considered America's first botanist. William began drawing his father's specimens and became a legendary artist and naturalist. From 1773 to 1777, he journeyed throughout the American South and drew much of the flora and fauna there. He also gathered botanical specimens that had never been seen by European eyes.

ERIKA: And thus, invasive species migrated to
      other areas.

His famous journal is now known as *Bartram's Travels* and is often described as the most astounding written artifact of the early republic. He described visiting the council house on the mound in the book:

"The council or town-house is a large rotunda, capable of accommodating several hundred people; it stands on the top of an ancient artificial mount of earth, of about twenty feet perpendicular, and the rotunda on

HISTORICAL PHOTO OF NIKWASI MOUND IN FRANKLIN, NORTH CAROLINA FROM THE 1940S. PROVIDED BY MACON COUNTY HISTORICAL SOCIETY.

NIKWASI MOUND AS IT SITS TODAY. PHOTO BY AUTHOR.

the top of it being above thirty feet more, gives the whole fabric an elevation of about sixty feet from the common surface of the ground…"

ERIKA: It sounds like it was amazing to see.

He then went on to write about the entertainment he and some of the other white traders were given. They observed a great dance followed by an elaborate feast. A Wataree chief told Bartram that many people had lived at the site and each generation added to it or changed its shape.

According to some modern spiritualists, the Nikwasi mound is a confluence of many ley lines that pass through here on the way toward many other ancient sacred sites. In the 1960s, the Ley Hunters Club mentioned this mound and The Great Serpent Mound in Ohio as the two largest intersections of mystical energy in the northern hemisphere, and outside of Stonehenge, one of the largest in the world. Many say the large number of gems and crystals here, along with the mound, make it a major spiritual and natural energy source.

ERIKA: It is amazing because they didn't have anything to tell them about this, scientifically-speaking. They just had to do this based on feeling and stories.

Apparently, this mound marks one of the edges of the territory of Tsul'kalu' as designated on Judaculla Rock. One of the petroglyphs there may mark Nikwasi mound next to the Little Tennessee River that runs nearby. The Cherokee say this would make this the edge of his hunting

293

territory and the beginning of lands that may belong to others like Spearfinger or Stone Head.

ERIKA: I know which side of the mound I would stay on.

The mound was privately owned until sold to the town of Franklin in the 1940s, which kept it from being excavated or demolished. In 2019, it was purchased by a non-profit that, working in partnership with the Cherokee Tribe, intends to protect and preserve the mound for generations to come. It is the largest and best-preserved mound in western North Carolina, even if it is only a fraction of the size from when William Bartram came here.

AN ETCHING OF A PAINTING OF WILLIAM BARTRAM. THE ETCHING WAS DONE IN THE EARLY 1800S TO PRESERVE THE PAINTING. PROVIDED BY THE JACKSON COUNTY HISTORICAL SOCIETY.

RUTHERFORD TRACE

WE HAVE TO GET BACK IN THE WAYBACK MACHINE. THIS time, we are traveling to September 10, 1776. Just a year after William Bartram noted the town with the council house on Nikwasi mound, a divisive piece of American history occurred right here. The budding Colonial forces were extremely scared of an alliance between the Cherokee and the British forces in western North Carolina.

This period of war was marked by the colonists' fear of British spies inciting Indian attacks. If you glance at the Declaration of Independence, you'll of course first see, "all men are created equal." However, farther down, you'll see that King George III of England, "…has excited domestic insurrections among us and has endeavored to bring on the inhabitants of our frontiers the merciless Indian savages, whose known rule of warfare is an undistinguished destruction of all ages, sexes and conditions."

The colonists were scared. In 1775, the Treaty of Sycamore Shoals had Cherokee chiefs agreeing to give 20 million acres of prime Cherokee lands to the white man in what is now Kentucky. Cherokee War Chief Dragging Canoe spoke out against it and vowed to fight the white settlers.

ERIKA: The lies that were told to the Cherokee and other indigenous tribes were horrible.

"Whole Indian nations have melted away like snowballs in the sun before the white man's advance," Dragging Canoe said in a now famous speech. "We had hoped that the white men would not be willing to travel beyond the mountains. Now that hope is gone. They have passed the mountains, and have settled upon Cherokee land…

"Should we not therefore run all risks and incur all consequences, rather than submit to further loss of our country? Such treaties may be all right for men who are too old to hunt or fight. As for me, I have my young warriors about me. We will have our lands."

THE **Dark Side** OF THE **Smoky Mountains**

The Colonists feared he would ally with the British as they had long-standing trade relationships with the Cherokee. They did not understand that the Cherokee and British relationships had become strained due to border disputes in recent years. There was a ton of friction in the area between the two nations.

> **ERIKA:** How would they have known? They didn't have the internet back then.

In August of 1776, Griffith Rutherford was given the command of around 2,700 men between the ages of 16 and 60. Rutherford was appointed Brigadier General. William Lenoir kept a diary of his expedition as he set out of what is now McDowell County and marched into the Cherokee lands of western North Carolina with his militia.

> **ERIKA:** I do not like where this is going.

ILLUSTRATION OF GENERAL GRIFFITH RUTHERFORD. PROVIDED BY BUNCOMBE COUNTY HISTORICAL SOCIETY.

Lenoir's diary would mark their passage through what is now Asheville all the way through Balsam Gap and even through Waynesville. By September, they began to burn and destroy Cherokee towns. Their tactic was to burn every house, cut and destroy every crop, seize and destroy all livestock, and kill any Cherokee who attempted to fight back. Then they would move on to the next town.

> ERIKA: This is terrible.

The total numbers of destroyed villages and towns are hotly debated. Estimates range between 50 and 75. At Nikwasi, Rutherford destroyed the town that was noted in accounts as being five miles long and two miles wide with over 90 houses. All this destruction led to most of the towns being abandoned, though some were eventually rebuilt.

This act by the colonial militia became known as the Rutherford Trace. It was utterly devastating for the Cherokee. Many fled into the hills and tried to make it to their towns in Tennessee, but those towns had been hit by similar tactics by Colonel Christian and his Virginia men.

How many of the Cherokee died of diseases or famine later that winter? We will likely never know.

> ERIKA: I can't even imagine the devastation.

In 1780, many of Rutherford's men and other frontier militia groups would band together to defeat the British at the Battle of Kings Mountain. To some, it was a crucial military campaign in the early days of the Revolutionary War, and the beginning of a National Guard that paved the way for American independence. To others, it was a brutal march of terror that killed and starved many innocent Cherokee, far worse than even the Trail of Tears. Sherman's march through the South would be the only close contender for the volume of destruction in its wake.

> ERIKA: Before we travel out of Franklin, I want to throw in a couple of stops for food or libations I love before you whisk us out into nature.

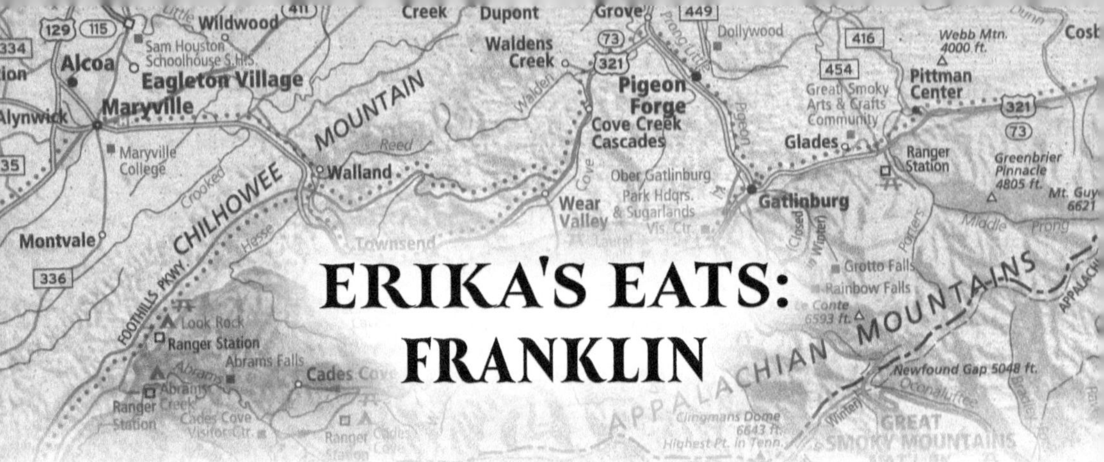

ERIKA'S EATS: FRANKLIN

Gracious Plates on Main

This cute restaurant right on Main Street serves tapas along with its own spirit. Because it is haunted, I had to grab a drink (or two). I could not help but grab a Tequila Mockingbird. After downing two of those, I grabbed blackened tuna bites and Brasstown ribeye steak and frites. Mark loves their buffalo wings. With full bellies and maybe a little buzz, we learned about the figure that walks through the dining room at night. Servers and patrons move out of the way until they realize this ghostly visitor has no real form. So, you may have a visitor pass your table when enjoying this amazing place.

Kountry Kitchen

This fun family-owned hole-in-the-wall diner serves break-fast and lunch—along with a serving from the other side of the veil. This is a favorite of Mark's as he, of course, loves their fried baloney sandwich, and I love to dive into their Mountain Man hashbrowns, piled high with just sausage, peppers, onions, and your choice of cheese or gravy. Although the food is yummy and filling, we don't suggest you linger at night. There is purportedly a spirit that prowls the dining room. That may be why they are only open for breakfast and lunch.

> **VALERIE:** My god. The country fried steak at this place is to die for! No mermaid picture here.

Erika's Eats: Franklin

Motor Company Grill

Now that we are done at the haunted restaurants, we can head to a truly fun burger joint. The Motor Company Grill has a retro diner vibe with milkshakes and all. My favorite is the burger with peanut butter! You might be saying "Yuck" but don't knock it 'til you try it. Mark loves their bacon peanut butter burger. Naturally, I also grab their flavor of the week milkshake!

THIS WATERFALL IS ON THE BARTRAM TRAIL JUST PAST THE WALLACE BRANCH TRAILHEAD NEAR FRANKLIN, NORTH CAROLINA. PHOTO BY AUTHOR.

WAYAH BALD MOUNTAIN

JUST OUTSIDE THE EDGE OF FRANKLIN IS THE WAYAH BALD observation tower built by the Civilian Conservation Corps in 1937 for fire detection. It is on a treeless open area on top of Wayah mountain. The tower marks where the Appalachian Trail crosses the Bartram Trail and makes it an important stop for hikers on either hike. On a clear day, you can see mountain peaks in three states from the top of the tower.

> **ERIKA:** That is very cool and *very* high up.

The name comes from the Cherokee word for wolves: "Wa ya." Red wolves once frequented this peak and were hunted by the natives for thousands and thousands of years. Some spear points found in this area date back to more than eleven thousand years ago.

The Cherokee say that the reason no trees grow here is that the Nûñnë'hï keep it clear so that thunderbirds and eagles could watch for game like rabbits or evil spirits like Spearfinger and Stone Head.

> **ERIKA:** I love the idea of Thunderbirds launching from
> that peak.

Coneheetah, a legendary Cherokee Chief, came up here to listen to the stars and gain guidance. He even named his grandson Wayah. Stories say that one day his grandson came up to the peak and Coneheetah (translating for the stars) told him of an enemy coming from the north to fight the Cherokee.

Wayah took his grandfather's advice and went down the mountain to prepare for the enemy. The ensuing battle allowed Wayah to make a name for himself and marked him as a great Cherokee leader. He would return up to the mountain many times to seek Coneheetah's guidance until he joined the stars. Wayah learned to listen to the stars himself until he, too, joined them in death.

> **ERIKA:** I would love to be that in tune with nature.

MARK: Talking to the stars is easy. It's getting them to talk back that's hard.

Sometimes hikers claim to hear the unnerving howls of red wolves, now long extinct. Some have even claimed to see the spectral pack running just under the tree line. Park rangers claim to have no knowledge of any of these reported sightings.

ERIKA: Park rangers are not allowed to discuss preternatural things.

The rangers do, however, seem to strangely clam up when asked about Bigfoot sightings in the Nantahala and around Wayah Bald. There were several reports of sightings during a rash of wildfires in 2016. The Sasquatch sighted near here moved in a pack of four or five and seemed to have that same gray fur that helped them blend in with the wintry peaks of these mountains.

ERIKA: There are so many sightings of them in the Smokies!

Keep your eyes peeled for them when hiking or visiting the tower. There is a gravel road up the mountain for those not eager to climb over Wayah Bald at its 5,000 feet altitude.

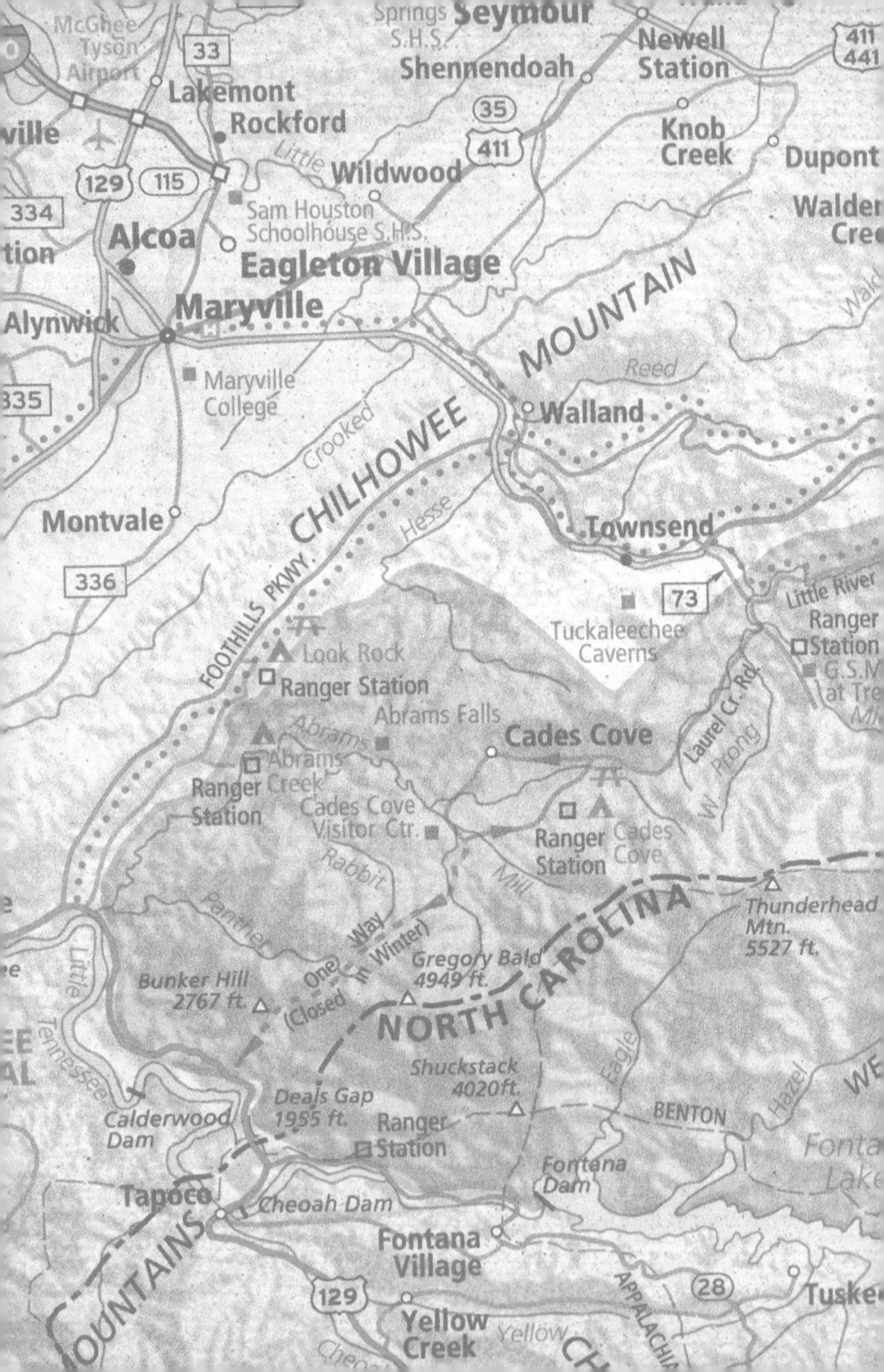

McGhee Tyson Airport
Lakemont
Rockford
Springs
S.H.S.
Seymour
Shennendoah
Newell Station
411 441
Knob Creek
Dupont
Walder Cree
ville
33
Little
Wildwood
35
411
129
115
334
Sam Houston Schoolhouse S.H.S.
Alcoa
Eagleton Village
Maryville
MOUNTAIN
Walden
Alynwick
Reed
335
Maryville College
Crooked
CHILHOWEE
Walland
Montvale
Hesse
Townsend
336
73
Little River
Ranger Station
FOOTHILLS PKWY.
Tuckaleechee Caverns
G.S.M.
at Tre
Mt
Look Rock
Ranger Station
Abrams Falls
Cades Cove
Laurel Cr. Rd.
Abrams
Abrams Creek
Ranger Station
W. Prong
Cades Cove Visitor Ctr.
Ranger Station
Cades Cove
Rabbit
Mill
NORTH CAROLINA
Panther
One Way (Closed in Winter)
Gregory Bald 4949 ft.
Thunderhead Mtn. 5527 ft.
Little
Tennessee
Bunker Hill 2767 ft.
Shuckstack 4020ft.
Eagle
BENTON
Hazel
WE
EE
AL
Deals Gap 1955 ft.
Ranger Station
Fonta
Lak
Calderwood Dam
Fontana Dam
Tapoco
Cheoah Dam
Fontana Village
APPALACHIA
28
Tuske
MOUNTAINS
129
Yellow Creek
Yellow
Cheo
CH

HIGHLANDS, NORTH CAROLINA

HIGHLANDS

THERE'S A GREAT LEGEND ABOUT THE FOUNDING OF THE town of Highlands in North Carolina. The story goes that, in 1875, two land developers, Samuel Kelsey and Clinton Hutchinson, drew a line from Chicago, Illinois to Savannah, Georgia. Then they drew a line from New York to New Orleans. They decided these would be the biggest trade lines in the coming years now that the Civil War was over.

> **ERIKA:** I wonder if they were a few whiskeys in when making that decision.

Where the lines intersected is where Highlands now stands. They decided to build a resort and spa there, and the town has been an epicenter for artists, authors, actors, photographers, scientists, and scholars ever since its founding.

ONCE YOU WERE ALLOWED TO DRIVE UNDER DRY FALLS ON THE WAY TO HIGHLANDS. NOW YOU CAN WALK UNDER IT AND SEE THE FAMOUS "BACKSIDE OF WATER." PHOTO BY AUTHOR.

LOG CABIN RESTAURANT

Sometime between 1922 and 1935, Joe Webb built what would become the Log Cabin Restaurant at 130 Log Cabin Lane. No one knows the exact date because Joe Webb built about 30 buildings in that period using only native resources and hand tools. A little over 35 years ago, this structure was turned into a restaurant.

Restauranter Jason Cancilla runs the establishment. He used to work at the Grove Park Inn in Asheville. "The Grove Park Inn was built in 1913, so my time there was a great introduction to the historic properties of the region," he says. Having taken care of presidents, senators, and countless celebrities over the years, Cancilla says that Highlands and the Log Cabin brought a new set of opportunities.

"We've become a place that locals can be proud to bring friends and family from out of town," he says. "For the visitors from out of town, most of them come to Highlands to shake off the heat and traffic of their home in bigger cities or maybe see a little snow in the winter. This is a great place to do it."

At the Log Cabin, menus are changed and printed daily to feature fresh local produce and seasonal ingredients. Seafood arrives nearly every day from all over the country, so there is always something new and fresh. Do not skip their seafood offering. Check out the latest menu at LogCabinHighlands.com and call for reservations.

Erika: Why do I think this is about to get spooky?

While you are there, you may notice that the restaurant offers something … unearthly. Witnesses have reported seeing yet another "Lady in White" walking through the dining room. Sometimes, just out of the corner of their eye, they'll notice the darting movement of a white dress. The staff frequently report the strange feeling of being watched

Erika: I love all these Ladies in White!

THE **Dark Side** OF THE **Smoky Mountains**

MARK: It truly deserves some research as to why so
many are reported.

The staff mentioned lights turning off and on. One mentioned seeing the lady in white, but there is nothing they fear. The lady seems to only be a spectral remnant of a time long past, here in Highlands.

MARK: A brief side note: The Log Cabin Restaurant closed
just before we went to print and does not appear
to be reopening as it is for sale. Hopefully, it will
return to operation soon as it dodged any
damage from Hurricane Helene.

THE LAST REMAINING SANITARIUM TENT FROM "BUG HILL." THIS ISOLATION TENT WAS PART OF THE TREATMENT FOR TUBERCULOSIS AT THE HIGHLANDS SANITARIUM. PHOTO BY AUTHOR.

BUG HILL

TUBERCULOSIS HIT AMERICA AND THE WORLD VERY HARD in the early 1900s. From 1908 to 1918, Dr. Mary Lapham created a Highlands Tuberculosis Sanatorium, colloquially called Bug Hill. In the 1880s, one in seven people died from "The White Plague" of TB. Doctors quickly discovered it was primarily spread by coughing, so patients were quickly spurned and isolated. Moving patients to open air lands with high elevation seemed to work as a moderate cure. Good nutrition seemed to also help. Highlands was already a spa and resort, so the town became the go-to destination for those seeking treatment.

ERIKA: It is amazing how quickly things like this spread.

Mary Lapham built the health center to begin trials of a new therapeutic modality. Pneumothorax was to be a cutting-edge treatment for pulmonary tuberculosis. Her method involved gradually collapsing an infected lung by injecting it with nitrogen. In its compressed state, the lungs could rest and heal. It was high risk, but the center and the cure worked surprisingly well.

ERIKA: Wow! That seems like a very scary idea back then.

Her talks, demos, and medical journal entries helped other physicians achieve similar success. In 1940, just four years after her death, 80 percent of patients in treatment were undergoing some type of pneumothorax therapy. This remained the treatment of choice until the 1950s, when Streptomycin wiped out TB in the United States.

ERIKA: Yay for vaccines!

Today, only the Highlands Sanatorium tent still stands, one of the 60 open air cabins built for the patients around 1908. During a fire in 1918, this building was saved.

THE **Dark Side** OF THE **Smoky Mountains**

There are stories that a ghostly doctor walks to the cabin as though checking on a patient. Others say you can still hear phantom coughing echoing from the building. While a reminder of a terrible tragic time, you can still marvel at the treatment and success rate here at the Highlands Sanatorium.

ERIKA: Nope! I'm not going in there.

HISTORICAL PHOTO OF BUG HILL WITH ITS MANY HEALING CABINS FROM 1910. ONLY ONE REMAINS TODAY. PROVIDED BY HIGHLANDS HISTORICAL SOCIETY.

WHITESIDE MOUNTAIN

JUST OUTSIDE OF HIGHLANDS IS A NATIONAL RECRE-ational trail that climbs to the top of Whiteside Mountain; there are amazing 700-foot-high cliff walls and spectacular views. This moderately rough hike is not for the faint of heart, but it is worth the trip.

ERIKA: I am bringing snacks and water.

Whiteside Mountain, or Sanigilâ'gǐ in Cherokee, houses another Devil's Courthouse—not to be confused with the other one 20 miles away back in Transylvania County. This one takes its name from the last home of Spearfinger and Stone Head. Here, they built a bridge between Whiteside and another nearby peak using their powers of stone manipulation. The Thunderbirds came and destroyed it, as it grew too close to their domain in the sky. This would also end their only team-up which the Nûññë'hï felt gave them too much power.

ERIKA: Wait, you didn't tell me the liver eaters were up here.

It was also in these woods where the infamous Devil Monkeys were first spotted in the 1940s. These creatures are similar to the Puckwudgies or Stump Jumpers of Lumberjack lore in the northern forests. They tend to come down from the trees in times of famine and raid the nearby farms for livestock. There are some reports of them being vampire monkeys. They tend to be three to four feet in height with chimpanzee-like features but with extremely sharp claws and fangs.

ERIKA: Vampire monkeys?

The Devil Monkeys are thought to have a cave somewhere in Whiteside's Devil's Courthouse area. The caves here are thought to be honeycombed throughout the mountain and might even be the former home of the Little People of the Cherokee, the Moon-Eyed People, or even

the **Dark Side** of the **Smoky Mountains**

the Leftunders also known as the Bogeymen of the caves. They might even have been carved by the rolling of Stone Head. The Devil Monkeys have supposedly forced out whomever lived in the caves and now rule the domain beneath the mountains.

These beastly little creatures have been reported here for decades now. Their howls echo along the trail to warn those who are getting too close to their territory.

Murphy, North Carolina

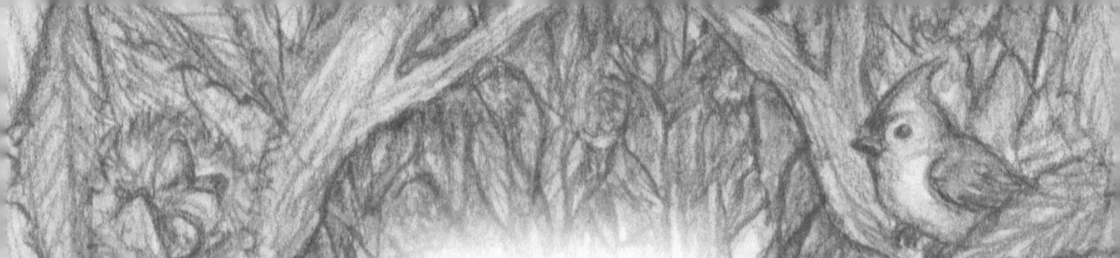

MURPHY

THE CHEROKEE LIVED FOR A LONG TIME IN THIS AREA where the Hiwassee River meets the Valley River. This connected the Cherokee trading path from their lands to the east to the European "Overhill Towns" in what is now Tennessee. It was named Tlanusi'yï, or "The Leech Place," after a great creature that lived here.

ERIKA: A creature? I just got away from the Vampire Monkeys.

The town was named for Archibald Murphey, an influential educator, but in a twist of irony, it was misspelled by a clerk and the name "Murphy" stuck. Fort Butler was built here during the Cherokee removal in 1836 and became a famous part of the Trail of Tears.

MURPHY, NORTH CAROLINA HAS MANY BEAR STATUES THAT ARE PAINTED BY LOCAL ARTISTS. THIS ONE OUTSIDE THE CHEROKEE COUNTY HISTORICAL MUSEUM PRESENTS THE TRAIL OF TEARS AND THE SUFFERING OF THE CHEROKEE PEOPLE. PHOTO BY THE ARTIST.

THE LEECH PLACE

I wasn't sure about including this one. You see, we only have one account of it from 1900 wherein James Mooney recounted his talks with some of the Cherokee storytellers. Mooney added a few tall tales to his records of the Cherokee, and since many other storytellers don't include this one, I wasn't sure about adding it to our road trip guide.

> **Erika:** Is this where the creature is? NOPE! I'm
> not going.

The story goes that there is a ledge of rock running over the stream just where the Valley River meets the Hiwassee. If you stand on the ledge, you can apparently see a very deep hole. One day, a Cherokee hunting party saw a great red object lying on that rock as they came down the trail toward it.

As they watched it, it unrolled, and they realized it was alive. It was a great giant leech with red and white stripes along its body. It rolled up again and then crawled down into the deep water.

> **Erika:** NOPE! NOPE! NOPE!

The water began to foam as if it was boiling, and a waterspout came down on the very spot where the men had just been standing. If they had not moved, it would have washed them all into the water and the hole.

The story goes that many fell victim to this trick of the Great Leech. It's supposedly still down there to this day as people say they can see movement down the hole. There's supposedly an underground river that heads to the nearby town of Nottely, and they also have a Leech Place where the creature sometimes travels.

The Riverwalk here notes the location of The Leech Place with a marker. It also notes that there is a mineral vein there that is red and white striped that can be seen when the water levels are low.

THE **Dark Side** OF THE **Smoky Mountains**

ERIKA: That sounds like a horrible way to die!

Besides the Nûñně'hï of the rivers and mountains, there is also a race of cannibal spirits that inhabit the deep waters of the mountain rivers. They are particularly fond of the flesh of small children. They, too, find the waters of this area a feast.

ERIKA: This is not a great place to visit!

THE LEECH PLACE IS MARKED ON THE MURPHY RIVER WALK TRAIL. YOU CAN SEE THE RIDGELINE MARKING THE CREATURE'S SUPPOSED HOME IN THE WATER ON THE RIGHT. PHOTO BY AUTHOR.

CHEROKEE LITTLE PEOPLE

THE LITTLE PEOPLE OF THE CHEROKEE, WHAT WE WOULD call Brownies, seem to be the kinder spirits of the area. They play drums to chase away the cannibal spirits and drive the Leech deep into its hole.

> **ERIKA:** I do love the Fae.

The Little People have three main tribes: the Laurel People, the Rock People, and the Dogwood People. The Rock People are the mean ones who practice "getting even" and steal children and the like. But they are only like this because their space has been invaded. The Laurel People play tricks and are generally mischievous. When you find children laughing in their sleep, the Laurel People are being humorous and are sharing their joy with the children in their dreams. Then there are the Dogwood People, who are good and take care of others.

> **ERIKA:** Now you tell us about all the nice Little
> People here.

The lessons taught by the Little People are clear. The Rock People teach us that if you intentionally do mean things to other people, it will come back on you. We must always respect other people's limits and boundaries. The Laurel People teach us that we shouldn't take the world too seriously, and we must always have joy and share that joy with others. The lessons of the Dogwood People are simple: if you do something for someone, do it out of the goodness of your heart. Don't do it to have people obligated to you or for personal gain.

> **ERIKA:** The lesson of Erika is to stay away from giant
> leeches, vampire monkeys, and liver- eating
> immortals!

THE Dark Side OF THE Smoky Mountains

THE LITTLE PEOPLE OF THE CHEROKEE ARE VERY SIMILAR TO STORIES OF THE FAE IN EUROPE.
ILLUSTRATION BY KARI SCHULTZ.

THE MOON-EYED PEOPLE STATUE

WHEN YOU GO TO THE CHEROKEE COUNTY HISTORICAL Museum, you'll find a plethora of Cherokee artifacts. It's here you can truly begin to realize the vast scope of their culture, perhaps even more than in the town of Cherokee itself. It truly is awe-inspiring. In the basement, there is one piece that stands out.

ERIKA: Are you trying to trick me into the basement?

Here, you'll find the effigy of the Moon-Eyed People. This unassuming, three-foot sculpture looks like what we would now call grey aliens. It makes us wonder, "What *were* the Moon-Eyed People?"

ERIKA: You think they might have been what we now call the "Greys"?

MARK: There are some who think that.

As we wrote in the Cherokee chapter, there are many theories. They were not spirits like the Nûñnë'hï. They were not immortals or monsters. They were people. Short, sometimes bearded, they created the area's pre-Columbian ruins before being driven away during a conflict with the Creek and the Cherokee; the reason for the conflict has, unfortunately, been lost to history.

ERIKA: I wonder what they could have been fighting over.

The debate continues as to whether they were simply folklore or real people from a pre-historic period. Not too far away lies Fort Mountain State Park in Chatsworth, Georgia. There are ruins of a wall that predates all known settlers, even the Cherokee, and the historical markers

THE **Dark Side** OF THE **Smoky Mountains**

here denote the stories of the Moon-Eyed People who may have built these ruins.

> **ERIKA:** Wow! I want to know more about the conflict though... Maybe the Moon-Eyed People cast spells on the Cherokee?

Again, this must lie in the realm of the preternatural. We simply don't know. Who were they? Were they from the sky as some legends say? Were they the descendants of a lost Welsh prince who sailed across the Atlantic even before the Vikings? Were they underground albino cave dwellers who came to the surface from time to time? Did they even ever exist at all? We can never truly know. The effigy here is all we have.

> **ERIKA:** It's a cool effigy, and now I want out of the basement.

THE MOON EYED PEOPLE effigy carving at the CHEROKEE COUNTY HISTORICAL MUSEUM IN MURPHY, NORTH CAROLINA. PHOTO BY AUTHOR.

CHEROHALA SKYWAY

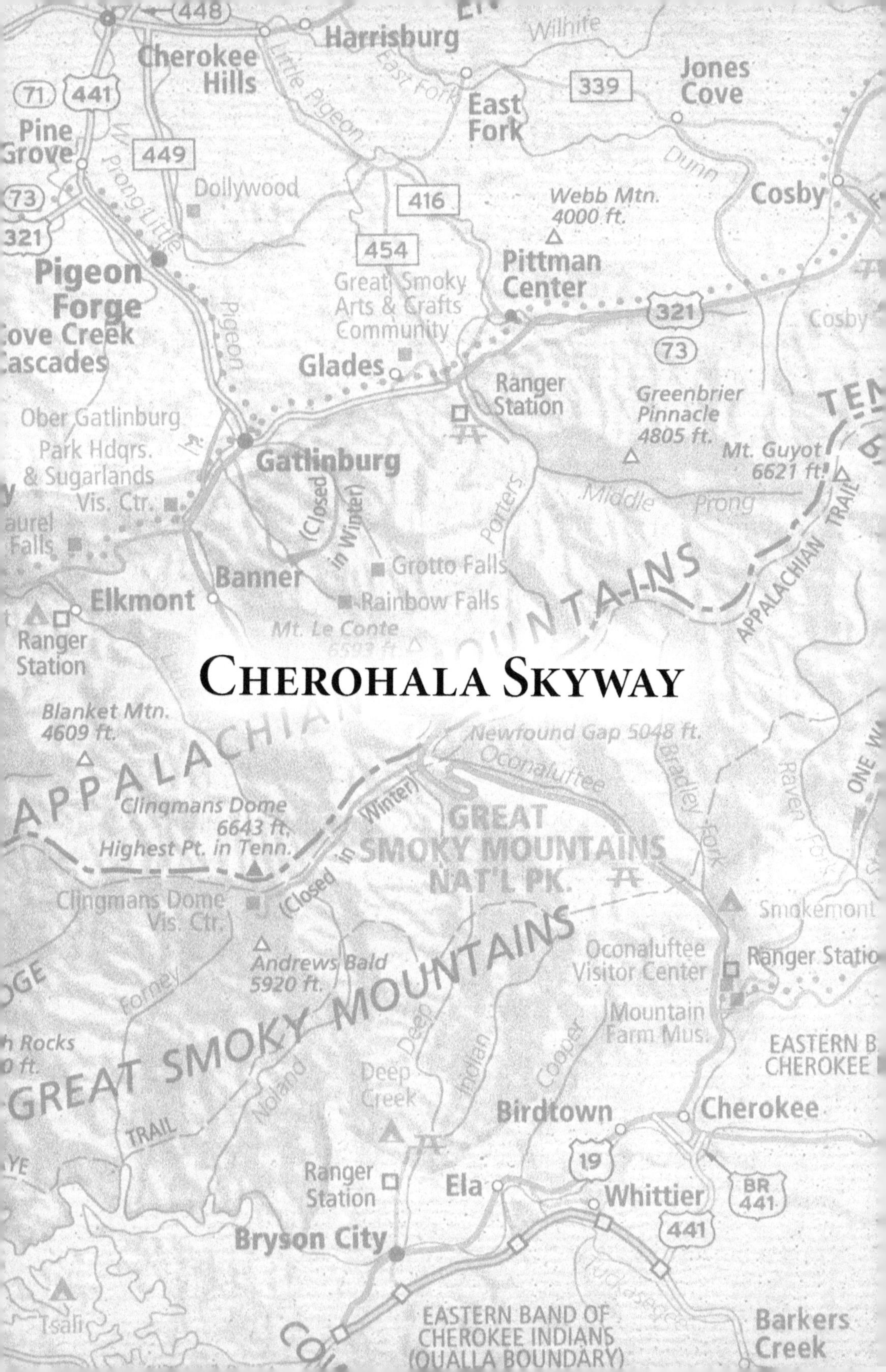

CHEROHALA SKYWAY

OUR LAST LEG BACK ACROSS THE SMOKIES IS A NICE DRIVE along the national scenic byway of the Cherohala Skyway. Just a short drive from Murphy, we head to Robbins, North Carolina. This road is named after the Cherokee and Nantahala National Forests that it crosses, thus: "Chero … Hala." The road didn't open until 1996, and it treats you to scenic view after scenic view as you ascend to nearly 5,400 feet in elevation.

> **ERIKA:** Snack time!

The Cherokee Nation once occupied these mountains, and their legacy is all along this road. The signs are written in both English and Cherokee. These roads were once the very footpaths used by the ancient Cherokee and even the animal paths before them. It is an amazing drive.

> **ERIKA:** Yes, it is!

The road itself sprang from an idea had by Sam Williams in 1958. Television was America's new entertainment king, and the Western was its dominant form. *Wagon Train* and *Gunsmoke* were at the top of the ratings boards. Sam dreamt of running his own wagon train from his home in the Tellico Plains of Tennessee to the mountain towns of North Carolina. Sam brought up the idea at his Kiwanis Club meeting and said the roads between the nearby towns were only fit for covered wagons.

> **ERIKA:** Have you ever ridden in a covered wagon? Sounds bumpy!

> **MARK:** I'm just glad we don't have to worry about dying of dysentery.

40,000 Greet Wagon Train at Murphy

MURPHY, N. C., July 5 (UPI) —A big wagon train rumbled into Murphy Monday, paraded through the downtown area and then retired to the fairgrounds for an old-time July Fourth celebration featuring games, contests and speeches.

An estimated 40,000 persons were on hand to welcome the train.

Thus ended the train's two-day, 70-plus mile journey over the mountains from Tellico Plains, Tenn. More than 100 wagons and 800 riders supplied the pioneer-like atmosphere.

The return trip started today.

Pushes Road Need

The train was organized three years ago to publicize the need for a shorter highway across the mountains between the two towns.

Dedication ceremonies were held Saturday near Tellico Plains for a highway link.

ARTICLE DESCRIBING THE TELLICO TO MURPHY WAGON TRAIN AND THE NEED FOR THE CHEROHALA SKYWAY. KNOXVILLE NEWS SENTINEL, JULY 5, 1960.

THE **Dark Side** OF THE **Smoky Mountains**

Within six weeks of that fateful meeting, the first wagon train traveled with over sixty-seven covered wagons and three hundred horsemen. With the huge success of its inaugural run, it became an annual event. Politicians loved it so much they proposed a highway be constructed from Tellico Plains to Murphy.

Sadly, in 1962, it was determined that the original route to Murphy wouldn't be feasible for the highway. However, nearby Robbinsville allowed it to pass through their federal land. Thirty-four years, and over one-hundred-million dollars later, and the highway in the sky was completed.

ERIKA: That is very cool and very expensive.

The Forest Service estimated that over five million cars a year would use the road. This means ten cars per minute, year-round. Today, the actual figure is around 50-100 motorcycles and cars a day. The Skyway is beautiful, but dangerous in the winter months with icy conditions and deep snow.

ERIKA: So, visit in the spring or fall.

A couple of things to watch out for while driving along: In 1912, the Hooper Blad Mountain Farm received eleven sows and three boars from the Ural Mountains in Russia. Each hog was around 60 to 70 pounds. Within days, the hogs broke free of their pen and freely roamed the farm on the mountain. By the early 1920s, the wild hog population on the mountain was considered to be in the hundreds, and hunts were organized to capture them. Only two were caught, and ultimately, a lot more of the hogs escaped into the wild.

ERIKA: Again, can we say "invasive species?"

Today, the population of the Russian Blue Boar is still growing. While it's unlikely to see one from your car while driving by, the hogs are usually expected to weigh over 180 pounds. They tend to stay in the deepest woods along the road.

ERIKA: Be careful if you stop and hike. I have seen *Game of Thrones*; it can end badly!

Cherohala Skyway

If you go for a hike on one of the trails along the highway, you might find the remains of one of the old settlements, long abandoned. You'll typically find corner stones and old stone chimneys. If you happen to see a fire in one, that may be the Heart of the Hearth. Legends say that these are spirits of flame that are there to provide shelter for those wandering the woods.

The stories say that if you write your fondest wish onto a sheet of paper and throw it into a Heart of the Hearth's magical flame, it will be granted within the next full moon. So, keep your eyes open for these phantom lights on your hikes. They might even be the cause of some of the other ghost lights seen throughout the Appalachians.

One last thing to be wary of out here: the Smoky Mountain gamecocks. Supposedly these turkeys are the only thing that could survive against the blue hogs. They were bred for pit-fighting in the 1850s. Eventually, they grew so large they were able to turn on their masters and escape. They supposedly thrive in the wilds of these border mountains as vicious pack hunters.

If you found those stories to be unbelievable, well, you might be partially right. The blue hogs are very real. The Heart of Hearth and the gamecocks might be tall tales, but there are those who swear they've experienced sightings of both here along the Cherohala and this side of the Smokies.

Now we're on our way back to where it all started. We can either head to Knoxville or back to Chattanooga. There's a few more stops we could have made on our trip that were a little out of our way, but let's include them as some bonus trips for those who want more adventure.

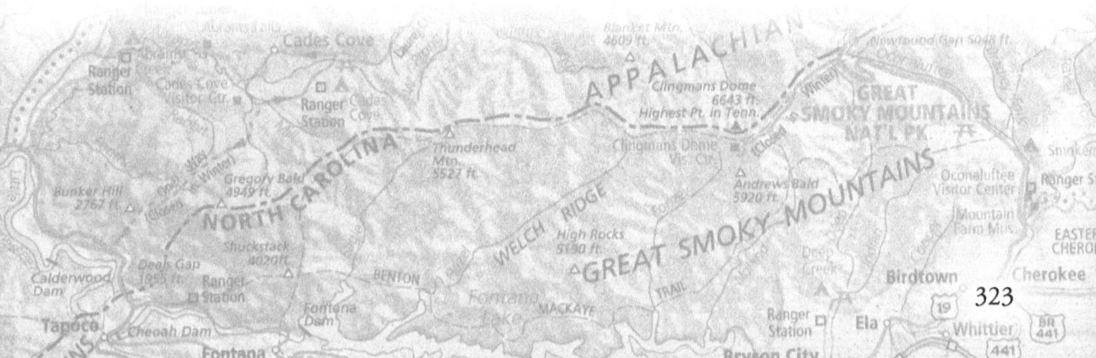

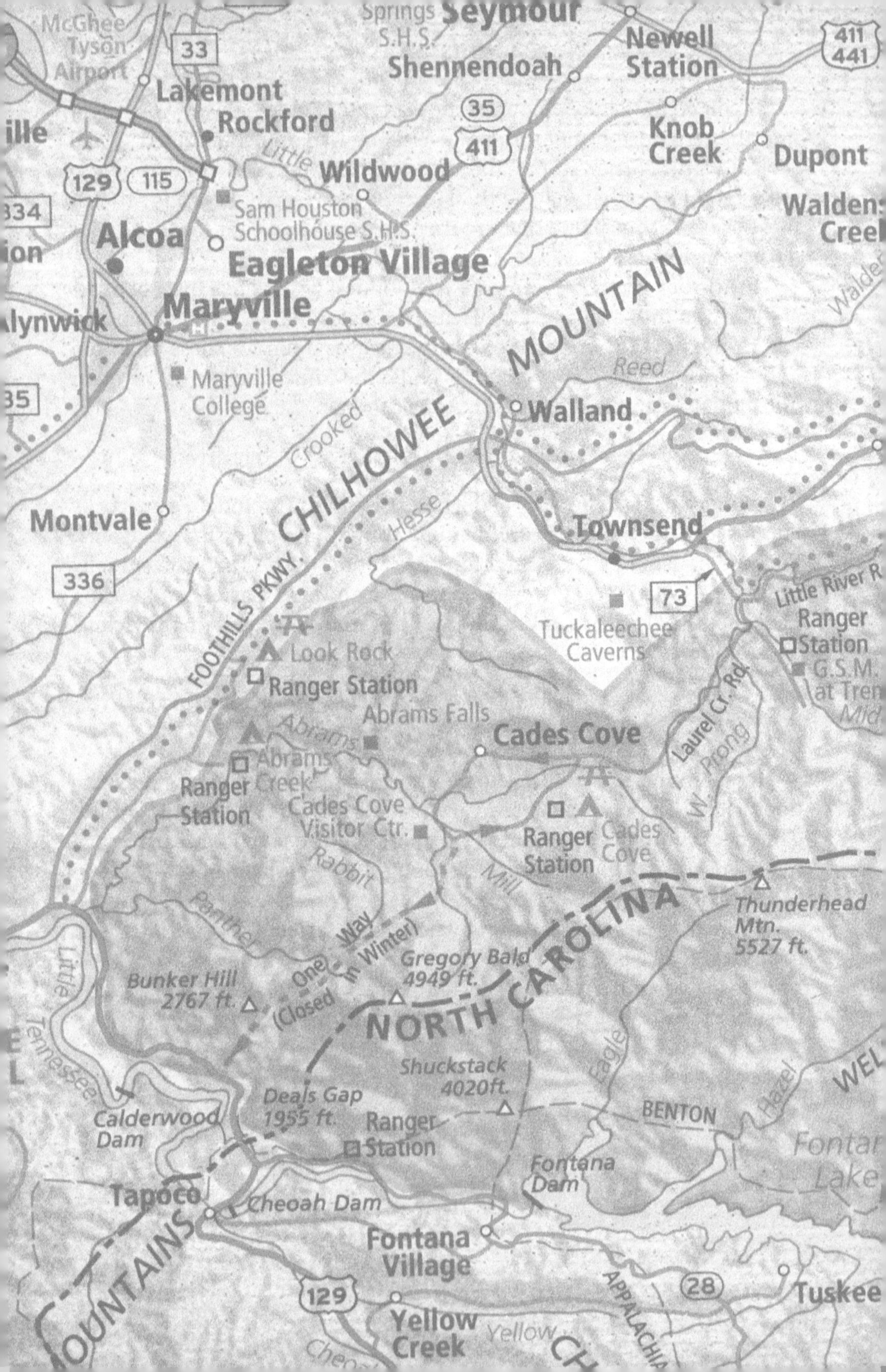

McGhee Tyson Airport
Lakemont
Rockford
Alcoa
ille
334
ion
lynwick
129
115
33
35
Little
Springs S.H.S.
Seymour
Shennendoah
Wildwood
Newell Station
411 441
Knob Creek
Dupont
Walden Creek
411
35
Sam Houston Schoolhouse S.H.S.
Eagleton Village
Maryville
Maryville College
Crooked
CHILHOWEE
Hesse
MOUNTAIN
Reed
Walland
Townsend
Walden
Montvale
336
FOOTHILLS PKWY.
Tuckaleechee Caverns
73
Little River R.
Ranger Station
G.S.M. at Tren Mid
Look Rock
Ranger Station
Abrams Falls
Cades Cove
Laurel Cr. Rd.
W. Prong
Abrams
Abrams Creek
Ranger Station
Cades Cove Visitor Ctr.
Ranger Station
Cades Cove
Rabbit
Mill
Panther
One Way (Closed in Winter)
Gregory Bald 4949 ft.
NORTH CAROLINA
Thunderhead Mtn. 5527 ft.
Bunker Hill 2767 ft.
Eagle
Shuckstack 4020 ft.
BENTON
WEL
Little Tennessee
Calderwood Dam
Deals Gap 1955 ft.
Ranger Station
Fontana Dam
Hazel
Fontana Lake
Tapoco
Cheoah Dam
Fontana Village
APPALACHIA
28
Tuskee
MOUNTAINS
EL
129
Yellow Creek
Yellow
Cheoa
CH

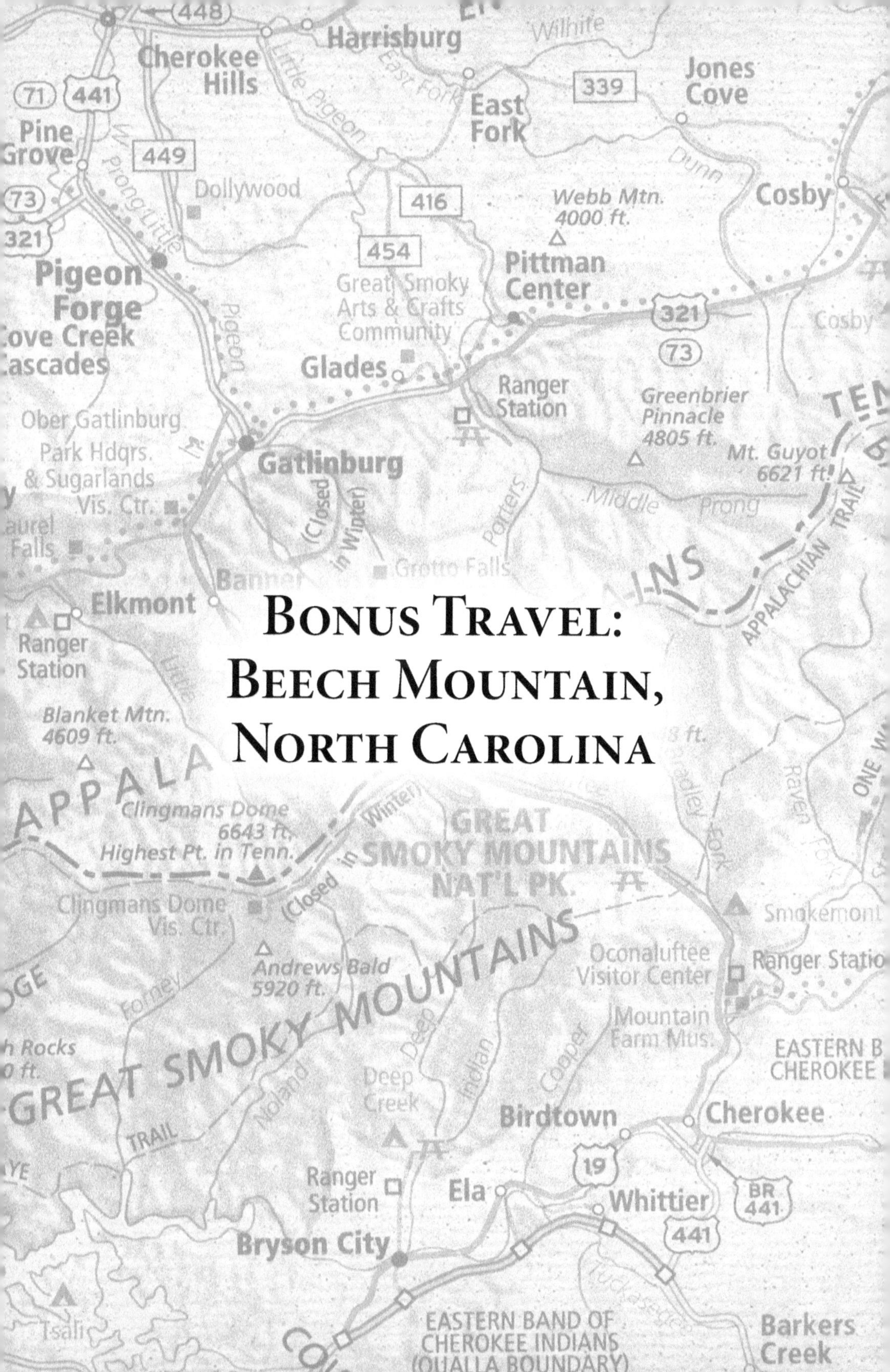

Bonus Travel: Beech Mountain, North Carolina

LAND OF OZ

INSPIRED BY SOME OF THE NEARBY THEME PARKS LIKE THE Tweetsie Railroad in Blowing Rock, NC., Grover Robbins purchased land on the peak of Beech Mountain in 1962. He hired Jack Pentes to help figure out a design. They were inspired when they realized the land was similar to the Land of Oz from the books and the legendary film.

Construction would continue for nearly a decade and new music and lyrics were added. Robbins passed away in March of 1970, just months before the grand opening. The official ribbon cutting included Debbie Reynolds and Carrie Fisher. Reynolds co-owned many of the props from the original film and put them on display in the park. It was an immediate hit.

Sadly, a huge fire in 1975 would destroy much of the park. Many of the film's costumes and a bronze bust of Judy Garland commissioned for the park were stolen in the aftermath. The whole park was sold and redeveloped by a new investor. By the 1980s, it was considered a "tourist trap" and not worth the price of admission. Attendance dropped dramatically. It closed in 1981.

It became an urban explorer's paradise during the 1980s as it sat vacant and abandoned. There were plans to demolish it and turn it into a gated community of homes. It was saved in the early 90s, and an Autumn Festival at Oz event has brought in guests for over 30 years. Now the event draws thousands each year to walk the yellow brick road on Beech Mountain.

Vintage photo of the Land of Oz attraction on Beech Mountain in North Carolina. Photo provided by Land of Oz.

Follow the Yellow Brick Road at the Land of Oz. Photo provided by Land of Oz.

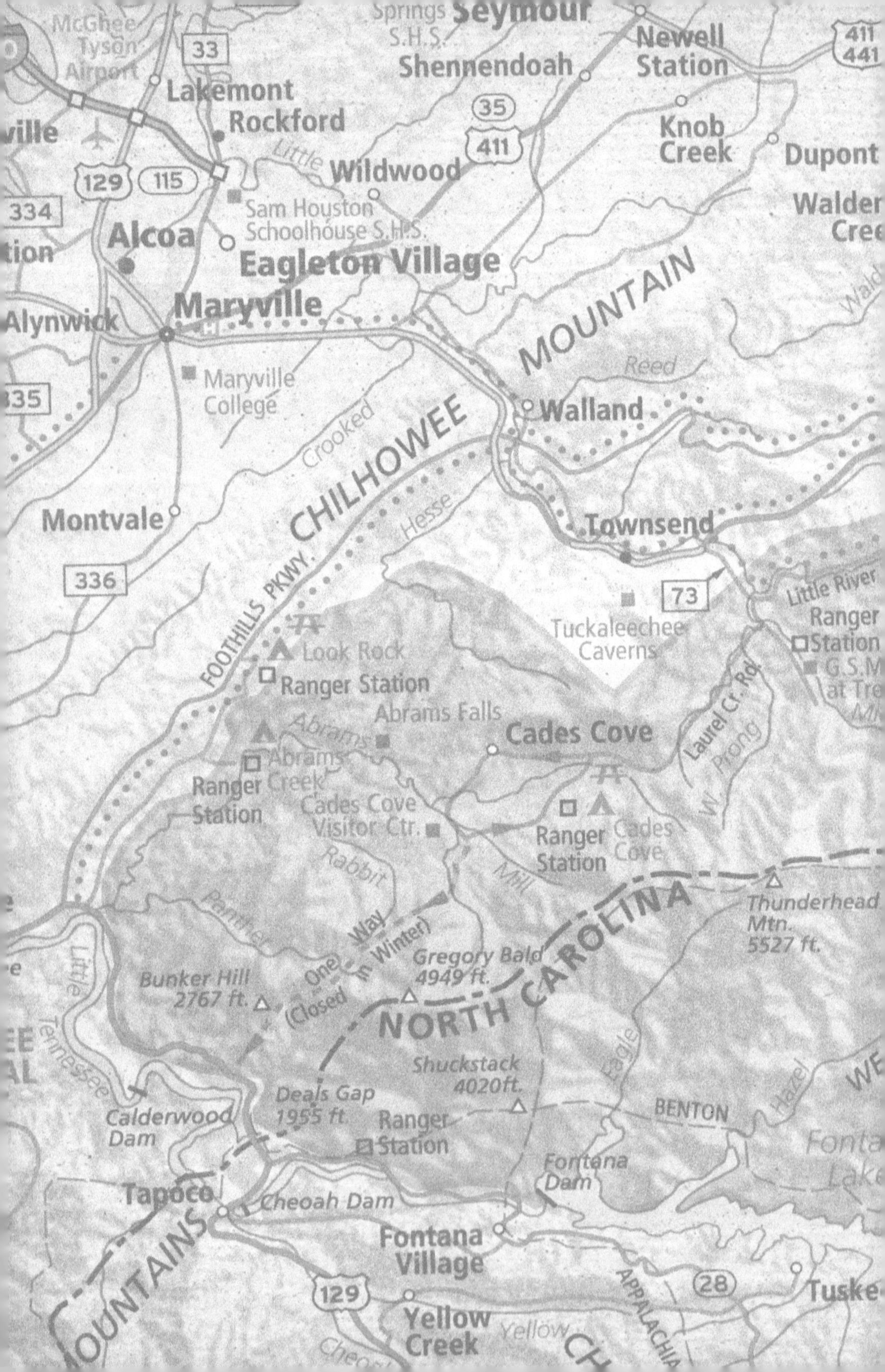

Springs
Seymour
S.H.S.
Newell
Station
411
441
McGhee
Tyson
Airport
33
Shennendoah
Lakemont
Rockford
35
Knob
Creek
Dupont
US 411
129
115
Wildwood
Little
Walder
Cree
334
Sam Houston
Schoolhouse S.H.S.
Alcoa
Eagleton Village
Maryville
MOUNTAIN
Reed
Alynwick
335
Maryville
College
Crooked
CHILHOWEE
Walland
Hesse
Townsend
Montvale
336
Little River
Ranger
Station
73
Tuckaleechee
Caverns
G.S.M.
at Tre
FOOTHILLS PKWY.
Look Rock
Ranger Station
Abrams Falls
Cades Cove
Laurel Cr. Rd.
Abrams
W. Prong
Abrams
Creek
Ranger
Station
Cades Cove
Visitor Ctr.
Ranger
Station
Cades
Cove
Rabbit
Mill
NORTH CAROLINA
Thunderhead
Mtn.
5527 ft.
Panther
One
Way
(Closed
in Winter)
Gregory Bald
4949 ft.
Little
Bunker Hill
2767 ft.
Tennessee
Shuckstack
4020 ft.
Eagle
BENTON
Hazel
EE
AL
Deals Gap
1955 ft.
Ranger
Station
Fontana
Dam
Fonta
Lak
Calderwood
Dam
Tapoco
Cheoah Dam
WE
MOUNTAINS
Fontana
Village
APPALACHIA
28
Tuske
129
Yellow
Creek
Yellow
Cheo
CH

Bonus Travel: Burke County, North Carolina

HENRY RIVER MILL VILLAGE

THE HENRY RIVER MILL VILLAGE WAS FOUNDED WHEN two families formed the Henry River Manufacturing Company, producing cotton yarn. They built 35 homes for the workers, a boarding house, a company store, and a dam to provide the necessary waterpower.

Visiting the village takes you back in time to when the textile industry dominated North Carolina. It is currently under maintenance and preservation after being purchased in 2017. The current owners are protecting and restoring the property's original buildings.

ERIKA: But why is this a bonus travel?

For those visiting here, you might recognize it as District 12 from the *Hunger Games* franchise. When taking a tour, you can opt for the historical or the Hollywood tour. The general store is the Mellark family bakery in the movie. You can even visit the Everdeen home where Katniss wakes up prior to the "Reaping."

ERIKA: I love the *HUNGER GAMES*!

The village is about halfway between Asheville and Charlotte. They have several events each year, including a guided paranormal investigation of the buildings in the village. In order to attend these ghost hunts, you must pre-purchase tickets.

ERIKA: May the odds be ever in your favor!

HENRY RIVER MILL VILLAGE WAS USED IN THE HUNGER GAMES FILM SERIES AS DISTRICT 12. PHOTO PROVIDED BY HENRY RIVER MILL HISTORICAL SOCIETY.

Bonus Travel: Blue Ridge, Georgia

EXPEDITION BIGFOOT

WE'VE DISCUSSED BIGFOOT THROUGHOUT THIS TRIP. THE "Old Man of the Woods" was well- known by both the Cherokee and the European settlers in this area. To this day, there are frequent sightings from Brushy Mountain to Cades Cove, to Wayah Bald, and all the way thorough the Great Smoky Mountain National Park. Hikers speak of him in hushed tones. The rangers all joke and laugh when asked about them in public but will tell whispered stories when off-duty and off the record.

ERIKA: Don't forget about my favorite: the Boojum!

Whether you are a believer or a skeptic, there is an amazing place to visit not too far from the Smokies and still in the southern Appalachians. A short drive down the round takes us to Blue Ridge, Georgia and the excellent museum known as Expedition Bigfoot.

This huge museum contains interactive exhibits and life-sized displays of some famous historical encounters with Bigfoot. The museum also has the largest permanent display of footprint casts. They even have the only displayed Bigfoot butt-print that we've ever seen.

ERIKA: Bigfoot has a nice round behind.

Photography is encouraged. Check their calendar for events and speakers as they are an active research center. New evidence is sent to them nearly every day for cataloging. They have an active encounter log and map for documenting sightings.

ERIKA: They are a great place to report sightings as well!

Make sure to check out the theater and gift shop while you are there. Tell them *Eerie Travels* sent you.

THE **Dark Side** OF THE **Smoky Mountains**

THE *WHITE THANG* IS A LIGHT-HAIRED TYPE OF SASQUATCH SEEN IN THE *SMOKY MOUNTAINS* AND THROUGHOUT THE REST OF THE *APPALACHIANS*. ILLUSTRATION BY *KARI SCHULTZ*.

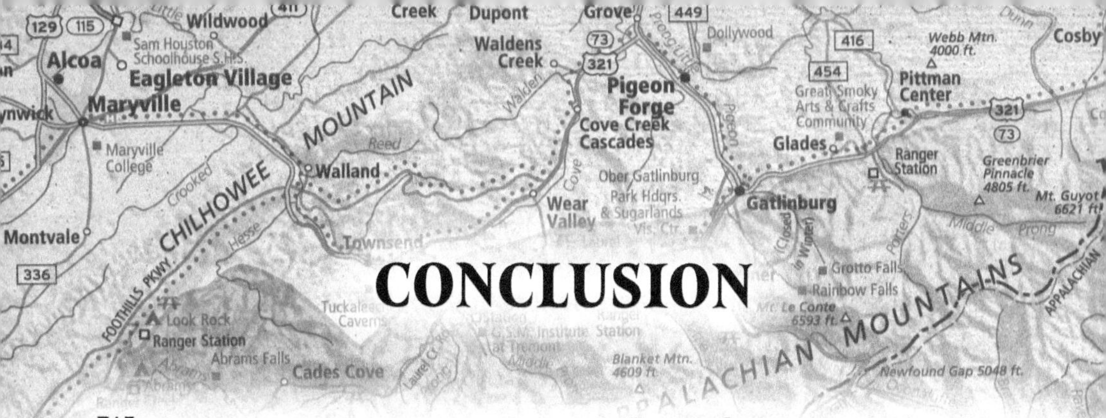

CONCLUSION

WELL, WE MADE IT THROUGH THE *DARK SIDE OF THE SMOKIES*. It's been a long ride, but we've visited some amazing locations, eaten some amazing food, and traveled in the footsteps of history. We've discussed folklore, monsters, ghosts, cryptids, and even some legendary tall tales. It's funny, but I think we've still only scratched the surface of all the strange goings-on in the shadows of these mountains.

We didn't even touch on some of the legendary monsters of the Appalachians like those mentioned in Manly Wade Wellman's *John the Balladeer* stories, like the Behinder, the Tree-Squeezer, the Flat, the Gardinel, or the dreaded One Other. The problem with those is he based them on true Appalachian legends and added a bunch of sci-fi and fantasy elements to make them into modern folklore of their own. Kind of like early Creepypasta, in a way. It makes them hard to research objectively.

I'm just glad we didn't bump into any Not-Deer, the Wokalor, or the Bench-leg on this trip. I'm certain we're going to bump into all of them on future *Eerie Travels*.

ERIKA: This has been a truly amazing, beautiful, breathtaking, and sometimes spooky journey. I hope our Travelers have had so much fun! Please don't forget to post photos and videos from your journey and tag us @eerietravelsshow. You can also share any of your stories with us! Just send us a message or jump on our website. We would love to hear suggestions of places we might have missed or hear your spooky tales. And with that, Mark, take us away!

THE **Dark Side** OF THE **Smoky Mountains**

MARK: Well, Travelers, we've reached the end of this journey. We hope that you've discovered some new places to visit. We hope that you've found new places to experience beyond the tourist traps and typical hot spots on your next trip to the Smoky Mountains. We hope you'll take a few moments to consider the amazing history here.

There is so much more to learn about Cherokee culture and history; it would easily fill hundreds upon hundreds of books. The folklore of the early European settlers here could easily fill a hundred more. For those, we'll have to look to the future. Perhaps they'll be included in future episodes of our podcast and maybe even more guidebooks.

Until then, guard your gems from the Boojum, beware the curse of Spearfinger, and keep your eyes open for the many ghosts, haints, and spirits in the coves of the Smokies.

And we will see you … on the other side.

THE EERIE TRAVELS TEAM AT THE OLD MILL RESTAURANT IN PIGEON FORGE, TENNESSEE. PHOTO BY AUTHOR.

ABOUT THE AUTHORS

Mark Muncy is the best-selling author of *Eerie Florida*, *Eerie Appalachia*, and many more books. He is the co-host of the "Eerie Travels Podcast." Currently he lives in the Smoky Mountains collecting further stories for future adventures.

Erika Lance is the CEO and Founder of 4 Horsemen Publications and its imprints since January of 2020. She started both these presses under the belief that the publishing world needs to change in how it treats authors, artists, and readers.

She is the host of the "Drinking with Authors" podcast, which has over 300+ episodes that showcase authors that are just starting out to those who have been published for decades. As an author with both fiction and nonfiction works, she writes horror/suspense/thriller as Erika and humorous romance and erotica under the pen name Dalia Lance.

Kari Schultz, the illustrator, lives with Mark Muncy in the Smoky Mountain woods and works with him on his best-selling books. When not keeping Mark upright, illustrating, photographing, or crocheting, she tries to befriend the local wildlife.

Special Thanks to Beau Lake, Kathy Schultz, and Kimberly Gallo for early edits. Thanks to Valerie Willis for our typesetting.

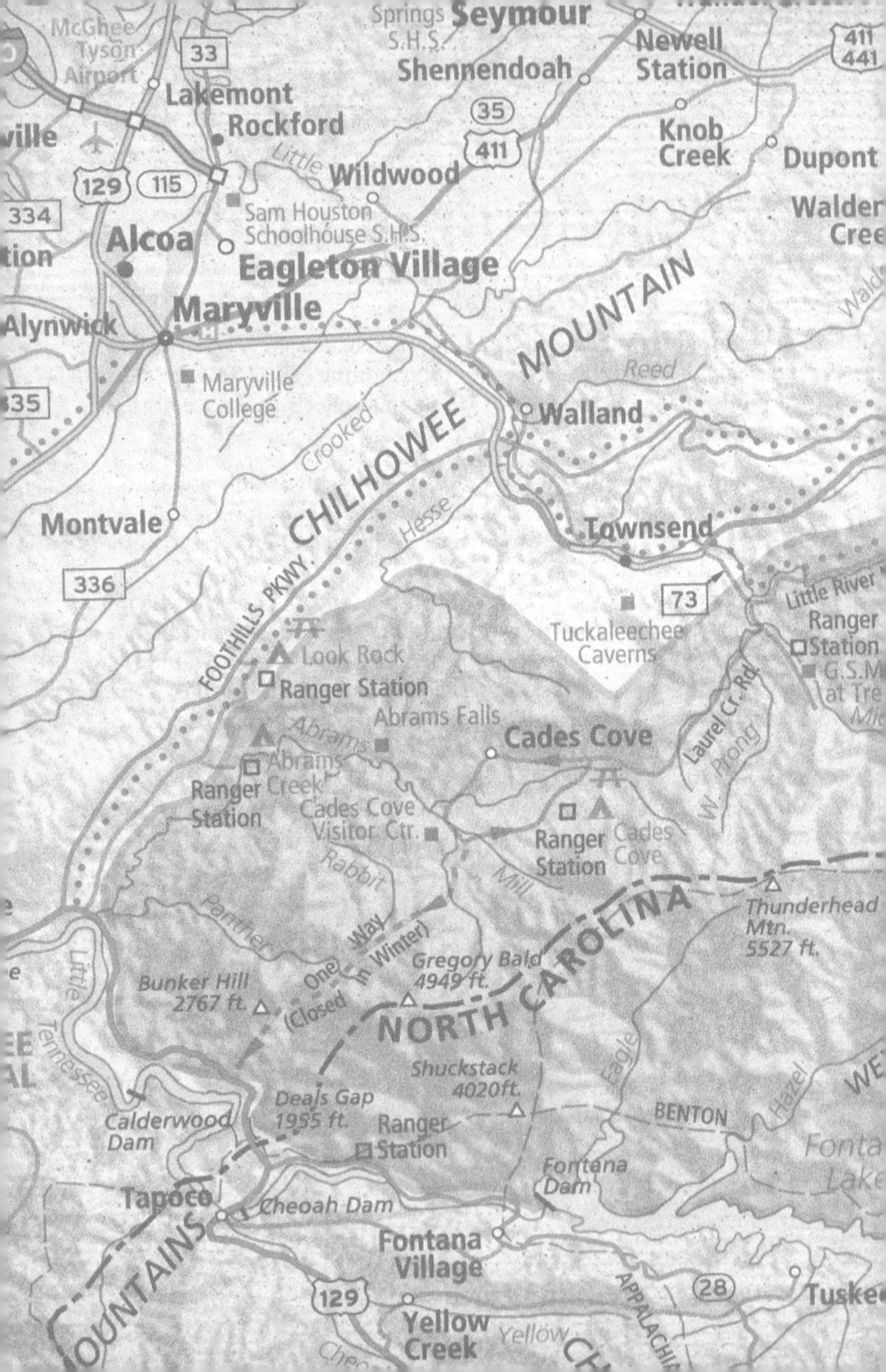

McGhee Tyson Airport
33
Lakemont
Rockford
Springs
Seymour
S.H.S.
Shennendoah
35
411
Newell Station
411 441
Knob Creek
Dupont
ville
129
115
334
Alcoa
tion
Sam Houston Schoolhouse S.H.S.
Wildwood
Eagleton Village
Walder Cree
Alynwick
Maryville
MOUNTAIN
835
Maryville College
Reed
Crooked
CHILHOWEE
Walland
Montvale
Hesse
Townsend
336
FOOTHILLS PKWY.
73
Tuckaleechee Caverns
Little River Ranger Station
G.S.M. at Tre Mt
Look Rock
Ranger Station
Abrams Falls
Cades Cove
Laurel Cr. Rd.
Abrams
Abrams Creek
Ranger Station
Cades Cove Visitor Ctr.
Ranger Station
Cades Cove
W. Prong
Rabbit
Mill
NORTH CAROLINA
Thunderhead Mtn. 5527 ft.
Panther
Little Tennessee
One Way
In Winter
(Closed
Gregory Bald 4949 ft.
Bunker Hill 2767 ft.
EE AL
Shuckstack 4020ft.
Eagle
BENTON
Hazel
WE
Fonta Lake
Calderwood Dam
Deals Gap 1955 ft.
Ranger Station
Fontana Dam
Tapoco
Cheoah Dam
Fontana Village
APPALACHI
28
Tuske
129
Yellow Creek
Yellow
MOUNTAINS
Che

Appendix

448
Harrisburg
Cherokee Hills
Wilhite
East Fork
Jones Cove
339
71
441
449
Pine Grove
Dollywood
73
416
Webb Mtn. 4000 ft.
Cosby
321
454
Pittman Center
Great Smoky Arts & Crafts Community
321
Pigeon Forge
Cosby
Cove Creek Cascades
73
Glades
Ranger Station
Greenbrier Pinnacle 4805 ft.
TENN.
Ober Gatlinburg
Park Hdqrs. & Sugarlands Vis. Ctr.
Gatlinburg
Mt. Guyot 6621 ft.
Middle Prong
APPALACHIAN TRAIL
Laurel Falls
(Closed in Winter)
Porters
MOUNTAINS
Grotto Falls
Banner
Rainbow Falls
Elkmont
Mt. Le Conte
Ranger Station
Blanket Mtn. 4609 ft.
Newfound Gap 5048 ft.
Oconaluftee
APPALACHIAN
Clingmans Dome 6643 ft. Highest Pt. in Tenn.
(Closed in Winter)
GREAT
Bradley Fork
Raven Fork
ONE
Clingmans Dome Vis. Ctr.
SMOKY MOUNTAINS NAT'L PK.
Smokemont
Ranger Station
Forney
Andrews Bald 5920 ft.
Oconaluftee Visitor Center
Rocks ft.
GREAT SMOKY MOUNTAINS
Noland
Deep
Indian
Mountain Farm Mus.
EASTERN B CHEROKEE
Deep Creek
Cooper
Birdtown
Cherokee
TRAIL
Ranger Station
Ela
19
Whittier
BR 441
Tsali
Bryson City
441
EASTERN BAND OF CHEROKEE INDIANS (QUALLA BOUNDARY)
Barkers Creek

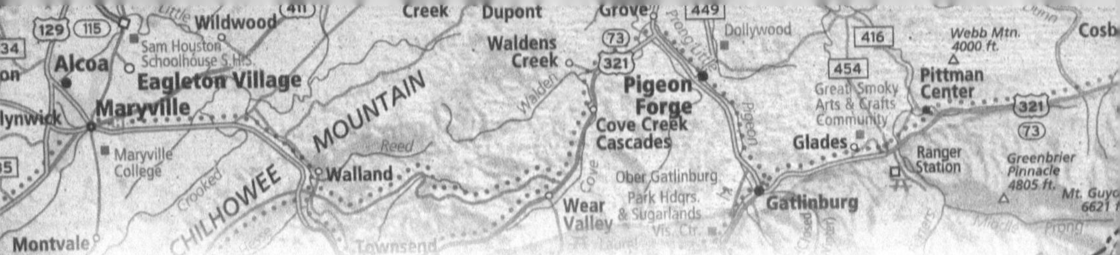

Asheville Botanical Gardens - 151 WT Weaver Blvd, Asheville, NC 28804 - https://ashevillebotanicalgarden.org/

Asheville Mystery Museum (with the Haunted Ashville Ghost Tour) - 80 Broadway St, Asheville, NC 28801 - https://hauntedasheville.com/

Asheville Pinball Museum - 1 Battle Square Ste 1b, Asheville, NC 28801 - https://ashevillepinball.com/

Babettes: A New Orleans Coffeehouse - https://bebettescoffeehouse.com/

Basilica of St. Lawerence - 97 Haywood St, Asheville, NC 28801 - https://saintlawrencebasilica.org/

Battery Park Hotel - 1 Battle Square, Asheville, NC 28801

Beaver Lake - Coordinates 35°38'04"N 82°33'48"W – Directions: Beaver Lake Directions: The sanctuary is on Merrimon Avenue about two miles north of downtown Asheville. Take exit 5-A from I-240 north onto Merrimon. In about two miles, look for Fresh Market grocery store and library on left. The small parking area is immediately past the library on the left. To reach the sanctuary from the north on US 19/23, take the Merrimon Ave. exit, and at the bottom of the exit ramp, turn right onto Merrimon. In about 1.5 miles, you'll see Beaver Lake on the right; the sanctuary parking lot is another .8 mile.

Beech Mountain: Land of Oz -1 Yellow Brick Rd, Beech Mountain, NC 28604 https://landofoznc.com/

Biltmore McDonalds - 35 Hendersonville Rd, Asheville, NC 28803

Boojum Brewery Taproom - 50 N Main St, Waynesville, NC 28786 - https://www.boojumbrewing.com/

Bug Hill: Highlands Historical Society – 524 N. 4th Street, Highlands, NC 28741 -https://www.highlandshistory.com/

Burke County: Henry River Mill Village - 4255 Henry River Rd, Hickory, North Carolina 28602

Appendix

Chicken Alley - 41 Carolina Ln, Asheville, NC 28801

Church of the Redeemer 1201 Riverside Dr, Asheville, NC 28804 - https://churchoftheredeemer-episcopal.com/

Church Street - Put "Church St, Asheville, NC 28801" in Map app.

City Lights Café – 3 E Jackson St, Sylva, NC 28779

Craggy Prison - 2992 Riverside Dr, Asheville, NC 28804 - https://www.dac.nc.gov/divisions-and-sections/institutions/prison-facilities/craggy-correctional-institution

Craven Street Bridge - 192 Riverside Dr, Asheville, NC 28801

Daddy Mac's Down Home Dive – https://www.eatatdaddymacs.com/

Earth and Sky Dwellings in Asheville - https://www.earthandskydwellings.com/

Earth Magic - www.earth-magick.com 80 North Lexington Ave, Asheville, NC 28801

Expedition Bigfoot - 1934 GA-515, Blue Ridge, GA 30513 - https://www.expeditionbigfoot.com/

Fletcher School of Dance - 4 Weaverville Rd, Asheville, NC 28804 - https://www.ashevilleballet.com/our-story

Foragers Canteen - 42 Depot St, Dillsboro, NC 28725

Fryemont Inn - 245 Fryemont St, Bryson City, NC 28713- www.fryemontinn.com

Gracious Plates on Main – 46 E Main Street Franklin, NC 28734 graciousplatesonmain.com

Great Smoky Mountains Railroad - 45 Mitchell St, Bryson City, NC 28713 - https://gsmr.com/

Helen's Bridge - Put "Helens Bridge College St, Asheville, NC 28801" in your Map app.

THE **Dark Side** OF THE **Smoky Mountains**

Hell's Half Acre - At the corner of Sycamore and Valley streets, in what is now part of Asheville's East End, was a neighborhood known politely as *The Acre* and more widely as *Hell's Half Acre*.

Highland Hospital - 450 Montford Ave, Asheville

The Highlands Sanatorium - 524 N. 4th Street, Highlands, NC 28741-0670 https://highlandshistory.com/exhibits/sanatorium

Innovation Station - 40 Depot St, Dillsboro, NC 28725

The Jackson Building - 22 S Pack Square, Asheville, NC 28801- https://www.exploreasheville.com/architecture-trail/jackson-building/

Jarrett House - 518 Haywood Rd, Sylva, NC 28779

Judaculla Rock - 552 Judaculla Rock Rd, Cullowhee, NC 28723

Kountry Kitchen - 351 Carolina Mountain Dr, Franklin, NC 28734

Last Shot Memorial - The monument is located on the east side of Sulphur Springs Road just north of the intersection with 5th Street. (Latitude: 35.48687 Longitude: -83.00399)

The Leech Place - Murphy River Walk looking toward "The Leech Place" and Valley River. Following the boardwalk in this direction will lead you toward Konehete Park.

Log Cabin Restaurant - 130 Log Cabin Ln, Highlands, NC 28741

Lucy in the Rye - 612 W Main St, Sylva, NC 28779 - http://www.lucyin-therye.com/

Merrimon and Broadway - Put "Merrimon Ave & Broadway St" in Map app.

The Moon-Eyed People Statue (Cherokee County Historical Museum) - 87 Peachtree Street, Murphy, NC 28906

Motor Company Grill - 86 West Main Street, Franklin, NC 28734 - https://www.motorcogrill.com/

Pinnacle Park Trail - https://www.discoverjacksonnc.com/outdoors/trails/pinnacle-park-trail/

Appendix

Pop-N-Jacks - 225 Everett St Suite B, Bryson City, NC 28713 - https://www.pop-n-jacks.com/

Riverside Cemetery - 53 Birch St, Asheville, NC 28801- https://cityofasheville.github.io/riversidecemetery/Main/

Riverwood Shops - Old Dillsboro shops, 90 Webster St, Sylva, NC 28779

Rosabees – https://rosabees.weebly.com/

Smoky Mountain Roasters – 444 Hazelwood Ave, Waynesville, NC, United States, North Carolina

The Biltmore Estate - https://www.biltmore.com/

The Great Escape Room - www.thegreatescaperoom.com

The Jackson Building - 22 S Pack Square, Asheville, NC 28801- https://www.exploreasheville.com/architecture-trail/jackson-building/

The Omni Grove Park Inn - 290 Macon Ave, Asheville, NC 28804- https://www.omnihotels.com/hotels/asheville-grove-park?utm_source=gm-blisting&utm_medium=organic

The Princess Anne Hotel - https://princessannehotel.com/

The Road to Nowhere - https://www.explorebrysoncity.com/the-history-of-the-road-to-nowhere-in-swain-county/

The Scotsman Public House - https://www.scotsmanpublic.com/

Waneta Street - Put "E Waneta St" in Map app.

Wayah Bald Mountain - https://www.romanticasheville.com/wayah_bald.htm

Western Carolina University - 1 University Dr, Cullowhee, NC 28723 - https://www.wcu.edu/

Whiteside Mountain - Parking lot, 91-170 Deville Dr, Highlands, NC 28741

Getting caught in a "Bear Jam" at Cades Cove.
Photo by author.